QWYRK

Thousand Acres Press
825 Wildlife
Estes Park, CO 80517

ISBN: 978-1-7362988-1-7

QWYRK

Tim Rayborn

"I liked this book a great deal! Charming and funny, the characters are delightful, and it's scary exactly where it should be. I wouldn't have missed it for anything."

~ Peter S. Beagle, author of *The Last Unicorn*

"*Qwyrk* is, for starters, delightfully... quirky. Rayborn's ear for culture is as good as his ear for music, and his fantasy romp through a small British town has some of the same wacky flavor we find in the mythic send-ups written by Tom Holt/K.J. Parker. Rayborn's elves may be updated, but human nature remains the same. As Qwyrk herself tells Jilly, her kind visit our world 'To give children a little nudge when they need it and sometimes remind adults of what they've been missing.' In times when we all need distraction, here is a tale to take your mind off your troubles for a while."

~ Diana L. Paxson, author of *Sword of Avalon*

"Bringing the familiar modern world together with the fantastic and mythical in a smart and witty way, *Qwyrk* is a delightful foray into magical realism. Fans of Pratchett, Gaiman, Beagle, and de Lint will absolutely feel at home in this story! Rayborn takes figures from traditional folklore and gives them a wonderfully fresh and believable update. You'll be hooked right away on both the human and magical characters—they're engaging and familiar in such a way that you simply must know what happens next. Strong and capable female characters, the challenges of negotiating magic in a world that's largely forgotten it, effective world-building, and a good dose of sarcasm all make this book such a fun read. I can't wait to read more about the further adventures of Qwyrk!"

~ Laura Tempest Zakroff, author of *Sigil Witchery* and *Weave the Liminal*

"You will never look at a rose bush the same way again! A fun romp through a modern English fairy encounter, written with a light heart, a clever mind, and a wicked sense of humour. Enjoy!"

~ Elizabeth Kerner, author of *Song in the Silence*

CHAPTER ONE

Will they eat my brain first, or my eyeballs?

The question ticked over and over in his mind.

Jimmy Eckleson was scared. No, terrified. It was late, well past midnight, but sleep wasn't an option. His eyes were wide open. He clutched the covers up around his face, and his fingers ached and were getting numb. The almost-full moon glowed through the window, illuminating his rather large bedroom with a ghostly light, and casting shadows on the walls in strange shapes.

And that's what worried him: those shadows.

The last two nights he'd seen things, really weird things. Really, really weird things. Things like a shadow with human form moving around his room in strange ways, no doubt doing some evil ritual. A shape with glowing red eyes had lingered by his bed, its arms outstretched to strike him dead and drag his soul to hell; well, he was pretty sure that's what would happen. On both nights, he lay quivering with the covers pulled over his head, hoping he would live to see the morning. So far, whatever it was, it had left him alive, but he knew it was only a matter of time.

After that first night, he'd told his mother about it.

"Oh Jimmy, you're just playing too many of those horrid video games," was all she could offer in response. But it was enough. Mums are good that way.

She's probably right, he thought, and for the rest of the day, he was relieved. He went to bed with new-found confidence, and even smiled as he turned out the light... until later on when it came back. There it was again, just hovering in silence, and he hadn't even looked at a video game all day, as a test.

Now, he was near panic.

*If it comes back again, it's gonna do me in. It's just waiting and biding its time, looking for the best way to strike. It's probably out there right now, hiding in the darkness, a big evil smile on its face, I mean, if it even **has** a face. Or it can smile. I bet it does. I bet it's got fangs. And brain suckers.*

A creak in the well-weathered house startled him, and he almost cried out. His heart pounded, and he stared into the murky moonlit room, not daring to hope that tonight he might be left in peace. His eyes darted back and forth; he heard every sound, every slight movement. His hands shook, and he clutched the covers even tighter, desperate to believe that they might give him some protection, no matter how meager.

Bollocks! I need my Crossbow of Might right now, or the mega chain gun...

Then, it all started again.

There was the slightest distortion in one of the shadows near his wardrobe. He held his breath, eyes now so wide open that his eyelids hurt. The distortion changed to a flicker, and then, before his horrified gaze, a shape emerged, a shape with glowing red eyes that must have been from hell itself. And then another shadow appeared. And another.

More of them?

Jimmy couldn't stand it any longer. No matter what happened, he couldn't stay in his room.

I'll escape or go down trying!

Summoning all of his courage, he leaped from his bed in one quick bound and dashed to the bedroom door, grabbing the handle in panic. Throwing the door open, he rushed into the safety of the hallway, yelling at the top of his lungs: "Mum! Dad! HELP!" He didn't dare look back. If he had, he might have noticed one of the shadows turning to the others, flinging its spectral arms up in the air in... exasperation?

* * *

"Oh, bloody hell! Sorry girls, we've been spotted. We'd better get out of the way."

"Nice one, Qwyrk!" snapped one of the other Shadows. "Bring us all the way up here, and as soon as we arrive, we've got a flippin' screamin' kid to greet us. That's just spot on, that is!"

"Look, it's not my fault he's got insomnia, or dyspepsia, or Black Death, or whatever, is it? His parents'll be back in here any second, so we need to hide, all right?"

The other two Shadows swore and grumbled between them, but dissipated into nothingness in the dark, leaving just the first one standing there. But it also melted into the moon-made murk of one corner, near the old wardrobe where it first appeared.

* * *

Jimmy's parents came storming into his room a moment later, Jimmy following from behind at a safe distance. His father turned on the light, which revealed nothing. Squinting in the brightness, the annoyed Mr. Eckleson had a quick look around, which assured him that the lock on the window was as secure as it had always been, and that the room, large though it was, could not possibly be hiding burglars, evil shadows, monsters under the bed, politicians, or anything else.

"Jimmy," his father began, "I've had enough of this nonsense!"

"But dad..."

"Your father's right, Jimmy," his mother broke in. "There will be no video games for a week, young man. I think those dreadful things are giving you horrible dreams. Now, I want you to go back to bed, go to sleep, and stop all of this. Think of something pleasant for a change. And if you can't sleep, go downstairs and warm yourself some milk!"

"But make sure you do it quietly," his father added.

Both of them again ordered him back to bed. Sulking and protesting, Jimmy obeyed, muttering that they'd just signed his death warrant. "Some parents they are," he mused like the condemned man he was.

The light went out and the door slammed shut. He could hear his parents grumbling as their voices faded into the distance, and he was certain that it was the last time he would ever hear them.

"They'll be sorry," he sulked. "They'll be right sorry when they come in tomorrow and find nothing left of me but scorched ash on the bed... and maybe a finger or two."

No sooner had his sight adjusted to the dark again, when he saw one of the shadows, its red eyes glowing in the dark like coals from Hades. He swallowed hard as it approached; it looked annoyed.

"Well, I hope you're happy with yourself," it said, in a young woman's voice that spoke with an accent that sounded southern English, or something, but with an otherworldly tone mixed in. "You couldn't just go to sleep and stay asleep could you? Me and the girls were just going to check in on things and then do a spot of yoga down in your living room, that's all. Now, thanks to your caterwauling, your parents are right furious, and we haven't had a chance to do what we're supposed to do. Thanks a lot mate!"

Jimmy screamed again.

"Oh, bloody hell!"

* * *

Qwyrk and her friends sat on the slanted rooftop of the Ecklesons' large old home a little later on, quite annoyed. Now they were just trying to avoid all of the clatter and the obnoxious human adults stomping around below. Jimmy's second outburst had no doubt earned him a grounding for the next month. Mr. Eckleson had let out a few stern words that were decidedly inappropriate for young Jimmy's ears.

So Qwyrk, and her mates Qwypp and Qwykk, sat and surveyed the scene. It was a nice detached Edwardian home, with a lovely yard. Well, it would have been lovely except that it needed more tending than the Ecklesons were prepared to give it.

An old rosebush had grown to quite a size, such that its thorny branches often grabbed people as they walked by, often to gasps of surprise that then turned to annoyance as new victims found themselves unable to walk any farther until they became untangled. Those that ventured forward to smell the roses risked never being seen again.

At least twice a month, Mr. Eckleson threatened to hack the whole thing down, but somehow, he always got distracted by other weekend activities, such as football on television. And secretly, he harbored a slight fear of the thing, as if it were watching him. He worried that if he cut it down, a mob of rosebushes might return one night to enact a brutal vengeance. Mr. Eckleson needed a bit more fresh air.

Yes, it could have been a charming entryway to an old house, even with the disagreeable rosebush. But the plastic pink flamingos that Mrs. Eckleson had brought back from their Florida holiday and displayed with pride out front ensured that "charming" was not a word on the lips of guests. So did the bright blue ceramic garden gnome.

So, the trio looked down on the yard now: gnomes, flamingos, petulant rosebushes, and all. Humans could only see them as shadows with glowing red eyes, but up here, all alone, they saw each other on their natural form, which was basically like humans, except for their pointed ears. Humans would probably be disappointed by that. The occasional human—like a witch, a druid, a shaman, or some such—who could see them in their true form called them elves or fairies, which the Shadows resented. Elves were pretty silly, after all.

"So... what are we looking at?" Qwypp asked. Her bright red bob haircut clashed with her blue overalls and purple Doc Marten boots in a noticeable way.

"The rosebush," Qwyrk sighed, as she ran her hands through her short but oh-so-stylish blonde hair.

"The rosebush," Qwypp repeated. "And we're looking at this rosebush because..."

"Shhh! Did you see that?" Qwyrk interrupted.

"What?" asked Qwykk, curling a strand of her long, wavy brown hair around her finger, and smoothing out wrinkles in her new designer exercise outfit. She obviously prided herself on being the glamorous one of the three.

"One of the branches moved."

"Oh. My. Goddess!" Qwypp exclaimed. "You mean they have... *wind* up here in the north? We got here just in time!"

Qwykk stifled a giggle.

Qwyrk shot both of them an angry look. "It bent a little, like an elbow, you idiots! The rosebush is taking on anthropomorphic qualities. I'm sure I just saw it."

"Anthro-what?" Qwykk asked.

"It means it's becoming animated, moving like a bipedal being," Qwypp answered, looking quite proud of herself, and smiling a smug smile.

"I don't care what its sexual orientation is! That's its own private business," Qwykk answered in an equally snooty voice, clearly trying to sound impressive.

Qwyrk sighed and rolled her eyes. "Look, let's just focus on it for a while, all right? It may do something else. We have to find out."

"I wonder how that would work?" Qwykk mused after another minute of the three of them watching in silence.

"How *what* would work?" Qwyrk knew she'd regret asking.

"I mean, if you was a rosebush, how would you know who you fancied? Like, what if you had a knob with thorns? That wouldn't be very pleasant! And even if you did know, what could you do about it? I mean... suppose you liked the rosebush on the other side of the street, how would you know if *it* fancied you back? And even if you knew it did, how would you actually get over there to get a snog? It's not like you could move or anything. And how would you actually snog? Like, with what? Rosebuds on your branches? And suppose you actually fancied the oak tree next door instead, well, *that* opens up a whole new set of problems!"

Qwyrk almost put her face in her palms. Almost.

"Why can't we just go downstairs and do some yoga?" Qwypp interjected, and for once, Qwyrk was glad for her whining.

"I told you..." Qwyrk started.

"You didn't, though!" Qwypp said, annoyed. "Just that you've got a job up here to do, because of some funny reports."

"Yeah, Qwyrk, what's up? You dragged us all the way up here from London, when we were going clubbing this weekend, and we have a right to know why."

Qwyrk assumed a mock pleasant voice. "Look, here it is again, in small words, so you'll understand: that big rosebush has been doing some strange things over the last couple of weeks. It's been moving like a human, and people have also been seeing things like ghosts, goblins, strange lights, and apparitions in the neighborhood; there was even a little earthquake a few days ago. When a plant starts moving by itself, it's usually not a good thing, and if there're ghosts and goblins involved, and the earth starts rumbling, it doesn't usually lead to snogs and chocolate. All clear now?"

"But what are we supposed to do about it?" pouted Qwykk. "Now I can't use my VIP pass to London's 'Club Nitro Ibiza Hedonistic Fun Dome' this weekend."

"The council wants us to keep an eye on it for a bit, to watch over everything. Our mate Jimmy down there is making that a bit difficult and making me question the wisdom of that order. I've a good mind to gag him tomorrow night."

"The fact that we're the ones that scare the bejeesus out of most kids who see us is somehow lost on the council, eh?" snarked Qwypp.

"I don't make the rules," Qwyrk answered. "I just follow them."

ONE

Qwyrk did ponder the irony of it all. "Well, what can I say? Sometimes kids are up far past their bedtimes and spot us. Then they get more scared of us than of the dangers we're supposed to be watching for."

It's time for a change in policy.

* * *

From nearby, it watched, it sniffed the night air, it growled in a low rumble. This was what its master sought: the source, the resting place. And if these ridiculous Shadows got in the way of what was to come, it would take pleasure in devouring them. But not yet; it was being held back, being made to bide its time. Soon there would be blood, and soon the killing would begin. For now, it sensed itself being pulled back to its own world, and it hissed in fury that it couldn't remain, couldn't attack. These Shadows were lucky, but their lives and countless others were only prolonged for a little while longer. With another growl, it vanished into the dark, taking with it vital information.

* * *

"Why are you even up north?" Qwykk asked. "It doesn't seem like your kind of place at all."

"I don't know," Qwyrk sighed. "These days, I like being up here; London's already overrun with enough of us as it is. I like things a little more wide-open and less congested. Leeds, York, the country... it's more my kind of place right now. Still, watching for trouble from Nighttime Nasties gets damned tedious sometimes. Not that the Nasties are tedious, mind you, just, that I don't see them as much these days. From what I've heard, they've decided there was enough nonsense in the world as it is and they aren't needed right now. They're holding back for a while, having a bit of a holiday, and biding their time until the world gets nicer again. I heard something about there being a union vote on it. So yeah, it's all rather quiet these days, the odd situation like this notwithstanding, and *that* is why I asked you up: to keep me company, and because this might just be something."

"Or, it might be nothing at all," Qwypp answered.

Qwyrk was already regretting this little get-together.

"Well, it seemed like a good idea at the time: invite you up, watch the weird bush from the window in Jimmy's bedroom, and then head off downstairs for a bit of exercise and gossip. A few days of observing, and we could make a report. Except of course, now Jimmy has seen us and ruined it. And sitting up here on the roof is hardly comfortable."

Qwyrk was tiring of even this quiet suburban location, she'd started telling herself. It would be so much nicer to go a bit farther north, to one of those quaint little towns or villages that Americans who watch public television seem to think are the main form of habitation in England. Qwyrk decided she'd have to go to the States one of these days to clear up that little misunderstanding. No doubt to the sound of many screaming and terrified children.

She mused as the trio sat for another half hour or so, watching the thorny plant with intention, passing the time making idle talk about the weather, Qwypp's and Qwykk's thwarted weekend plans, and the general state of the economy. Well, not so much that last one. Qwypp brought it up, and then Qwykk asked, "What exactly is stocked in a stock market, and where do you go to buy all those stocked up things? And what makes them crash, and what did playing footsie have to do with people's money, anyway? And where are all the bulls and bears?"

And still the rosebush made no movements.

"Is there supposed to be a monster under it or something?" Qwypp said, rather out of the blue, "like a 'monster-under-the-bush' sort of thing?"

"I had a run-in with a monster-under-the-bed once," Qwykk volunteered in answer.

"Oh yeah?" Qwypp asked. "What was he like? Was he all furry with fangs and claws?"

"Not really. Actually, he was a fit bloke. Don't know why they call them 'monsters' at all. Well, I mean the only thing about him that was a monster was his huge..."

"All right, thank you very much!" Qwyrk interrupted, quite sure that she didn't want to know why Qwykk was under a bed to begin with.

"Well, we're not gonna get much done sitting up here all night," Qwypp quipped.

"Like we ever get much done, anyway," Qwykk quacked.

"Oh, bollocks!" Qwyrk snapped. "If you're both so bored that you're just going to whine about everything, why don't you take the rest of the night off? I'll stay here for a bit longer and go try to find a quiet place to do yoga on my own. We can catch up tomorrow."

Qwykk and Qwypp brightened at this suggestion.

"Cool!" cooed Qwykk. "Hey Qwypp, let's go try some clubbing down in the city center. I've got this amazing new blue stretchy mini I've wanted to wear for a night out!"

"Oh yeah," Qwypp countered, "a shadow with glowing red eyes, wearing a mini that humans can't see, that'll really turn the folks on!"

Qwykk cursed. "Well it's better than that slaggy pair of silver shorts you wear with those pink platform boots. Thank Goddess humans can't see that outfit, or I'd die of embarrassment bein' seen near you!"

"Oh yeah?" Qwypp cried. "What about that atrocity of a swimsuit you wore when we were floating around Ibiza last year? What the hell was that? I'll tell you what! Two strands of flipping dental floss held together by some surgical gauze!"

"Girls," Qwyrk interrupted, with a fake and pained smile stretched across her elfin face. "If you keep this up, you're going to wake up little Jimmy again. I think we've done enough damage to the poor boy's emotional state for one evening. Besides, the night's already middle-aged, and if you want to have any fun, you'd best be off and get on with it."

Qwykk and Qwypp considered Qwyrk's carefully constructed concern. They looked at each other and burst out laughing.

"You fancy coming with us, Qwyrk?" Qwykk asked. "There'll be fit blokes and lovely girls to admire, flirt with, maybe dance with…"

"No, I'll be fine around here, thanks."

"Right. Suit yourself."

The two of them jumped off the roof as they said good night to Qwyrk, landing in the yard thirty feet below, avoiding the rosebush from hell, and skipping off, arm-in-arm to adventures unknown and better left untold.

Qwyrk looked at her own clothes and was grateful for her plain shirt and favorite jeans. She rolled her eyes again as her friends pranced off. Then she stood up and also jumped off the roof, landing gently on the lawn, and paying no heed to the nefarious bush lurking nearby.

"It's brilliant that silly human rules like gravity don't apply, unless we want them to. At least I'll never have to worry about saggy anything," she said to herself with satisfaction, marveling once again at how her kind interacted with this world.

"I need to get out of here for a bit," she said as she strolled down the middle of the quiet, deserted street in the opposite direction of her friends. "That stupid plant isn't going anywhere; it's barely moved, anyway. Whatever's happening can't be all that bad. A rose-bush is hardly going to take over the city at that pace.

"Maybe I'll pop up to the country for a day or two and see what's going on up there. Now, what was the name of that lovely little town I visited back in the 1680s?"

* * *

From underneath the rosebush, a faint glow grew just a little bit brighter.

CHAPTER TWO

Knettles-on-Nidd is one of those delightful English towns, where virtually every portion could fit as a picture on a postcard, and in fact, most have. Sitting atop a rocky outcrop over the River Nidd in Yorkshire, it offers commanding views of the countryside, at least on those days when clouds don't obscure such things, i.e., about seventeen a year.

It is famous for many things, including the romantic ruin of a medieval castle (exactly how are ruins "romantic," anyway? Do they recite love poems? Do they send each other flowers? Maybe roses from the Ecklesons' bush?), a medieval house built into the rock wall of the outcropping, and a cave where an old woman—said to be a witch and mystic—once lived a long time ago. Some people thought she was just a confused and grumpy old lady; those she turned into toads for thinking this were convinced of it. Perhaps due to her influence down the centuries, the place became known for its odd and unexplained occurrences. A famous New Age store now thrives in town as well, the *Aloe Plant Swapping Shop*.

In all, the town is a perfect place for tourists to stop for an afternoon or a few days, the kind of place that Americans who've never ventured much farther than the sixteen-plex movie theater on the outskirts of the town where they grew up can come to and gawk, wonder where the dragons are, and when the special effects will start. Most of these folks end up just settling for one of the pubs, where after a few pints of the local ale, the dragons and visual effects show up anyway.

It happened one June day that a group of tourists from west Texas ventured into Knettles, on a big flashy tour bus that stopped in the town square and seemed quite out of place next to the town's olde-worlde charm, however modified to meet visitors' expectations it might have been.

This particular group of seniors had something unusual about them, at least as far as the locals were concerned. They all wore matching outfits consisting of aqua-colored T-shirts and white baggy shorts. Tan cowboy hats all around completed the ensemble. The shirts had a little map of Texas on the left-hand side, with a large star placed on the western half of the state, to show where they came from. Not a bad idea, considering that west Texan and North Yorkshirese are essentially two different languages, and should one of them become lost, a map pointing back home might be far more useful than trying to communicate by speaking.

One of these colorfully-adorned tourists, Dottie Lee Jefferson, is important to our story. Dottie was a free-spirited widow who had the tendency to wander off on her own and get so caught up in things she would become lost and miss her ride back. She once inadvertently ended up spending a week in the home of a Moroccan carpet seller in Fez. After seven days, wherein the merchant resorted to putting out the word to all of his cousins to look for a flying carpet that would take her far away, the tour operators finally caught up with her.

Yes, Dottie had been banned from more than one tour group for stunts like this. In fact, the tour operators for this particular side-trip had considered putting maps on both sides of her T-shirt. Actually, they considered not letting her off the bus.

While several people in her group were wandering through gift shops, looking for those essential take-home artifacts like tea mugs with Benny Hill's face on one side and Benny Hill's face dressed up as the queen on the opposite side, or aprons illustrated with twenty-three of the best breeds of Yorkshire sheep, Dottie had, yet again, slipped off in search of bigger adventures.

And so she wandered down a long flight of stone stairs near the castle, leading to the river below town. And then she wandered a little farther. And then she found the house.

It had been built right into the side of the cliff on which the town rested, just like the guide book said, with one old wooden door and a small window facing the outside world. No one was quite sure when it had been made, probably back in the Middle Ages. No one was quite sure why. People did strange things back then, like believe in shadows with glowing red eyes. And elves.

It had been listed as off-limits by the town for the past few weeks, after the council voted to evict its resident, Vernon, well-known as the town eccentric (though "loony" was the actual term used). He was in the habit of stepping out of the odd little home, shaking his fists, and yelling at no one in particular. Sometimes he would launch into long lectures about the state of the nation. Churchill had it all wrong and was leading the country into ruin, apparently. Almost no one listened. Well, maybe the elves did.

Anyway, the place was now shut, pending absorption by the

government's heritage commission, to be reopened as a tourist trap. The tea mugs and key chains were already stored in a warehouse in Manchester, waiting to ship, though without Benny Hill's face on them. People could walk by and gawk, but that was all for the moment; the town brochure did not, of course, insist that people gawk, but it was understood to be perfectly acceptable to do so. It was just the sort of place that required Dottie's extra attention.

"What a strange lil' ol' house!" she said with glee, stepping over the old fence in front, and marching up to the door, ignoring the "Do Not Enter" signs posted every three feet. Approaching it, she knocked. No answer. She tried again. Still nothing. So she tried the door handle, and to her surprise, it worked and the door pushed inward.

A rush of excitement ran down her spine. She stepped inside and closed the door behind her to keep out the draft of the English weather. Never mind that it was summer and warm for a change. This was what all the guidebooks told her to do, so she was sticking to it.

It was dark inside; the one window had been boarded up, but just enough light peeped through the cracks for her to see well enough after a minute or two. But there wasn't much to see, and Dottie was rather disappointed. Exactly what she had expected to find was not clear even to her, so why she was disappointed was an equal mystery. It was just one room, and not even a big one.

"Them midevil folks weren't very discriminatin'," she thought out loud.

There were some newspapers scattered about, an old couch, a bed, and a rusted sink, but one oddity caught her eye: a toilet plunger standing upright in one corner of the room.

"Well ain't that strange!" she said, walking over to pick it up and have a closer look. It seemed stuck to the floor, but she was persistent, and after a few tugs, it came up with a popping sound. As it did, a funny kind of tingle went through her, like a tickle. She almost giggled. And then, something odd happened. Something extremely odd.

A loud, disembodied, evil-sounding voice boomed around the whole room.

"FREE! I AM FREE! WE ARE FREE!"

The room became even darker for a moment, if that was possible, and then the door blew open. Something shadowy soared out from where the plunger had stood and rushed out the door, like a wind. It disappeared in an instant, a cold laughter fading into the distance.

Dottie fell flat on her behind and sat on the floor in shock. She just stared at the now-ajar door with her eyes and mouth wide open.

"Oh no! Oh lordy! What did I do? I gotta tell the others!"

She struggled to her feet and ran out of the house, not bothering to shut the door behind her and knocking over several of the warning signs on the way back to the path. For the first time in her life as a tourist, she wanted to be back on time.

* * *

Jilly Pleeth sat in the local park enjoying the afternoon sunshine, sketching pictures in her art pad. At age eleven, she showed quite a talent for drawing. While other children were spending the far-too-few warm summer days playing and running about, Jilly liked to do what she did best: draw.

Her parents were gone for the evening, off to one of their important "grown-up functions," something to do with buildings and managing properties and other such boring things.

"Apparently, adults like to get together after a hard day's work and talk to each other about work," she said to herself. Adults were weird.

They told her, "Be home by six o'clock," and had left her a meal to be microwaved. This would, of course, reduce its meager flavor quotient to that of a cardboard box, and make it dry, tough, and chewy, whatever it was, though it might be an improvement over her mum's usual cooking. Knowing that they would already be gone by six, Jilly had thought to be a bit naughty, get some proper food in a shop, and go home later, just because she could.

"Besides," she decided, "it won't be dark for ages, so it's fine to get home a bit later. I can always give mum's meal to Odin."

Jilly had come up with the name of the Norse god for the family bulldog, because Odin always seemed to be squinting out of one eye—the dog, not the god, that is. Well, the god might have done so, too. Odin the god wore an eye patch, hence her little joke. Her father never got the connection, but he liked the name anyway; he said it sounded important, and he would only own an important dog.

Adults were weird.

She sat there for a while longer, content to sketch birds and dogs and trees, and dogs chasing birds into trees, and then, tying back her long, sandy blonde hair, she decided to pack up and hatch her devious little plan to provide herself with some proper nourishment. There was a shop nearby that sold pies of all kinds: meat pies, vegetable pies, cheese pies, mushroom pies, and pies with various other mystery animal parts that Jilly thought were best left alone.

Not long ago, she'd decided to become a vegetarian, as much to shock her parents as out of personal conviction. They hadn't even noticed. Her mum had said something like, "That's lovely, dear," which just annoyed Jilly. Since she couldn't rebel and get a rise out of them, she'd decided to rebel in secret, on her own terms, hence her clandestine mission to the pie shop. At least *she* would know.

Arriving at said shop, she walked in and bought two pies—one cheese and one vegetable—from Mrs. Thackeray, a charming little woman whose head always seemed to be tilting one way or another. Jilly's mother called this a nervous tic, but for a long time, Jilly didn't know what an alarmed insect had to do with Mrs. Thackeray's head. She had started imagining all sorts of scenes of the little bug running rampant in the woman's hair, making her head shake back and forth to try to get it to fall off. Why didn't she just wash and comb her hair and be done with it? One day, she looked up what it really meant and then felt silly.

In any case, she thanked Mrs. Thackeray, left the shop, and began eating the vegetable pie as she walked home.

"I'll save the cheese pie for later, maybe even eat it in bed!" It was good to be a wild child.

Her walk was uneventful, and in the sunshine that lingered in summer, quite pleasant. She had a thought to go down to the river and sketch some more, but her hand was tired, so she decided to save that for another day.

"Still, it might be nice to walk along the river for a bit," she said, since she had nothing else to do. Except make sure that Odin was fed the incriminating evidence of the non-eaten "meal."

She made her way to the ruins of the old fourteenth-century castle that still towered over the rock outcropping by the river. It was a powerful reminder of the history of the region, and Jilly always liked to look at it and imagine what life could have been like back then.

It must have been dreadfully cold living in there in winter, she always thought as she walked by, and decided that, as fun as it might be to dream about living in a castle, central heating was more far acceptable in the real world. And the idea of outdoor toilets in the middle of January was even less appealing than whatever food was waiting for her at home.

She wandered down the twisty, winding steps and path from the castle's high position to the river and found a nice little patch of grass to sit on. The river calmed and relaxed her. She gazed at it for a short time, watching patterns in the current and thinking about how good it was to be away from school and doing important things instead.

Her attention was soon drawn to a little old woman wearing an aqua-colored T-shirt, white baggy shorts, and a cowboy hat. The woman hobbled along as fast as she could, heading past Jilly and toward the steps that led back up the hill to the castle. As she drew near to Jilly, she stopped, breathing hard. She looked scared.

"Run for your life, sweetie!" she panted in an accent that Jilly recognized as American and southern, from that funny cartoon show she'd seen about people in Texas. Jilly noticed the map of Texas on the woman's shirt and was pleased with herself.

"Excuse me, but why?" Jilly asked, bringing her attention back to the woman's panic, trying to be polite.

"Somethin' evil and unnatural's out there, darlin'! I'd say it was the devil himself that done gone and got loose. He was hidin' in a toilet plunger, and I accidentally set him free and he flew away! Lordy, it was awful!"

Jilly stared at her blankly. *Is this really what happens when you grow up?*

"I don't have time to explain," the woman continued, "but you'd best get on outta here before he comes after you... it might be the end of the world!" And off she went, huffing and puffing without another word.

Jilly watched her for a minute as she struggled up the multitude of steps and inclines toward the castle. Then, deciding that she should leave (though not because some Lord of Darkness was about to strike), she picked up her things and stood up.

Just keep walking by the river and join up with the streets a little farther up, she thought, *then you can avoid the crazy woman.*

She wandered a little farther on, when she noticed something strange down by the water. It looked like two people were struggling with each other. She didn't want to get too close, and there didn't seem to be anyone else around that she could run to for help; all of the river shops were already closed. Hiding behind a nearby tree, she peered around and tried to see what was happening.

A man dressed in a white robe with a red cross on the front of it seemed to be fighting and wrestling with... a shadow? Jilly squinted to try to get a better look, and yes, it *was* a shadow! It was dark, but she could still see through it. It looked like it was trying to strangle the man.

"This is crazy!" she whispered.

Fear washed over her, and she remembered what the old woman had said. She looked around in panic, desperate to find someone nearby, but she couldn't see anyone. It was upsetting that no one else was around. And worse, she had no mobile to phone for help.

The man was losing the fight; in another moment, he went limp, his hands slipping from the arms of the creature to fall lifeless at his sides. Jilly let out a horrified gasp, and regretted it at once. The shadow let the body fall into the river and turned its face toward her. Its eyes glowed red and seemed to bore right into her, like it was probing her mind. As she stood still, numb with fear, it let out a hiss and moved toward her, seeming to float over the ground.

Jilly was in shock, her mouth open and trembling. She wanted to scream, but no sound came out. Tears formed in her eyes, and her whole body shook. The creature was getting nearer now. Somehow finding the will to move, she turned and ran as fast as she could, dropping her cheese pie but keeping a tight grip on her sketchbook, as if it would afford some protection. She could hear the thing hissing and growling behind her, drawing closer, no matter how fast she ran. Her heart pounded, and she was already out of breath.

This has to be a bad dream! Please, let me wake up in the park!

But there was no such relief, and the thing was closing in; she could feel it.

She couldn't stop, she couldn't think, she couldn't even slow down and try to find an adult to help. She risked a glance behind her, but didn't see her pursuer anywhere.

Did it give up? Is it gone?

She didn't dare to hope. She didn't dare to stop. As she ran, her mind raced.

If I get away, where do I go? The police? And tell them I just saw a shadow with red eyes murder a man? They'll go tell my parents, and then I'll really be in trouble.

Being a rebel wasn't so much fun after all.

She could only rationalize that she had to get home. Once there, she could think things through; somehow she'd be safe there. Making leaps and bounds up a flight of steps to rejoin the town, she decided to take a shortcut though some side alleyways.

"That'll save time, and if it's still following me, I might be able to lose it!"

Gasping for breath, her sides hurt now, and she fought back tears of fright and confusion. She rounded the corner of an old building and headed toward a narrow alley straight ahead. She fled into it, and glancing behind herself again, she slammed straight on into something. The force of the impact knocked her down and backwards, and also knocked over whoever, or whatever, she'd hit. She let out a gasp from the impact and heard one from her unintended target.

In pain, she sat up and saw a young woman a few feet from her, also getting up and rubbing her stomach where Jilly had just collided with her. She had short blonde hair and ears that seemed... pointed? She looked almost like an elf. She wore a long-sleeved white shirt and blue jeans, with brown ankle boots. Jilly thought she was pretty.

"I'm so sorry miss," Jilly said through gasping breaths, forgetting her hunter for the moment. "I didn't see you, and I was running rather quickly, I guess."

"Oh it's all right," the elf-woman responded. "I'm not hurt and it was an... hold on!"

Jilly saw shock on her face.

"You, you, just called me 'miss,' and you... you're talking to me, and you can see me?"

"Uh, right," Jilly answered, picking up her sketchbook and sliding away, remembering her peril at once and feeling nervous.

"What do I look like?" the woman demanded.

Jilly didn't know what to make of the question. Her day was getting weirder by the minute. But she answered anyway.

"You've... got short blonde hair, you're wearing jeans, and you have pointy ears. Are you an elf? Like from *The Lord of the Rings*?"

The woman put her face in her hands. "Oh, bloody hell," she repeated several times. She looked up again after a few moments.

"Sorry, I shouldn't be swearing. And no, I'm not a flipping elf! Why do you lot always think that? Elves are just, well, *silly*, that's all. But since you can see me, there's no point in lying, I suppose. My name's Qwyrk. I'm what's known as a Shadow person, being, whatever."

Jilly eyes widened in terror, and she let out a short cry, jumping to her feet and making to run away.

"Wait!" Qwyrk exclaimed. "What's wrong?"

"I… I just saw one of you… things," Jilly stuttered, halting for a moment, but ready to flee at any second, "back down by the river. It killed a man and pushed his body into the water. And now it's after me!"

"What?" Qwyrk gasped. "No, that's not possible! Please, please understand, we don't kill people!"

"Well that one did!" Jilly protested, taking another hesitant step away and holding her sketchbook to her chest like a shield. She was ready to run in an instant if this "Quirk" person made any sudden moves.

"Look, honey," Qwyrk said in a soft voice, holding out her hands, maybe trying to show that she was no threat. "I don't know what you saw, but I promise you, I'm not a killer, and others like me aren't, either. We help people, especially children."

"Then what was that thing?" Jilly asked, halting her backwards inching.

"I don't know, but I can help you; I can protect you until I find out."

Jilly looked at Qwyrk for a long moment, not sure if she could trust her, or if it was just a trick. But there was something about Qwyrk's kind and concerned look that made Jilly feel safe. She moved back toward this stranger and timidly held out her hand, still clutching her sketchbook with one arm.

"I'm Jilly," she said with a half-smile.

Qwyrk smiled and shook her hand. "Nice to meet you Jilly. Now, tell me everything that happened."

Jilly recounted what she'd just seen, recalling the crazy Texan woman and the Shadow strangling that poor man. Qwyrk listened without interrupting.

"I don't understand. What does it mean? What's happening? Where did it go?" Jilly asked at the end of her story, exasperated and frightened.

"I won't lie to you. There could be some real trouble," Qwyrk answered, looking worried. "You see, Shadows help humans. We've been around for quite a long time. We live in our own world, our own dimension, I guess, but we're over in this one all the time to check on people and chase off bad things that might be causing trouble. Normally, no one can see us except like how you saw that one down at the river. We just look like shadows with glowing red eyes."

"Why's that?" Jilly asked, struggling to believe any of this and thinking that someone was having a joke at her expense.

"I don't even know, to be honest," Qwyrk answered. "It's just the way it's always been. Something mystical and magical, I suppose. It probably has to do with the fact that we're made of different stuff than humans. We see each other just as you can see me now. This is what I really look like. But the fact that you can see me in my real form at all is very odd, and added to everything else you've told me, it's even stranger."

"Is that thing going to come after me again, now that I've seen it?" Jilly asked with alarm.

Qwyrk smiled and put her hands on Jilly's shoulders.

"I'm not going to let anything hurt you, Jilly."

Jilly gave her a weak smile, but she knew that Qwyrk hadn't answered her question.

CHAPTER THREE

"Look, the best thing to do right now is to get you back to your home as soon as possible," Qwyrk offered. "We can talk more there in safety, and maybe figure out what to do, yeah?"

"All right, but I really want to know what's going on," Jilly replied. "I mean, I've always been open to strange things, but this is too much all at once, like when you eat ice cream too quickly and then your head hurts like crazy."

No doubt about it, today had turned into one big ice cream headache.

Jilly wasn't sure why she trusted Qwyrk, but the elfin woman had done nothing to alarm her, and she seemed genuine and caring, so Jilly reasoned it was safe to bring her home. It wasn't a great idea, but it was too late to do anything about it, anyway. The only problem, of course, was that Qwyrk (so she said) looked like a shadow with red eyes to everyone else, which could raise some eyebrows, even in a small town famed for its weird history.

She was relieved when Qwyrk said, "I'll follow you at a distance, and use back alleys and side streets where possible. That's how I navigate in daylight when I need to get around. It's all right, I do it all the time. That way, I can keep an eye out for the other Shadow, too!"

It took a little effort, and more than once, Qwyrk got lost in the maze of old streets that had no logical plan, requiring Jilly to backtrack and find her. After a bit of a hike, they made it to Jilly's home, a pleasant detached brick house on the northwest side of town, with a green lawn and a nice hedge in front (and thankfully, no rosebushes). As Jilly had figured, her parents were already gone for the evening. Looking around from the front step to make sure that no nosy neighbors were watching, she gestured for Qwyrk to come inside.

* * *

But she didn't notice the curtains ruffling from a window in a house across the street.

* * *

Qwyrk didn't need to use the door, but she decided that it would unnerve Jilly if she just walked through the front wall, so she obliged her young hostess. And she knew Jilly wasn't ready to see her teleport, not yet, anyway. Also, dematerializing was something that became more difficult and painful to do the longer she spent in the humans' world. Something to do with the different way our world is structured from theirs, but nothing a nice stay back in her own realm wouldn't fix.

Like I've got time for that, she thought.

Qwyrk stepped inside, and Jilly shut the door in haste, leading her guest into the living room.

At least these people have better taste than the Ecklesons, Qwyrk decided as she looked around.

"Do you want some tea?" Jilly asked.

"No thanks," Qwyrk answered. "We don't need to consume human foods, you see. I mean we can, but it's not necessary."

"Then what do you eat?" Jilly responded. "Sorry, I dropped my cheese pie, and I'm still hungry."

"Well, most often we don't, really," Qwyrk answered. "I mean, there are foods and drinks where I'm from, fruits and wine, and things like that, but those are more for celebrations and such, rather than sustenance. And humans who eat our food often end up in a bad state. They get so enamored of it that they can't go back to their own food, and they just starve. It's rather awful, actually. So, we never offer our food to humans without precautions, and we don't think to accept any of theirs. I guess we just don't have a taste for it."

"Not even things like fish and chips, or scones and jam?"

"No, sorry."

"Then how do you stay alive?"

"Well, Shadows are immortal, so things are different for us."

"That must be wonderful!" Jilly exclaimed.

"Well, it's not all great," Qwyrk answered. "Living forever has its drawbacks. I mean, it's easy to get bored, because after a while, you feel like you've seen and done everything. And if you get attached to mortals, it can be very hard to let them go..." She gazed out the window for a moment, looking a bit sad. If Jilly sensed that Qwyrk was remembering someone, she didn't pry, which was nice of her.

"Where *do* you come from?" Jilly asked, drawing her attention back to the conversation.

"It's a place called Symphinity. Well, that's what we call it now.

It used to be known as a part of Faerie, because humans thought it was so magical and wonderful. It still is by a lot of people."

"What does the name mean?" asked Jilly, sounding excited that she was speaking to a real live representative of the land of the Fae, even under a different name.

"Well, I guess it's like infinity, but they wanted to combine that with something artistic, like 'symphony' or something. Personally, I think it sounds like a New Age record album title, but lots of folks thought the name sounded more 'modern,' like some big corporation or something, making our realm ready to interact with humans in your twenty-first century. Every once in a while, the council who governs the realm likes to shake things up a bit, just to prove they've still got a sense of humor."

Or any sense at all, she thought, holding her tongue.

"It's just a symbolic change," she continued. "It doesn't really mean anything."

"What's it like there?"

"It's not that different from here in some ways. I mean, there are trees and grass and sky and such. I have a little home by a forest and a lake, though I don't spend much time there; too busy over here lately. Our world looks sort of medieval and fairy tale-like, but it's all a bit, I don't know, nicer somehow. Cleaner, more magical, older in a good way, if that makes sense. This world used to be much more like it."

"I thought so," Jilly answered. "We're not doing a very good job these days with taking care of things, are we?"

Qwyrk nodded. "And a lot of humans have forgotten how to dream and find magic in their lives. That's part of why we Shadows are here, too. To give children a little nudge when they need it and sometimes remind adults of what they've been missing."

"So, why are you up here in our town?" Jilly asked.

Forgetting herself, Qwyrk blurted out, "Because my two mates just wanted to slack off and go clubbing, I couldn't find a good place to do yoga, and the rosebush wasn't moving around as much as they said it was."

Jilly scrunched up her face in confusion. "Eh?"

Qwyrk laughed, realizing how ridiculous it sounded, so she recounted for Jilly some of her personal story, and how she, Qwypp, and Qwykk had ended up in the north of England. She left out the bits about her friends' tarty looks and behavior.

"This all must seem really strange to you," Qwyrk added with sympathy.

"Well, I must say, if I hadn't seen that Shadow creature, sorry... person, with my own eyes, I wouldn't have believed it."

"Didn't you ever believe in fairies and such when you were younger?"

"Sort of, I suppose. But since I never saw one, I guess I didn't think much about it. I remember hearing about those 'Cottingley fairies,' and how it was all made up with paper dolls, so I guess after that, I never thought about it much."

"Oh, no, they were real."

"What?"

"The Cottingley fairies, they were real. Edith, Emma, and Ethel. They've been known to be a right pain in the arse, as well. Oh sorry, I shouldn't be saying words like that around you."

"It's all right, I say it all the time. You mean they *were* real?"

"Oh yeah. I just spoke to them a few months ago. They still get giggles about the whole thing. They did it on a bet with their boyfriends, who were gnomes, you see. Gomer, Godfrey, and Abner."

"Abner?"

"Never mind. The point is they bet their blokes that they could get photos taken of them, and people would believe them. A lot did, including that Arthur Conan Doyle chap, who was right smart. He knew they were real.

"The important thing is, that all of those things children see and imagine are real. Well, most of them. Thank Goddess those bloated things in those colored jump suits with television antennae on their heads aren't real, or I'd be leaving for another dimension, let me tell you! And before you ask, no, there's no secret school for witches and wizards. Also, you're not going to get to my world by pushing your way through the back of a wardrobe. But most of the other things are real, like when children have imaginary friends that grown-ups can't see."

Just then, Jilly looked over Qwyrk's shoulder and squinted. Qwyrk saw that she had a perplexed look on her face, and turned to look in the same direction.

"What's that?" Jilly asked, pointing to a small figure standing in the corner of the room. It seemed to have appeared out of the blue, and wasn't making any effort to conceal itself.

It was a mottled avocado green, shaped like a frog with a pudgy face. Very like a frog face. Except for the bushy eyebrows. And the mutton chop beard. And the beefeater moustache.

"Oh no, oh Goddess, no," moaned Qwyrk, a look of mingled frustration and mild horror falling over her face.

"Oh no, what?"

"That's Blip," Qwyrk said with annoyance.

"Blip?"

"A jirry-jirry," Qwyrk answered.

"A what?"

"A jirry-jirry."

"What's that?"

"An imaginary friend, like I said. Lots of children have them."

"I don't."

"Well, lots do."

"But he's not imaginary. I can see him!"

"Yes, but that's what people call them."

"Why?"

"Because parents can't see them, so they assume they're imaginary."

"But you can see him."

"I'm not a parent. And they only come around if children imagine them."

"Then why is he here?"

"What do you mean?"

"You just said he was real!"

"What?"

"That, that... Blip. You said he was real."

"Yeah, so?"

"So, if he's real, how come he has to be imagined?"

"What?"

"You just said that he only comes around if you imagine him, but I didn't, and if he's real, why doesn't he just come around anyway?"

Qwyrk was getting a headache, which was rather remarkable, considering that Shadows don't get headaches.

Jilly looked at Blip again. "I'm quite sure I don't have that much imagination."

*   *   *

Jilly was even more confused. *What is going on today?*

"Look, it's real easy," Qwyrk started to say.

"My dear young lady," Blip addressed Jilly, interrupting and striding forward to both of them in a rather pompous walk on his hind legs. As he spoke, Jilly was wondering why a two-foot-tall frog would sound like one of those news presenters on BBC news or a proper gentleman from one of those Victorian television dramas.

"Please forgive the less than satisfactory answers to your conundrum given by the Shadow girl," Blip continued. "She can be a trifle unintelligible, even at the best of times, and I fear that with the situation facing you now, she shall be less than hopeless in explaining to you the intricacies of your unfortunate situation, offering instead mere persiflage. Therefore, I must humbly apologize on Miss Qwyrk's behalf. She cannot help it; it's in the breeding, you know."

Qwyrk fumed. Her eyes started to glow red, and she looked like she was about to explode.

"Now then," said Blip, clearly ignoring her. "My name is Bernard Beresford Bartlesby Blippingstone the Third, and I have just today been assigned to you. This rather uncouth girl," he motioned toward Qwyrk with disdain, "is in the habit of calling me Blip, a name I both abhor and detest."

Jilly wondered how one could abhor and detest something at the same time, and what the difference was in any case, but she kept quiet and nodded with a polite smile. She didn't want a lengthy explanation, anyway.

"The jirry-jirries perform a most important duty in the realm of childhood development," he continued. "We see to it that young minds are stimulated and that imaginations are activated. However, we can only show ourselves to children under the age of thirteen, give or take a year, and only when they have expressed a specific desire for an imaginary playmate. That creates the means by which we are able to manifest ourselves to them. Don't bother asking about the mystical technicalities; it's all quite complex. That's just the way it works.

"Those of a more, shall we say, parental nature, are limited by their adult-eroded cognition, and therefore cannot perceive anything other than that their children are talking to thin air, a jolly good defense mechanism, if I do say so!"

Jilly felt like she was back in school, listening to the most wretched teacher alive. Or even worse, one of those "guests" that was invited to her school for an auditorium talk, where every student had to attend for the betterment of their character.

"Exactly what I just said," interrupted Qwyrk, "only I said it with twenty words instead of two thousand."

Blip snorted, but said nothing else.

"What do you really want, *Blip?*" Qwyrk asked.

"Having listened to your conversation," he answered, "it is my understanding that there may be extraordinary qualities to this entire heinous situation that both of you have not yet surmised, implied permutations of such exquisite complexity that only the finest of intellects shall be able to unravel and extrapolate the oblique secrets, and thus propose adequate solutions that will resolve the crux of the matter satisfactorily. We must be impavid in our undertaking."

"Huh?" Jilly asked, a blank look on her face.

"He means that there's a lot more going on here that we don't know about yet, and it's going to take some smart thinking to figure it out," Qwyrk translated. "For once, I agree with him."

"Precisely what I just said," Blip answered with a cool and superior tone. "I offer myself as just such an intellect for this matter."

Qwyrk tried to hide her smirk, but didn't do a good job of it.

Jilly was more confused than ever.

Blip snorted in defiance again.

"Now then," he continued, "what do we know about the situation? If we're going to make a good start on it, then we must have all the facts arrayed before us. I daresay it wouldn't suit us to begin this venture with anything less."

"Mr. Blip," Jilly said, conscious that she was interrupting, but not wanting him to launch off into another auditorium speech.

"Mr. Blippingstone, if you please, child," he corrected.

Qwyrk rolled her eyes, which were now fading back to their normal color.

"Uh, right," said Jilly. "I'm wondering why your folk have such a peculiar name. Do you jeer at people because they can't see you?"

No, no, dear, no, child," Blip answered, waving his hands in a negative motion. "It's 'jirry' with an 'i.' No, you see, the name derives from the Latin motto of our noble stock: *Jiridicum omnium semper scientium*. 'All jirry-jirries are always knowing.'"

"Oh, bloody hell!" exclaimed Qwyrk, rolling her eyes again. "That's not Latin! You haven't got your declensions right, and there's no such word as 'jiridicum' in Latin!"

"And what would *you* know about it?" Blip shot back, taking umbrage.

"I was around when it was spoken the first time! I picked up more than a few things along the way," Qwyrk retorted.

"I'll have you know I was present at the sealing of the Magna Carta," Blip bragged.

"A lot of good that did you, since you don't know the sodding language!"

"The intent of the document was more than clear."

"And they were speaking French too. Or, are you a master of

that, as well?"

For Jilly, it was like she was watching a surreal tennis match.

"You just don't want to admit that I might possibly know more about something than you do," Blip sulked.

"More than what? If you don't believe me, go pick up a Latin language book; there's no such word, and your grammar's shite!"

She turned to Jilly.

"Jirry-jirries got their name because a young child once thought that one of them looked like jelly, the way he was jiggling about and all, but she couldn't quite pronounce the word correctly, so she called him 'jirry,' and then 'jirry-jirry.' We all thought it was funny, and so we started calling them that."

Blip scowled. "Jilly, jelly, jirry-jirry. I'm beginning to feel as if I'm looking at a crossword in the *Bedlam Weekly News*."

"But... jelly hasn't been around for all that long," Jilly noted, with far too much inquisitiveness for her own good. "And you said you've both been here for centuries. What were they called before?"

"A lot of things," Qwyrk whispered to herself, but Jilly heard her, anyway.

"Various things," she spoke up, "but nothing permanent. They are imaginary after all."

Now it was Jilly's turn to have the headache. "But you just said... oh never mind!"

"What I want to know," Qwyrk continued, "is why you're *really* here, Blip? Jilly didn't imagine you, and you didn't just suddenly take an interest in her, so what's going on?"

"I cannot comment."

"Oh, I think you can."

"I am not permitted to say."

"Oh, I think you are."

In a flash, she grabbed him by one ankle, hoisted him upside down and began tickling him on the stomach.

"WAHAHAHAHA! OOOH! OHHH! BWAAHAHAHHAA!! Damn it girl, stop it! I'm not going to tell, I'm not... HEEEEHEHEHEHEHOOHOHOHOHO!!" Blip thrashed about, trying to knock her arm away, with no success.

"Just tell me what I want to know, and I'll stop," Qwyrk said with an impish grin.

Blip laughed even harder, but managed to gasp out, "All right, damn you, all right! Just put... me... down!!"

Without another word, she let go of his ankle and he crashed to the floor in a heap. Swearing and cursing as if Jilly were not there, he pulled himself upright, rubbing his head.

"Nice job with the language there, Mr. 'Childhood Development,'" Qwyrk said, clearly enjoying this spectacle.

"If you're quite finished," he scowled, "I'm here because the council is not happy with your decision to abandon the haunted rosebush."

"I didn't 'abandon' anything! I'm just checking out a few other places that might give me some clues about what's actually going on. I think what's happened to Jilly qualifies as an important development! In fact I'd wager they're probably related."

"Undoubtedly," Blip retorted, "which is precisely why I am here. The child needs guidance, even if she did not request it. This is a most unusual situation, and the council wanted someone with experience to look into it."

"And they sent you, because?"

"Because I am just such a qualified individual: scholar, linguist, omniligent, philosopher, polymath... a natural leader."

Qwyrk choked back a guffaw. "No, more likely you were

'volunteered' for this because no one else wanted to touch it. They either thought it wasn't worth their time, or they viewed you as expendable in case it was something really bad. Also, I'm doing just fine without their 'help,' thank you very much! I'm going to have words with them when this is over. And that was a really rapid response to my running into Jilly, by the way; this whole thing just happened an hour ago! And the last thing I need is some pompous jirry-jirry telling me what to do, so why don't you just bugger off back to the council and tell them everything's under control?"

"I cannot do that, much as the thought is a tempting one," Blip said in an icy tone. "I am to remain here until this ostrobogulous mystery is solved. And since the girl has become involved, I now have to keep an eye on her. That's all I know; that's all they told me."

"Ah, now I get it. You were sent here because you *did* something, right? Screwed up badly on your last assignment? Managed to convince another child that Father Christmas isn't real?"

"Wait, he *is*?" Jilly asked in disbelief. "Oh, come on!"

"Of course he is," Qwyrk answered. "He and Blip have a long-running feud over something; I don't even know what it's about. And Blip's gone around in the past saying he doesn't exist; he's upset more than one child by it."

"That's horrible!" Jilly said, scowling at Blip.

"It was not my fault!" Blip defended himself. "I assumed the child in question was already past the stage of believing in him, so I saw no harm in discouraging that belief. It's not like Nicholas doesn't deserve a little scorn and derision from time to time, bloody arrogant pillock!"

"What made you two start arguing?" Jilly asked him.

"No one knows," Qwyrk interrupted. "Both of them refuse to talk about it, and it's been going on for decades. Anyway, we're getting way off track here. The point is, I don't need Blip helping me with this!"

"Do you see, young Jillian?" Blip turned to her, just ignoring Qwyrk now, but pointing an amphibious finger in her direction, "Do you see the lack of respect and rudeness that abounds in this woman? No manners, no etiquette, just the brash arrogance and impertinence so common in young people these days. It should not be allowed, I say!"

"I'm over two thousand years old..."

"In any case, I assure you, Miss Qwyrk, that when I am elected to the House of Lords, things will be quite different," Blip declared with all the authority a two-foot, moustachioed frog could muster. "We shall at last command the respect that we have deserved for so long. Ah yes, The Right Honourable the Lord Blippingstone of Upper Symphinity, member of The Right Honourable the Lords Spiritual and Temporal of the United Kingdom of Great Britain and Northern Ireland in Parliament Assembled. What a marvelous ring it has, don't you think?"

Jilly watched him gaze off into the distance, lost in the moment.

"Blip," Qwyrk said with a look of drained exasperation, dragging his attention back to the living room, "you can't be in the flipping House of Lords! You're not human, you're not a lord, and they're not electing people!"

"Trifling matters of no consequence," Blip replied with a dismissive wave of his arm. "My campaign shall be one of compelling arguments about substantive issues, which will sway the people and the Prime Minister over to my position. I shall have their full backing presently."

"That'll be a good trick," Qwyrk laid on the sarcasm, "considering they can't even see you. And who's going to vote for you? All those civic-minded ten-year-olds?"

"Hmmph!" was all that Blip said in reply.

"I don't wish to be horrible," Jilly said after a moment of icy silence between them, "but I *did* see somebody get killed this afternoon, and I'm still frightened about it. While you've been lovely company, I think I'd just like to go to bed and forget about it."

"I can't leave you alone, Jilly," Qwyrk answered with genuine concern, putting her hand on the girl's shoulder. "We don't know who did that horrible thing, and I'm afraid that if I leave you unprotected, you might be in danger."

"Quite right... for once," Blip interjected. "You'll be far safer with us."

Jilly saw Qwyrk wince in response, clearly not thrilled with the "us" part of it.

"But I could tell my parents," Jilly said. "Dad could go to the police. It would sound better coming from him than me, anyway. We don't have to say it was a Shadow. And what about that poor man's body?"

"I don't think it's a good idea, Jilly," Qwyrk answered. "More than likely, they'd end up thinking you were lying, and if they did find a body, they might even think you know more than you're telling. I'm guessing the dead man knew who the Shadow was, and maybe he could even see the Shadow's real form. Something really strange is going on, and I don't want to involve any more humans in it until I find out what."

"But I can see *you*," Jilly protested with frustration. "You're not just a shadow to me. What does it mean?"

Qwyrk looked away and out the window at the setting sun, but didn't answer. Jilly realized that she had no answer.

CHAPTER FOUR

Qwyrk and Blip spent the night in Jilly's room upstairs, but nothing disturbed their watch. Her parents returned around midnight and went straight to bed. Qwyrk sat at a chair and kept to herself, while Blip sprawled on the floor nearby, lying on his back, looking rather ridiculous.

Jilly's room had enough space not to feel cramped. It wasn't decorated in the typical manner of an eleven-year-old girl. It was a bit plainer ("and not all pink and fluffy, thank Goddess!"), but had some impressive prints of art masterpieces on the walls. Jilly liked Renaissance and Surrealist art, so the poster of the "Mona Lisa" next to Magritte's "Le Château des Pyrénées" made perfect sense in her mind. She'd wanted a poster of one of Bosch's paintings (a Renaissance Surrealist, she liked to call him), but even her not-over-ly-bothered parents thought the images were inappropriate; not until she was older, they said. Parents were so annoying. So, she just went to the library, looked up books of his works, and copied some of the whimsical and strange images into her sketchbooks, another triumph for the aspiring subversive artist.

"Can I sketch you?" she'd asked a distracted Qwyrk earlier that evening, when she was looking out the window with worry on her face.

"What?" She turned to her new friend.

"You know, draw a picture of you? Since I'm not supposed to be able to see you, I thought I'd like have a sketch of you, just because."

"Um, sure, I suppose. Do I need to do anything?"

"No, just sit there and kind of look in this direction."

"Excuse me," Blip interjected, raising his hand. "I should like to offer myself as a more suitable candidate for portraiture. A future Lord should be immortalized in the plastic arts of course: sketches, painting, sculpture. I may as well become accustomed to it. So, I would gladly volunteer myself to you for such an artistic endeavor. Simply tell me how you wish me to array myself and I shall be happy to oblige. Of course I do not have the appropriate accoutrements with me at this precise moment, but perhaps those could be filled in later."

"Um, right…" Jilly answered, flummoxed about what to say. She glanced at Qwyrk, who rolled her eyes and then resumed her gaze out the window.

She had a sudden idea. "I tell you what? Why don't I do a sketch of Qwyrk first, just for practice, and then we can arrange something more suitable for you tomorrow?"

"Ah yes, an excellent notion, child! Draw her now, and get all of the potential mistakes out of your system on a subject that does not matter. Then we can attend to the proper portrait in the morning."

Qwyrk shot him an evil look that seemed to communicate just how much she'd like to wrap her hands around his thick, but almost non-existent neck, and squeeze hard.

In any case, Jilly was pleased that she'd managed to deflect Blip's generous offer, and, taking up her pencil and drawing pad, she hoped that come morning, he would have forgotten all about it. She drew Qwyrk's picture and then fell asleep.

She slept well, oblivious to the dawn.

* * *

A nice feature (depending on your point of view) of northern England in the summer is the sun rising extra early, so that by five o'clock in the morning, it's broad daylight. On days when it's not cloudy, the sun is out in all it luminous glory, making it difficult for many to be late sleepers. All right, maybe it's not so great, after all.

The light made Qwyrk restless. She watched Jilly as she slept, feeling envy for the peace that humans can have every night by the simple act of closing their eyes. Neither she nor Blip needed to sleep, though she was sure she had seen him dozing more than once, probably just to irritate her; at least he didn't snore, as far as she knew. In any case, they couldn't talk while Jilly was still asleep, and they had agreed the night before that they were not willing to leave her unattended, even in broad daylight.

Not that she wanted to talk with Blip, anyway.

He's far too stubborn for his own good, and why, oh why, has he, of all jirry-jirries, been assigned to Jilly? He's probably sent to spy on me, even if he doesn't know it. Maybe he's been duped into doing it for some other reason; all it would take was a little flattery about his skills and his "noble lineage." But how the hell did they find out so quickly about Jilly?

Qwyrk was determined to take it up with the council, once this whole mess was cleared up. In fact, she was considering going to them right away to get some straight answers about what was going on, but she didn't want to leave Jilly alone.

She turned over the previous day's events in her mind for the hundredth time. The clock now read 6:00 AM. She was about to get up and peer outside when Jilly sat straight up in bed, her eyes wide and a look of awful realization on her face.

"Bollocks!" she half-whispered, half-shouted.

Qwyrk was on her feet and facing her, fearing that another Shadow may have entered the room, and Blip stood up at once from his faux-sleep, assuming what looked like a karate stance, arms extended and one leg up, in that crane pose from the movie about the martial arts kid, or something. Qwyrk didn't want to know.

"What is it?" she asked with alarm, looking all around the room to spot any potential threat.

"I forgot to feed mum's meal to Odin last night!" Jilly whispered.

"Odin?"

"Our dog. He'll eat anything, and I didn't want to eat the slop mum left me to microwave. So I thought I'd feed him with it last night, but then Mr. Blip showed up, and we got to talking, and I got sleepy, and we came up here... and I forgot all about it!"

Blip grimaced at his name yet again being taken in vain.

"If they find it's still in the refrigerator," she continued, "I'll be in trouble. I mean, they ignore me a lot, but they *do* notice things like that. It's pretty stupid really. They'll want to know why I didn't eat it, and where I was when I should have been home, and all sorts of rubbish. I'm not good with that kind of pressure on the spot, and I might just accidentally tell them everything!"

"Well, what time do they get up?" Qwyrk asked.

She looked at the clock. "In about ten minutes."

"That's not our only heinous situation," Blip announced, looking disturbed, and relaxing from whatever his martial arts stance was supposed to be.

FOUR

"What do you mean?" Qwyrk asked with ever-increasing annoyance.

"During our conversation last night, I must have mistakenly left my walking cane on the coffee table. It's magical; if I'm holding it, it's quite invisible, but if I set it down, that is not the case. If a human attempts to pick it up, or even touches it, it will fly up and about to avoid capture. Oh, and it screams. A smashing good trick if I do say so!" He smiled, which disappeared as he saw Qwyrk's glare,

"Bollocks!" Qwyrk swore, her eyes flaring red again and trying not to lose what little of her temper was left. "Jilly, you go downstairs, get the food, and get rid of it. Blip, you go get your stupid cane, and I'll keep watch!"

* * *

In a moment, Jilly crept out of her room, followed by her two most unusual new friends, past the closed door of her parents' bedroom, and padded downstairs. All was quiet.

Jilly snuck into the kitchen, past a sleeping Odin, and opened the refrigerator. There, in a sealed clear plastic box, was the so-called meal from last night. It appeared to be a mixture of some kind of meat (hadn't she told them several times that she was now a vegetarian?) and boiled vegetables, and it all looked rather grey in the morning light. Jilly lifted the box out and closed the refrigerator door, turning to take it outside and dump it. So pleased was she to have gotten this far, that she didn't notice where she was walking and tripped right over the sleeping dog, landing face down on the floor and sending the box of grey-colored food substances flying across the kitchen, to splat against the wall above the sink and spill its contents all over the counter.

Odin was up in a flash, barking. But that wasn't bad enough; his keen canine senses told him something was amiss in the living room. He bounded off into it as fast as his stubby legs would carry him.

"Oh no!" Jilly whispered in horror as she picked herself up, too late to catch hold of him and whisk him outside.

* * *

Meanwhile, Qwyrk stood at the foot of the stairs, and Blip made his way across the living room to where the cane was lying on the coffee table. While Qwyrk kept an eye out to make sure Jilly's parents didn't come out of their bedroom, Blip, nodding to her, started for the table.

He was no more than a foot away from reclaiming his odd little magical artifact when he heard Qwyrk hiss a profanity. Turning to see what the commotion was, he cried out as a massive growling bulldog bore down on him. Recoiling and throwing his hands up in front of his face, he ducked so that the dog missed him, but knocked the cane clean off the table in his clumsiness.

At once, the enchanted object rose up into the air and flitted about, zooming back and forth around the room in random, nonsensical patterns.

But at least it didn't scream.

No, it started singing a soprano solo from a Wagner opera; Brünnhilde's aria from *Die Götterdämmerung*, "Starke Scheite schichtet mir dort," to be precise:

"Starke Scheite

schichtet mir dort

am Rande des Rheins zuhauf!"

In a panic, Qwyrk dashed into the middle of the room and tried to grab hold of it, but each time she drew near, it would soar away to another part of the room, its vibrato becoming more piercing and obnoxious with each moment, threatening to break the windows. Blip jumped from the table trying to catch hold of the end, and missing it, fell on his backside in a most undignified manner.

"Hoch und hell

lodre die Glut,"

It was clear that Odin didn't know what to make of it all. He crouched down in a corner, growling and trying to look fierce. He watched as it soared from one end of the room to the other, but made no attempt to chase it.

*　*　*

Jilly stumbled into the living room, having forgotten about the food oozing like a mudslide down the kitchen wall.

"What's going on?" she hissed in panic, her voice all but drowned out by the not-so-dulcet tones of the operatic walking stick.

"die den edlen Leib

des hehresten helden verzehrt."

"The dog can see us and he hit the bloody cane, didn't he?" Qwyrk answered, not even trying to whisper, "and now it's gone all flipping operatic diva on us. Blip! What the hell kind of defense is that? I thought you said it screamed!"

"I personalized it," he retorted with irritation, as if that were obvious. "I found the screaming too much to take, rather like a scene from a medieval torture chamber. Now, if someone tries to steal it, at least I can expose them to some culture. It might help with their rehabilitation!"

"I don't even believe this," Qwyrk said, a blank look on her face, not even flinching as the cane whizzed by over her head. "Actually, I do."

"Sein Roß führet dahrer,

daß mit mir dem Recken es folge:"

"Jilly?" a woman's voice called from upstairs. "What's all that racket down there? Why are you up so early? What's going on?"

"Right, I've had enough of this," Qwyrk said, looking well beyond annoyed. Not taking her eyes from the cane, she waited until it began its next circle across the room. She jumped up, and to Jilly's astonishment, stayed suspended in mid-air. The tuneful walking stick soon rushed over in her direction.

"denn des Helden heiligste

Ehre zu teilen,"

Qwyrk reached out with remarkably quick reflexes and caught hold of the end.

"verlangt mein eigener Leib.

Vollbringt Brünnhildes Wunsch!"

SNAP!

The singing stopped at once (well, just as the first stanza ended, anyway). Qwyrk descended to the floor, holding one piece of the cane in each hand. Blip regarded her with a mixture of outrage and horror; he was almost shaking.

* * *

At that moment, the sound of footsteps on the stairs was a signal to both of them to remain quiet. Qwyrk blended into the shadows near the curtain, and Blip would not be seen, though he looked ready to swear like an army sergeant and give himself away.

Jilly's mother appeared, bedecked in a pink robe, her hair pinned up in several places. In fact, she had so many pins sticking out in all directions that Jilly thought she looked like that bald-headed creature from those horror movies she wasn't allowed to watch, but had managed to see anyway, late one night at a sleepover at her friend's house. They were gross.

"What's going on?" her mother asked again.

"I'm sorry mum. I couldn't sleep, and I was playing with Odin, and... I hit the stereo and accidentally turned it on." Jilly hoped that her mother wouldn't notice at just past six o'clock in the morning that she never played with Odin, and that they had no Wagner in their CD collection.

"Well, stop messing about," her mother carped. Without saying another word, she turned around and went back down the hall to her bedroom and husband, who had apparently slept through the whole thing.

Jilly leaned against a wall, breathed an audible sigh of relief, and looked over to Qwyrk, who also looked relieved.

"I have to go and clean up the mess in the kitchen," Jilly whispered. "They'll be back out before long."

* * *

Qwyrk let out a sigh of exasperation and sank to the floor. Blip stormed over to her, a look of righteous indignation on his face (if such a thing is possible on a frog with a moustache). He snatched the two pieces from her hands.

"And just what am I supposed to do with these?" he asked sourly. She glared back at him. "Do you really want me to tell you?"

* * *

The trio laid low until Jilly's parents were out of the house some ninety minutes later. Jilly had managed to scrape the pseudo-food off the wall and counter and get it into the rubbish bin outside, after discovering that even Odin wouldn't eat it. She then headed back up to her room and shut the door, pretending to be asleep.

Qwyrk watched as Jilly's parents drove away, and then turned to the others.

"Entertaining as this morning has been," she sneered, "we have a lot of work to do today if we're going to find out what the bloody hell is going on."

"I completely concur," Blip responded, apparently over his sulk about the cane. "This will require meticulous research of a most scholarly nature to uncover the multi-faceted plots which have insidiously woven themselves together in such an inextricable manner, as to be nearly impenetrable in their density and opacity. Indeed, there is likely a phenakism here, and the consequences of our not unmasking it are such that..."

"Blip, shut up," Qwyrk said without any emotion one way or another. Blip snorted.

"Now, Jilly," she started, "I want you to tell me one more time what happened yesterday. Try to remember everything. I've got some ideas about what may be going on, but I'm still not sure."

So Jilly once again recounted the frightening events of the day before, when her life rather rudely became too weird, even for her liking. Qwyrk listened, and even Blip paid attention. It was the same version, Qwyrk decided, but she was glad that her new friend humored her in telling it again, anyway.

"You said that funny American woman told you she released something from under a... toilet plunger," Qwyrk noted. "Did she say *where* she was when this happened?"

"No, just something about setting it free. It could have been in a house, a shop, anywhere, really."

"Well, it must have been near the river, because she couldn't have gotten too far, and it sounds like it had just happened when she saw you. She was running from it."

Jilly nodded. "I wonder about the poor man that creature— sorry, Shadow—killed. Won't the police find his body soon?"

"Maybe, but maybe not. It might have already washed down river and won't be found for days. Or maybe whoever did this has the power to conceal it. Maybe he can prevent others from seeing his victim."

"But then why did I see him?" Jilly asked. "Why do I see you? And why was he a shadow to me, but you're just as who you really are when I look at you?"

It pained Qwyrk to see her frightened and confused. "I don't know. Somehow, you've slipped into our level of awareness. It may have started when you saw the murderer, and finished up when you ran into me. But as to what's caused it, I don't know. Not yet, anyway. But we have to figure out what's so special about the place down by the river, and why a man was killed by... whatever it was."

Qwyrk realized that she was as confused as Jilly, which wasn't helping.

Blip stood up. "What we need is to obtain a good general knowledge of the area, and possibly a map that would show all nearby buildings that could be candidates," he offered, then paused for a moment.

Qwyrk looked at him in surprise. "You're right, Blip."

He continued, "It would be even better if we had someone with a good accounting of all the toilet plungers positioned thusly as supernatural restraints in the vicinity."

Qwyrk's face fell. *You had to spoil it, didn't you?* she thought.

"We should try to find the funny woman from Texas who let it out," Jilly spoke up, obviously hoping to head off another fight between the two. "She might be able to tell you a bit more; she was right odd, though."

"Good idea," Qwyrk nodded. "Do you think those tourists will still be in town?"

"I don't know, but I doubt it," Jilly answered, her face falling as if a good chance had just been wrested away from them. "Those groups just come in for the day, and then they're off somewhere else, or back to where they came from. They probably left sometime last night. We'd need to find out where they went."

"Over at the coach depot, then."

"Yes, but we don't know which one they were on, and I doubt they'd know just from my description of her, strange as she was."

"There might be some people in town who saw them and heard where they were going next; just thinking about how they were dressed, they'd be pretty hard to miss," Qwyrk thought out loud. "Or, I could always just head on out and try to find them." She realized that would mean leaving Jilly alone with Blip, and her stomach turned a little, yet another non-Shadow affliction. She decided she might have to risk it.

"I wonder if anyone over at the store would know?" Jilly asked.

"The store?"

"The *Aloe Plant Swapping Shop*. It's a big New Age place up on the high street. It's quite popular with tourists. Folks come from all over to buy things there, have psychic readings done, attend workshops, get enlightened in a weekend, that sort of thing. Some of those tourists might have gone in and we could ask about the Shadow person, too. This kind of thing may be right up someone's alley over there."

"Mmm, I don't want to involve too many humans," Qwyrk answered, worried about this getting out of hand. "If more people know about what happened, that will put them in danger too. I have a feeling this murderer has an agenda; he'll likely leave most people alone if they don't know about him, at least for now. I'm not sure, but I doubt his victim was random."

"But we don't have to say much of anything," Jilly answered. "We could just sound out a few people about history and landmarks. I mean, *I* know some things about the town, but not that much. If this sort of thing has happened here, it might have happened before. Or at least there may be someone who's heard of some spirit being locked... in a toilet plunger."

All three realized just how preposterous that sounded.

"Sound reasoning, child," Blip said in an encouraging voice. Qwyrk was almost proud of him. "I vote that we make for this establishment at once, and continue our investigation there."

"And just who are you going to question?" Qwyrk grinned, "some world-famous child occult historian?"

Blip sniffed, but otherwise ignored her.

"It's a good idea, Jilly, but are you up to doing this, since you're the only one who can ask questions?"

"Well, I'll just go in and be myself. The people there are nice, and a few of them know me. Mr. Blip could come with me, since they can't see him, and you could follow us along back streets and alleys. If I find out anything, I'll just come back to you."

"It's Mr. Blippingstone," Blip interjected.

"And I suppose I can find some place dark to linger while you're asking," Qwyrk reasoned.

"How about down in the London Underground in front of an

approaching train?" Blip muttered to himself.

"What?" Qwyrk asked.

"Nothing, nothing. Just clearing my throat."

"We'll just see if we can find out anything at all," Jilly offered. "Maybe there's a book on the town's weird history. There are lots of strange things that were supposed to have happened here over the centuries, and someone might have written them down."

"Right then," Qwyrk said, standing up with a smile. "Let's go get enlightened!"

CHAPTER FIVE

Jilly and Blip left the house at around 10:00 AM, followed by Qwyrk, who, not finding many shadows on a bright, sunny, summer morning, elected instead to hop from roof to roof back into town, explaining that she would be mistaken for a shadow of a cloud or bird by the unobservant below. The sight rather unnerved Jilly, seeing Qwyrk in her true form skipping with ease over large distances.

"Does she always do things like that?" she asked her diminutive companion as they strolled along a sidewalk.

"Hm?" Blip answered, his mind obviously on other things while he fiddled with a shiny monocle. "Oh, yes, that. Well, you must understand child, that Shadows are a bit... oh, how should one say, undisciplined for the most part. I mean, the council instructs them perfectly well in how to carry out their duties, but repeatedly, the Shadows act in very improper and insubordinate ways. I'm afraid there is nothing to be done about it. However, when I am a member of the Lords..."

Blip was interrupted (and to Jilly's relief) by the sound of a toddler laughing. They passed a young mother pushing her little girl in a pram. The child saw Blip and began to giggle with delight, pointing at him and trying to get her mother's attention. The mother, of course, saw nothing but Jilly. Feigning ignorance, Jilly shrugged at the woman and hastened up the street, Blip following behind in a jog.

"Does it bother you that grown-ups can't see you?" she asked as they rounded a corner and started for the main street.

"Oh, not at all," Blip answered. "We could not perform our duties if we were to be seen by every low-born commoner who happened to look."

Jilly rolled her eyes and decided not to pursue the conversation any further.

After crossing a tall road bridge over the train tracks, they made their way up to the main market street of town. Things were quiet this morning; the buses of tourists wouldn't start pulling in until about noon, giving the locals at least a few hours' peace every day. The town center was all cobblestones and Dickensian buildings and charm, rebuilt to look like it had been that way for centuries. It was a clever trick that worked; few visitors ever questioned any of the buildings' ages. Jilly liked it; it gave her a feeling of connection with the past, even if it was a bit manufactured.

Their destination was in one of those restored buildings, and but for the store's name on the window and its odd collection of objects displayed, it could indeed have been an old Victorian curiosity shop. However, the wands, crystals, and electric-powered meditative fountains in the window ruined that illusion.

Arriving at the *Swapping Shop*, Jilly saw that few people were inside yet. She looked up and saw Qwyrk crouching on the edge of a roof on the opposite side of the street. With a nod to her, Jilly entered the store and motioned to Blip to follow right behind to avoid the door slamming shut on him.

Inside was a strange and wonderful mixture of all manner of things designed to aid spiritual seekers on every path in whatever way they wished. Three floors of candles, crystals, incense, oils, books, CDs, statues, feathers, flutes, drums, art, and everything else one could imagine, plus more. Jilly always liked coming in here; it gave her a break from the humdrum world outside. Here, all of the things she wanted to believe might exist actually did. She doubted that her parents would approve, which made it an even better place to be. And now, her strange new visitors had offered confirmation of those magical things she longed for, which thrilled and unnerved her at the same time.

"Good morning, Jilly!" a kindly, middle-aged woman said. Jilly turned and saw that it was Janet, the store's manager. Her long brown hair was streaked with grey, braided, and tied back. A pair of gold-rimmed wire spectacles perched just at the edge of her nose. If not for the rustic, homespun, neo-hippie clothing, she could have been quite at home in one of the town's many antique shops, or some such similar establishment.

Jilly smiled and strode up to the counter. Blip stayed behind her, saying nothing. Apparently, Janet couldn't see him at all. Good! She decided he just had to stay quiet; being invisible did not mean being inaudible.

"Good morning, Janet," Jilly answered with a big smile.

"What brings you in here so early, dear?"

"Oh, no reason, really, just thought I'd look around, see what's new. You always get new things in mid-week, don't you?"

Janet nodded. "There's not much new today, though. I did get some lovely incense burners in, but that's not your sort of thing, is it?"

"No, not really. The smoke just makes me sneeze. Say, did you see those funny tourists from Texas yesterday, the ones in the cowboy hats and horrible T-shirts?"

"So much for subtlety," Blip muttered, rolling his eyes. He scowled at her, but she pretended not to see or hear him. *Shut up!*

Janet smirked. "Oh, they were a giggle! I had a few come in here and look around. Quite puzzled, they were. I managed to sell some candles to one, but the others left in a hurry, saying something about it all being the work of the devil."

"I wonder where they went off to?" Jilly laughed.

"Oh, York. The one lady who bought the candles was quite excited about it. She said they were going to stay in that area for a couple of days. I'd love to see them all at the Viking Centre, on the cars, and sniffing the Viking latrine!"

Jilly smiled and turned to give Blip a look of smug satisfaction.

"Yeah, that would be a right laugh! Say, I was wondering, do you know anything about the weird things that were supposed to have gone on here over the centuries? Like people seeing shadow beings and fairies and such?"

Blip groaned. "Why not just fill out a full report and hand it to the police? Or shall we inform the local branch of the BBC as well?"

Jilly shot him a quick glare, but was glad to discover that again, he'd not been heard.

"Shadow beings?" Janet said with obvious amusement. "Dear, I think you've been watching too many horror movies. But you might want to check out the local history section upstairs. We have some books on old Granny Boatford, who lived here in the sixteenth century. She was supposed to have seen some strange things, and said even stranger things."

"Right, I'll do that, thanks."

Jilly turned to head up to the next floor.

"Child, I do not recommend a career as a detective in law enforcement," Blip announced as they climbed the stairs.

"Hmm! I got answers, didn't I?" Jilly whispered with annoyance.

"Crudely. A bit more eloquence would have been appropriate. Certain protocols observed under such distressing circumstances will always yield the expectant results with the least amount of unnecessary burden."

"Shhhhh! Someone will hear you!"

Jilly kept her decidedly not-well-mannered thoughts to herself as they reached the next floor. Fortunately, no one else was up here yet. They found the history section, a hodge-podge of books about various odd topics, none of which would have impressed a historian, with titles like *The Secret History of the Atavistic Frogmen of Thule* and *5,000 Years of Prune Juice: An Illuminati Conspiracy*.

Looking through the titles, she found some promising ones and flipped through a few of the books on Granny Boatford, but none of them had anything to say about any Shadow people that she might have seen. Blip kept insisting on seeing each book for himself to double-check, so she would set them on the carpet, and he would turn pages, after checking to make sure no one else had joined them on this floor. Seeing a book turn pages all by itself would have been a bit too much, even for the shop's usual customers.

After a while of futile searching, she was ready to give up, when she found a passage on the page of a facsimile edition of Boatford's biography, from 1608:

And so it was that one James Goodkinne, Esq., thus belieu'd by all to be sorely afflict'd with the most lamentable humour of Tom of Bedlam, didde go unto Grandemother Boatforde in her cave for to seeke a remedie to his ill temper'd disposition. He tolde her that he had oft times and in diuerse ways been uisited by a shadowe man with eyes that glow'd as from the very depths of Hades. Afear'd that he had become thus possess'd, the Grandemother dismiss'd his frighte, saying unto him that suche creatures were in the service of goode and would do unto him naught that inclin'd to evil. She summon'd his ghostlie haunt, who thus spake unto him his true purpose, whiche was for the guarding of his children. Thus cur'd of all terror, James went away in laudible solace.

"Did they really speak and spell like this back then?" Jilly was incredulous, struggling to understand the archaic language.

"Oh yes, absolutely!" Blip answered with pride. "A very good time to be around, I daresay. Shakespeare, Marlowe, Sidney, Jonson, Donne, Spenser. The folk of those times knew their manners and graces, unlike the uncouth masses of today, in fact..."

"Mr. Blip," Jilly interrupted in a lowered voice, hoping to avoid another auditorium lecture, "we should tell Qwyrk about this. It's obviously referring to Shadow people. It's not much, but it's a start."

"It's 'Mr. Blippingstone,' child, but I agree. I shall fetch her at once." And off he bounded before Jilly could stop him.

*   *   *

Leaving her to peruse the rest of the obscure books for any more references, Blip hopped back down the stairs, to be confronted by a problem he had not thought of: how to open the door and leave the shop without drawing any attention to himself.

"I could go back and retrieve Jilly; no, no, I am supposed to be educating *her*, it wouldn't do to ask for her help. Plus, it would seem odd for her to open the door for no reason, and then go back upstairs. It might draw unwanted attention. If I simply teleport through, I might leave a magical trace and draw even more unwanted attention."

He mused a while longer.

"Now, let me see," he said, stroking his handlebar whiskers, and gazing at the floor.

The door opened and a potential customer walked in. The door shut.

"I could create a slight distraction. Perhaps knock over a few candles or some such."

Another customer paid for a book and left the store. The door swung open and shut.

"No, no, much too anarchist. It wouldn't be proper. One must maintain a certain sense of decorum, even in distressing situations."

A magazine delivery man pushed open the door and propped it open with his foot, as he picked up his bundle of journals.

"Ah, I have it!" he said with a snap of his froggy fingers. "When the proprietor goes to lunch, I shall follow deftly behind and sneak past while the door is open. Ha! Brilliant! Except, that luncheon is a long way off yet, or at least should be if done in the proper manner. There is elevenses, of course, but I doubt that they adhere to that noble custom this far north. A bit uncouth up here, they are. No real manners."

Blip looked up for a moment. Through his monocle, he spied the still-propped-open door. He thought. It dawned on him. Time was wasting. He had one chance. He made his move. The door began to swing shut as the delivery man moved into the store. Blip panicked. He ran. He dove for the doorway. He made it through just as it closed. Almost. The door slammed on his foot. He crashed face-first onto the pavement, his monocle rolling off into the street, where it was crushed by a passing car.

"OH, BLASTED BLACK PUDDINGS!" he yelled in agony at the

top of his lungs. Fortunately, no one was around to notice why the door to that unusual shop was swearing of its own accord. On the other hand, most of the locals wouldn't have cared, anyway.

* * *

Just then, Qwyrk appeared, jumping off the rooftop opposite the store and landing in front of him. She hadn't even bothered to worry about who might see her.

"Blip, what the hell are you doing?"

"Get...my...foot...out...of...the...door... Please!"

She let out an exasperated sigh and pushed the door open a little. Blip withdrew his foot with more swearing and stood up. He clutched it and hopped around on his remaining good one.

Qwyrk choked back a laugh, but couldn't hide her smile. Still, she was mad.

"We have to get off the street!" she snapped without a hint of sympathy, grabbing him and dragging him away from the front door.

Ducking into a nearby alley, with Blip still hobbling on one foot, she turned to face him.

"Now what the hell is going on?"

"We found something," Blip grunted. "In an old facsimile edition of the life of Grandmother Boatford, a sixteenth-century mystic who dwelled in these parts in..."

"Oh, bloody hell, I know who she was. What did you find?"

"Hmph! Apparently, she could see and speak to Shadows, and even summon them."

"And?"

"And... that's all we've learned so far. I was coming outside to tell you, so that you could have a look at the book yourself. But such courtesy is obviously something you do not appreciate."

Qwyrk let out a sigh. "All right, I'm sorry. You're right, I should take a look at this. I'll need to find a way to sneak inside."

"It's not as easy as you might think," he answered, his foot still aching.

"You all right there?"

Qwyrk whirled around to see a young man looking at her in astonishment. He had long brown, platted hair, a scruffy beard, and a couple of facial piercings, one each on the nose and eyebrow. He sported a white long-sleeve Tibetan shirt with colorful tie-dye patterns in the middle, baggy olive green pants, and a pair of scuffed Doc Marten boots.

"What?" was all she could say in reply. It didn't even occur to her that he shouldn't be able to see her at all.

"Oh, I don't mean no harm," he answered in a sing-song tenor voice. "It's just that, well, a minute ago you were like all shadowy and see-through, and now you're this really fit bird. That's dead cool. Can you teach me how to do that?"

Rather than try to deny anything or worry about why yet another human could see her in her actual form, she just went with it. "No, no, I can't actually. It takes years of practice. I learned how to do it in Nepal, and that's the only place you're allowed to study it. Maybe you should go there. Right now."

"Sweet!" he said. "I knew it was going to be a cosmically import-ant day today. Me guides told me in the bath this morning."

"Your guides... in the bath?" Qwyrk asked.

"Oh yeah, Zixytar, and Zzazznapo'ti'ak, the two higher alien beings from the Council of 27 that I channel. That's where they always appear to me. But it's all right; they are beyond the lure of the flesh, and so are not aroused by the sight of my naked body."

"Can't imagine why," Qwyrk said to herself.

"Eh?" he asked.

"Nothing."

Blip sat on a crate nearby, ignoring them, rubbing his foot, and sulking, muttering about the loss of his monocle.

"I thought when I first saw you that you might have been that freaky looking shadowy thing I saw yesterday down by the river; real ugly vibe coming off that one. Evil, actually. Didn't want to be anywhere near it."

Qwyrk shot him an alarmed look.

"But you seem cool enough," he continued. "You related to him or something?"

"N-no," she answered. "He's not someone I know at all."

"Fair enough."

"What's your name?" she asked with a sigh, now losing hope of keeping this nightmare a secret.

"Well, that's the thing," he replied. "I've actually got several. My full name is Star Shine Moon Tao Who-Prances-With-Hedgehogs. I had it changed to that legally a few years back, right about the time I got me eyebrow piercing. It was only twenty-five quid, the name change, that is. The piercing I had done for free by me mate. I adopted the name after a really freaky vision quest, where the Great Hedgehog Spirit appeared to me and told me the secrets of the universe."

"The 'Great... Hedgehog Spirit'?" Qwyrk raised one eyebrow.

"Yeah, but he said I could go by 'Star Tao' for short, so that's what I do most of the time."

"So... Star Tao, what did you learn from the, um... Great Hedgehog Spirit?" She fought back a smirk.

"Well, I can't remember much about them universal secrets. Shame really. I always thought I could write a book on the whole thing and make a fortune like that Deepra Chopak guy, but maybe the mortal mind cannot hold such knowledge for too long."

I doubt your mind can hold much of anything for too long, thought Qwyrk, fighting the temptation to say anything.

"What's that?" she asked, noticing he held a handful of flyers, and trying to be polite, or at least change the subject to something less absurd.

"Oh, right!" He beamed, holding up the pile and trying to even them out. "This is me workshop coming up this Sunday. We meet here at the store, and then we walk on out to the country. Yeah, I've done a lot of work to get it all together. Have a look and see what you think."

He handed her a flyer, which she took and glanced at.

Star Tao, Now, Wow!

A day of enriching, enlightening, non-fattening, non-animal tested, non-environmental impact sound experiences channeled from the Pleiadian Star Sisters and Brothers of the Eighteenth Dimension.

6:00 AM – 7:00 AM

The day begins with "Reiki-Wakey" at dawn, a simple and effective means of awakening the honoured seeker to the joys and treasures that await them throughout the day, accompanied by Tibetan singing bowls and sweet grass incense. And nose flutes.

7:00 AM – 8:30 AM

Breakfast will be served in the first workshop, "Yogurt with Yoga (Soy Options Available)." The goal will be to feed yourself with your feet. In addition to spoons, chopsticks will be available to advanced students, who may also choose the "Tarot with your Toes" option for £25 extra.

8:30 AM – 10:30 AM

"Feng Shui and the Art of Reiki with Aromatherapeutic Crystals whilst under Self-Hypnosis using NLP during Hatha Yoga augmented by Shiatsu, and Reflexology in the Nude" is fairly self-explanatory, but additional details can be provided on request.

10:30 AM – 12:00 PM

Learning to channel whilst practicing short yang form Tai Chi will allow your chosen higher entity to slide into your being with greater ease, refreshing you both and clarifying your transmissions. The last half hour will focus on DIY acupuncture, to further fine tune your messages. Aromatherapy oils will be provided.

12:00 PM – 1:00 PM

A wholesome lunch of organic, vegan, non-GMO, fairly-traded, gluten-free, refined sugar-free, fat-free, cholesterol-free, non-environmentally impacted delicious fare will be served (menu to be announced). No microbes will be harmed in the creation of this food, and it will be cooked solely through the directing of energy through crystals. For Breatharians, a selection of imported airs will be on offer. If you eat or drink too much, relief can be found in the Iron John. There will also be two informal discussions: "Mu and You," and "The Bonsai and I." Thereafter will follow a Dreamtime rest period. Lucid dreaming is recommended.

1:00 PM – 2:30 PM

Gregorian chant with Tantric Chi Kung in the "Hildegard the Corn Mother" Sweat Lodge will begin right after lunch. Bring djembes. This is followed by beginning instruction on out-of-body Tantric sex whilst in the presence of your Power Animal (and how to do it in public and not be noticed), accompanied by Indian bells, whale song, and wind chimes.

2:30 PM – 3:00 PM

Time for you to pause, reflect, and just be. Or use the toilet.

3:00 PM – 4:00 PM

Coal walking in a Native American shamanic trance-dance-as-soul-work for the wounded Holy Fool within will be followed by soothing massages for anyone with sore feet, administered by women who run with wolves. Dowsing rods are optional, but encouraged.

4:00 PM – 5:00 PM

Star Tao speaks: Counseling the self god-consciousness to nurture the playful performance artist inside, and raise the kundalini of your inner child. Bring digeridoos. This will be followed by smudging in a medieval-style, permacultural monastic herbal garden, modeled on a crop circle design.

5:00 PM – 5:30 PM

The day will conclude with a rune casting, done in a clockwise progression in robes around a maypole positioned on a ley line to honor the sun, which by then will be on its way to setting (well, in another five hours). But by doing this, we will send a powerful summoning prayer with our collective energies for it to rise again the following day. This has never failed to work.

So come, find yourself, come again, and unleash the Atlantean-Isis-Dolphin-Pyramid power within!

Cost for the day: £399, excluding VAT

Please note that astrological readings will not be given at this workshop, as we would like to be taken seriously.

"Pretty cool, eh?" Star Tao said, swaying back and forth a little, and bobbing his head up and down, clearly pleased with himself.

Watching him made Qwyrk feel a bit sick, and Shadows don't get seasick. In fact, a lot of things that don't happen to Shadows seemed to have just popped by to say "hello" in the last two days.

"Exactly how many participants do you have signed up for this... thing?" she asked, handing him back the flyer and trying to focus on something in the distance, while still appearing to be looking at him.

"Well, one so far, a bloke from down in Sheffield. I sort of know him, well... he's me other cousin, actually. But we still got a few days! I think there's going to be a swelling of interest at the last minute. That's the way it always is."

There's going to be a swelling on your head in the next few minutes if you don't stop swaying, thought Qwyrk, but instead saying, "How many of these have you run before?"

"Well, uh, this is me first. But I've had a lot of experience listening to others who've done 'em, right? So, I think I have a really good take on what to do."

"Ahem. I'm sorry to interrupt, but I'm wondering what all of this rubbish has to do with our ongoing investigation." Limping into their presence, Blip looked peeved at having been ignored all this time. Never mind that he had ignored them first. And he was undoubtedly still upset about the fate of his shiny new eye piece.

"Oh right!" Star Tao said, looking down at Blip with wide eyes. He knelt down and put his hands together. "You're the great Amazonian Frog God! Cool! I channeled you once. Hail, bimba-bumba, mega-moga thaaaloooooo! Say, did you ever find out what really happened to Jim Morrison like I asked you?"

The fact that Star Tao could even *see* Blip didn't surprise Qwyrk at all at this point. Nothing did.

Blip motioned to Qwyrk to bend down to him. She did, and he said into her ear, "What on earth is this miscreant talking about?"

"I think he saw the murderer, too, Blip," she whispered. "Go along with him; he could be useful. He thinks you're a god, which should please you."

"Ahem, yes, right, well," Blip started, clearing his throat and making himself audible again. "I am indeed that god to whom you refer, young man, though I daresay I haven't been in the Amazon for quite some time. A god is needed all over the world, you see, and one of such a stature as me could never be confined to one geographical location for too long."

Qwyrk already regretted her suggestion.

"Now as for this Mr. James Morrison, I'm not sure I recall you making that request; I'm a very busy god, you know, and even a god can become somewhat forgetful, what with his multitude of duties. What does he do, this Mr. Morrison? Is he in Parliament? What's his constituency?"

Qwyrk buried her face in her hands.

"Parliament?" Star Tao answered with a laugh. "That's really funny, mate. You're like a trickster god, aren't you, one who's always messin' about and doin' our heads in to teach us new things. I can groove on that. You're all right, mate. Instruct me and I shall follow."

Blip turned to Qwyrk again with a large smile and whispered, "Despite the uncouth nature of this youth, I seem to have acquired a loyal follower, perhaps even a disciple. Despite my continual lack of accolades, the tragic loss of my cane and monocle, and an extremely sore foot, this is turning out to be a good day, after all." Qwyrk just wanted to be somewhere far away.

CHAPTER SIX

Golden light from elegant chandeliers bathed the hall in a warm, arcane glow, accenting the Gothic architecture. Sumptuous tapestries and red carpets adorned the floors and the walls. The sight made him both proud and humbled him. This was his day, at long last.

The most exalted in the land had gathered together in this place, arrayed in the finest aristocratic robes and wigs of purest white. They were here to honor him, a rare gift. The Prime Minister beamed with pride in the distance.

As the sound of *Rule Britannia* played on trumpets and horns, he began his procession, in a stately manner, something to which he was utterly accustomed. He was dressed in a robe of velvet, and behind him, his servant was clad in the garments of an eighteenth-century page, which somehow suited him; the horrid platted hair was tucked away under a powdered wig, and he held the edges of his master's robe as he walked. He had even removed his dreadful piercings, at his master's insistence. The hair would have to be chopped off, of course, but that was a matter for another time.

Ahead of them, on the throne, was their goal, the queen herself. She sat in regal splendor on her throne, as she had for more than half a century, her purple robe with ermine trim trailing off to the left. No sign of emotion showed on her face, though he knew that she was delighted to welcome him into the fold at last. He approached with all due reverence and motioned for his page to take his designated place on the side.

The queen rose and took up the sword of state. He knelt before her, head bowed. He beamed as the sword caressed each of his shoulders in succession.

"For services excellently rendered to the Crown, for your staggering intellect, your immense wisdom, and for your many other incomparable attributes, I dub thee 'Sir Bernard Beresford Bartlesby Blippingstone the Third of Symphinity,' and create for you the title of Baron Blippingstone, to be carried in perpetuity by your heirs and descendants. Arise, Sir Bernard!"

"Your majesty," he replied with a broad smile and a reverential bow. He began to retreat from the throne, never, of course, turning his back on royalty. The crowd began to applaud, breaking into full cheers.

He smiled at them, waved and bowed, promising to uphold his new positions with honor and dignity. The Prime Minister reached down to shake his hand.

"Well done, Sir Blip!"

"Blip."

"Blip!"

"What? What?!"

Blip looked around and saw Qwyrk standing over him, the unkempt youth nearby, swaying back and forth with his eyes closed, chanting something. Blip's foot still ached, and his triumph was ruined. He resumed sulking.

* * *

"Look, I don't know where you'd gone off to, but cut it out!" Qwyrk warned. "Star Tao here thinks he can help us find out some information. Since he can see both of us just fine, I filled him in while you were off wherever you were. Now it looks like he's gone off somewhere too."

"Yeah, mate. I can help," he said, snapping out of his mantra. "Oh, sorry, oh lord, I didn't mean to be disrespectful."

"Hm, well, it's all right just this once, but do have a care in the future," Blip answered with authority. "We must observe the proper protocols, you see, even in times of stress."

Qwyrk let out a heavy sigh. "Can we please just go see what Jilly has found out?"

"I'm right here," came the answer, and Jilly stepped into the alley. "I bought the book and stepped out to see where Mr. Blip had gone off to..."

"Mr. Blippingstone," he muttered.

"...and I heard your voices over here."

She looked at Star Tao with suspicion. "Who are you?"

"He saw the murderer, too, Jilly," Qwyrk answered before Star Tao could launch into another monologue about his name. "And apparently, *he* can see me as I really am, too."

"And that's a right nice thing, too," Star Tao said with a grin.

Qwyrk resisted the impulse to leave him in an unconscious heap on the ground, but only just. Gritting her teeth, she looked Jilly.

"What did you find in the book?" she asked, now managing to ignore Star Tao completely.

"Lots of things actually. Apparently, this Granny Boatford

talked to the Shadow people a lot, and could see them in their real forms, too."

"It's funny that I don't remember hearing much about her," Qwyrk pondered. "I mean, I know who she was, but I never knew she had any real contact with us. Of course, I hadn't been up north in a while, a few hundred years at least, so I might have missed out on that."

"You haven't come up here for a few hundred years?" Jilly asked, sounding astonished.

"Well, there wasn't that much to do up here. It's got a rather bad reputation, you know, 'it's grim up north' and all that. I mean, that's not fair, but it did used to be all Picts painting themselves blue, and lonely Romans, and then Vikings pillaging, and solitary monks and things. Besides in Elizabethan times, it was even colder than it is now, and I preferred to be off in the south of France, or Italy."

"Such selfless dedication to duty," Blip muttered, just loud enough for Qwyrk to hear.

"Does the book say anything about a Shadow that murdered people or caused harm?" she asked, ignoring Blip.

"Well, it does say something," she said, flipping through the pages, "here. Not much, though, and it doesn't say anything else about it, before or after."

She showed the page to Qwyrk, who read it aloud:

And once, Grandemother Boatforde was sore aware of the malice done by the shadow, Red Cappe, and didde resolve forthwith to strengthen the banishement it had borne in a confin'd space, wherein it would knowe only torment and grief. Makinge many a fine potion, she conceiv'd of a most excellente conceit, and sought thereafter the services of one Sir Simon the Coy, and olde Knight of the Temple some three hundred and fifty years of age. Sir Simon agreed that it should be best to continue its confinement in his dwelling, under a newe and better chamber potte, for the greytest indignitie of alle.

"Now just a damned minute!" Qwyrk exclaimed, interrupting her reading. "A 350-year-old knight guarding a Shadow locked in a chamber pot? That's ridiculous!"

"Any more ridiculous than me seeing a Shadow jumping across rooftops, or an old lady releasing one from a toilet plunger?" Jilly said with a grin.

"Touché, my dear," Qwyrk conceded.

"Something about that name," Qwyrk continued. "'Red Cappe.' Red Cap. I know I've heard it before, but I can't recall where. I'm sure it wasn't good."

"It's not impossible that the Knights Templar did this, you know," Blip offered. "They were very clever. Who knows what magical secrets they discovered? What alchemical complexities they unearthed? What mystical conundrums they..."

"I just wonder," Jilly pondered aloud, to cut him off. Qwyrk almost hugged her for it. "There's an old house down by the river, built right into the side of the rock. It's medieval, and I think the Templars used it once. I don't know if anyone's been there for a while, though. Do you suppose that's what the book's talking about?"

"Not to be pedantic, my dear," Blip answered, "but books do not, technically speak. Well, of course, some magical books do, but I've always felt that it was a bit of cheating, really, robbing the reader of the whole purpose of opening the pages of a dusty old tome to peruse it for..."

"It could be," Qwyrk interrupted. Telling Blip to shut up wouldn't work, so she decided just to pretend he wasn't there. "You were by the river when you met the frantic lady. Maybe she did something in there to set it loose?"

"But she said it was a toilet plunger, and why would it still be in an old abandoned house?"

"Wait! This is like, really freaky!" Star Tao exclaimed. "Me head's tingling. I think I'm getting a message from me guides."

"But you said they only contact you... in the bathtub," Qwyrk answered, now regretting going along with him.

"They do mostly, that's what makes this so groovy, 'cause it's new! But hold on, something's coming through..."

His eyes rolled back, and he stuck his tongue out; Qwyrk had not imagined until now that he could look any less appealing.

"Greets!" he said in a soft, monotone voice, somewhat lower than his own. "We are of the Council of 27 (three times greater than the Council of 9). We are Zixytar and Zzazznapo'ti'ak. Love we send, and many blessings for harmony and totality. Come we do because we feel you are perplexed, and thus spake we through this little fleshy vessel for your beneficial enlightenmentism. Breathe you must unlike we who are pure energy in spirit form. We come to bring you to Light and Lifelove and Laugh, for Laugh is the godsong of the cosmos. Tremble you not in our presence, for once we were as ye, little and small and afraid and little... and small. But now we advance to the higher levels of soul-life and bring with us the song of the cosmic joy bond.

"Ask what you will, oh little ones, and we shall reveal all that can be known, within the limits of our own directives not to interfere with your developmentism."

Jilly stared at Star Tao, looking lost. "I didn't understand a word he just said."

Qwyrk let out an exasperated sigh. "Oh, all right, what the hell... I'll play along. What are we facing here? What kind of Shadow kills, and why did it get free?"

Star Tao spoke again. "Shadows are many and made by the sun, but shadows are only false and mimic the life force. To find answers look within and you will hear the god song laugh-laugh that enables joyness. That is your true face and the way to finally be free happy happy joy joy."

Qwyrk turned to Blip and Jilly, a blank look on her face. "Isn't it amazing how they never channel anyone useful, like 'Bob, a recently-deceased plumber from Chelmsford,' or something?"

She turned back to Star Tao. "Thank you very much for your... help, Zix... er, both of you. You have been most useful to us."

"Help we are in the light of lifesun. Help we do as the cosmos parades. Help we see in the essence of being. Help we become through our ancestral star bond."

"Now he's making up Jon Anderson lyrics," Qwyrk sighed.

Star Tao shook and flailed. He opened his eyes (back in their proper place) and looked around.

"Bloody hell! That was AMAZING! It was like a surge of pure, divine energy through me whole body!"

"Well, a short circuit maybe," Qwyrk mumbled.

"Was it any help?" he asked, a stupid grin on his face.

"Oh very," Qwyrk answered flatly, "if we were looking for some New Age song titles!"

"Cool!" Star Tao said with that stomach-churning swaying of his body picking up again. "You know, it almost felt like an erotic experience that time, kind of Tantric, yeah? In a whole-body orgasmic kind of way."

He grinned at Qwyrk, "If you ever want to try it..."

*　*　*

Moments later, Star Tao rubbed his cheek, still red and painful from Qwyrk's slap, as the four of them emerged from the alley.

They'd resolved to go and look at the old Templar house set into the cliff, and so made their way past the old castle and down the many steps nearby that led to the river. Blip hobbled along on one leg, grumbling to himself. Jilly seemed uneasy about retracing her steps, the horrors of yesterday no doubt still clear in her mind.

"I don't like this," she said as they began their descent down the endless flights of steps to the river. "I'm afraid he might still be around watching. What if he attacks again?"

"Don't worry, honey," Qwyrk said, trying to sound as reassuring as possible. "I doubt he's still around here, and in any case, he wouldn't try anything in broad daylight."

"He did yesterday," Jilly said, perhaps a little more bluntly than she intended.

Qwyrk didn't have an answer, and looked away.

"Not to worry, child," Blip offered. "In my many years as a companion to the young, I have delved deeply into the martial arts, and have mastered several of them: kung fu, kendo, karate, judo, and jujitsu."

"Right, because those two subjects go so naturally well together," Qwyrk cracked.

"Mock if you will," Blip retorted, "but in the East, I am known as 'Sensei Blippingstone Bernard-san.' They reverse the name order there, you see," he explained to Jilly. She tried not to look at him and just nodded instead, her face somewhere between grinning and crying.

"And the fact that this is the first time I've ever heard of this in all the centuries I've known you indicates what?" Qwyrk put to him.

"That the secrets of the East are not meant to be divulged to the foolish and the frivolous," he answered with a haughty air.

"Hey, he's right," Star Tao interjected. "Some things just shouldn't be shared with lesser minds. Lead us on, oh great god and ascended master."

Blip beamed.

Qwyrk imagined a near future where both Blip and Star Tao just waded off into the river below and never came back. The thought made her smile.

* * *

After a good deal of time spent navigating down the steps with care in order for Qwyrk not to be seen ("more trouble than she's worth," Blip muttered), they came to an old boarded-up house carved into the cliff face, just like the guide books said (the ones next to the Benny Hill mugs). The gate was open, and it appeared as if the door was ajar. There were also several "Do Not Enter" signs, some lying flat on the ground. There was a faded painting on the rock wall next to the door, which looked medieval, and might have been a heraldic shield, or a cross, or some such.

"Well, it looks like someone's been here recently," Jilly offered, at once regretting voicing her firm grasp of the obvious.

Glancing around to make sure that no one was looking, she and Star Tao walked up to the door, followed by their mystical companions. Once inside, Jilly closed the door most of the way. Blip flinched for a moment at the sound.

The house was dark and dusty and smelled of mold and earth. An old table and overturned chair sat in one corner, and what looked like the sad remains of a bed slumped in another. There was a broken toilet and sink against one wall, and next to it, Qwyrk spotted the overturned toilet plunger. It seemed to have arcane magical writing in several languages inscribed all around it: Latin, Greek, Enochian, Hebrew, Esperanto.

"I don't believe it!" she exclaimed, picking it up and looking it over. "They really did have this bloke imprisoned under it!"

Jilly looked around on the ground, squinting in the dark to see anything as she waited for her eyes to adjust to the lack of light. Other than a few old newspapers, there wasn't much to see.

Then she spied what looked like a rolled-up piece of parchment lying squished underneath a small stack of papers near the collapsed bed.

"What's this?" she said, bending over to pick it up.

The document was old, crumbling at the edges, and covered in dust. Jilly unrolled it with care and held it open for the others to see. Blip painfully stood on his tiptoes, but to no avail.

"Hello! Down here!" he protested, but no one seemed to listen. He scowled. "When I am knighted and titled, all of this will change."

"Blip, go open the door a bit more so we can see what's written on it," Qwyrk commanded.

"You realize after the incident in the store that I am probably most likely unable to do so, and in any case am still suffering from a post-traumatic stress incident!" he snapped. Again, no one paid attention. Still grimacing, he stomped back over to the door, or hopped, really, in a manner as close to angry stomping as his tender foot would allow, but that just made it look like his other foot hurt was hurting, too.

"I've a good mind to slam it shut and startle everyone," he whispered, loud enough to be heard. "No, no, that would be childish and a future lord is far above such things. Still, it's a momentary pleasure to think about their possible reactions."

"Hey! Don't be disrespecting him like that!" Star Tao protested.

"He's a god, show him some respect."

Blip smiled. "Indeed! A fine young man," he replied.

Qwyrk scowled at Star Tao, Jilly noted, and turned her attention to the parchment instead. With a wave of her hand, a small orb of golden light appeared, hovering in the air nearby and providing enough extra light. Jilly marveled at this, but decided to wait to ask her about it later. Star Tao also looked impressed. Blip scowled, because he must have figured out that she had just sent him to the door to get rid of him.

Qwyrk could make out archaic lettering and what looked like the remains of a wax seal. It had faded over the centuries, but most of the script was still legible.

"It's an old medieval charter, I think," she said. "The inscription is in Latin."

"Latin?" Blip's voice picked up, and he strode (limped) with confidence back to the others. "Here then, show it to me. I shall provide the necessary translation."

"Oh right," Qwyrk rolled her eyes. "Mr. 'jiridicum' is going to give us the definitive reading. Move over, Oxford dons."

Blip grunted, apparently ever more indignant that his divinity could so persistently be mocked.

"What does it say?" Jilly interrupted, by now skilled at heading off their confrontations. She'd already lost count of how many it had been today; had they really been doing this for centuries? She looked on as Qwyrk scanned the page for a few moments.

"In nomine domine," she began, "umm... Let this seal act as a protection against the incursions of the... I can't make the next part out; something about 'de Souls,' maybe? It shall dwell in misery and shame for all eternity under the... something, protected by the virtuous Sir Simon of Wakefield, Knight of the Temple. He shall be granted the gift of long life, forgoing paradise, to fulfill the purpose of... it's all blotted out. Made in the Year of our Lord, 1321, enacted and enspelled with the sacred seals of Solomon and... Rupert."

"Rupert?" Qwyrk looked up, confused.

"It's signed and sealed with the seal of the Grand Master of the Templars himself," she added. "They weren't messing around with this. But... I thought the Templars were destroyed in 1314."

"Well," Blip spoke up, "that's what they wanted the world to think. In actuality, their original purpose was no longer relevant, so they allowed themselves to simply disappear from human reckoning. A whole series of silly legends popped up over the centuries about them, too. For example..."

"So, this Sir Simon was given eternal life to look after whatever this seal was, well, sealing?" Jilly interrupted, and Qwyrk was clearly grateful for her clever redirection of the conversation.

Qwyrk nodded. "Apparently so. And that's what you saw yesterday. And I'll bet that Simon was the old bloke who used to live here, until he got carted away so the town could turn this place into another tourist attraction. Idiots! They have no idea what they've done!"

"Oh, the indignity we knights must face in this age," Blip mused to himself.

Star Tao, who had been trying to look closer at Qwyrk while he was leaning over, (and don't think she didn't notice!) and pretending to try to read the parchment said, "Cool! So, like this old knight bloke did some freaky medieval mojo to keep the evil spook in that bog and not bother anybody. That's brilliant! But why did they have to lock it up in the first place?"

For once, it seemed that Qwyrk didn't have the urge to slap him, barely.

"That's what we still have to find out," she answered, moving away from him when she realized what he was up to. "If the Grand Master of the Temple got involved, Shadows must have put him up to it. The Templars had regular dealings with us back then, so the council must have instructed them to do this. But why here? And why in a damned chamber pot, or toilet plunger, or whatever? That's about as non-secure and stupid as I can imagine!"

"Or perhaps it's utterly brilliant," Blip countered. Jilly eyed him with a mixture of curiosity and dread that he was going to start another pompous pontification.

"Think about it," he went on. "A dreadful menace to medieval society, perhaps plundering the countryside, pulling peasants from their cottages at night to do Goddess-knows-what horrid things to them in various and sundry manners: killing livestock, bringing plague, turning cow's milk, putting dust in the miller's flour, smudging ink on manuscript pages, carrying off and ravishing virgins, giving bagpipes to musicians..."

"Blip! Get to the point!" Qwyrk snapped, obviously having had just about enough of everyone today. Even Jilly was weary of it.

"All I'm saying is that for some reason, council members and Templars alike needed to put a stop to it, and since Robin Hood was no longer around to take care of matters..."

Qwyrk glared.

"They enacted a means of trapping the thing and punishing it with the humiliation of consigning it to a chamber pot, or some similar such artifact. That it was hidden in a simple poor knight's dwelling such as this and in a tiny village, rather than a Temple stronghold makes perfect sense, you see. Hiding in plain sight; oldest trick in the book. No one would ever think to look here, in case some minion or follower wanted to free the killer. This Sir Simon would have had a fairly easy task, and could have officially 'retired' from the order as a hermit, or some such, without any fanfare or fuss, thus ensuring the safety of the seal and of the magical prison. Whatever was in it would simply have disappeared from all reckoning."

The others gazed at Blip in disbelief. This all made perfect sense. Qwyrk glanced toward the door.

"What are you looking for?" Jilly asked.

"I'm waiting to see the flock of winged pigs that's about to fly by outside at any moment."

Star Tao fell to his knees. "Hail, mighty god of the Amazon!" he exclaimed, bowing low and placing his arms out in front of him to touch the floor. "You know and see all!"

"Yes, well, I like to think so," Blip said with obvious extreme satisfaction. He smirked smugly at Qwyrk, who looked too stunned by his deductive logic to even react with annoyance. He'd won for once, and he knew it, and it was time to gloat. She winced.

"So, Sir Simon was actually old Vernon?" Jilly asked, still not convinced (or perhaps it was at Blip's new-found reasoning skills). "He was a bit mad, they said. He'd come out and talk to things at night, when no one was there."

"Well, no one *you* could see," Blip said in a chiding tone.

"That's true," Qwyrk added. "Bloody hell, I've just agreed with you for the second time in less than a minute, or a decade, for that matter." She looked back at Jilly. "You couldn't have seen me before yesterday, so how do you know Vernon wasn't talking to real beings, Shadows or others?"

"Well," Jilly replied, "I've heard that he used to have arguments, and yell in the middle of the night from his doorstep here, so I just assumed he was crazy."

Qwyrk smiled. "Take a look at Blip and me. Does Vernon's

yelling make sense now?"

Jilly nodded with a smile, seeing her point.

Star Tao was still genuflecting.

"For shite's sake, will you get up?" Qwyrk snapped.

"I am just trying to show proper respect for a divine being. You should be as well."

"Indeed," said Blip, beaming and puffing up his chest. "Very wise boy."

"In fact," Star Tao said with a brave tone and standing up, "if you don't stop yelling at me and hitting me, I might just go off you, and then you'll never know what you're missing. I am a master of the Tantric arts."

Jilly gave her a confused look, which was enough to make Qwyrk hold her tongue for the moment.

"I think we need to find Simon, and fast," she said instead, "and see if there is some way to stop this thing, or at least get it back into where it was and reseal it, before it does any more harm. And I want to know what the hell this thing is, why it was put away to begin with, who it killed yesterday, and if it's somehow letting mortals see me!"

"Well, I'm glad it did that, at least," Jilly said with a smile.

Qwyrk smiled back, and put her arms around Jilly, giving her a big hug. "Me, too."

Star Tao smiled a crooked grin and held his arms out. "Me too!"

"Now which eye would look better blackened, the left one or the right?" Qwyrk said, just loud enough for Jilly to hear her.

CHAPTER SEVEN

Jilly peered out of the door, looking in every direction to make sure no one was about. Motioning to the others to follow, she stepped out into the eye-hurting sunlight, and crept past the fallen-down signs and back onto the pavement. Looking back at the house with a smile, she turned in triumph to walk on ahead.

And ran right into someone. Someone tall. Someone dressed in black and blue and white. With a uniform. And a radio. And an air of authority. She looked up at the rather stern face of a police officer, who was gazing down on her with suspicious eyes.

Oh, bollocks! she almost said out loud.

"Now, young lady," the officer began, "you wouldn't have been creeping around on that old property would you? Because, as far as I can see, there are at least four 'Do Not Enter' signs standing and scattered about in front of it. Now, I don't know the exact nature of schools these days, though I'm sure they're in a sad state, but I assume you've had enough time in one of them to be able to read at least those two words, and have a general understanding of what they mean?"

Jilly gritted her teeth. Condescending adult prat! She was so mad; she wanted Qwyrk to turn him into a toad. If she could do something like that, of course. But she held back her anger and forced a smile.

"I wasn't inside, sir. I was... just walking by, that's all. I did a school report on the old house once, and I like to come by sometimes and look at it." She began to gain confidence. "I do wish they'd hurry up and fix it, so that it could be open to the public. Wouldn't that be great?"

Her optimism vanished as she saw that he was completely unimpressed with her creative prevarication, and her attempt to change the subject.

"I see a door slightly open, and a couple of signs knocked over," he stated. "Now, I am no Sherlock Holmes, it must be said. I do not smoke a pipe, use cocaine, nor do I have a doctor as a sidekick, and I've probably never said the word 'elementary' even once in my life, except for just now. That being said, it does not take one with a superior fictitious detective's intuition to see that something is seriously amiss here."

Jilly closed her eyes. Authority with a generous helping of sarcasm; lovely.

"I am willing to bet that you, and maybe some of your young mates, have been creeping around where you shouldn't be, maybe daring each other to go into the scary, dangerous old house in the cliff, hoping it isn't haunted and that you won't get caught. Now, being young once myself, I can understand the exciting lure of such temptations, but being an officer of Her Majesty's law, I cannot allow such improper behavior and illicit actions to go uninvestigated."

Jilly stared at him in disbelief. Had Blip just possessed this man's body?

He took hold of her shirt sleeve. "Now, we are going to walk back up there and see if any of your mates are still hiding inside, and then I will decide what to do with you."

He marched her back up to the door, which he pushed open wide. Jilly saw Blip standing still, like some bizarre Art Deco statue, or a lamp she'd seen at one of her mother's friend's houses once. Qwyrk stood in one corner, away from the light, with her eyes closed. Jilly knew the policeman wouldn't be able to see either of them, and wasn't worried. The problem was... *Where's Star Tao?*

Trying hard not to seem like she was looking, she scanned the room for him, but he was nowhere to be found.

"I told you," she said with a smug expression, which she realized was a bad idea. "I was just looking at the outside. There's no one in here, see? I don't go around breaking laws, honest!"

The policeman walked about the room a bit, trying to act thorough, even though it was obvious that the place was empty. Jilly watched impatiently, waiting for him to make his rounds and then concede her point and leave. He looked at the bed, examined the sink, avoided the toilet, ignored the plunger (thankfully), and turned to face her. As he did so, his right shoe's heel came down directly on top of Blip's still-sore foot. Assuming he'd stepped on a rock or piece of wood, he gave it no notice and walked back over to Jilly.

Blip winced. Then his eyes widened. He whimpered. He put one hand over his mouth and clenched it shut as hard as possible. His other hand clutched his re-injured foot, and he hopped on his one good leg, yet again. He obviously wanted to shout. He plainly wanted to scream. Tears formed in his eyes.

Meanwhile, Jilly saw that Qwyrk had opened her eyes just long enough to see what had happened. She had covered her face with her hands, and seemed to summon everything she could to keep from bursting into laughter. She shut her eyes tightly and tears also began to form in them. She started shaking as her silent guffaws became more severe.

Between Blip hopping in place in silence and Qwyrk desperately trying not to burst into audible hysterics, Jilly found she had to place a hand over her mouth, too. She coughed a couple of times, using the excuse of the mustiness of the place.

"Can I please go now? I don't like it in here, and as you can see, I haven't done anything illegal."

Her would-be inquisitor was clearly still suspicious, but in his Holmesian logic, concluded that he had no real evidence to pin on her.

"Get on off, then, and don't be playing around here anymore. It's not safe."

Jilly ran away without another word, and disappeared behind a nearby building, where she waited until the officer had walked a long way off on his rounds. Once she was sure he was well out of sight and wouldn't be back for some time, she hurried back to the house. Inside, Qwyrk was doubled over in giggles, tears streaming from her eyes, while Blip sat on the floor rubbing his foot anew and swearing colorfully, disregarding the fact that Jilly had returned.

"Oh now, be careful Mr. Blippingstone," Qwyrk managed to say through her laughs, "that kind of language is certainly not appropriate for young ears!"

Blip grumbled and lowered his voice, "I don't give a cask of brandy about what's appropriate at the moment!"

"Oh, don't worry about me," Jilly said. "He hasn't said anything I haven't heard before... except that one thing about..."

"Never mind, dear!" Qwyrk interrupted, catching her breath at last.

"Um, where'd Star Tao go?" Jilly asked after another moment.

"Oh, crap!" Qwyrk said with a look of sudden realization that wiped the smile off her face and made her ignore watching her own language around Jilly. "I'd actually forgotten about him already. I sent him off to Symphinity when I heard you approaching."

"You sent him off?" Maybe she *could* have turned the policeman into a toad.

"Well, it's not something we like to do, but in emergencies, we can transport mortals back to our own world, for their protection. But I have to get him back! He's the last kind of person that should be there for too long!"

She waved her hand in a circle and some purple lights formed in a ring; she stepped into them and disappeared. A moment later, there was another violet flash, and she was back with Star Tao in hand. His eyes were wide, and he was shaking a little.

"Bloody hell!" he said. "I think I've just had an out-of-body experience! Except, like, me body was still with me, so it was more of an in-body-out-of-body experience. I was in this brilliant place, right? All beautiful and green and forests, and there were like people around in fancy clothes... they looked a bit like you." He pointed at Qwyrk. "Actually, they kind of looked like elves."

Qwyrk sighed.

"And now I'm back here. Shame really. I'd have loved to look around a bit, and maybe talked to them elf people."

"Oh yeah, they would have *loved* that," muttered Qwyrk.

"What happened?" Star Tao said, after a moment of trying work things out on his own.

Qwyrk looked like she was going to tell him the truth, but then abandoned that idea. Instead, she said, "You must have somehow teleported yourself to Elf Land in a moment of crisis. I imagine it's all that channeling you do. You've probably picked up some unknown talents along the way."

"Oh, brilliant!" he answered, grinning wider and stupider than ever.

"In fact, if you practice really hard," she continued, "I'll bet you could harness that talent and go back there some time, but you're probably going to need to go off and meditate for about, oh, twelve hours a day for a few years to do it again. Why not start right now?"

"Look, we need to get out of here, before that policeman comes back," Jilly spoke up. "The last thing I need is the police talking to my mum and dad about how I'm a breaking-and-entering case."

* * *

They left the old house, leaving the immediate area with haste. Blip was in too much pain to walk, so Qwyrk offered to let him sit on her shoulder. He was forced to wrap his arms around her neck to avoid falling off. It was a situation that neither of them relished. In fact, Blip probably would have died of indignant embarrassment had anyone else been able to see him, Qwyrk decided, which made her grin. They wandered back along the river, mindful of being watched, and climbed the stairs back toward the castle as fast as they could, huffing and puffing in the last third of the journey to the top.

"We need to get back to your house, Jilly," Qwyrk said. "We can read some more from the Granny Boatford book and also do a bit of online research. I want to look up those names. They're familiar, but I just can't place them."

"You use computers in your world?" Jilly asked, surprised.

"Well, no, but we do try to keep up with humanity's techno-logical innovations. They can come in very handy. I thought home computers were just brilliant when they were invented!"

"Hm!" Blip said. "Give me parchment and a good scribe any day. Or at least a good Gutenberg press. All the digital this and high speed that and MP5 nonsense."

"3," Jilly corrected.

"What?"

"It's MP3; you're probably thinking of MI5, you know, the spy agency."

"No matter. All a load of rubbish, if you ask me."

"Well," Qwyrk said. "When we get back to Jilly's, Blip, you can nurse your foot with a medieval poultice and listen to a minstrel recite the *Song of Roland*."

"It's quite inappropriate and uncouth to mock a warrior injured in battle, you know."

"Oh? Have you been fending off hordes of carnivorous hobgoblins with a battle axe at various points this morning when no one noticed?"

"We are in the midst of a potentially deadly war, girl. It matters not if the injury occurs in combat or at times of strategy."

"Or when tripping and falling flat on your face."

"Hmph! Churchill would be ashamed of your attitude!"

"Well, it's a good thing he's not here then, isn't it?"

"Right," Star Tao spoke up, as they reached the top of the steps. He looked a bit dejected. "I hate to say good bye, 'cause this has been groovy and brilliant, but I really have to go now. I was goin' on up to the store to drop off these flyers when I ran into you lot. I need to get them out so as many people as possible can see what I have to offer. In fact, I wish I'd given some of them out to those elves."

Qwyrk shuddered.

"So, I guess I'll see you 'round some time... right?"

"Yes, absolutely," said Qwyrk, with a broad smile. "Lovely to meet you. I'm sure we'll see you again sometime. Keep on meditating, and I'm sure you'll get back to Elf Land someday. Bye, now!"

Star Tao turned to leave. "All right then..."

Jilly looked remorseful. "Star Tao, wait!" she said as he was leaving. "My address is 12 Middlemuck Lane. Come on by later if you like."

"I'll do that, thanks!" His face brightened up. He turned to Blip and bowed again.

"Farewell, oh great god! I am your committed servant. You have but to ask, and I shall obey!"

"And I shall hold you to that! Farewell!" Blip answered with pride. "Fine young man! Very fine indeed!"

"And I'll see *you* later," he said with a wink and a grin to Qwyrk. She shuddered again.

And with that, he bounded away from the steps and off toward the *Swapping Shop*.

"Jilly, why did you say that? We were almost free of him!"

"Oh, come on, Qwyrk. He's not a bad bloke. He's nice, actually, and he means well. And besides, since he saw the murderer, he might well be in danger, too. Or doesn't that matter to you?"

She gave Qwyrk one of those frowning, pouty, squinty-eyed looks that children do so well, designed to induce as much guilt as possible. It worked. Qwyrk let out a heavy sigh, and now she was the one feeling horrible.

"You're right, I'm sorry. I've been mean. But I'm just so stressed about this right now, that having to look after one more person, especially one that's not exactly all there, is not what I need. But yes, you're absolutely right, he could be a target. We'll keep an eye on him, I promise."

Jilly smiled. "Now, we just have to get back to my house without you being seen."

The sun was high overhead, a bit past noon, with few clouds, and there were little in the way of hiding-in-shadows options for Qwyrk, were she to walk with them.

"My best bet would be to do what I did before I think. You just go on ahead and we'll follow."

"A moment please," Blip interjected. "What do you mean exactly, by 'what I did before' and 'we'll follow'? Surely, you do not expect me, in my most fragile state, to hang on to your neck for dear life while you go bounding over rooftops like a madwoman out of some inane comic book. I insist on going with the child. I'm not that heavy; she can carry me."

"Come on Blip! Live a little!" Qwyrk said with a mischievous grin, glancing at Jilly, who caught on. She hoisted him up onto her back.

"Right then, bye, you two! See you in a little bit," Jilly said with a not-so-innocent smile, as she hopped off past the castle and on to the main street, not looking back.

"Jilly! Come back here at once!" Blip exhorted. "I will not be left here with this rapscallion to be subjected to this torture!" But she was already gone.

"Hang on tight, Blip!" Qwyrk began a run to the castle, ready to bound upwards to the top of its remaining tower.

"Now just a damned minute, girl! You may think you can act all important around the others, but you have no authority to do so with me! I insist that you put me down at once, and AAAAAHHHHHHHH!"

Qwyrk leapt up with Blip clutching her neck with all his strength. She prepared to jump to a nearby roof.

"Put me down, damn you! PUT ME DOWN! AAAHHHHHHHHH!"

*　*　*

Later, back at Jilly's home, she and Qwyrk sat down in front of the family computer in her parents' office, while Blip sat on the sofa in the living room, his foot bandaged and his head and stomach recovering from motion sickness, so he claimed. Jilly thought he looked a bit greener than usual, and it made her grin. She'd been tempted to break out her sketchbook and draw him in this state, but she knew she wouldn't get away with it. Still, she tried to remember the look on his face, so she could draw him later...

After the online program welcomed them and informed that they had mail, Jilly started searching. "Let's try 'red cap' first," she said, typing it in to the search engine.

Within seconds, dozens of results came back:

Red Caps! Get the best prices on woolen hats for winter!

The Aurora **Red Cap**s are off to their worst season in ten years.

Red Capper: the caffeine energy drink that gives you propellers.

...with government figures in the **red, cap**s on spending will be likely this year.

Red capybaras make great pets!

Red Capsicum: the ultimate ultra-sized dildo for her supreme pleasure.

And so on...

"Not very useful," Qwyrk said with disappointment.

"What's a capybara?" Jilly asked.

"It's a large rodent from South America, I think," Qwyrk answered.

"Hm. What's an ultra-sized dil..."

"Let's try de Soulis instead," Qwyrk interrupted.

Jilly typed "di Solas."

Grazzie! Welcome to the website of **di Solas'** pizza! Now serving the greater Sheboygan area with our eight-cheese specialty. Diet version (with six cheeses) also available.

Spanish skiing champion Marco **di Solas** crashed face-first into a tree Sunday in Lillehammer, Norway. One ski is said to be still embedded in the tree, along with three of his teeth.

"I think it's actually spelled d-e_S-o-u-l-i-s," Qwyrk said, eager to avoid any more unfortunate search results that Jilly shouldn't be seeing. Hadn't her parents ever heard of web search controls?

Jilly typed in the new spelling:

De Soulis: the finest in erotic adult entertainment. A world-class gentlemen's club in Miami where all your desires come true, nightly.

"Oh, bloody hell," Qwyrk cursed.

She scanned the page until her eyes caught one reference.

"Jilly, click that one," she said as she pointed. "William de Soulis, medieval necromancer and sorcerer. That's it!"

Jilly clicked the link, and they were then viewing a simple text page, simple except for the animated bats that flitted across the screen, and the doom-laden background music that was reminiscent of a soundtrack rejected from a long-forgotten 1960s Hammer Horror film, something with a title like *The Bleeding Coffin of Dr. Insanity*, or some such.

"I can stop the music; it's just one of those MP5's," Jilly joked. Qwyrk chuckled.

She shut off the music, and the two of them commenced reading. Jilly read aloud:

"Lord William de Soulis was the hereditary Butler of the Scottish King and lived in the later thirteenth and early fourteenth centuries. He was said to have become a powerful necromancer and sorcerer after a battle wherein an opponent used magic to escape harm. De Soulis lusted for that kind of power, determined that he would learn all he could to make himself invincible by evil magical means.

"From his home at Hermitage Castle in Roxburghshire along the border with England, he is said to have engaged in many foul deeds, including theft, murder... and child sacrifices... ick!

"Um, through black magical means, he was rumored to have conjured up an evil spirit, or demon, called Robin Redcap... there's the name, Qwyrk! So-called because he used to dip his cap in the blood of his victims... ugh, nasty! Redcap did his bidding for some time, and the two terrorized the lands around de Soulis' estate. It is said that Redcap stole his soul somehow, and that eventually, some local folk, aided with good advice and wisdom from Thomas of Erceldoune, also known as 'the Rhymer,' succeeded in capturing de Soulis in 1321, and... melting him alive in lead and boiling water.

"Oh, Qwyrk, this is horrible!" She looked at her friend with disgust and fear.

"It's just awful," Qwyrk answered with a nod. "I knew there was something really bad going on. I don't know that much about what happened, but now it's coming back to me, and I heard some stories at the time. I think the council tried to play it down for whatever reason. Redcap is a renegade Shadow. He went bad a long time ago, at least 500 years before de Soulis, and from what I remember, he's evil and dangerous. I can absolutely see why the Templars locked him away forever."

She put her arm around Jilly and gave her a hug, seeing how upset she was.

Blip came hobbling into the room at that moment, having recovered his balance, and presumably put his stomach back where it properly belonged.

"What's going on? What did you find?"

"Blip," Qwyrk said in a solemn tone. "We have a big problem."

* * *

He moved with silence and haste through the countryside, avoiding mortals and hiding in the shadows of hills, dells, and forests. Sometimes, he had to cross the strange new roads, which seemed to be made of a smooth, dark rock, and across which humans in bizarre wheeled, metal carriages sped without any visible means of motion. One almost struck him, though it would have not harmed him, he was quite sure. Perhaps next time, he would let one hit him, just to see what would happen.

These mortals may have learned new sciences, but they were still cattle to him. Oh, he could kill them with ease, it's true. He would love to rip their hearts out and do even worse things if he had time; nothing would please him more. He should have killed the girl who saw him take his first revenge on that foolish Templar, but that other Shadow was nearby, and he was too weak for such a confrontation. At least the look of terror on her face had been exquisite, even more satisfying than killing one of those hated knights.

But for the moment, he had another task, a task he was compelled to accomplish, being driven by the one bound to him. And that one wanted no more killing, for now. That one feared detection and demanded secrecy.

The other was always there, this mortal; ever since he had died, the two of them had been as one. Now, tasting his first freedom in more than a century, he wanted to run free, to rampage, to destroy and hurt, to maim and kill. But he could not, not yet. There was this task to perform first; somehow, the mortal still commanded him, and he hated it.

"It cannot be far; my beloved pet showed me the place," the mortal said, through his mouth, but with a different voice. "Have things changed so much in so short a time?"

"Things in this world change quickly these days, I think," he answered in his own hoarse, cruel voice. "This search would be faster, were I simply to take a few of the local peasants and torture them for the information we want!"

"There will be none of that!" the other chided. "Not yet. We do not even know if any of them would know where it is, any more. My plan will be beneficial to both of us. Surely you, the immortal, should have learned patience after all this time?"

"A self-imposed boundary for the weak, nothing more," he spat.

"We have been locked away for more than a century since our last escape, I believe. What harm will a few more days be? When this works, we shall be free of one another, and you may do as you wish. That is what you want, is it not?"

"You have deceived me before."

"And you me."

"So it is. I shall play your little game for now, mortal, but beware that I have none of your cherished patience. To be free forever, and rid of you for all time is reason enough to stay my killing, but I will not wait long."

"You will not have to."

And so this Shadow and the mortal trapped inside, freed from a magical prison by a foolish woman's mistake, continued on their way farther south, still searching, but not yet finding what they sought.

CHAPTER EIGHT

"Redcap! Of course, it's coming back to me now. Damn it! Damn it all and double damn it!" Blip swore, paying no heed to the young ears of his charge as he paced about the living room, his previous injuries apparently forgotten. "I thought we'd seen the last of him in the fourteenth century. Or the sixteenth. Or was it the nineteenth? I seem to remember something about him then..."

"We'll have to look into it," Qwyrk answered, for once not taking issue with him. "I remember hearing something about that too, but my memory's weirdly fuzzy; it's like there's a big stone block in the way. It's sort of on the edge, but I can't quite reach it." She sat on the couch and gazed out the window, rubbing her hands together, looking nervous.

"Yes, yes, the same for me," Blip concurred. "I'd swear I know more about this than I seem to recall. Damn it all!"

Jilly watched them both. If they were agreeing and not fighting, this must be serious. She was afraid.

"So... what do we do?" she asked after an uncomfortably long silence.

"*You're* not doing anything," Qwyrk admonished, turning to look at her. "Now that I know what we're dealing with, I've got to make sure you stay as far away from all of this as possible... and no arguing about it!"

"Quite right, quite right," Blip agreed. "This is far too dangerous. Even with my extensive skills in the martial arts, I have a strong sense of dread about the whole situation. We simply can't have a child involved who might be put in harm's way hindering our efforts."

Jilly fumed in silence. Not only were they telling her she was useless, Qwyrk even ignored Blip's boast about his fighting abilities, *and* they were agreeing with each other again! It was all so annoying.

"All right," she said, "what are *you* going to do?" She added a sarcastic tone to her voice; at least she hoped that's how it sounded.

"We have to figure out where they've gone," Qwyrk answered, apparently oblivious to Jilly's sarcasm (which just annoyed her even more). "It depends on who's in control, de Soulis or Redcap. If it's de Soulis, they may lie low for a bit. But I'm sure he'll be planning something, even though it may take a while to set it in motion. We may have a few days. But if it's Redcap..."

She looked at Jilly with a genuine fear, and Jilly was less resentful, even a bit ashamed, realizing how bad this all was becoming. She sat down next to Qwyrk and gave her a big hug; she found that she took great comfort in Qwyrk's embrace.

Then she noticed two thin but strong arms wrapped around her from behind her. Blip had jumped up on the couch, and she realized that he had decided to show his concern at that very moment. His embrace was tight. Rather too tight.

"There, there, child, don't worry your young head about this. It shan't be as bad as it seems at the moment."

"Um, Mr. Blip..."

"Mr. Blippingstone, child. However, under these exceptional circumstances of great duress, I am prepared to forgo the normal formalities."

He patted her on the head (which felt more like he was swatting her) before returning his right arm once again to his ironclad hug. Actually, it was tighter the second time.

"Um, right," Jilly panted. "It's just that..."

"Now I know this is a frightening situation, but I can assure you that it is not the first such dangerous encounter I've faced in my time. No, most certainly not. There have been many close calls and adventures of daring-do in my time, of that I promise."

"Um..." Jilly said again. She was beginning to have trouble breathing in. She squirmed in his arms and tried to wrestle free, with no luck.

"I may be a cultured gentleman of the finest order, but I'm an old soldier, too. I remember once in 1754, there was an incident with a renegade hobgoblin in Surrey; a perfidious nuisance he was! I was called in to take the situation in hand, of course, and while I thought that it would initially be a simple matter, it revealed itself to be of considerable more difficulty than I had at first anticipated. You see, he had enlisted the aid of a band of rogue hedgehogs armed with poisoned porcupine quills..."

"Um, please!" Jilly gasped, all attempts at unlocking his arms having failed.

Qwyrk reached over and removed his arms from around her with amazing ease. "I think it might be best if we actually protect her and don't do Redcap's work for him," she said coolly.

Jilly inhaled a glorious breath of air and rubbed her arms to get some sensation back into them.

Blip jumped off the couch and turned his back on them in a sulk, arms folded. "That's the problem with the youth of today; no appreciation at all, and they've gone soft. I weep for the future."

"If you're quite done feeling sorry for yourself," Qwyrk shot at him after a moment, "we have work to do, or we won't even have a future."

Jilly smiled. They were bickering again; maybe things were going to be all right after all.

*   *   *

A short time later, they were in front of the computer again, Blip apparently over the insult of being rejected while baring his soul.

"Everyone who's seen them is in danger," Qwyrk explained, "regardless of whether they attack now or later. We know the tour bus with that woman went to York, but we have to find out where Simon was taken after they removed him. He's a likely target, and I have to get to him first; I'm sure he can help us. Is there any way you can find out where he is?"

"I don't know," Jilly replied. "It's probably private information. I can check, but even if I found out the details about him being taken away, I'd be surprised if most of it weren't protected by passwords, and such. I'm not even sure where to start looking, actually."

"Just try anyway," Qwyrk said. "Check about the old house, maybe? There might be some references to... Vernon was it?"

"Well, that's what everyone called him," Jilly answered, "though I don't know how he got that name. No one really knew who he was or where he came from; he just always seemed to be there. I guess he really had been!"

Jilly typed some words into the search engine.

"Mostly just things about the house itself and its history," she said, scrolling through the results.

Qwyrk breathed a silent sigh of relief that no links to sites like "Temple of Pleasure" or "Knights in White Satin" came up this time.

"Here! What about this?"

She clicked one promising link: a news story.

"June 10," she read aloud. "Vernon Templeton, a long-time resident of the old Templar house in the rock, was removed from the premises today, evicted so that necessary repairs can be made to the structure, which will begin in July. Locals cannot recall how long Vernon had lived there, or if he even had any legal right to be on the property, but most said that he had been living in the structure for as long as they could remember. Some added that their parents recall him being there from before the Second World War; others dismissed this as nonsense.

"Vernon initially resisted arrest, but eventually surrendered to police without further struggle. Witnesses report that as he left, he was muttering over and over something about protecting a seal, and appealing to the shadows for help. Given his suspected fragile mental state, he is being housed temporarily at the *St. Cornelly's Hospital for the Potentially Troubled*, near York, until it can be determined if he has any living relatives."

"Not likely!" Qwyrk exclaimed. "But this is brilliant news! Now I can go and talk to him, protect him if I have to, and check on the woman who started all this. I have to make sure she didn't let them out deliberately."

"I doubt that," Jilly answered. "She looked pretty scared. Stupid cow! It's all her fault!"

"If she didn't mean to, then how could she have known, Jilly?" Qwyrk said. "It was a disaster waiting to happen. Anyone could have accidentally done it, even you."

Qwyrk saw Jilly fuming; she clearly didn't like being wrong. She glared at Qwyrk, got up without another word, and stomped upstairs.

Blip offered, "Well, that was rather tense. Shall I go and speak to her?"

"Uh, no, I imagine that would be just about the worst thing you could do. I'll go up in a bit. I need you to stay here with her, though, and keep a close watch. If anything happens and de Soulis and Redcap show up here, take her to Symphinity straightaway. Don't even try to fight them."

"I'm quite capable of handling myself!"

"Blip! I'm serious! If it were just you, I honestly wouldn't care, but you're *not* going to risk her life for any reason, understand?"

"Fine! What if the lad shows up, as well? I assume I'm to take him there too if trouble develops."

Qwyrk sighed. "Yes, yes, of course. I'm not too keen on that idea, to be honest, but we can't risk any mortal lives over something that's our problem. And I am damned well going to have words with some of our superiors before this is all over! I mean, why the hell haven't they already dispatched someone to handle this? Why are we groping around on the internet, needing an eleven-year-old human girl to help us find basic answers?"

"Good questions, indeed," Blip mused. "Perhaps they don't know about it yet?"

"I find that hard to believe. You were sent over here soon enough, unless someone is keeping information from them?"

"I must admit that thought had crossed my mind. Look at the trouble we're having with even remembering things."

"But who the hell would do that? Who would want these bastards on the loose again? Everyone knows what they're capable of."

"Not everyone agrees with how the council governs things, you know."

"Well, I don't always agree with them either, but that doesn't mean I'm going to go and release some murdering monster and a depraved wizard who share a body!"

"Nor I, but I fear there may be some who might."

"What? Have you heard something?"

"No, nothing especially. Just whispers here, murmurs there; the usual grumbling and complaining about wanting to shake things up. I hadn't really given it much thought until now."

"I wonder," Qwyrk pondered. "Me and the girls were sent to check on a house in Leeds. We were told about some unusual disturbances there, ripples in the magical web, and such. We didn't find much, but I wonder if it's related to what's been happening here. De Soulis might be planning something, and there may be something in that neighborhood that he needs. I don't know, it's a guess."

"Possibly; a logical deduction in any case."

"Oh damn it, for all I know, he may on his way to York right now; I can't sit here. I'm going to go up and talk with Jilly, and then I have to go. But here's what is really bothering me: why didn't either of us remember Redcap and de Soulis until we saw those websites that jogged our memories? We both know who they are. It's like something was clouding our thoughts about it, and keeping us in the dark."

"Yes, I'd thought of that as well; some sort of incantation, perhaps. A mind-scrambling cantrip to put us off the trail."

"But who the hell would cast that to slow us down? And why would they be allied with those two?"

"It's damned bothersome, I agree. There are always factions that want changes, but I never thought one of them would go this far; what's their ultimate purpose, I wonder?"

"I don't know; we're just guessing now, anyway. I'm going to stop in Symphinity on the way to York, though, and see my old mentor. Then if I have time, I'll be off to the council. I have a few pointed questions to ask, believe me!"

"Well, give them a damned good box on the ears from me, as well, and tell them if they don't get this in hand, then I bloody well resign!"

Qwyrk smiled, and, for once, was glad Blip was here. Then she decided she must be delirious.

* * *

Jilly ignored the knock on the door, knowing it wouldn't do any good, but she wanted to put off talking with Qwyrk for a few more seconds. She sat on her bed with her sketchbook, hoping that feeling frustrated and angry would lead to an amazing masterpiece; she'd read about how many artists had experienced this, and gone on to create their finest works. So far, no luck.

"Jilly..." Qwyrk said as she peered around the door. Jilly didn't look up, but instead kept circling her pencil over the paper, certain that at any moment, inspiration would strike.

"Look," Qwyrk continued, opening the door, stepping in, closing it behind her, and sitting on the edge of the bed. "I'm sorry if I was a bit blunt with you earlier. You know it's not because I don't value you, or think you can't help, but, oh sweetie, this is so serious, even worse that I thought.

"You have to understand that Redcap and de Soulis are

absolutely evil. I mean, separately, they were horrible enough, but together in one body, it's just crazy! I don't think there's anything they wouldn't do, and no one they wouldn't harm to get on with whatever it is they're up to. I mean, I'd guess that after being trapped for so long, de Soulis must have some plan for doing something awful. And Redcap, well, he just wants to hurt and kill.

"I'm remembering a bit of it now: Redcap stole his soul while he was alive, see. He held on to it by keeping it inside of him. But after de Soulis was killed, they merged into one being, basically two personalities trapped in one Shadow's body. If they weren't insane already, that would have been enough to drive them both mad. De Soulis was stronger, and he controlled Redcap's need to murder, but he couldn't always keep that control. So now that they're free, there's really no way of knowing what they'll do next."

"What do you think they *will* do?" Jilly asked setting down her pencil and looking up.

"I think de Soulis is up to something, because as far as I know, there haven't been any killing sprees reported across northern England yet, thank Goddess. But it's only a matter of time. I have to find Simon and make sure he's all right, and I *have* to go alone, Jilly. This is far too dangerous."

"But I want to help."

"I didn't say you couldn't. Look, if you want, get back on the computer and start finding out anything else you can about these two and their history. It may give us some clues as to what they're up to. I was down in Leeds a few nights back because I was told there was some kind of disturbance, a magical one. I didn't find out much, but it's odd that this would happen so soon before they were set free. My guess is that once Simon was gone, those two could sense it and knew that they could be set free at any moment. Maybe they were causing something to happen."

"Does that mean they're going to Leeds?"

"I don't know, maybe. I have to go back and check on that, too. Anyone living in that neighborhood could be in terrible danger."

"When will you be back?"

"I don't know. I'm going to try to be quick, but it might be a while. I need you to stay here. Blip will stay with you..."

Jilly gave Qwyrk a cold stare.

"Yeah, all right, I know, but really, he's good to have around right now. And I gave him strict instructions that if anything happens, he's to take you to our world right away. They won't be able to get to you there."

"Go to your home? Oh, that would be brilliant! But... what about mum and dad? I mean, if Redcap and de Soulis found me and came back here, we'd have to protect them as well, right? And Star Tao? He said he was going to stop by later."

Qwyrk sighed. "I hadn't thought about your parents. This is getting way too complicated. Yes, yes, of course. I'll let Blip know."

She leaned in and took Jilly's hands. "It's going to be all right. And I *do* want your help, really. Anything else you can find out will help me. There might be information in this world that we don't have in our own records back home; things can get a bit careless there sometimes. We've lost more than we should have over the centuries. And I'm starting to worry that some records may have been deliberately destroyed."

Jilly gave her a weak smile. She was happy that Qwyrk said she needed her, but she didn't believe that things were going to be all right. She'd seen way too much already to believe that.

* * *

EIGHT

After a flash of violet light, Qwyrk stood in the clearing of a forest. The trees were verdant and green, flowers bloomed, and a sweet floral smell lingered in the air. Birdsong sounded in the tree branches above her. The sunlight was more golden here and shimmered through the magical mists, weaving between tree trunks as if alive. Even the air was pure and fresh. She smiled. Despite her fondness for the human realm, it was always good to be home.

"No time for taking in the sights," she sighed aloud, and made her way down a nearby path. There was one Shadow she trusted in a time like this, her old mentor and friend.

His home was set in another clearing, a short walk from where she manifested. It was a curious hodgepodge of different styles culled from human architecture over the centuries: three stories tall, with gables and chimneys, a bit of a castle here (a crenellated turret in need of some repair, unless he designed it that way on purpose), some Tudor there (leaded glass and wooden support beams), a few gargoyles peaking over various edges... all woven into a delightful and odd blend that somehow harmonized well enough. Slovenly, unique, charming, and even a bit inspiring; it was befitting of one of her people's leading scholars of the human world.

She approached the broad wooden front door. A brass bell hung down to one side. "Always his preferred method for callers," she said with a smile. He always liked to swap the bells out, leading her to wonder what happened to all the old ones. "Has he changed it again?" The new one was engraved with a large, ornate letter "Q," just as the previous one had been.

She grasped the clapper and struck the bell twice to make sure it really sounded. It had a deep resonant tone, far too deep for a bell of its size, but since this was a magician's house, it wasn't too surprising.

Before the last of the tones had faded, a grotesque stone

creature peered down over the arch above the door. It had pointed ears and a snout like a dog, but there was something dragon-like about it, and it seemed to have wings folded on its back.

"Alloooooo! Who are you?" it snapped. "What's your business?" Its voice sounded, well, stony, and it seemed to be putting on a rather bad (but thankfully, faint) French accent.

"I'm Qwyrk," she answered, not missing a beat and treating this as totally normal. "The master of this house knows me well, and always greets me with good cheer. He has said that I'm welcome any time. Go and tell him I'm here, please."

"And just why should I do zat? How do I know you are zis... Qwyrk? You could be absolutely anyone! You could be Attila the Hun, come to sack the treasure room... oh damn, I shouldn't have mentioned the treasure room! Or, you could be Genghis Khan, determined to burn ze house to the ground by undermining the wooden beams in the wine cellar... damn! I shouldn't have said anything about ze wine cellar. Grrrrr! Look, just go away, whoever you are. He's not seeing anyone today!"

"And who are you?" Qwyrk demanded, getting well past the point of annoyed now, and somewhere far along the well-worn road to quite irritated.

"I'm Gargula, of course, spokesman for ze master of the house, and guardian of its arcane secrets. Damn! I should not have mentioned ze arcane secrets!"

"Well, you're doing a bang-up job of *that*, mate. Look, would you please just let him know I'm here, so he can make up his *own* mind about whether to let me in?"

"Gargula!"

Another voice shrieked from a bit farther up, and in a moment, a beaked face peered over a ledge. It was rather like an eagle, except for the ears, which looked like a pig's. Qwyrk thought the voice sounded a bit more feminine, somehow, if such a thing was possible in a stone statue.

"Leave me alone, woman, and let me perform my duties! We have an intruder! Would you have me giving my consent to every visitor who came here with ill intent?"

"And just what exactly am I going to do?" Qwyrk asked interrupting him. "Do I bloody well look like Attila the Hun?" Her eyes narrowed and she pointed at him. "And if you say 'yes,' I'm getting a sledgehammer after you, and then you'll really learn about 'ill intent'!"

"See? See? I knew you were hostile! Thank goodness I stood firm. Ha! 'Stood firm.' A very fine jest, if I may say so myself! Yes, I am rock-solid in my commitment to guarding this home. Ha, ha, ha! Rock-solid!"

"Oh, effing hell," Qwyrk swore, looking around for something to throw at Gargula, who was still chuckling at his self-perceived wit.

"I apologize madam," the female said.

"What's your name?" Qwyrk asked.

"I'm Babewyn. I try to keep old Gargula here under control, but he can be quite the stubborn ass some days. I shall go and fetch the master."

"Thank you," Qwyrk replied, grateful that this idiotic ordeal was about to be over. Arguing with gargoyles was not high on her list of preferred things to do at the moment.

Gargula had ceased his laughter and slipped into something like a cough. He made a disgusting hacking sound, like clearing his throat, and then spit in Qwyrk's direction. She winced and stepped aside as several small pebbles clattered on the stone walkway beside her.

She was grateful when, a moment later, the door opened.

The fellow in the doorway was quite a sight to behold. He wore a rich, dark blue velvet robe, lined with gold trim that seemed always to change shape, back and forth from Celtic knots to floral patterns. The silver stars and planets on the robe seemed to twinkle and move of their own accord in random directions.

He had long white hair, from which his pointed ears protruded. His face didn't look as old as his hair suggested he might be, and his thin white beard didn't add much to his age, either. His gold wire-rimmed spectacles rested on the edge of his pointed nose. Since Shadows are immortal, Qwyrk had long suspected that he just wore this guise because it amused and suited him.

There was a kind and wise air about him, though, one that she always sensed right away. It was one of her favorite things about him.

"Qwyrk?" he said in a soft voice.

"Qwyyz!" she smiled, throwing open her arms.

He let out a belly laugh and embraced her. "My dear Qwyrk! How lovely to see you! It's been far too long!"

"At least a year in human reckoning," she said, knowing he would delight in her calendric reference.

"I should think it's been longer than that," he said in a mock chiding tone, like a parent scolding their offspring for not writing or phoning often enough.

Meanwhile, Babewyn had climbed back up to the arch above the door and began arguing with Gargula. They seemed to be slipping into some form of old, medieval French. She smacked him on the snout. He growled and let off a torrent of curse words best left to medieval French.

"Oh, don't mind them," Qwyzz said hearing the commotion. "They're a bit testy, but they have their uses. I picked them up off of an old church in Normandy six or seven centuries ago, but only got around to animating them recently. Every home should have a good watch-gargoyle or two. But, come in, come in!"

She stepped inside to a large wood-paneled sitting room, over-crowded and adorned with everything imaginable, collected over several centuries. Multi-colored candles lit the whole area, burning from several iron candelabras. As their wax overflowed, it fell to the floor, where it reformed into various Classical and medieval-style statues, which then picked themselves up and wandered out of the room. In one corner, on a small table, a set of wooden Viking chess pieces played a game with itself, and the pieces were getting rather irritated, shouting at each other in the Old Norse language and threatening to make illegal moves. Nearby, the obligatory suit of armor was busy polishing itself, complaining about a few spots that were too hard to reach. It bowed as she walked past it.

A smiling woman stood at the opposite entryway, similar in appearance to Qwyzz, with long flowing white hair and a robe that was more of a long dress, and not so outlandish. She waved at them.

"You remember my wife, Qwota," Qwyzz said, smiling back at her.

Qwyrk snickered. "You ask me that every time I come here, silly! Hello, Qwota! So nice to see you again."

"And you, dear," she answered. "It's been some time since we've seen you around here, you know; you really must come by more often. Anyway, I wish I could stay and chat, but I have so many things to do today. I'll be out for a bit, Qwyzz darling, but it was lovely to see you, Qwyrk."

"Likewise."

With that, Qwota turned, exited out the back garden door, and left them alone.

"Please, please, sit down." Qwyzz motioned to the rather grand divan covered in a rich burgundy velvet fabric with gold trim. "May

I offer you some tea? Or port, perhaps? I have a lovely one, an 1895 just begging to be tried." Qwyzz delighted in his rituals, despite not having the need to consume food or drink.

"I'd love to," she answered, sitting down, "but I can't really stay long. I just want to talk to you about the problem."

"Problem?"

"With Redcap and de Soulis."

Qwyzz looked lost. "What about them?"

Qwyrk couldn't believe her ears. "You know! Their escape..."

"My dear, that happened way back in the 1800s."

"You mean you don't know, either?"

"What should I know?"

"They're free now, Qwyzz! They escaped yesterday!"

"Impossible! Simon of Wakefield is guarding the seal, it should be quite safe."

With a heavy sigh, Qwyrk relayed all of the events of the last twenty-four hours, while Qwyzz looked more and more horrified.

"Oh dear. Oh dear, oh dear..."

"Yes, it *is* just a bit of a problem. I can't believe no one told you."

"I haven't heard a word. This is a total shock to me."

"No one's been sent to take care of it either, and Blip and I are the only ones who seem to know. And it's odd. Somehow, we forgot about who they were, too. It wasn't until Jilly looked them up online that our memories were jogged."

"Online? Oh yes, that internet contraption," Qwyzz mused. "I've heard of that. I must study it sometime. After I finish my commentary on Gutenberg's printing press; a wondrous creation that!"

Qwyrk ignored his charming out-of-touch demeanor, and said, "Look, it seems like someone has gone to great lengths to hide the fact that these two are free and to erase all memory of them from the

Shadows on earth; or maybe it was just Blip and me, I don't know. We only broke the spell by accident when we read about them. That scares me, because if someone targeted us, they know that we know, and that puts Jilly in danger. This is serious, Qwyzz. Someone *wants* them free to do whatever horrible things they're going to. Someone *here*."

Qwyzz chewed his lip with worry and nodded. "There certainly is one faction that might be responsible, the Korrigan, but I can't imagine that even they would resort to this."

"The Korrigan?"

"The night faeries who live in Brittany. They're trouble sometimes, to be sure, and I suspect that more than one of them has dabbled in the black arts. Generally, they're more pranksters, but lately, there seems to be a growing malevolence in their actions, more akin to goblins and such. I fear we may be losing a portion of them to evil, to the Darkfae."

"Well, that's a start, anyway. Do you think one of them might be using magic to blind us to what's going on and help de Soulis and Redcap?"

"It's disturbing, but I suppose it may be possible."

"Well, I can't worry about them now, I have to go to York and find Simon, as well as that other human, the woman who we think accidentally set them free. Both are in danger."

Qwyzz shook his head. "Maybe, but maybe not, at least not yet. I agree that Simon will certainly be a target, but I suspect de Soulis wants to revive his work and unleash hell before he strikes at his jailer."

"What work? Look, my head's still fuzzy about all this, and I can't remember a whole lot, so anything you know is vital."

"It might be best if I let Simon fill you in on the details, as he'll probably have a clearer picture of it than even I do. I can pinpoint his exact location to save you some time."

He pulled out what looked like an old astrolabe that glowed a soft, golden color. He studied it for a moment, squinted, strained, and then smiled.

"Excellent!" He tapped Qwyrk on the forehead, and a picture formed in her mind of the facility and the specific room where Simon was being kept.

"It always disturbs me a little bit how you can do things like that," she said with a smile. "Thank you so much! Now, I should get over there and learn everything he can tell me."

Qwyzz sighed and made a motion with his right hand. A bottle of port appeared on the small table in front of them, along with two glasses.

"Have a drink before you go, my dear, I've a feeling you're going to need it."

CHAPTER NINE

Qwyrk stood behind a group of trees and looked at the institution. She always opted to appear outside when traveling between worlds; the idea of materializing inside a wall didn't bear thinking about. *St. Cornelly's Hospital for the Potentially Troubled* was not nearly as sterile and hospital-like as she had thought it might be. In fact, it looked a bit more like a nice retirement home, being a series of old nineteenth-century stone buildings built in a neo-medieval style. Of course, that could also imply it was a big dungeon.

"Right," she said to herself. "So I know where Simon's room is, but getting there is still going to be a bit of trick."

She looked around. It was a bright, sunny afternoon, and just strolling across the lawn and walking in the front door might raise a few eyebrows; a pair of glowing red eyes attached to a translucent body was hardly an everyday sight. But the bigger problem was actually locating Simon.

"He might be in his room, or he might be in the refectory, the television lounge... anywhere. Bollocks, why didn't I think to ask Qwyzz?"

She couldn't just waltz in and ask where he might be found (not that she would have waltzed in to begin with... that would be silly). She glanced around again. There was a larger group of trees in the rear of the buildings that could help.

"Right, then. Off we go."

Darting from tree to tree, sometimes crawling behind a low bush (and feeling quite undignified about it), she made her way around to the back and into a well-groomed garden.

From here, she could see the wing where Simon was housed. He was just one floor above ground level, which made his room easier to access, unless the window wasn't open or he wasn't in there. There were a number of people milling about in the garden, some residents, some visitors, rendering any chance of sneaking in the back doors impossible.

"Damn it!" she whispered. "Every way in means walking right past a pile of people. Even if I jump up to the first floor of windows, I don't know where I'm going. And why the hell am I still talking to myself out loud?"

Given the urgency of the situation, she was tempted to just run and leap, but thought better of it. She stood there for several minutes, stumped about what to do.

Then she noticed a robust staff member dressed in blinding white making his way toward the back entrance and pushing a large wheeled cart filled with folded towels and bed sheets. Squinting, Qwyrk made her way to a nearby tree and looked at the cart. It was just big enough.

NINE

Bloody hell, she thought, *I don't believe I'm going to do this!*

Feeling like a star in one of those "I-dare-you-to-do-something-completely-stupid" reality TV shows, she made a quick dash for the cart. Well, a dash that involved sneaking up behind the cart-pusher without alerting him or anyone else. Fortunately, there was only one nearby resident couple admiring a new array of flowers and two squirrels quarreling over the right to a particularly savory acorn.

Damn it! She swore to herself. *Why is his outfit so damned bright?*

Squinting again, she tried to move around him and slip into the lower rack of the cart. But it proved to be trickier than she planned. The cart-pusher was a large man and tended to sway from side to side as he lumbered along, in no obvious hurry. First right, then left, all the while humming some inane tune. It reminded her of Star Tao's incessant swaying, which only irritated her more.

Right, that's it!

Without another thought, she stood up and kicked him hard on the behind.

"OUCH! HEY!"

The poor fellow turned around to see who his attacker was, his arms raised in some kind of bizarre defensive pose.

Flipping hell, what is it with these damned martial arts people?

Qwyrk ignored how much it looked like Blip's and dove past him, proceeding to trip and land on her face, scraping various parts. Stifling the urge to swear like an army sergeant, she scrambled into the lower rack of the cart and pulled some sheets over herself, quite sure she was going to bleed all over them, leaving the staff to wonder why there were blue-green stains on the fabric. For someone who could jump off of a tall building and land on the ground below with no effort, this was embarrassing.

After a moment, the man grunted in confusion and turned around. Resuming his tune, he began to push the cart again, a most uncomfortable and bumpy ride. Qwyrk sighed with relief. Well, there was no relief, because the constant shaking of the cart, combined with the pain of the fall, was making her feel sick.

*Lovely. I can bleed **and** yack all over the linens.*

Approximately two days later (or so it seemed), she sensed the cart being pushed through some doors. Resolving to wait until her unknowing porter had left, she heard the door shut again at long last. With relief, she climbed out of the cart and was pleased to see that she hadn't suffered any real damage from her fall.

Finding that she was in a laundry room, she made for the door. Which refused to open, of course, being locked from the outside and all.

"Of course," she sighed. "He must have locked it on his way out, because *nothing* can go smoothly today." She sighed again. "Only one thing for it; going to hurt something awful, though."

Squinting hard, she summoned up an ancient technique she learned centuries ago.

"Always a chance you'll muck it up and not get through," she said.

Keeping her mind focused, she began to dematerialize her form, just enough to be able to pass through solid objects. Stepping forward, she walked right through the heavy wooden door, emerging a few seconds later, re-materializing, gasping, and feeling like she'd been knocked down by an especially irritated bull.

"Damn, damn, damn!" she swore as she stumbled forward, rubbing her aching head, and shaking it to ward off the fog that came along with the pain. "This had better well be worth it."

Finding the room she wanted was easier than it should have been, which gave her pause. After everything else that had happened today, she half expected Simon to have been transferred to some facility in Cornwall. But no, a nearby list on the wall detailing which tenants got which laundry pointed to where he was lodging.

Making her way upstairs to the first floor, and dashing down the hall, she found his room. Looking around, she knocked on the door, and trying the handle, found it to be unlocked. She pushed it open and peered around into the room.

"Simon? Sir Simon of Wakefield?"

Inside was a wizened old man, dressed in a simple grey linen shirt with blue trousers. His hair was snow white, but still thick, and flowed to his shoulders. He wore a thin, well-trimmed beard.

He was reading a small book with a dark brown leather cover that was cracked and worn with age. He looked up as Qwyrk spoke.

"Well, I was wondering when I would hear from one of you," he said in a bitter tone. "If you're expecting me to quiver in fright at the sight of a Shadow with glowing red eyes, I'm afraid I will disappoint you, young lady. I have the Sight and can see you as you are."

"I'm Qwyrk," she said, entering the room and quickly shutting the door behind her.

"So then," he said, paying no attention to her introduction and closing his book. "Tell me, what news? The seals are secure, I take it?"

"Ummm, well, we have a little bit of a problem with that."

"How little?"

"Um... not so little, actually. Kind of a proper, ginormous nightmare."

She relayed everything that had happened so far.

Simon sat in silence for a bit, looking down, as if lost deep in thought. Qwyrk wanted to press him for some response, but held her tongue.

"So," he said after an uncomfortable silence, "they murdered

Henry, and right in front of that poor child. I'm very sorry. He was a good knight, you see. She should never have witnessed something so terrible. He must have arrived only a few minutes too late."

"Henry was a Templar?" she asked.

Simon nodded. "We recruit quietly these days and stay out of history's way. Henry was young and promising; he might even have been a suitable permanent replacement for me one day. When the order learned of my... incarceration, he was sent here first, to try to get me released, claiming to be my grandson. But we medieval knights don't exactly carry the proper modern identification, you see. They wanted blood tests and all sorts of rubbish to prove the relation. Can you imagine what they'd have found if they drew my blood? Over 700 years old, traces of the Black Death, among other afflictions, and no modern vaccinations of any kind. That would have caused quite a stir! So he abandoned that plan, and I sent him back there to guard the seals while I worked out how to get out of here. Now look what's happened..."

"Please, sir, I need to know what to do," Qwyrk said, impatience gnawing at her. "I have to know exactly what I'm dealing with. Please, tell me everything you can."

"Right then, have a seat and listen carefully," he began. "It started in the late thirteenth century, at Hermitage Castle in Scotland, near the border. William de Soulis was the butler for the Scottish King. Not much is known about his youth. In any case, he lusted for more power and a higher station than he had, and so he turned to sorcery. He learned many arcane arts, some benevolent, some forbidden. His servant was whispered by locals to be a demon. In reality, he was a renegade Shadow, Robin Redcap, whom de Soulis had contacted and managed to free from prison by magical means. As you know, Redcap had escaped captivity more than once in the past."

"Actually, I didn't know that, until you just mentioned it," she said. "It seems to come back more with each bit of information that I hear, like it's being 'un-erased,' or something."

Simon nodded. "A confusion cantrip, most likely. Someone doesn't want you to remember." He continued, "The two of them terrorized the countryside for several years, stealing, looting, destroying, and taking what they wanted, whether in treasure or flesh. De Soulis was feared, and his power began to rival that of the king himself. Eventually, a minstrel and magic-worker named Thomas of Ercildoune, known to history as 'the Rhymer,' was called down from the Tomnahurich Hill in Scotland, and he intervened."

"That's a gateway to the Fae realms; I remember him," Qwyrk said. "Wasn't he in love with a Shadow woman, and they married or some such?"

"Not a Shadow, but a faerie queen, Glorienne. I heard that he passed on some years ago, even though his life was abnormally lengthened by his stay in your world, though I'm not certain he's gone. I will pass too one day, you know. The magic is not perfect, and we humans are simply not meant to live as long as he and I have. But let's not worry about that now.

"Thomas discerned a way to kill de Soulis, and he told the local people how it could be done. In 1321, they succeeded, though many died in the attempt."

"Yeah, we read about that online. Melted alive. Gruesome, but it didn't really work, did it?"

"Well, it destroyed his body, but his soul belonged to Redcap, who had managed to steal it via the magical connection they shared. But Redcap didn't count on de Soulis' will being so strong. Even beyond death, he was far more powerful in mind than Redcap, and he took control of the Shadow's body, though the two always struggle for the upper hand. Sometimes Redcap wins out temporarily, but de Soulis always wins out again.

"De Soulis revels in the power of Redcap's Shadow form, and since his aims are largely those of death and destruction, Redcap is more cooperative than he would otherwise be. But he hates de Soulis with a passion, and no doubt wants to be free of him and any of the constraints on his behavior that de Soulis imposes."

"What would happen if they could be separated?"

"Well, de Soulis would probably go on to his deserved fate, so that's something, but Redcap would be free, chaotic, and murderous. The magic needed to separate them would have to be quite strong, I fear, and I don't think anyone even knows how. It wasn't possible all those centuries ago, so I don't know if it could even be accomplished after all this time. We tried just about everything, from separating them to destroying them utterly and concluded that locking them away was the only solution. We sealed them under protective sigils and hid them in a small, unremarkable village. It seemed a good strategy."

So Blip was right, Qwyrk thought, much as it pained her to admit it.

"But they managed to escape more than once, most often when my duties took me away from guarding them. In fact, old Grandmother Boatford gave them a good thrashing right in my home town of Knettles in the sixteenth century!

"You may remember stories of a character known as Spring-heeled Jack in the nineteenth century? He was a sensation in the Victorian newspapers. That was the two of them. They'd go jumping about, scaring people, shooting fire at them and such. Fortunately, only a handful of people were hurt, though a few unfortunate souls were also murdered. That part never made it into the papers; I suppose it was considered too shocking, or perhaps just too unbelievable. They had the whole of England in an uproar for decades. No one could understand how one man could live for so long. But it was actually two, and they were in one form."

"Bloody hell! No wonder he was never caught. So how did they escape, then?"

"We... I got careless. The seals had held them for centuries, but the chamber pot was old and cracking. Once, while I was gone for a short duration, I left the watch in the hands of a young and quite capable Shadow. One afternoon he accidentally knocked it off of a shelf while cleaning my little home, trying to be kind and thoughtful. They made quick work of him, poor boy, and disappeared. I still blame myself for his death.

"They had been in that limbo state for so long that they were a bit disoriented I think, and neither seemed to have control. I imagine that's why many of Spring-heeled Jack's attacks were more like pranks at first, but as time went on, they become more dangerous. We were able to bring them back. By the next time they escaped, Redcap was in a particularly murderous frame of mind, and did much more damage, though the newspapers never reported it."

"How did they escape again so soon?"

"It was not my fault the second time, though I wish I could take the blame for it, you see..."

"Actually, never mind that for the moment," she interrupted. "How did you recapture them? That's what we need to know now."

"Both times, a group of your people was dispatched to hunt them down and trap them. I don't know the means, and it obviously took some time and effort, but they were successful. In each case, they brought them back to me, trapped in a magical orb; I have no idea how it worked. From there, some magic-makers transferred them into a new plunger, the seals were re-established, and that was the end of it. I assume they've sent a group of Shadows after them again?"

"Not as far as I know, and that's the whole problem! No one in Symphinity even seems to know that they've been freed, and my friend and I," she winced momentarily at using that word to describe Blip, "seemed to have had our memories of the two of them erased, by this... cantrip thing. I'm only piecing it all back together now, as you're telling me these things. Someone in our world seems to be helping them by keeping their escape a secret, and messing with my mind, altering my memories... and yeah, I am well furious about it!"

"Oh dear, this is bad, very bad indeed," Simon answered, his face becoming pale.

"I think it's likely they'll come after you, but we can keep an eye on you," Qwyrk said, sensing his fear and wanting to calm it.

"They will eventually seek me out, true, but that's not what I'm worried about. They could have easily found me by now, and I would already be dead. That I'm still here means that de Soulis is most definitely in control of the body and obviously without a team of Shadows out there to stop him. They are under no confusion this time, if they're receiving help. They'll be heading toward Leeds. He's looking for the wyrmroost."

"The what, now?"

"A dragon's nest filled with drakelet eggs. Back in the thirteenth century, a Fire Drake awoke from its hibernation and caused some problems in the North, but she was eventually subdued and put back to sleep for another millennia or so. Unfortunately, we learned that she had a nest, which was never found. They don't need to mate to lay eggs, you see, a survival adaptation when male dragons are scarce or still sleeping.

"De Soulis learned of this nest while he was alive and had plans to hatch the drakelets and ensorcell them to be his servants, about a dozen of them. Imagine the horrific destruction they could have caused! He searched far and wide for the nest, and finally found it. He cast a number of spells to keep the eggs safe and hidden, in a kind of hibernation, while he made his plans. He was always a grand schemer, you see.

"In any case, nothing came of it, fortunately; he was killed a few months later. But the wyrmroost remained, buried deep in the ground. Templars and Shadow scholars later determined that it must have been somewhere in the countryside beyond Leeds, but de Soulis' shielding magic was strong, and they were never able to locate it precisely.

"It was decided that as long as he'd enchanted the nest and hidden it, no further harm could come from it, since he was no longer alive to undo the magic. I didn't like that idea at all, for this exact reason, but I was overruled, and by then, we Templars had already been scattered by that bastard King Philip in France... 'The Fair' my shriveled old arse! I had to keep a low profile and continue on with my assigned duty, pretending to be a regular knight. It wasn't the time to argue. Decades and centuries passed without incident, and the search for the nest was abandoned, mostly forgotten. I don't need to tell you what happens if he finds the eggs and hatches them now."

"I can use my imagination. Twelve young fire dragons under the control of an evil sorcerer and a psychopathic Shadow... equals a very unhappy ending." Qwyrk nodded.

"It must certainly be under the city by now, which has sprawled out considerably in the last hundred years," Simon added.

"Oh, I know exactly where it is, even what house it's near. It's in a residential neighborhood on the outskirts, lots of families and children. I was sent there a few days ago with two mates of mine to check out some disturbances. We didn't find much, but there were reports about strange phenomena happening in the area for a time beforehand: weird lights in the sky, even small earthquakes."

"No doubt coinciding with my eviction." Simon looked sad. "They must have sensed my absence and de Soulis may have begun preparations by undoing some of his charms. I don't know how, but that has to be it. Or, as we fear, he had help. This is sounding more and more like no mere accident."

Qwyrk nodded, wondering to where all of this conspiring led.

"Right," she said after a moment's pause. "I have to get down there and try to stop them."

"You can't do this on your own, it's far too dangerous! They've already killed a fine Templar knight with no effort."

"I don't really have a choice, do I?"

"At least go to your world and seek some help."

"My old mentor is taking it up with the council, but who knows what that will do? For all I know, everyone on the council may be in on it, and he might already be in prison, or worse. I don't have time to sit around and wait, hoping that someone comes to the rescue."

"You have no idea what to do once you actually get there and confront them."

"Yeah, all right, so I'll improvise! I haven't made it this far without having learned a few things about how to handle myself in fights."

"You will die," Simon said curtly.

"A risk I have to take, since I'm the only one available. Let's face it, you're not exactly in prime fighting condition." She regretted her words.

"No, I'm not, but others in my order are. They could be summoned to help."

"And how long will that take?"

"They could be in Leeds by tomorrow, maybe the day after."

"And the dragons could be hatched and roaming free by then. Look, if this is his plan, maybe he's going to try to wake them up tonight. He'll wait until it's dark; it's what Shadows always do to avoid detection. I don't know if he can free the eggs in that short a time, but do we really want to wait around and find out?"

Simon looked at her with a frustrated gaze. "You're right, something must be done, and you're the only one who can help right now. I'm impressed by you; I also fear that this is the first and last time I will ever see you." He sighed.

Thanks for the vote of confidence, mate, she mused.

"Can I ask you a rather personal question?" she asked after a moment's silence.

Simon nodded.

"Why were you chosen to guard the seals? How did the Templars decide on you and give you your extended life?"

"That is another story altogether, and a long one." He sighed again, a sad tone to his voice. "I'm tired and would like to rest for a bit."

Qwyrk took the hint and let the matter drop.

"I should call on my friends to come and keep an eye on you," she offered.

"There's no need, my dear. I'm in no imminent danger, and their attention is focused on far worse things than killing me. In any case, I'm an old, old man; I've lived far longer than I should have. If it's my time, then it's my time. I am ready to pass on if need be."

"It's *not* your time, and you're going to be guarding these two monsters for many years to come when we stuff them back where they came from, I promise!"

Simon smiled. "I admire your courage and your spirit, and I wish you the best. I shall summon my brothers, and pray that they are not too late in coming to your aid."

Qwyrk smiled and held his hands. "Thank you. One other question, if you don't mind: why can the child, Jilly, see me as I am? And also the other bloke? Both of them saw de Soulis and Redcap yesterday. Does that have anything to do with it?"

"Oh, it does, indeed. It was a spell that de Soulis cast on Redcap. As long as Redcap was nearby, de Soulis would be able to see any other Shadows in their true forms. It was created to protect him from any surprise attacks." He grinned. "Something you all excel at. That magic still lingers around them, so now, anyone who sees them is enspelled and has the same ability, at least temporarily."

"How long does it last?"

"It should wear off in a few days."

"I'm sorry I'll disappear from Jilly so soon. One other thing..." she said. "Why on earth were they kept under a chamber pot... and a toilet plunger?"

Simon chuckled. "Just a bit of humor on our part. It was the most humiliating thing we could think of to contain the man who wanted to rule the world."

"Look, thank you, truly," she said. "I need to go. I have one other human to check on out here before I head off to Leeds. She's the one who set them free. I need to make sure she's all right... and isn't involved in this in some way. Maybe I can even learn a thing or two from her. I assume she'll be able to see me as well?"

"Very likely. You'll know for sure if there's not an inordinate amount of screaming when you greet her. Good luck, Qwyrk."

Qwyrk smiled. She squeezed his hands again, and then exited

his room. *Now, how to get the hell out of here*, she mused to herself.

* * *

How can I get out of here? Jilly thought.

"Now then," Blip instructed, "in order to carry out my instructional duties to you, I would like to review the entire corpus of Western Philosophy. Not all at once, of course, but we should be able to make a suitable summation in, oh, say, three or four lessons, five at most. I understand that the subject can be a bit daunting to the neophyte, and accordingly, I shall tailor these lectures with the beginner in mind. Therefore, I have chosen as our starting text, Kant's *Kritik der reinen Vernunft*, known in the Mother Tongue as the *Critique of Pure Reason*, a jolly light read that will guide you painlessly into the fascinating word of philosophical theory and inquiry."

"Um, Mr. Blip..."

"Lesson one, the Preface, and I quote: 'Human reason has this peculiar fate that in one species of its knowledge it is burdened by questions which, as prescribed by the very nature of reason itself, it is not able to ignore, but which, as transcending all its powers, it is also not able to answer...'"

"Um..."

"'The perplexity into which it thus falls is not due to any fault of its own. It begins with principles which it has no option save to employ in the course of experience, and which this experience at the same time abundantly justifies it in using...'"

"Mr. Blippingstone!"

"Yes? Very good, child! Very good, indeed. Proper use of my name, you get a bonus mark for that."

"Um, I'm sorry, but Qwyrk's not back yet, and I'm a bit worried.

It seems like she's been gone for ages."

"Two hours at most, I would expect. But, there's nothing to worry about, my dear, nothing at all! We have the situation well in hand. Now, where was I... oh yes! 'Rising with their aid (since it is determined to this also by its own nature) to ever higher, ever more remote, conditions, it soon becomes aware that in this way—the questions never ceasing—its work must always remain incomplete...'"

"I think I saw someone outside!" Jilly exclaimed.

Blip dropped his lesson book and assumed his karate crane position once again. Jilly gave him a blank stare.

"I was going to say that I think it's Star Tao, so you don't have to fight or anything."

"Oh, right, well, carry on then. Fine young lad, that boy!"

"We may have to postpone the lesson for a bit, I'm afraid." Jilly breathed a huge inner sigh of relief.

"Hm? Oh, well, yes, I suppose under the circumstances. A pity, though, I was just getting started."

Jilly shuddered at the thought.

A moment later there was a knock on the door. She ran and opened it. Sure enough, the gawky young man was standing there, flopping plats, a big toothy grin through his thin beard. She hugged him.

"All right, Jilly?"

"Yes, thank you! Come in."

"Cheers!"

"You get everything done, then?"

"Yeah, got all me workshop flyers distributed, talked to a few people who are interested, and confirmed me one student so far. It's all brilliant! Nice place you have here. So... where's Qwyrk?" He looked around the living room, obviously disappointed not to see her.

Then his eyes fell on Blip. He sank to his knees and bowed, his head touching the floor.

"Hail!" he uttered. "Thank you, oh great Amazonian God for blessing us with your presence once again."

Blip was clearly over the moon, waving his hand. "Yes, well, you may recover. It seemed to me that circumstances warranted my staying on the mortal plane for some time longer, until we can reach a satisfactory conclusion to the problem we've encountered."

"You are wise beyond all mortal knowing, my lord."

"Indeed. Indeed I am!"

* * *

Qwyrk decided that she couldn't waste time with a sneaky exit (and her covert entrance hadn't gone all that well, anyway), so she found the nearest open window at the end of the hall, and just jumped out. Unfortunately, she landed right in front of an elderly woman sipping tea at a table on the lawn.

The woman shrieked and dropped her cup, staring in wide-mouthed horror at the menacing-looking Shadow with glowing red eyes standing before her.

"Um, look," Qwyrk improvised. "I'm not really real, I'm just a side effect of your... medication, all right? Actually, it's probably your tea that set it off. Or both. Nothing to be afraid of, I'll be gone in just a moment. Actually, I won't be gone at all, because I was never really here to begin with. Make sense? Bye, then! Byeee!"

With that, she bounded off, leaving the poor woman whimpering and looking at her teapot in disbelief.

"Lovely job, Qwyrk," she said to herself, leaping over a small clump of trees. "Scaring old ladies. And guess what? I get to do it all again in a few minutes! Lovely."

In a short time, she stood some distance away from the *Shoulders' Arms*, an historic inn situated on the outskirts of York. Sure enough, the tour bus was parked nearby. There appeared to be a line of folks boarding the bus. They were wearing matching T-shirts and cowboy hats, just like the one Jilly had described. Actually, they looked even sillier than she had made them out to be.

"Right, please hurry up, everyone!" a man's voice called out. "The coach is leaving in ten minutes sharp for the castle."

"Damn!" Qwyrk swore. "There won't be time to talk to this woman, and who knows when they'll be back?"

"Where's Dottie?" Qwyrk heard a woman say in a Texas accent.

"Oh, she's staying here," another answered. "I don't think after her scare yesterday that she'll be going anywhere for a while."

"Yes! Thank you!" Qwyrk whispered. "I just have to wait for this lot to bugger off, and then go find her."

The next ten minutes seemed to drag on for hours. Qwyrk was quite sure the sun was much closer to setting than it had been when the announcement was made. Actually, there probably had already been a whole General Election. She sighed as the bus did finally roll on out to whatever exotic destination was on the itinerary for the afternoon. With no one around on the grounds, Qwyrk wasted no time and just strode right across the lawn to the entrance, enjoying her bold frontal assault.

Once there, she slipped inside and found the lobby to be empty. Making her way to the stairs, she dashed up two flights, and found the room after spying on the list at the desk. This no longer seemed like an easy task, as the knot in her stomach reminded her, yet another little physical ailment not normally experienced by

~ 146 ~

Shadows.

Taking a deep breath, she knocked.

"Who is it?" a woman's voice asked in a southern drawl.

"Um, can I talk to you for a minute. It's about the tour." She winced. She didn't like having to lie, but she knew the door might never open if she said why she was really there.

She heard the lock slide, and the door began to open. Standing there was a short, rotund woman who looked like she had had the life scared out of her. Though Dottie was the cause of this mess, Qwyrk felt sorry for her.

"What do you need to know?" she asked in a timid voice.

"Look I'm sorry, it's not really about the tour, but I need to talk to you about what happened to you yesterday..."

Dottie backed up, a terrified expression her face. "Oh lordy! Has the devil come for me?"

Qwyrk held up her hands and shook her head. "No, no! Nothing like that, I promise! I won't hurt you."

"You're not a demon, then? You've got pointy ears!"

"No, no, I'm... an angel." Qwyrk winced again to herself. She wasn't a good liar, especially under stress. "Nothing's going to happen to you, I promise. In fact I want to help you. I know what you're afraid of, and I can stop that horrible thing you saw."

"I don't think anyone can do that, sweetie," Dottie replied, "especially not a pretty young lady like you, angel or not."

"Look, I just need to know, did that thing speak to you, threaten you, anything?"

"No, thank goodness! He just said something about being free and rushed right on out the door. Actually, he may not have even seen me. Oh lord, I hope he didn't!"

"Can you tell me exactly what happened, from the beginning?"

"Well, I was just lookin' around. I get curious that way, and like to look at things. And I found that cute little house, and just had to have a better look-see. I didn't mean no harm; I just wanted a peek. Well, I got in there, and it was an awful mess, and there was this strange little toilet plunger with all sorts of funny writing on it in the corner. I just picked it up to have a look, and it kinda tickled all up and down my arm. Then that horrible shape came out of it, knocked me on my patootie, and flew right on out of there, laughing. It was the most horrible sound I ever did hear."

"I'm sure it was, but really, you're safe now. It's not going to come back for you. It's not interested in you. The best thing for you to do is to put it behind you and get out there and enjoy the rest of your holiday."

"Oh, I'm done with travelin'. After I get home, I'm never leaving Texas again!"

"All the more reason why you should enjoy this trip while you're here. Look at it this way: this country is a magical place, and you got to see a little of that magic, the bad and the good, both yesterday and right now. That's a lot more than most people ever get to see in their lives! You've seen proof that there are worlds beyond your own. And with that knowledge, think how much more special all those old places your group is visiting will look now."

"Well, that's a nice way of thinkin' about it, now that you mention it," Dottie pondered. "Maybe I will go on the trip tomorrow..."

"You do that, and have fun. Really! Everything's going to be all right, I promise! I have to go now, but thank you."

"Thank you, angel, whoever you are." Dottie smiled for the first time in a day.

Qwyrk smiled back, said goodbye, and left back down the hall

NINE

she came up, satisfied that this human hadn't deliberately set them free. That was something, at least.

CHAPTER TEN

"Yes, yes, it's not easy being a god," Blip mused, seated on the couch and sipping a cup of Earl Grey. Star Tao was a captive audience of one, and Jilly craved doing something else, like mathematics homework for school that wouldn't start for months.

"We have so many responsibilities, you see, my young gaber-lunzie," Blip continued, "determining the order of the universe, answering prayers, seeing to it that our worshippers remain happy and content. Oh, yes, it's all well and good to say that we're 'omnipotent,' but it's rather more complex than that. It requires a certain type of, how shall one say, personality, I suppose, and not all gods are up to the task. Oh, they might be good at hurling a thunderbolt, or bringing rain, or some such thing, but they have not fully grasped the enormity of the duties set before them.

"Concerning our followers, for instance, we must maintain an adequate propinquity, whilst also seeming distant enough to retain our regal and mysterious air. Too much familiarity would risk denigrating our celestial nature, while if we were too aloof, people would simply stop believing in us altogether, a problem that has plagued many a god in the past. Ask old Zeus about that one! Finding the balance between those two extremes is an ever-challenging task, I can well assure you. Of course, if it were simple, anyone could do it, and then we wouldn't be gods, would we?"

"Wise words, my lord." Star Tao seemed to be in some kind of half-trance.

On the other hand, Jilly just felt half-awake. She stared out the window, desperate to see Qwyrk return, as Blip's self-aggrandizing symphony to the virtues of his divinity moved into its second movement. His words faded further and further from her ears as she thought more about everything that was happening, and still might happen. How simple and mundane life had been just yesterday, before everything got dumped into her life. There was no evil sorcerer and his monster companion trying to take over the world, no Blip and his tedious lectures, no proof of any worlds beyond her own... and no Qwyrk.

She regretted being angry before, and now she feared she might never even see her new friend again. They'd met less than day ago, yet Jilly's attachment, even love for Qwyrk, surprised her. In no time at all, Qwyrk had become like her older sister, something that Jilly, as an only child, never knew she even wanted. What would happen if Qwyrk were...

"Wouldn't you agree, young Miss Pleeth?"

"Umm, what?"

"Now, now, child, you must not let your mind stray, especially when instruction of such an important nature is being given. I mused about the eternal question of predestination versus free will, and what role a god might play in it. I merely stated that it is a vexing conundrum of seemingly irreconcilable paradoxes, but that the real truth of the matter is that mortals are not simply prepared to understand it as of yet. Wouldn't you agree?"

"Um, yes, I suppose so." She had no idea at all what he was talking about and was happy when he paid her little attention as he launched into some new pontification about the nature of supplication and worship, much to Star Tao's rapt delight.

"Right, I should really be writing this down," he said.

"Yes, yes, indeed; quite right, my boy. Go and fetch the appropriate implements and then we shall continue. It shall be a new scripture for a new time."

Star Tao looked at Jilly for a moment, in a questioning gaze.

"Over there, in the office," she replied pointing in its direction as she returned her gaze to the window.

"Right, back in a mo' with paper and pen," he said and scooted off.

"What's wrong with you child?" Blip asked. "Your mind is wandering off farther than an untethered mule, and, if I do say so myself, you're missing quite a fine discussion on the nature of the universe as a result!"

"I'm sorry, Mr. Blip..."

"Mr. Blippingstone..."

"But I just can't stop thinking about Qwyrk. I'm so worried about everything. I wish she would come back. She's been gone far too long."

"Child, she is more than capable of taking care of herself. While Miss Qwyrk and I do have our differences, and a damned good number of them, I've known her for many centuries, and I do know that she is resourceful and intelligent, if a bit headstrong and irritating. Well, more than a bit. However, if anyone can look after herself in such a dangerous situation as this, Qwyrk can. Of that I have no doubt. She'll be back, and probably sooner than you expect." He smiled at her, and Jilly was somehow reassured.

Star Tao reappeared, looking eager and ready.

"Right, I got me pen and paper. Where did we leave off, master?"

"Ahem, yes, as I was saying, the duties of a worshipper are many and can be demanding at times, but they are also rewarding, precisely because they build character and lead to a more formal relationship with the chosen god, a situation which can only bring multifarious benefits to said supplicant and enhance his or her life immeasurably. Consider it a kind of social contract, though one of a mysterious and metaphysical nature, rather than one of the more philosophical and earthly bent. Though it could be said to be some-where between the theories of Hobbes and Locke, rather than the more permissive musings of Rousseau..."

Jilly gazed out the window again and wanted Qwyrk back more than ever.

* * *

Qwyrk stood outside, a good distance from the hotel in a copse of trees, musing over everything she had learned. She didn't know which one of these things disturbed her more: the release of de Soulis and Redcap, or the fact that someone from her own realm seemed to be helping them and clouding her and others' memories about it.

"Nothing else for it, then," she sighed aloud to herself. "I've got to get back to Leeds and stop them. But I'd better check in on Jilly first, and get Blip to come along." For once, the thought of his companionship didn't make her feel ill. She was oddly comforted that he would be there with her. It was that fact that made her feel ill.

TEN

"Qwyrk?"

She spun around in the direction of the voice. "What the hell?"

She was confronted by two young women, one with long, wavy brown hair and wearing a short, sleeveless, blue stretch dress with black, sparkly high-heel shoes. She was joined by another young lady, adorned with a bright red bob haircut, white T-shirt, and tight, silver shorts with pink platform boots.

"Qwyrk, it *is* you! Goddess, what are you doing all the way out here, love?" Qwypp asked.

"I might ask the same of you... and what the hell are you both wearing?"

"Oh we were out clubbing till like six this morning," Qwykk offered up. "It was brilliant! We just haven't gotten around to changing. Didn't need to, really."

"All right, but what are you doing out *here*?"

"Well, last night we were at the Big Bad Venue in Leeds," Qwypp answered, "and it was Mexican alcohol night, and we met these blokes who were pissed off their heads on Tequila, and... I think if humans have too much alcohol they can sort of see us, at least a little, and we got in a taxi with them after the club closed, and they rode around for a while not remembering where they lived, until they were well out of the city, and we couldn't really tell the driver where to go without scaring the hell out of him, so we just rode with them while the meter was clicking away, and..."

"Look, never mind," Qwyrk interrupted. "Listen. Things are bad, really bad. Remember the other night? The rosebush, and all that? Well, it's a lot worse than we could have guessed. De Soulis is back, and Redcap with him."

The two of them gave her blank stares.

Qwyrk rolled her eyes. "I didn't expect either of you to know anyway, and I doubt it has anything to do with the cantrip."

"Isn't that the herb that drives cats wild?" Qwykk asked, looking confused.

"No, you pillock!" Qwypp interjected, "Cantrip! You know, an overnight camping trip!"

Qwyrk's hand went to cover her face, almost as a reflex.

"Look," she said from behind her palm, "just listen. Some really evil magic has been stirred up, and that rosebush we were looking at by Jimmy's home is the focal point for it. That's why it was doing all those weird things."

"You mean that android-morphical thingie you were talking about," Qwykk offered, trying to sound informed.

Qwyrk gazed at her, wondering how some Shadows could survive so long. "Uh, yeah, that. I'm going to head back over there tonight with Blip and try to take care of it."

"We'll come, too!" Qwykk volunteered with a smile and a bouncy demeanor that made her look like a model from a shampoo commercial. Qwypp seemed less enthused at the thought.

"Oh, Goddess, no!" Qwyrk shot back in anger and frustration, realizing that she had startled her friend, who even looked a bit hurt. "Look, I'm sorry, I'm just really stressed out about all of this right now. It's better if Blip and I handle this; we know what to do." Though in reality, she had no clue. "There *is* something the two of you can do, though. There's an old Templar knight who needs looking after for a bit in a hospital nearby. I'd appreciate it if you could keep an eye on him and see that he's safe."

"Of course," Qwypp answered, "we'd be happy to. But... you'll be all right, yeah?"

Qwyrk nodded. "I'll be fine, and I'll feel a lot better knowing that someone is looking after Simon."

"What are we looking out for?" Qwykk queried.

"Nothing, really," Qwyrk lied. "I just want to make sure that he's all right, and feels safe. He's had a bit of a rough go of things recently, and has been working hard for a long time. He can tell you more if he's so inclined, but I wouldn't bet on it. Look, he's at *St. Cornelly's Hospital for the Potentially Troubled*, just a few miles back down this road. The room number is thirty-four, one floor up. You'll have to sneak in, but I have no doubt you're both real good at getting into places you don't belong. Just mind the laundry rooms in that place, all right?"

They gave her a puzzled look.

"And," she added, "you might want to change into some other clothes, like hospital uniforms or something, because he can see us. Just saying."

"Are you sure you don't need us?" Qwypp questioned.

"No, honestly, I'll be all right. If I change my mind, I'm sure I can find you. Now get off, both of you, before I get sick looking at that appalling club wear!" She grinned, and they smiled back, taking the hint. With a flourish, they set off down the road, all sass and attitude, heedless of traffic, or of causing any sensation.

Qwyrk shook her head, wondering if Simon really was going to be any safer.

* * *

He stood in the cover of brambles and trees, looking down the hill at the street lined with brick houses that seemed a little like those he once knew during his last escape, but they were also different. Strange cables crisscrossed their roofs, and odd wires and metal dishes sat atop many. Those strange metal carriages lined the street, and sometimes one would zoom by, making that terrible noise they all did, leaving behind its obnoxious stench. Beyond this street was another, and here the houses were not attached to one another, but stood free, larger than their siblings, and beset with gardens, trees, hedges, and... rosebushes.

"Why do you bring me here?" he asked the other who shared his form, the acid of his voice betraying the hatred he had for the mortal he was bound to.

"Can you not sense it, you fool?" His mouth moved but another's voice sounded. "It's nearby, just as my pet confirmed: the wyrmroost! The eggs are buried deep in the ground, and they are stirring, called to life by our presence. Exactly as I'd hoped!"

"So?"

"Do you not see, you idiot? When I free them and hatch them, the young fire drakes will do my... our bidding. We can reclaim the rule of these northern lands that we once had, and most importantly, I will sacrifice one of them. With a dragon's blood, I can separate us at last!"

"You seem quite sure of yourself."

"Sure enough that after all these centuries, I don't wish to be in this form with you any longer than I must."

"And where will you go, or had you forgotten that it is my body you inhabit, human?"

"With the power of the drakes and their blood, a new human body will be mine for the taking. I can easily possess another, whoever I like. When I tire of one, I can move on to another, forever."

"And you would give up the strength and power of this form to retreat back into one so weak as a frail little human? I'm glad to hear it. Perhaps you are sentimental and soft. In which case, I shall enjoy killing you in that new form you are so eager to adopt."

"You can try, you fiend, but I think you'll be disappointed. And your efforts may be painful for you."

"We shall see. Now, what must we do?"

"We shall wait until cover of full darkness and then proceed to the source."

"Of course. More waiting. Always waiting. I grow weary of your schemes, little man."

"My schemes offer a way back to our true freedom, to power. I think, whereas you merely act, and that is why I control you and not the other way around. Or had you not noticed?"

Redcap growled, but made no further answer.

The summer sun would still be in the sky for many hours. They would wait. A little while longer, they would wait.

* * *

"...and so, the Delphic Oracle was one means by which the ancient Greeks sought to commune with their divine benefactors, and while its mystical approach may have been of some use to invoke the general awe of the commoners, it was not the most effective tool for communicating divine wishes to the masses. However, for sheer theater and pomp, one could scarcely do better than what many of the ancient Greco-Roman rites could conjure up, if you'll excuse the joke, heh heh..."

Jilly was beginning to wish de Soulis would just destroy the world and be done with it.

While Star Tao scribbled on his notepad in haste (she reckoned he'd already filled at least twenty pages of the *Gospel According to Blip*), she again gazed out the window. Once, she tried to excuse herself, but Blip insisted that he was coming to the most important part, and that she wouldn't want to miss the ensuing revelations.

Maybe if I fake a seizure or a ruptured appendix...

There was no need for faux medical crises, however, for at that moment, she spied out the window the event she'd wanted for the last several hours.

"Qwyrk! She's back!" And with that, she jumped up from the couch and ran to the front door.

"Ah, brilliant!" Star Tao exclaimed, and he stood up to follow her.

"Um, excuse me, we're not finished," Blip cautioned. "I was about to provide specific examples of the relative ineffectiveness of Thracian Bacchic Rites in the quest for more rain for the spring crops; it's quite scintillating..."

Jilly heard nothing, but flung open the door to see Qwyrk's smiling face.

"Oh, Qwyrk! Thank goodness! I was so worried!" She threw her arms around Qwyrk, who laughed and embraced her. They stood there for a long time, Jilly not wanting to let go.

"I think we'd better go in," Qwyrk said at last. "It's going to seem rather strange if someone outside looks at you hugging someone they can't see!"

"Oh, right!" Jilly realized, feeling a bit embarrassed. In they went, and she closed the door behind them to keep out prying eyes.

"All right, then, Qwyrk?" Star Tao offered a meager smile. For once, she seemed rather glad to see him. She even gave him a quick hug, only to begin sniffing the air; her nose twitched.

"Patchouli?" she asked.

"Only the very finest!"

Star Tao was obviously so taken aback by this gesture of friendship that he didn't even know how to react. Jilly saw him just stand there for a bit, trying to process it after Qwyrk had already gone into the living room.

"First, an illuminating lecture from a god," he said with a smile, "and now a hug from a fit elf maiden; can this day get any better?"

Qwyrk sat down, and after a moment of greetings and small talk, explained to Blip and Jilly (and Star Tao, who wandered in, still in a daze of pleasant confusion) all that had happened: her trip back home, her meeting with Simon, her contact with Dottie (though she left out the bit with Qwypp and Qwykk), and what it all meant. The happiness at her return took on a somber feel.

"A grave situation, indeed," Blip stated, now apparently off of his godly high horse about dispensing necessary crop rotation advice.

"Blip, you and I have to do something about this. The Templars may show up, or they may be days away. We don't have that kind of time. We have to get down to Leeds tonight. I don't think it will take long for de Soulis to discover where he's hidden that nest. He might be there already. This is our only chance. If he gets those eggs and disappears, we won't find him before he's done, well, whatever it is he's going to do."

"Quite right, quite right, we must go, I agree." But for once, Blip didn't sound as confident.

"And we're going too, right?" Jilly thought that if she included Star Tao, an adult (well, sort of), she might have a better chance of stating her case. But no such luck.

"Honey, you know I can't allow that. This sorcerer is appallingly dangerous. He kills people without a thought, especially if Redcap gains any control. Right now, I don't know how much de Soulis has the upper hand. It's bad enough that he's in control, but if he loses it... there could be a bloodbath."

"Qwyrk..." Blip cautioned.

"No Blip, she needs to know the truth. This isn't a fun adventure to a bookstore any more or a search on the internet. If we fail, all of Britain could be in danger. If there's more to what's been happening, and de Soulis is getting help from other Shadows, our own world might be in peril, too."

Jilly shivered. As much as she wanted to go, she was afraid for herself and for Qwyrk. She didn't want either Qwyrk or Blip to go. After being ignored by her parents for so long, these two had become, in a short time, like a family to her. Admittedly, a rather odd family, but the sentiment was there. She was terrified of what might happen to them. But she held her tongue and just nodded.

"I know, I get it. I'm not all that eager to go, anyway. But that doesn't mean I have to like staying here, and I most definitely don't want you two getting hurt."

"I know, and I promise you, we'll be careful." Qwyrk leaned over and kissed Jilly on the forehead. It offered little comfort.

"There, there, child," Blip offered in one of his rather poor attempts at opening up; at least his bravado was back. He patted her in the head, a bit too hard, but she was grateful for the sentiment, regardless. "I know it all seems hopeless, but I can assure you, things are not as grim as they seem. It will be like Agincourt or Trafalgar. Don't count us out just yet!"

Jilly smiled. "Thank you, Mr. Blippingstone."

Blip beamed. "You can call me Blip this one time, if you like," he said in a quiet voice.

"What was that?"

"Ahem. Er, um... I said, well, you may call me 'Blip' just this one time, if you like. However," he said as he stiffened and stood up, "do not get used to it! We have many hours of serious instruction in the arts and sciences ahead of us when I return, and I insist on proper formality in all such cases. The student must respect the tutor, and an air of casual relaxation simply will not do."

He hopped off the couch and made himself to look busy by polishing his broken monocle at the other end of the room, but Jilly noticed that his back was to them, and that he was trying to hide the tears forming in his eyes.

"Uh, right, what do you want me to do, then?" Star Tao had stayed out of this bonding experience and clearly looked a bit awkward having to say anything at all. But seeing his god looking a bit flustered, he no doubt figured he would be a good follower and step in at that moment.

"I want you to stay here, too," Qwyrk answered, for once without a hint of annoyance. "Keep an eye on Jilly for us, will you?"

"Oh, absolutely! I'd be honored! She'll be safe and sound for when you get back!"

Qwyrk's pained look in response made them all realize that maybe she wasn't going to be coming back. "Bloody hell," Star Tao swore to himself.

"Actually, you might want to hide up in my room this evening," Jilly suggested to him after a moment of uncomfortable silence. "I'm not sure how I would explain you to my parents."

"Yeah, that would be a puzzler wouldn't it?" Star Tao offered. "They'd get bent right out of shape having some dodgy bloke like me on the premises hanging out with their underage daughter, I reckon."

Qwyrk let out a guffaw of laughter, in spite of herself. "I suppose they'd want to take you out and beat the crap out of you!"

Star Tao laughed, but the idea seemed to rob him of some of the humor it might otherwise have had.

"It's going to be hard enough staying at home with mum and dad tonight as it is," Jilly offered. "I'd offer to sneak you up some of mum's food after we have dinner, but it would probably kill you!"

They all shared in another laugh for a moment, which faded too quickly, as the grimness of the situation came back to their thoughts.

"It's all right, Jilly," Star Tao offered. "I'll run out and get something to eat meself and then come back later. What time are your parents getting home, anyway?"

"Oh, I don't know, really, whenever they get home, basically. Could be in an hour, could be at half past eight. I didn't see any more of that grey muck in the refrigerator, so I just assumed they'd be home at a sensible hour tonight."

"Never mind, we'll sort it out. I will practice an astral yogic meditation to blur the atoms in my physical form, and they won't even know I'm here. I could walk right by them in that state and help meself to food off the table, and they'd never see it."

Jilly wasn't quite sure what he meant by that (and wasn't sure that Star Tao knew either), but she was glad for the effort he was willing to make, whatever it required.

Qwyrk sighed. "We should probably get going... Blip?"

Blip turned around, having wiped his eyes and placed the monocle away. "Yes, yes, of course. All set, ready to go!" He strode back over in his confident swagger, but Jilly knew it was all for show. He was afraid, and so was Qwyrk, and so was she, and maybe Star Tao was, too. None of them wanted to admit it.

"I think our best plan is just to flash back home and go on to Jimmy's from there," Qwyrk offered. "That will save time, even though it's tiring, and I don't expect you'll want to go bounding over roof tops with me all the way to Leeds." She grinned.

"Quite right! Damned uncivilized, that. My foot is still sore, and my stomach has no desire for a repeat of the hellish carnival ride it was atop your shoulder!"

"Right, then," Qwyrk said with a sigh. She took Jilly's hands. "It's all going to be fine, Jilly. We're not going to let de Soulis hurt anyone. We have a lot of things going for us, and a lot of experience. Who knows? Maybe we'll even get some extra help in time."

"But you don't know what's going to happen, and you don't know how strong he might be now," Jilly said, blinking back tears. "You can't promise you'll be back."

Qwyrk teared up as well and hugged her. "No, I can't. But I'm not about to give up easily! He won't win if there's any way I can prevent it!"

These words offered no comfort to Jilly, who just hugged her friend and cried. Blip and Star Tao stood aside to give them their moment. After a short time, Qwyrk parted from her, squeezed her hands again, and kissed her on the head. Then, saying nothing else, but giving a nod and a smile to Star Tao, she made some circular gestures with her hand and disappeared with Blip in a purple flash, leaving an herbaceous, lavender aroma behind in the air.

"That's spot on!" Star Tao exclaimed. "I've got to have her teach me how to do that!"

Jilly broke down, sobbing into the cushion. Star Tao sat down beside her and patted her shoulder.

"I don't know about you, Jilly, but I'm not about to sit round waiting for the world to end, or whatever's gonna happen. I mean, come on, you don't really think we're gonna let them go off all alone and deal with this monster with no back-up, do ya? The one you all call Blip may be divine, but he's still gonna appreciate help from a loyal follower. And Qwyrk, well, she's finally warming up to me! I mean, yeah, they may be angry at first, but they'll appreciate it in the long run. This all sounds like some crazy bad mojo, and they're going to need my skills and your smarts. I can maybe even ask some of me spirit guides for help. So, maybe write a note to your mum and dad? Tell them you're staying over at a friend's house, or something. I'll go get me van, and we'll be on our way!"

Jilly flung her arms around Star Tao and kissed him on the cheek, though her joy was tempered by a sudden realization.

"But we don't know where they're going! She never said where the house was. I know it's in the outskirts of north Leeds, but that could be anywhere. Why didn't I bother to ask? I always think I'm so clever and I didn't even think to find out. Arrrrghhh!" She punched the couch.

"Right, that is a pisser... oh, sorry!"

Jilly gave him the "I'm-not-a-child-and-I've-heard-much-worse" look.

"Did she mention the name of the family that lives in the house?" he offered.

"I don't think so. She just said it was a big house in north Leeds. Wait! No, she did! It was Eckmond, or Eckhart, or... Eckleson! Yeah, that was it!"

"So, why don't you go online, right, and see if you can find an address for that name in Leeds? Worth a shot."

Jilly was already on it, jumping up from the couch and bounding into the office. The computer seemed to take an extra-long time to boot up. It was well past time that they got a new one and entered the twenty-first century, but her father seemed to prefer his late 1990s model. At least she'd convinced him to move beyond dial-up.

"Come on, come on!" she grumbled, tapping her feet so hard against the floor that it made the room shake. After what seemed like ages, the computer connected, and Jilly began searching.

"Any luck?" Star Tao popped his head around the corner and looked in.

"Not yet. I might have to widen the search a bit, and... no, wait!

Here we go!"

And there it was.

"Mr. Edward Eckleson, complete with a telephone number and a north Leeds street address. It's the only matching name in the area. That's it, Star Tao, it has to be! I'll get a map and print it out."

"Groovy! I'll go and fetch the van. Oh, and your dog, he's here in the hall looking a bit hungry."

"Odin! Bollocks, I completely forgot to feed him today! And he didn't even have mum's slop for breakfast. Poor thing, I'll bet he's starving!"

"Right then, I'm off. Back in a few, and don't forget that note to your mum and dad; otherwise they'll think I've kidnapped you or something, and that won't look too good for me, with trying to hold me workshop and all!"

Off he went to get his vehicle, and off Jilly went to the kitchen to find something more suitable for the family canine than her mother's microwaved gruel and to pen an appropriate fib concerning her whereabouts for the evening, something about an evening of group drawing and girl-talk over at a friend's house, which her parents would only half-read, anyway. It hurt, but sometimes she was glad she was ignored. She grabbed a notepad and wrote a convincing story about her activities and left it on the kitchen table. Even *they* wouldn't fail to see it there.

She ran back to the office where the map had printed. Snatching it up, she ran upstairs, grabbed her coat and sketchbook, and wondered if she should bring anything else.

"It's not like I have any weapons," she mused, pausing for a moment to think that maybe she should have found a way to keep her mother's food from last night until now. Then she came to her senses.

She ran back downstairs, out the door, locked it behind her, and sat down on the front step to wait. And wait. And... wait.

"Damn it, where are you?" she pouted after at least twenty minutes of sitting. Her bum was getting sore, and she was growing impatient. Not that she was looking forward to whatever might happen, but sitting around doing nothing made it even worse. She was beginning to think he'd changed his mind and dashed off, leaving her all alone.

She also began to worry what the neighbors might think of her sitting here doing nothing. Well, not all the neighbors, just one. Ms. Agnes Burdockweed across the street could be more than a little nosy and had a habit of peeking out from her curtains to see what the hostile world beyond was up to. If Star Tao drove up in some sort of crazy hippie van, undoubtedly Agnes would make a note of it, and probably report it to her parents, and the police. She swore again, wishing she'd agreed to meet Star Tao farther up the street. She thought about getting up and walking down a block or two to meet him, but then realized she didn't know what direction he'd be coming from. So all she could do was sit and fidget, and wait some more.

Then she had a horrible thought about what would happen if her parents came home while she was waiting on the steps. She didn't want to have to lie to their faces about where she was going, and her lack of any overnight supplies would make her story fall apart in no time. And with her luck, Star Tao would pull up right in the middle of her story. She contemplated giving up and going back up to her room to wait out the night, never mind how awful that would be.

Somehow, she stuck it out and decided to keep waiting. Another ten minutes went by, and her heart sank even more.

She was frustrated to the point of tears. "He's abandoned me, I'm sure of it."

CHAPTER ELEVEN

"Over there," Qwyrk pointed as she and Blip observed the large garden from behind a nearby hedge. It was more than a little overgrown and marked by rather garish pink flamingos. Still, there was a certain rustic charm to the place, and it looked much nicer in the summer sunlight, almost inviting... until one spied the garden gnome.

"What?" Blip replied, standing on tiptoes, straining to get a better view over the foliage.

"That's the rosebush." It moved a little in the late afternoon breeze that was picking up, but otherwise seemed normal enough.

"Very well done, my dear. I'm glad to see that some of that horticultural education you received all those centuries ago has stayed with you. Ouch!"

She smacked him on the head, not caring what sound he made.

"That's the source, Blip! That's where the wyrmroost is. The eggs are buried under it, and that's where de Soulis and Redcap will be going, if they're not hiding around here already. Got it?"

"Then stop smacking my head! Do you want to alert them?"

"They won't do anything until dark."

"How can you be sure? Subtlety doesn't seem to be their strong point."

"I don't think they'll risk the exposure. They probably don't know how many of us might be around waiting for them. Huh! It's just as well they don't know that!"

"Maybe they do. If we've been betrayed, then perhaps someone is already in contact with them. Maybe they've already gotten what they came for and absconded."

"No, we'd see the evidence. And they'd be tempted to cause damage and harm others. There's no hole in the ground; nothing's been touched yet. We'll just have to sit and wait and see what happens. Unfortunately, it's their move."

"Well, perhaps we could remove said dragon's nest before they get here and spirit it away to Symphinity. They wouldn't dare go after it there."

"I'd thought of that, but we have no idea what kind of protective wards and charms he's set on it, and believe me, he has. It could well kill us before we even got close to it. I'm not willing to risk that, are you? As much as I hate it, we don't have a lot of choice but to wait until they get here and then try to stop whatever they're going to do. I just wish this were somewhere else and not in the middle of a damned residential neighborhood. People will get hurt tonight, Blip. People could well be killed."

"I know. I don't like it any more than you do. But, barring the arrival of a rather impressive cavalry, I don't think there is anything we can do about it. The Templars won't be here in time, I presume?"

"That's what Simon said when I told him the location. I can't believe there aren't a few knights in this city, though! It's big enough to warrant their presence. I'd go get them myself, if I even knew where to look; they're so flipping secretive. Simon was going to summon them, and they only respond to calls from their brothers, no matter what the crisis. It keeps them secret and alive, I suppose. Damn it, I swear, if we make it through this, I'm going to wring some flipping necks back home. I want to know exactly what's going on and who the hell is behind this!"

Qwyrk wanted to go to the house, to find Jimmy at least, and tell him to take his parents and run. But given how traumatized he'd been the other night, and how harshly his mum and dad had treated him, it would do far more harm than good. Also, Jimmy would be able to see Blip, and that would just make matters worse. It didn't look like anyone was home, anyway. *Maybe*, she hoped against hope, *they've gone away for the evening, or even overnight?*

She sighed and looked up. The sun had another two hours hour or so to set. She was beginning to wish that someone, anyone, could be here with them as backup, even Qwykk and Qwypp. Yes, she realized, the situation was that desperate.

* * *

"That's it!" Jilly determined. "He's got five more minutes and then I go in, and I don't care if he comes back!" Tears formed in her eyes at the thought of being left behind.

"Maybe Qwyrk asked him to do this. Maybe the three of them already had a plan, and they had to come up with some way to leave me out of it."

The more she thought about it, the more logical it seemed, the more she was sure she was being excluded, and the angrier she became. She began to let her imagination run away with her, dreaming up all sort of plots and counterplots about how all of this had been discussed behind her back.

"Maybe they talked about it in secret before Star Tao came over earlier. Maybe all of his note-taking wasn't because of Blip's stupid lecture, maybe he was working out the details. I never saw what he did with those notes."

She scrunched up her nose thinking about it and gave in to a full-on dose of paranoia. They'd left her behind; she knew it. All was lost. Steam was about to come out her ears. She was ready to hit something, or someone. She resisted the urge to pace around on the lawn and draw attention to herself, but if Agnes Burdockweed happened to pop her head out the door to ask what Jilly was doing, she might just stomp over there and smack her.

"It's all so unfair!" she said to herself. "All right, fine, so I'm a girl, but I can still do things! I could have been a lookout. I could have warned other people to stay away. I don't have to do any fighting." Though, she wished she could have. Despite all the danger, what she really wanted was to be able to fight side-by-side with Qwyrk, and believing that was impossible frustrated her.

She heaved a heavy sigh and resigned herself to going inside, when she heard a vehicle up the street. It was a bit loud, and it seemed to chug along with an uneven rhythm. She didn't dare to hope, but stood up and ran to the curb. Sure enough, a van approached, and it had all the markings of the kind of vehicle Star Tao would own. It looked to be from the mid-1970s, was painted purple, and seemed to have other designs on the side, though Jilly couldn't see them from where she stood. It looked amusingly out of place in her neighborhood, and was a bit too wide for the narrow street. As it got closer, she could make out painted suns on one side, with rainbows on the other; there was no doubting it, this was his van!

Her whole mood changed in an instant, and, troubles now forgotten, she nearly jumped for joy, running down the street to meet him halfway. And sure enough, there he was, smiling and waving.

"Star Tao!" she laughed as he stopped and she jumped into the passenger's seat. "I thought sure you'd got lost, or gone off without me!"

"Nah, I wouldn't do that, Jilly! Sorry I'm late. I had a bit of a problem. I went back to the town center, and meant to eat and then come right back here, but I got pulled over by a copper a few blocks back, actually. Yeah, he wasn't very nice, either. Wanted to see me license and insurance and MOT and all that rubbish, which I *do* have, in case you're wondering. Said I have a back brake light out and I need to get it fixed. Gave me a sodding ticket! Can you believe it! I'm gutted, I have supplies to buy for me workshop! I can't be wasting money on rubbish like a ticket. It's a real pisser."

"Oh, I'm sorry, that's ridiculous; like you need both lights to let someone behind you know you're stopping!"

"Well that's what I told him, and he didn't look too happy about that! He threatened to search me van, so I decided to shut it and be nice, even though I wanted to clock him one. Then he mumbled something about the youth of today, and how he'd stopped a girl from messin' about in that old house down the cliff earlier, and left me with the bill. I'm thinking I should have channeled the Mystic Voice of Xenoglossia; it would have left him confused, and I could have just driven off."

"The what?"

"Oh, it's brilliant! Me guides sometimes give me knowledge of extraterrestrial languages that have all sorts of hidden meaning and power. When I'm speaking, it could be a language from some other galaxy. I could have used it to leave him totally messed up. Bollocks, I always forget to do things like that!"

"Well, maybe you'll get to use it tonight... it might come in handy." Jilly found Star Tao's random descriptions of his psychic powers amusing, unexpected, and, well, odd.

"Yeah, that's a brilliant idea! Qwyrk would be right impressed if I did that, I reckon. I'd be right in there! Anyway, I'll deal with the whole ticket thing later, yeah? Right now, we've got to get moving and help our mates. You got the map?"

She waved it in triumph. "Right here!"

"Righty then, off we go!"

She laughed again, so relieved and so happy that all of her fears had been for naught.

* * *

As they drove off, she didn't even notice the quick flourish of curtains in the window of the house of a certain Agnes Burdockweed.

* * *

"Clouds are moving in," Qwyrk noticed. "Looks like rain might be on its way; not sure if that's a good or bad thing. It might help hide what's going to happen and keep a few people off the street, but it might just make things worse for us. Slippery, wet conditions are hardly good for taking down a centuries-old sorcerer and his dangerous Shadow body."

"This waiting is interminable," Blip griped, not registering her words as they sat across the street on the pavement, keeping close watch on the garden. "Why don't they just damned well do something and get on with it? Yes, yes, I know, it's not dark enough yet," he offered before Qwyrk could answer, "but honestly, has that ever stopped any maniac in the past who wanted to destroy the world? They just did it. Or rather, they attempted to do so. Why do we have an arch-villain who's decided to obey the whims of cliché?"

"Maybe there's some reason beyond just not being detected," Qwyrk offered. "Maybe they need the darkness or the moon, or something to undo whatever magic is there. I don't know, so stop whining! And I can't speak for you, but I'm in no big hurry to die, so let's just wait it out."

"What if they don't show up? What then? Maybe we've miscalculated, and they're off somewhere else at the moment, preparing some other horror to which we are not yet privy?"

"I've thought of that, too. I don't have an answer. I just hope that's not the case."

"If it is, we may have made a terrible blunder. Perhaps they've doubled back and are attempting to terminate Simon, after all, or if Jilly..."

"Shut up!" Qwyrk hissed. "And not just because I don't want to think about that! There are people approaching, we have to be quiet."

She stood up and backed into a nearby yard, hiding in the shadow that a large oak tree afforded. Blip moved away from the pavement and joined her, so as not to be stepped on. Even Qwyrk knew he'd had rather enough of that for one day.

They heard voices as the humans approached.

* * *

"Now, Jimmy, isn't this a better way to spend an afternoon than being cooped up in the house with all of those ghastly games? A good walk and some fresh air will clear out those nightmares." It was a woman's voice, speaking in a manner that seemed both caring and condescending.

"I suppose," a boy answered in a weak voice.

"I think we should do this every day this summer. Yes, in fact, that's an excellent idea! Every day, rain or shine, we shall take a good brisk walk around the neighborhood. Why, there's so many interesting places to explore around here! Did you know that one of the houses nearby was once owned by Mr. Hezekiah Bottlewealth? He was a very influential business man in the 1870s and made a fortune in buying and selling hogs and hog futures. Isn't that fascinating? I never knew his house is right in this neighborhood. You can walk right by it anytime! When your father gets home, we'll plan out a special stroll this weekend, and we'll visit his house. Won't that be wonderful?"

Jimmy just grunted, thinking that he'd rather be left to his fate with the shadows than endure another afternoon like this.

* * *

"Crap!" Qwyrk whispered.

"What?" Blip looked at her in confusion. Or annoyance. One of the two. Or both.

"They live in *that* house, Blip! Damn, I hoped they were gone for a bit. We have to do something. If they're home when de Soulis gets here..."

"I could try to scare them off," he offered.

"Oh, and exactly how are you going to do that? Jump in front of them and growl? Kick them in the shins until they run away? The only thing that'll do is make Jimmy run *for* the house. No, we're going to have to find some way of keeping them inside for the night."

"And what of the father? There is a father, I presume?"

"I don't know. We'll deal with him when he gets home. Hopefully not while we're in the middle of trying not to get killed by de Soulis!"

"Speaking of which," he answered with a dry whisper, "do we actually have a plan, or are we just going to do one of those improvised flying-by-the-seat-of-our-trousers things and hope we make a good impression before being flayed alive?"

She glared at him. "I have some ideas. But until we see what they're going to do, we can't really plan much of a counter-attack."

"Assuming they show up at all."

"They will!" she insisted. "I hope," she said to herself. "Look," she continued, "I've a feeling we'll know when they arrive. My bigger concern is protecting Jimmy and his parents. No matter what happens, we have to keep them from harm if we can... Shhh! Here they come."

They were silent for a moment as Jimmy and his mum crossed the street, heading into their flamingoed and begnomed garden and up to the front door. A moment later, while she was praising the entrepreneurial spirit of a nineteenth-century pig merchant for some reason, the door shut behind them. It was an impressive old home, Qwyrk noted, different in the light than it had seemed when she sat on the roof two nights ago with Qwypp and Qwykk. But how to keep them from harm's way? Hoping for the best was not the strategy she wanted to use.

*　*　*

Star Tao and Jilly chugged south down the motorway, bound

for Leeds. His van didn't seem especially suitable for high-speed driving, and the ride was more than a tad bumpy. But she was in no position to be picky, at least they were going to get there, she hoped. The sun was setting and storm clouds moved in from the west, both of which made Jilly nervous.

"So..." Jilly ventured, "what exactly are we going to do when we get there? They're not going to be happy to see us, you know."

"Well, maybe not at first," Star Tao offered, "but I think they'll come to realize the unique skills we possess, and they'll be very happy in the end that we didn't listen to them."

"Just what skills are we talking about?" Jilly asked with more than a little sarcasm. Star Tao's channellings, real or imagined, were not going to be of much help, she realized. In fact, the closer they got to Leeds, the less enthused she was about this whole idea. Being rebellious had a certain thrill, to be sure, but pretty much all it had brought her over the past day was a lot of trouble. She shivered and pulled her coat about her, even though she wasn't cold.

"Well, consider this," he offered, "we may not have her elf magic or the Frog god's divine power and wisdom, but we can solve problems, yeah? Even if we don't fight, and mind you, I'm a pacifist for the most part and not all that made up about fightin' anyway, we can be the back-up team. We can, like, analyze the battlefield, and see where they're gonna be best used. If something goes wrong, we can help them regroup and recover. And if I can get a good cosmic connection going on, I might be able to summon members of the Council of 27 to sit in and give us their advanced alien perspective."

"Cosmic connection?"

"Yeah, well, it's almost like a mobile, right? Some places you get good universal reception, and in others it just drops out completely. It's a real nightmare, actually. I've had some amazing intergalactic conversations that got terminated because I drove through a tunnel or moved to the wrong side of a room. But you can't just redial, see, because the cosmic strands don't work that way. It may be ages before you can make that same connection again."

"So why don't you just stay in one place when you're channeling?"

"Well that's a good question! The answer is that sometimes the energy forces you to move about, almost like it has to be shaken off because one's small, mortal form can't hold it in. If you don't move, you get tremors and convulsions."

"So, why do you do it when you drive? You said something about losing reception going through a tunnel..."

"Yeah well, you see, sometimes they contact *me*, instead of the other way round. Since I can't control when that'll happen, it could be anywhere. And it happened once when I was on a motorway. I had no choice, because it was important, they said. So, since I couldn't walk, and couldn't get off the road right away, I just kind of started shaking, see? And then I was hoppin' up and down in me driver's seat. And I think I would have been pulled over, but I came to a tunnel and that was it. Connection dropped. They never did get back to me about what was so important, so I reckon they just changed their collective mind; they share one big brain, you see."

Jilly grimaced. "It must get crowded in there!"

Star Tao laughed. "Nah, they have a different cerebral structure to ours, so they're used to it."

Jilly was tempted to ask him how he got into all of this, but decided that would best be saved for another time, as he might, in the telling, inadvertently get contacted by some alien ambassador who wanted to fill in more details, and then he would start bobbing up and down and drive right by the exit they needed. Or into a ditch.

Fortunately, holding her tongue proved to be the wiser course of action; before too long, they saw signs for the road they wanted. Exiting the motorway (with Jilly feeling grateful that they hadn't been pulled over by any more tetchy policemen), they soon found themselves in a maze of streets in the northern suburbs of Leeds.

"Won't be long now," she observed, trying to sound more confident than she did, and seeing the ominous-looking storm clouds gathering.

* * *

The sky grew greyer and darker, and Qwyrk became ever more antsy. She had an urge to start pacing around the little grove of trees where they'd hidden themselves nearby. It opened onto a small park, but no one was out now. She could still see the house and the garden, though Blip had complained about being too far away. She stayed the urge to wander, but still shuffled around where she stood.

"Great northern beans, girl, will you stop your nervous fidgeting?" Blip snapped. "It's not doing anyone any good, and it's making me irritable!"

"And you have a better idea, I suppose? At least I'm keeping limber."

"Hmph! At times like this, it's better to calm the mind, prepare the battle internally. 'The victorious strategist only seeks battle after the victory has been won, whereas he who is destined to defeat first fights and afterwards looks for victory.' – Sun Tzu."

"Is this another one of those 'Blip the Ninja' philosophies that I've somehow never known about?"

"I've simply not chosen to reveal them until now, because the situation never warranted."

"Tell you what, if you manage to use... whatever it is you think you have in some effective way, I don't really care. In fact, I'll be right chuffed. Just don't get in my way, all right?"

"Get in your way? Get in *your* way?! I should ask the same thing of you! Undisciplined, unprincipled, disrespectful..."

"Blip, be quiet!" she whispered. "I just saw something in the yard!"

Scrambling to get a better look, Blip climbed a short way up the tree she was hiding behind, only to slip and fall back to the ground, luckily with a quiet and dull thud, rather than a spectacular crash.

"Well done, Bruce Lee."

He scowled. "What did you see?"

She sighed, though whether from relief or impatience, she wasn't quite sure. "I think it's Mr. Eckleson coming home. The door opened and someone went in. Now they're all in there, and we'll just have to deal with that when the time comes."

At that moment, she felt the first drop of water on her face. As she feared, the rain was about to start. "Great. It's going to get messy tonight. Maybe that will help us, maybe not."

She heard a vehicle approaching. She motioned for Blip to hide behind the tree, but he failed to see the sense in it.

"And you expect them to be arriving in an automobile, then?" he quipped. "Does de Soulis have a newfound taste for luxury cars?"

"Well, I don't know! Oh, damn it. My stomach is in such a knot, I'm not thinking straight anymore! Look, it's best if we just stay back out of sight."

"But humans can't see me, and you barely..." he started to lecture on the painfully obvious.

"Yeah, all right, fair point. Just... shut up!"

She needn't have worried. It wasn't de Solis and Redcap arriving somehow having mastered modern transportation. No, it was something worse. Far worse.

A purple van with suns and rainbows painted on the sides trundled towards them, rolling up the street in a slow crawl. Its occupants appeared to be looking for something, maybe a specific address. And its occupants looked an awful lot like...

"Oh no, oh Goddess no!" Qwyrk's stomach sank and a wave of horror passed over her. "It can't be. Please, no!"

Blip squinted and recoiled as well. "What in the name of damnation are those two doing here? I thought you gave them strict orders to stay put!"

"I did!" She glared at Star Tao who had noticed them and was smiling and waving through his rolled-down window. He parked the van and rolled up the window as Qwyrk started across the street toward them, her eyes beginning to glow red.

"Get out of the damned van right now, both of you!" she growled.

Sheepishly, Jilly and Star Tao obeyed, their presumed confidence that they would be welcomed and could be useful now clearly shattered in a matter of seconds. They stood in front of the vehicle as Qwyrk glared at them, her eyes blazing red with rage. Jilly obviously couldn't even bear to look at her, and so tried staring at the ground, maybe pretending she wasn't there. That failed as a strategy, too.

Qwyrk said nothing more but paced back and forth a little.

"I should just put you in that van and send you the hell out of here. But there's one slight problem: de Soulis is in the vicinity, and I don't know where. So if you happen to round a corner and he's there, he'll likely kill you both, since you've both seen him, and he's probably not too happy about that. You're damned lucky he hasn't offed you already. So, I've only got one choice, haven't I?"

She grabbed them by their collars and dragged them off the

street and into the small gathering of trees where she and Blip had been waiting. Jilly seemed shocked at how strong Qwyrk was and how she moved them with such ease. In actuality, Qwyrk could have lifted both of them up and carried them if she wanted.

"Right! You two are staying right here until this is over, and *if* we come back from this alive, I'm going to knock the living crap out of both of you! You're going to wish none of us had survived! Got it?"

They nodded in shame and avoided eye contact.

Jilly chanced a look at Blip, who turned his gaze away from her in disdain and rejection.

"If you are thinking that I might side with you on this, I will quickly quash your hopes, I'm afraid," he said in a cold voice. Qwyrk saw a genuine look of disappointment on his face as well as Jilly's sad reaction.

In any case, Qwyrk ignored her and turned to Blip. "We've got to make sure that the Ecklesons don't come out tonight, no matter what. It's either that, or we have to find some way to get them away from here. That'd be better, actually, but I don't see that happening."

"I could keep 'em inside, if you want..." Star Tao offered in a hesitating voice.

Qwyrk glared at him with an acid look that told him he would never have any chance with her. "How?"

"Well... I could go over there and make up some excuse about how there's a gas or water leak or something, somewhere in one of the pipes, and we need everyone to stay inside while the water company fixes it."

"And why exactly would they believe you?"

"Oh, right, well I used to work for King Alfred Water down south. Just for six months, but I remember enough of the lingo that I could convince them of it, I reckon. I'll just sit inside with them. I can always pretend to ring out on me phone for updates."

"Looking the way you do, and dressed the way you are, they're not going to buy it."

"Well, I'll just tell them I was off duty but got a ring on me mobile, and since I was the only one in the area, they asked me to stop by and tell everyone on this street. It's worth a shot, don't you think? It might help."

Qwyrk let out a heavy sigh. "I don't like this one bit. But, if you can pull it off, it will at least keep them inside, and keep your stupid arse a bit safer. That's probably the next best thing to getting them the hell out of here."

"I should go with him," Jilly offered, still not daring to look Qwyrk in the face.

"Yeah," Star Tao supported her. "I could say she's me niece, or something, and that I was on me way to take her home when I got the call. We'd be safer in there."

Qwyrk sighed again. "This is ridiculous, but all right, it's better than having you two idiots out here."

Her words obviously stung Jilly, whose eyes filled with tears.

"Well, get on over there," Qwyrk admonished, "and do it quick! We have no idea when they'll show up. Go!"

* * *

Jilly stole a quick glance at Qwyrk, who refused to even look at her. Wiping her eyes and turning to Star Tao, she nodded, and the two of them crossed the street and entered the Eckleson's yard. She marveled at the strange overgrowth, the flamingos, and the overall unkempt look of the place. The yard wasn't terribly English, being in a bit of a shambles like this. It was all a bit morose in the rain, which was increasing now, like she was walking through some horror movie. The scary part was that the reality was about to become a lot worse.

"Right, just let me do the talking," Star Tao said with a weak smile. "I'll have us in there in no time. We'll keep 'em occupied."

They strode up the walkway to the front door and rang the bell. After a short time, a woman, presumably Jimmy's mother, answered the door.

"Yes?" she asked, giving Star Tao an immediate look of distrust.

"Good evening, ma'am," he said with a smile. "My name is Connor Watson. I'm with Yorkist Water Works"

Connor Watson? Was that his name before? Jilly wondered.

"Well, what can I do for you?" the woman asked in a suspicious voice.

"Sorry to disturb you, but we've had a report of a water pressure build-up in one of our main pipes in the area. We're trying to locate the problem now, because if it's not taken care of, there's a chance of an explosion under the street. In the meantime, we're stopping by houses in the area to ask that all residents stay indoors and not venture out tonight, no matter what they might hear."

Mrs. Eckleson looked horrified. "My goodness! Will we be all right?"

"Oh yes, yes, everything will be fine, but just as a precaution, we want everyone inside. As I said, we don't yet know where the weak pipe is, or how severe it might be, so we can't risk having residents anywhere near it. We do know it's not under any of the houses, though, so you can relax about that."

"How do you know?"

"What?"

"How do you know it's not under a house? You said you don't know where it is."

"Ummm..."

Jilly had a moment of panic and bit her lip.

"We... have a computer grid detection system that can locate changes in pressure to a general area, and we discovered that it's under this street. Now it's a matter of pinpointing it exactly. Don't worry, even if it did blow, as long as no one is near it, they'll be fine."

Jilly gave a slight smile. *Nice one, mate.*

"Well, why aren't you wearing a uniform?"

"Well... that's because I'm off duty. This here is my niece... Fanny."

Fanny?! Jilly scrunched up her nose in irritation and, realizing that she might look suspicious, feigned a sneeze. It wasn't overly convincing, she decided.

"I was taking her home, see, when I got a message on me... my mobile telling me about the situation. Since I was nearby, I told them I'd go 'round to the houses and keep everybody safely inside. So, yes, I apologize for not looking a bit more, 'official,' I suppose."

Mrs. Eckleson still didn't look convinced.

"Look," Star Tao offered. "I'd be happy to come in and explain it a bit more, if you'd like; you're the last house on the street I have to inform."

"Henrietta? What's going on?" A somewhat portly man with a severe short haircut appeared in the doorway. Mrs. Eckleson repeated what Star Tao had told her. He didn't look convinced, either, but he shook Star Tao's hand. "Edward Eckleson."

"Connor Watson," Star Tao smiled. "And this is my niece, Fanny." Jilly scrunched up her nose again. She wanted to kick him in the shin.

"I should probably give them a ring," Edward said, "to find out when it will be done."

"Oh, no, no need for that," Star Tao hastily offered, a bit of panic in his voice. "I have a mobile right here, and I can check in. If we can come in, I'll happily sit here for a bit and give you updates."

Edward obviously wasn't that sold on the idea, but he agreed. In they went, and the door closed behind them.

*　*　*

Watching from a distance, Qwyrk and Blip saw the exchange, but couldn't hear it. When the door shut, she exclaimed, "I don't believe it. That git actually did it! He lied his way into the house of a complete stranger."

"Clever young man," Blip offered with the smile of an admiring father. "I keep telling you that."

The light was fading fast, and the rain began to fall in earnest. Qwyrk knew it wouldn't be long.

"Well, at least they're inside for the moment. Now, if he can just keep them there. I swear, I want to kick his skinny arse to Symphinity and back."

"You'll do no such thing! The lad is proving useful, and maybe the girl will, as well. Perhaps they're meant to help us."

"But they lied to me, Blip. They promised me they'd stay away and then did the exact opposite. That hurts. I don't know if I can trust either of them after this."

"I think we have bigger problems," Blip answered, pointing to the garden.

Qwyrk closed her eyes. "Crap! They're here!"

CHAPTER TWELVE

Emerging out of the shadows near the rosebush, a dark shape began to form, a whirlwind circling around it. In the fading light, they could see its glowing red eyes. It clenched its fists and raised its arms high. A gaseous golden light swirled around those fists, and the same began to emanate from the ground under the rosebush.

The figure raised itself up to its full height, drawing strength from the nearby dragon's nest. It lifted its head back and faced the sky as the rain began to fall in earnest. Its arms were raised up and its hands opened, balls of golden gas and fire swirling above its palms. The glow illuminated the drops of rain as they fell, giving the whole scene a haunting, otherworldly look. It stood there in defiance of the elements, triumphant and mighty.

It made no sound, but Qwyrk was sure she could see, or maybe just sense, something like a twisted smile on its face. A wave of fear swept over her, the worst she'd experienced in decades, maybe even centuries. De Soulis and Redcap were every bit as horrific as she had feared. And with each passing moment, they seemed to be gaining strength, even growing in size.

The rosebush vibrated, swaying and flailing its branches about. Qwyrk had never seen it move like that before, certainly not the other night. It seemed to be responding to the Shadow's movements, as if both were engaging in an evil choreography, a dance of the damned.

"Right, Blip, we have to do this now, we can't wait; they're getting stronger by the minute. There's something about the nest, like it's feeding them."

"I have a long journey to take and must bid the company farewell," he stated.

"What?"

"Sir Walter Raleigh. His last words."

"Touching, but I'm not ready to concede defeat and bugger off to the Summerlands just yet."

"Nor I. It just happened to come to mind... now then," he declared with his old Blip bravado, "shall we go over there and teach these nefarious upstarts a lesson in respect and common decency? I've had just about enough of their boorish behavior for one day!"

She smiled. Blip was an obnoxious twit, but right now, she was glad he was here.

As she stood to make her charge, she happened to turn and behold an astonishing figure emerging from the mist: he had shoulder length dark hair, slight stubble on the chin, and piercing blue eyes. He wore a long dark coat, a grey shirt that covered a shirt of chain mail, black leather trousers, and knee-high boots. At his belt was an impressive sword, his hand resting on the hilt. One corner of his shirt had a small red cross on it, and a gold medallion hung around his neck with two knights sitting on a horse. There was no doubt about his identity.

"You're a Templar knight," she whispered in shock.

He nodded. "Sir John Ashley of Ripon. Simon alerted the order some hours ago, and I was nearby. There aren't too many of us about these days, so you're lucky I was close. I'm glad I'm here in time."

"Ummm, thanks, I suppose. Look, we have to do something now. They're getting stronger by the minute. I think the dragon's nest is actually, well, feeding them somehow?"

He nodded again. "De Soulis stored away some of his power in it as insurance, for just this sort of thing. A large egg holds all the others, and it must be drawn out at night. Once he has enough power, he'll break his wards and remove it, and then be off somewhere else..."

"Look I'd love to know more, and we can talk about all this later—it'll be lovely, really—but let's stop him, all right?"

Sir John drew his sword without saying another word, and with eyes fixed on the hellish Shadow across the street, he strode toward it, while Qwyrk stood for a moment, watching him in astonishment.

"Ahem," Blip remarked, "if you're quite done making google eyes at the young man, shall we follow?"

"Goo-goo."

"What?"

"It's 'goo-goo' not 'google'. And besides, I was merely admiring his courage."

"So that's what you call it. It's always some lad or lass with you, isn't it? They must all be very brave."

"I am merely an appreciator of fine works of art, however they may present themselves."

"I see. Well, then, let's go help prevent that 'work of art' from getting himself eviscerated, shall we?"

Qwyrk was surprised that she smiled at his sarcasm, and then she and Blip followed the knight toward what was going to be a rather unpleasant evening.

* * *

"So the water flow has weakened one of the central pipes in the system, and there's a blockage which is building up pressure, and it could cause a rupture and blow a section of the street straight up into the sky?" Edward Eckleson sounded incredulous, as he eyed the platted stranger and his "niece," who were now sitting on their living room couch. They'd tried to position themselves so that the Ecklesons were looking away from the window, and not at the garden. The fierce storm meant that it was almost too dark to see anything out there now, and Jilly hoped that would be enough.

"That's right," Star Tao replied. "It's a rare occurrence, but I've seen it happen before. Once down in Cornwall. It was bad, really bad. The pressure built up way too high, and it blew a chunk right out of the pavement when someone was walking over it; it threw him up into the air. Yeah, broke a couple of bones, he did. It was a right ugly situation, and we don't want to see something like that here. So, the best thing everyone can do is just stay inside until we give you the all clear. It may take a few hours, so I hope you didn't have plans tonight."

Jilly sat next to him, saying nothing and smiling a pleasant smile, hoping that this ruse would be enough to fool them.

"No, no, nothing in particular," Edward said with a shake of his head. "But it is a damned peculiar situation. I can honestly say I've never heard of this sort of thing before."

"Well you wouldn't, because it doesn't happen too often, thankfully. I mean, it may not even take that long to repair. There's workers poking around under the street right now, and they may get it fixed in no time."

Jilly shot him a worried look.

"Or..." he continued, seeing her. "It could be hours, yeah, lots of hours. We, um, we just don't know right now."

"Would you like some tea?" Henrietta offered, and Jilly was grateful for the distraction. Star Tao needed a bit of time to plan out his made-up story a bit more.

"That would be lovely, Mrs. Eckleson, thank you," Jilly smiled.

"That'd be brilliant, thanks!" Star Tao echoed. "Tea," he continued, smiling at the still-skeptical Edward, who eyed him with a chilly expression. "You just can't beat it, eh? Nice, warming, especially on a night like this. I mean... not that it's that cold or anything, but, that wind and that rain, eh? I imagine it will get right violent out there tonight..."

Jilly glared at him.

"Could be all sorts of strange sounds and things from all the wind blowin' about, and then there's the whole pipe thing, so I wouldn't want to be out there anyway."

Jilly resisted the urge to stomp on his foot. Barely.

"Which... is why tea is so nice. Nice, eh? When you've got nowhere else to go? Heh, heh!"

Edward gave him a blank stare.

"Um... maybe I should try phoning to see if I can get a status update," Star Tao said, clearly trying not to let the situation get away from him. "I'll just pop into the other room; I reckon the reception's better in there, back soon!" And out he went.

Jilly tried to smile at Edward, but was sure he could see right through her.

"Dad?" a boy's voice sounded. A moment later, Jimmy walked

into the room. "What's going on?"

Edward relayed the information about their forced confinement for the evening in an abbreviated form.

"An explosion? Aw, that's brilliant!" Jimmy exclaimed, much to the annoyance of his father, who was obviously quite certain his son had taken this news in very much the wrong way.

"No, Jimmy, as I said, we have to stay inside while they fix it; they don't want anyone outside; it's too dangerous."

The excitement drained from Jimmy's face, and Jilly could see he realized that even if there were a grand blow-up that took out part of the street in a spectacular whoosh, he'd be stuck in the house and wouldn't see it.

"I'm going to review some legal papers before dinner," Edward said, standing up, and clearly not eager to be alone in a room with two children. "You two, uh, find something to talk about, won't you?" He gave a half-smile and a nod and exited.

"Um, hello, I'm Jimmy."

"Jilly," she smiled with little sincerity, though she already knew his name.

"Huh! Jimmy and Jilly! That's a bit funny don't you think?" He smiled, but it looked weird.

"I suppose..."

"So... you work for the water folks, then, too?"

"No," Jilly couldn't believe how stupid this conversation was already becoming. "My... uncle does. He's in there. We were on our way back to my house when he got an emergency phone call to stop by the houses in this neighborhood. The whole... explosion thing."

"Yeah, that's brilliant! Do you think it will blow up?"

"Don't know. I suppose it'd be a bit of a mess if it did."

"Yeah, but still, it'd be brilliant, though... what's that?!"

Jimmy pointed out the window, a look of horror on his face. Jilly had neglected to notice he was standing near it while he was talking to her.

"What?" She feigned innocence, turning around to look outside. It was too dark for the time of day. She couldn't see well, but winds were blowing fiercely, and there was a commotion down in the garden... sure enough, by the rosebush. It looked like a dark figure was rising up to stand near it. She choked back a gasp. It was him, she just knew it.

"Oh, it's just the wind, isn't it?" she lied with a nervous voice. "It plays tricks on your eyes. We've got this crazy tree in my yard that looks like it's moving all the time. You get a bit of wind through it, and you'd swear it was alive. Well, all right, I mean, it's actually *alive*, but you know, moving about and that sort of thing. It used to scare me like crazy until my mum showed me it was just the wind. I imagine that's all this is. Playing tricks on your eyes, and all that."

"I don't think so," Jimmy answered, looking back to her. "There's been some right weird stuff going on 'round here the last few nights." He sat next to her and lowered his voice. "Can you keep a secret?"

She nodded, trying to look as interested as possible to keep his attention off the yard.

"I've seen things in my room at night. They're... shadows, in the shape of people, but they've got glowing red eyes! And they... they speak to me."

"What do they say?" Jilly widened her eyes hoping to look fascinated and not amused.

"It was a girl's voice, at least the one that spoke to me the other night. She was going on about wanting to do yoga with her mates and such. I don't know what she... it, meant. But then, she warned me to keep my mouth shut and just sort of faded away into the dark, and I didn't see her any more. I probably shouldn't even be telling you. What if she's come back? What if that's her in the yard, come back to kill us all?"

Jilly bit her lower lip hard to stifle a laugh, and hoped it looked like she was thinking hard about what he'd said.

"So, she just left the other night?"

"Yeah, she just told me to shut it and buggered off. It was so weird. Mum thinks I'm playing too many video games and seeing things, but I stopped for a whole day, and it still happened. In fact, that's when the shadow spoke to me."

Jilly had a bright idea. "Look, I'm an artist. Maybe if you describe it to me, I could draw it. I brought my sketchbook with me, but it's out in my uncle's van, and I'm not going back out there! Do you have paper and pencils?"

"Yeah, up in my room."

"Great! Why don't we go up there and you can tell me more about. Doesn't sound like your parents are too keen on you talking about this, anyway."

Jimmy nodded and they set off upstairs. Jilly popped in to tell Star Tao (still pretending to check his phone messages) what they were doing; he seemed to get the hint and smiled at both of them with a nod. Jimmy shouted to his mother that they were going upstairs for a bit, and off they went.

Jilly was quite proud of herself for having created a perfect distraction. She stepped out of the living room without even a casual glance back out the window. She wouldn't have liked what she would have seen.

* * *

"Excuse me, are you Mr. Simon? Er, Sir Simon, I suppose. That sounds a bit better doesn't it? I mean, if you're really a 'Sir' and all, it wouldn't do to be calling you 'Mr.' That'd be sort of disrespectful and all. I mean, you earned the title and everything. Say, who knighted you?"

A smiling Qwykk stood at the door of Simon of Wakefield's room, Qwypp right behind her. Both were dressed as nurses, only they hadn't quite got the hang of it. Qwykk's white skirt was decidedly short, and she was wearing high heels with a tiara on her head, while Qwypp was still wearing her silver platform boots from last night's clubbing adventure.

Simon looked up from his evening newspaper, and regarded them blankly for a moment, wondering if death by stupidity was some sort of evil plan on the part of de Soulis.

"Um, hello," Qwypp interjected, popping her head over Qwykk's shoulder. "We were sent here by Qwyrk. She asked us to look after you. Said there was some real trouble brewing and that we should check in and make sure you're all right."

"Oh, she did, did she?" Simon replied, half relieved and half disappointed that they were on his side.

"Yeah, don't mind the outfits," Qwypp went on, "they were just a disguise to get us in here."

"Yeah," added Qwykk. "We're not real nurses, or anything. We're actually Shadows, like Qwyrk."

"You don't say?" Simon answered. He sighed, "Well, get in here and close the door before someone figures out your clever deception."

Obeying his request, they entered and shut the door behind them. Seating themselves down on the bed, they smiled.

"So," Qwypp started, but seemed unable to add anything to that thought.

"So, indeed," Simon finished it for her. He glanced back down at his paper.

"Ummm," she tried again. "Is there anything that you need?"

"Not particularly." He didn't look up.

"Right... so we'll just sit here... then, and sort of... stand guard."

"Well, we're actually sitting," Qwykk offered. "So, we'll be sitting guard."

"Right, right, yeah, sitting guard, good one, Qwykk!" Qwypp agreed. "So if you do need anything, just give us a shout, all right? I mean not a real shout, 'cause we're right here and all, and that might wake somebody up, if they're sleeping, or something... but metaphorically speaking and all, a shout, you know?"

"I'll keep that in mind." He turned the page of his paper.

"Yep," Qwypp nodded with a forced smile. "We'll be right here."

* * *

Grim determination showed on the Templar's face. His sword was grasped in hand and his will was like iron. It was as if the cavalry had indeed just arrived. Rain pelted at them, and fierce winds were whipping about now. Qwyrk wasn't sure if this was a supernatural storm brought on by the Shadow's nearness to its goal, but she was grateful for it. Before them stood a frightful sight.

The body of de Soulis and Redcap was engaged in a series of complex gestures and a low voice emanating from them chanted arcane words in a language Qwyrk didn't recognize, and didn't want to. Golden, gaseous light swirled around the Shadow's hands and the ground beneath the rosebush responded with a similar light. The plant itself seemed to be mimicking these movements, taking on an animated life of its own. And fortunately for them, the Shadow seemed oblivious to their presence, for now.

John brought his sword up into striking position and broke into a brisk walk. Qwyrk marched right there beside him. Blip struggled to keep up.

"Non nobis domine!" he whispered, as he charged, now perhaps twenty feet away. Bearing his sword in front of him, he ran and swung in a broad arc, striking the creature with a sharp blow on the back. The blade bit deep, so deep in fact that it passed all the way through. Bright golden sparks sputtered out with a hiss in all directions as his sword cut through the creature. Qwyrk stopped in astonishment; that strike should have lopped his opponent in two. Only it didn't.

But it had hurt, that was obvious. Immediately, the Shadow disengaged from its ritual and let out a yell that Qwyrk hoped would be masked by the fury of the elements. Their enemy stumbled and fell forward to one knee. John didn't wait for it to recover. He brought his sword down on its head, another killing blow that should have severed the head clean from the body, but again passed through with some effort instead. Still, it was enough to make their enemy fall face down to the ground.

John stabbed now, driving his sword into its back, pinning it to the ground. More showers of light scattered out in all directions. The creature grunted and writhed as if in pain, but was unable to release itself from its impaled position.

Qwyrk ran up to the creature, surprised she could only see it in its shadowy form. Whatever had once been there as a Shadow of good was long gone. While John held it fast, she grabbed its head and twisted it up to face her. Its red eyes burned with hate, scanning her, as if searching for a weakness it could exploit.

"It's over, you abomination!" she hissed. "You're going back into your prison forever!"

"Oh, I do not think so, child," it said a cold voice. A deeper voice with a growl added, "I will rip your throat out, pretty little one!"

"Both of you can shut it!"

Blip had reached them now. He strode over to the pinned form with confidence and kicked it in the side as hard as he could, with his good foot. It grunted, and he nodded in satisfaction.

"How will you recapture me?" de Soulis' voice taunted. "Or will you two hold me here indefinitely? Is this to be my new prison? What happens when dawn comes again, and all those pathetic little people you care for so much see this spectacle? That shall amuse me!"

"Others from my order are on their way, demon!" John said with an authority that surprised her. "It won't be long before you are confined and removed from here. We have powerful magic, more than enough to match whatever you can conjure."

"You boast, and you may even be correct, knight," de Soulis taunted. "But you know me not. Do you think those centuries of my confinement were spent dreaming only of escape? Or placating the idiot whose body I share?"

A low growl interrupted his reply.

"I have devised many plans during my long imprisonment, fools, and honed many skills... behold!"

Qwyrk glanced up just in time to see a rosebush branch encircled in gaseous light swinging at her. She had no time to react and it caught her squarely on the side of the head, knocking her several feet away to a hard landing in the mud, where she lay stunned, unable to move, though she could see that another thorny branch had hooked itself into Blip. He howled as it lifted him up and then sent him flying toward the house, disappearing into the dark.

* * *

At the same time, John tried to fend off a similar blow with his left arm while holding the sword fast into the creature, but even with his strength, it caught him, and pushed him over, sending a surge of supernatural energy pulsing through him. He cried out and let go of the sword for a moment, falling to the ground in a heap. It was all the Shadow needed to be free.

It pushed itself up with its forearms and staggered to its feet, John's sword still pierced through its body. Reaching around behind, it growled as it pulled the weapon out. Holding it fast, it gazed down at the now-stunned John, who groaned and rolled over to face what he knew was certain death.

"I could easily kill you little man..."

"Yes, yes! Let me kill him, now!" Redcap hissed.

"We have work to do, Redcap, a ritual to complete. There will be time enough for killing soon." He cast the sword aside.

Redcap growled in fury, but de Soulis once again kept him under control.

"Now," de Soulis whispered, as the Shadow's hands began to glow again. "Let the work be finished!"

* * *

"So it was about the height of a normal adult, you say?" Jilly was trying hard to keep Jimmy engaged, by sketching according to his description, and hoping that Star Tao had managed to do the same downstairs with Jimmy's parents. Henrietta had come up to bring them their cups of tea, but Jilly was grateful that she didn't stay long. Henrietta had seemed overjoyed that Jimmy had a visitor, and a young lady at that. Jilly hoped she wasn't trying to pair them up or some such horrid thing. Boys were still stupid, after all.

"Yeah, I mean I don't think it was any taller, but I was lying down, so maybe I'm wrong. But it had two eyes, glowing red! And, and they were so..."

"So what?" Jilly asked, raising one eyebrow.

"I don't know. Evil, I suppose?"

"So, you just assume that it was evil because its eyes glowed?"

"Well, what else would it be?"

"You're not dead, are you? I mean it told you off, but then left you alone."

"Yeah, but..."

"So, how do you know it was evil?"

"Well... what was it doing in my room in the first place? Why was it trespassing? Answer that one, miss smarty!"

"Maybe it was looking out for you. Maybe it was actually trying to see if you were okay, and you just panicked, without asking it what it really wanted. You said you shouted, right?"

"Wouldn't you?"

"I might have, but maybe if you'd just tried talking to it first, saying 'hello' or something."

"That didn't exactly cross my mind when I was worried about being impaled and fed to cacodemons."

"And just why did you think *that* was what was going to happen?"

"I don't know, it just popped into my mind. There's a scene like that in *Medieval Warlords of Endless War*, this brilliant video game I play. Except, my mum won't let me play it now, not for a whole month. She says I'm playing it too much, and it's giving me nightmares."

"Well, if you're over-reacting like you did to the shadow, maybe she's right."

"Over-reacting? What the bloody hell would you have done? You'd have screamed your head off, don't deny it! You're a..."

"A girl, yeah, I know, thank you very much; and I don't know how I would have reacted, but anyway, we're way off track now." She finished making her sketch. "I'm sure whatever it was is long gone, and you're perfectly safe, and have nothing whatsoever to worry about. Here, I'm almost done." She showed him.

Jimmy had a look. "That's good! Where'd you learn to draw like that?"

"I taught myself. It's something I've always been decent at."

"How do you get all the different shades like that?"

"There are lots of different ways. One trick I like is using the actual rough texture of a piece of paper to create extra shadows and markings. You can see things that aren't actually there, you just think you see them, because of the way the surface is shaped."

"That's clever, that is. What else do you..."

"...aaaaaaaaaaaaaAAAAAAAHHHHHHHHHH!!!!!"

There followed a loud thump on the side of the outside wall.

Jimmy jumped up in shock.

"What was that?!"

Jilly, trying not to sound overly alarmed, and failing because she herself was also shaken, tried to come up with something on the spot. "I don't know... probably just a tree branch or something smashing against the house in the wind. It's a frightful storm out there, in case you hadn't noticed."

"Bollocks! That was somebody yelling and hitting the side of the house! What if it's that shadow, come back to finish me off? I told you I saw something in the yard!"

Before she could stop him, he ran to his window, and threw open the curtains, but instead of seeing the terrifying events unfolding down by the rosebush, he was greeted by the strangest sight he'd probably ever seen in his young life (at least outside of one of those games). A two-foot tall frog with a moustache stood on the window sill, looking a bit perturbed. He knocked on the glass.

Jilly could see that Jimmy didn't have a clue as to what to do. He just stood there, his mouth open, shaking. She ran over, opened the window, and let Blip in. He hopped down to the floor, staggered about for a moment as if he were a bit tipsy, and then composed himself, looking up at both of them as if this were the most normal thing in the world.

Jimmy just stared and seemed almost catatonic.

Jilly glared at Blip with her what-on-earth-are-you-*doing* look, but said nothing.

"Um, yes, right, sorry to be a bother," Blip started.

Jimmy's stunned face showed that he wasn't expecting his visitor to talk. His already-wide eyes got even wider. He may have whimpered a little.

If he starts in with an auditorium lecture, I swear I'm throwing him out the window, she thought.

"Ahem. We have the situation under control, everything is fine, nothing to worry about at all. In fact, I'm just about to pop back down for the second round, wherein we shall wrap up things shortly. Cheerio!"

He hopped back up onto the window sill, nodded to them, pulled the curtains shut, and disappeared into the dark.

Jilly sat back down on her chair. Jimmy stood there looking beyond her to the wall, still silent and still shaking.

"Right," she started after a moment, casual as could be and looking at her paper, "back to telling me more about that shadow, then!"

TWELVE

* * *

The shared body of de Soulis and Redcap extended its arms to the rosebush, which responded, with two branches reaching out to meet them. If Qwyrk weren't unconscious (or nearly so) at the moment, she would have had some sarcastic remark to make about how the two of them should go on a television dancing show together.

The golden cloud surrounding the Shadow's arms drifted forward to surround the rosebush, and its branches began to convulse, sending off rose petals and leaves in all directions. Then, in one swift motion, it uprooted itself and "stepped" to one side, revealing a deep hole beneath. Within moments a large egg-like object rose up from its depths. Its bumpy, uneven surface was covered in dirt, but it glowed red and seemed to pulsate with life as it worked its way to the surface.

"You see, dear Redcap?" de Soulis spoke with arrogance. "Patience has its rewards! Here it is! The eggs are inside! Now, now my old friend, we can make all things happen."

Redcap growled with what sounded like a slight chuckle.

The Shadow knelt and picked up the larger egg, cradling it with surprising tenderness, stroking it, feeling its energy. The rosebush stepped back over the hole, and then became still except for the wind, its purpose accomplished.

"Feel it!" de Soulis boasted. "Imbibe the raw power coursing through it, through us! It's ours for the taking!"

Drops of rain hissed and steamed as they struck the egg, mingling with the crackling, pulsing sounds it made on its own. "It won't be long now!" de Soulis declared, "they are nearly ready to hatch. Does that not please you, Redcap?"

De Soulis surveyed the scene of his victory. "The Templar and the Shadow are fools, far too easy to defeat, and that dreadful little jirry-jirry is likely dead."

"Can I kill them now, since you have your precious prize?" Redcap spat out with venom.

"I would have to place the egg down for you to do so, my friend, and that I cannot do. I will not risk being parted from it now that I have it again after so long. However..." he kicked John hard in the side. John let out a gasp of pain and clutched at his midsection, groaning and trying to focus his eyes on his enemy.

"That felt good, didn't it, Redcap? Dealing out pain indiscriminately? There will be much of that, I can promise you. Leave these fools, they are no threat to us now. Let them contemplate their failure. We have more urgent matters to attend to, and once the ritual has been completed, there will be no one in all your wretched home world who will be able to stop me... us!"

"And where are we going now, oh, 'master'?"

"Why, back to the very place where we first met, and where I cursed myself by binding my soul to yours. Hermitage Castle, old boy! It will be a grand homecoming! I have many secret chambers hidden well beneath it that the fools who killed me could never find. From there we shall..."

"We shall do this, we shall do that! I am weary of your grand plans, and I want you out of my body forever!"

"Then hold your rabid tongue, you mongrel, so that I may accomplish that very task! Unless you think you are capable of such dark workings? I thought not. Once we are rid of one another, you may do as you wish, kill who you like. I care not, but for the moment, you will do as I say!"

Redcap growled again and kicked the Templar in the stomach

again, even harder. John let out a muffled cry and doubled over in a fetal position, gasping for breath. De Soulis reasserted himself, and started to walk away from where Qwyrk and John lay, stopping for a moment to look back at the house.

"Curious," de Soulis mused.

"What now?" Redcap growled.

"I sensed something... in that house. But it is probably just a memory stirred by the dragon egg; it is of no concern to you. Let us be off."

"I will take back this body, sorcerer. Just remember that!"

"When the time comes, you savage monstrosity, you may have it!"

The Shadow strode off into the rain-soaked night, its precious prize held tightly in its arms.

* * *

From behind a nearby tree, Blip had heard everything. He grimaced in anger to see the Templar and yes, even Qwyrk, lying injured on the ground. Once he was sure the Shadow was gone, he ran up to them, Qwyrk first. Taking hold of her collar, he rolled her over. She had a cut on her left temple and blue-green blood was smudged down her face.

She groaned and gazed up at him, confused.

"Blip? What happened? Why aren't we dead?"

"The damned thing got what it wanted, and left. I would have tried to stop them, but... there was nothing I could do. I'm sorry, but he... it... they... are just too powerful now. Damn it! I hate having to admit it, most of all to you, but this is not the time for bravado. A warrior must accept when he is beaten. We failed. We've lost."

* * *

"No, it's good actually," Qwyrk grunted in pain, sitting up. "You did the right thing. At least we're still alive."

Rain pouring from the sky washed away some of the blood from her face, though she was covered in mud and looked a complete mess.

"John!" she said with shock, looking over in his direction.

She pulled herself toward him, still too weak to stand. His eyes were closed and his breathing was shallow.

"We need to get him to hospital," she said.

"N-no," he whispered. "Call my brothers, they can take care of me far better. Please." He held out his medallion with the Templar seal on it. It glowed a faint yellow color and was warm to the touch.

"What do I do?" she asked.

"Just hold it in your hand, and concentrate. Think of Simon, since you know him. I'm too weak to do it myself. He'll hear you."

She closed her eyes and did as he asked, feeling a tingling warmth growing in the metal object as she held it. In her mind's eye, she saw an image of an old man sitting in a chair, reading a newspaper. It looked like two nurses were sitting on the bed near him, but they weren't doing anything, just looking around and at the ceiling. And they didn't look much like nurses.

"It's Simon, in the room where I saw him before, but who's that with him? Oh, bloody hell! It can't be. Nurses?"

"W-what is it?" John asked whispered, having lowered himself back down to the muddy ground, oblivious to the rain that was drenching them all.

"Oh, nothing to worry about. He's fine, I suppose, unless they find a way to chat him to death; but it looks like they're not doing much of anything. Just as well, really."

"Simon," she thought in her mind. She could visualize him. He frowned for a moment, but then clued in that he was being contacted.

"Who's there?" he projected, looking disturbed and guarded.

"It's Qwyrk. I'm here at the house in Leeds with one of your knights, Sir John Ashley. Look, we just fought de Soulis, but he beat us. Why he didn't kill us, I don't know, but he... they got away with the egg, er, eggs, whatever. John's injured pretty badly, and he asked me to use his medallion to contact you. What can I do? How do I help him?"

"Ah, we'll take care of him. I'll alert those who can help. I'm glad he was there with you; it probably saved your lives."

"Yeah, I expect it did. I almost thought we were going to beat the bastard. John gave him a right good thumping."

"Where are they going?"

"I don't know," Qwyrk was speaking out loud now, tired of having to think at him, but keeping her eyes closed so she could "see" him. "They disappeared after they knocked us for a loop."

"Hermitage Castle in the Scottish Borders," Blip interrupted, surmising what they were communicating to each other. Qwyrk opened her eyes.

"What?"

"I heard them. They're returning to the scene of their old crimes. It makes perfects sense."

"Did you hear that?" she said, closing her eyes again.

"Yes, yes, and I agree. It's where I thought they would go."

"So what do you want us to do?"

"I'll send help to John, and get the word out to the brothers. We'll convene and work out a strategy. I'm afraid we'll have to face them there. In the meantime, you should wait for my call. I'll have one of us contact you soon. We'll need all the help we can get. If there's anyone in your own world that you think can be of use to us..."

"Well, that's the problem. I told you. No one even seems to know about it!"

"Then I think you're going to have to go back and make them aware."

Qwyrk sighed, realizing he was right. "All right then, we'll wait to hear from you, but if I'm not around, it's because I've gone home."

"Understood."

"One last thing... they're not bothering you, are they? I mean I asked them to look in on you in a moment of desperation. But now I'm not sure it was such a good idea..."

"No, no, they're fine. Charming girls, if a little slow. They don't even know we're having this conversation. They just think I'm reading."

"Well, maybe you should send them on their way, then. Tell them to go back to Symphinity. I'd prefer if they were some place safe; believe me, they can't handle this."

"I'll try, but they seem rather determined to sit here and make sure that I do nothing whatsoever."

"Right, well, good luck with that. You want us to stay with John until help arrives, yeah?"

"I'd prefer if you didn't. Find a place to hide him and let us take care of it."

"I don't know if we should move him. He looks in a bad way. I'm worried."

"We can determine that. Find a place nearby where he can hide, and get yourselves out of there. Your battle is bound to have attracted some attention."

"Not that I've seen, but we do have a few other things to attend to." She remembered Jilly and Star Tao, and her anger came flooding back.

"Then get on with them. Go. We've dealt with this kind of thing countless times before. The lad is in good hands. Farewell, good luck."

The vision in her mind's eye disappeared. She let go of the medallion and looked at the fallen knight.

"John... John?"

He opened his eyes and looked at her, smiling.

"Can you move at all? We need to get you some place less conspicuous."

He nodded. "I can tuck myself under this damned rosebush. My brothers will find me soon. I'm wearing the medallion. You should go, do what you need to, don't worry about me."

"Are you sure you'll be all right? I don't want to leave you if there's any chance..."

"No, no, go... please. We prefer secrecy, even from Shadows and allies. It will be better if you're not here. I'll be well looked after, I promise."

He coughed and convulsed, and Qwyrk saw a trickle of blood on his chin. She winced. But she helped him sit up while Blip tried to recover the Templar's sword, and given his small size, thoroughly failed. He gave up a moment later, muttering something about fearing he might strain something. John staggered over to the fence behind the rosebush and sat down, brushing hair out of his rain-soaked face. Qwyrk retrieved his sword, and laid it across his lap.

He smiled at her. She smiled back, and on impulse, kissed him on the cheek. *Crap, what did I do that for?* She pulled back at once.

"Good luck," he said.

"And to you," she replied.

She stood up and was hit by a wave of dizziness. She shook her head to clear it, and could feel the side of her face swelling. She looked down at Blip, and saw that he had numerous scratches from his unfortunate encounter with the rosebush. Despite it all, she wanted to laugh, just a little.

"We're alive, at least," he offered after a moment. "And that means we can fight again."

"I doubt we're in any condition to do much else right now."

"Agreed. So, what shall we do then?"

"Wait for Simon to contact us, I suppose. Probably best to be back up in Knettles. At least it's a place we know."

"Indeed, a fine strategy for withdrawal and regrouping, an excellent notion."

"Right then," she said with irritation. "Let's go and collect our wayward children, shall we?"

CHAPTER THIRTEEN

Qwyrk wiped the wet dirt from her face. Her head still stung where the rosebush had caught it. Not the most dignified of battle injuries, she noted. She looked at the home, grateful that no damage had been done to it or the inhabitants. That was something, at least. Now that de Soulis was gone, the rain and wind were dying down. The smell of wet earth hung in the air, and something else, almost like a hint of brimstone or sulfur.

"Now, the question is, how are we going to get Jilly and Star Tao out of the house?" she asked. "We can't exactly go to the door and ring the bell."

"I'll attend to it," Blip replied. "I've already been up to the boy's bedroom once, and I believe that Jilly is up there."

"What? How? And how do you know that?"

"Never mind. Suffice to say that I can fetch them both and be back quickly. And I think the sooner we leave here the better. We'll be using the lad's vehicle, I presume?"

"Well, it's not my preferred method of traveling, but I don't think we have a choice. We can't leave it here, and I'm really not keen on taking them to Symphinity as a shortcut. They're damned lucky I haven't kicked both their arses."

*   *   *

Blip nodded and hobbled off toward the house, stopping at the foot of it and looking up. The window seemed far away.

"Now, the only question is, how am I going to get back up to the boy's bedroom window without the aid of the enchanted rosebush?" he mused. "I could toss a stone at the window to attract Jilly's attention. Hm. No, no, far too uncouth. Only hooligans do such things. I shan't wish to make a noise, either. That might bring the parents out. They couldn't see me, of course, but still, no need for them to suspect anything at all. If I had my singing cane, I could send it up to recite an opera aria; it would have the double effect of attracting the girl's attention and imparting some culture at the same time to both of their young minds. If only Qwyrk hadn't broken it in her damnable haste!"

"Excuse me," Qwyrk interrupted as she limped up behind him. "While you're figuring out your latest 'conundrum,' I'm going to go fetch Jilly."

*   *   *

With that, she leapt up with a painful grunt to the first floor window sill of Jimmy's bedroom, leaving Blip to look surprised, insulted, and indignant all at once. She peered in the window and could see Jilly sitting at a desk drawing something. Jimmy sat on the edge of his bed looking traumatized. This undoubtedly had something to do with Blip, and at the moment, Qwyrk didn't want to know.

"Ah well, there's nothing else for it," she sighed. "I'm just going to have to hope that poor Jimmy doesn't die of fright when he sees me again."

With some reservation, she crouched and knocked on the window. Jilly and Jimmy both looked up at her. Jilly ran to the window and opened it. Qwyrk saw that she looked guilty. For a moment, Qwyrk felt a pang of forgiveness and wanted to hug her, but not here, not now.

"Who's she?" Jimmy exclaimed, half frightened, half annoyed. "And how did she get up on my window sill?"

Damn it, of course! She cursed to herself. *Because de Soulis was close by, now Jimmy can see me, too. All right then, time to make up a convincing lie... such as... um...*

"Nothing to worry about, nothing at all," Qwyrk stammered in desperation.

"Yeah, she's my... aunt... Cinderella," Jilly interjected quickly, seeing Qwyrk falter.

Qwyrk shot her a look that said, *What the hell?*

"She works with my... uncle, who you met downstairs. They, um, they figure these things out, right? So, how's everything down there, then, auntie Cin? Have they got it all sorted out?"

"Oh, right, yeah, everything's fine, everything's great. The, um... thing that happened, the tiger that got loose? It's been captured, and put back in his cage, so people don't have to stay inside any more, they can go out again, you now, for walks and to the shops, and pubs and... and things..." She stopped as she saw Jilly standing behind Jimmy, shaking her head, mouthing "no," and looking nervous.

"Tiger?" Jimmy looked lost. "I thought it was a water problem in the pipes, and the chance of an explosion, or something?"

"Well it is," Qwyrk lied, only now remembering Star Tao's plan.

"The, uh, tiger got out, see, because he was being transported to another zoo, and when they heard about the pipe problem they had to stop and turn the lorry around... and, so... something must have come loose in the cage when they were reversing direction, and the lock sort of fell off, and it got free..."

"How did you get up on my window sill?" Jimmy asked, interrupting her.

"Um, a ladder?"

"But why?"

"Because... I needed to get a better view of the surrounding area, just to make sure no other animals, like gorillas and llamas... escaped in the confusion..." *Bollocks, this is getting stupider by the second.*

"But it's dark outside. You can't see anything from out there."

"I've got a strong battery-powered torch? Look, Jilly, just go and tell my... brother that we're done and we can all go. He's downstairs right?"

Jilly nodded. "I'll go tell him." Without another word, she bounded off downstairs.

Jimmy eyed Qwyrk with suspicion. "Um... Do you want to come in? You look a bit of a mess, if you don't mind my saying so."

"No, no, I'm fine here, thanks. And yeah, I slipped and fell in the mud a couple of times, stupid really."

"What's that stuff on the side of your face?"

"Um... oh, I spilt a little dish soap? Yeah, we use it sometimes to clean tools and things in our work, must have got some on me, heh." The children in this part of the world were far too inquisitive, precocious, and snarky, Qwyrk noted. "I'll just head back on down the ladder and be on my way, thanks! Have a lovely evening! Bye!"

"Hold on!" Jimmy started. "You... you've got pointed ears!"

"Oh yeah, those! Heh, Hallowe'en thing!"

"But it's June..."

"I know, but I'm just getting ready, right? Wanted to see how realistic they'd look."

"While you're on the job?"

"Well... I've got some fun mates at work, and they're always going on about how we should play jokes on each other, see? So I thought I'd break out the Hallowe'en ears early and see what they say!"

"Your voice," he said, looking suspicious. "It sounds familiar..."

"Right, really got to go, lovely speaking to you! Bye then! Byeeee!"

And with that, she jumped off the ledge, leaving Jimmy to ponder the strangeness of recent days. At least he didn't go over to the window and peer out, she thought, or he would have seen that there was no ladder at all.

* * *

"Little runt!" She swore to herself as she landed on the ground with a painful jolt. "I should have scared him more when I had the chance!"

"Well?" said Blip, impatient and annoyed at having been one-upped.

"They should be out in a minute. I told her to go collect Star Tao, so we can get the bloody hell out of here."

Sure enough, the door opened moments later, and Star Tao and Jilly made their goodbyes.

"Glad it all worked out safely," she could hear him say. "Thanks for the lovely tea and hospitality, I'll be sure to come round again sometime soon... I mean, that is, if there's another problem, which there won't be, 'cause we got it taken care of, and everything's fine now, so I guess I won't be seeing you ever again, after all... good night!"

He shut the door, and they shuffled down the front steps and back to their other-worldly companions.

Star Tao smiled at Qwyrk. "Everything all right then? You stopped him and it's all sorted? We fooled them in there, didn't we, Jilly? They never suspected a thing! Not bad, eh?" His face fell when he saw that Qwyrk was still not amused at all.

"No, we did not stop him," she answered coldly, "and everything is not 'sorted.' De Soulis has the master egg, and we're all damned lucky that we weren't killed. It was only because we had some help from a Templar knight that we even stood a chance."

"A Templar?" Jilly asked, presumably forgetting Qwyrk's continuing anger. "Where?"

"Over there behind the rosebush. He saved our necks, and yours, too, so you'd best be grateful!"

"I don't see anything..." she said scanning in the dark to where Qwyrk had motioned.

"Don't be silly, he's right over..." But she turned and saw that Jilly was correct. Where Sir John had been minutes ago, there was now just the tangled, bizarre plant.

*　*　*

"So, do you have any hobbies?" Qwypp was all smiles, desperate to make conversation.

"What?" Simon asked, annoyed as he looked up from his newspaper. He'd been trying so hard to ignore them that he'd almost forgotten they were there.

"You know, like things, you like to do. I mean there must be some things you picked up along the way, what with you being so old and such... oh, sorry! I didn't mean it that way. I mean, you're old, but not OLD, if you understand what I'm saying?"

"I'm not sure that I do," Simon answered coldly and looked back at his paper.

"What do you mean? You're not sure you have any hobbies, or you're not sure you understand what I said. They have like medications for that sort of thing... crap! Sorry! That's not what I meant! I mean... Qwykk! What was that interesting thing you were telling me about earlier?"

"Hmmm?" Qwykk sat twirling her long hair in one finger, chewing gum, and staring at the wall; she'd barely heard Qwypp... something about old bobbies, or boobies, or something.

"You know, that *thing*, you were telling me about? Just earlier? It was really brilliant!"

"I don't know what you're talkin' about..."

Qwypp fumed and leaned over to whisper in Qwykk's ear, though Simon could still hear her. "Look! I'm trying to make some conversation to pass the time, here. Just work with me, all right? Make up something!"

"Uh, right, that really brilliant thing I was tellin' you about? The thing that was brilliant? Oh yeah, that was nice wasn't it?"

Qwypp smiled. "Yeah, so?"

"So... it was all sort of brilliant, and I was well made up about it, and everyone I told was made up too, right?"

"Yeah, and?"

"And... so, we were all quite excited, and that was why I told you, because I knew you'd be too!" She grinned, pleased with herself, and said nothing else, turning her attention back to the wall while blowing a bubble with her chewing gum.

Qwypp scowled.

Simon stared at them both without expression for a moment before returning to the "entertainment" section of his paper, a concept which he found amusing, since there was virtually nothing entertaining about it.

"I have an idea," he said without looking up.

Both of them snapped to attention, obviously hoping for some alleviation to this dreary boredom Qwyrk had subjected them to.

"It might be a good idea to patrol the perimeter of this complex," he continued, "and make sure all is well. I can't guarantee that security hasn't been breached already, but with your obvious skills, it would go a long way toward setting my mind at ease. Remember, it's not just me, but a whole facility full of innocent human beings. You'd be doing everyone a huge service." He looked up at both of them and smiled.

"That's a brilliant idea!" Qwykk beamed. "Almost as brilliant as that brilliant thing I told you about earlier!" She smiled at Qwypp, who rolled her eyes.

"Yeah, all right," Qwypp added after a moment. "But what are we looking for? It's going to be a bit rough patrolling if we don't know what it is we're trying to watch."

"Anything unusual, of course," Simon answered. "It could be just about anything at all. A sound, a rustle in the bushes, a gust of air, a mysterious shadow against the moonlight... all of them deserve careful inspection. We don't want to let anything slip by, do we?"

"No, no, of course not. All right then, we'll get on that," Qwypp answered trying to sound authoritative. Qwykk had already stood up and adjusted her skirt, getting ready to leave.

"Um, are you sure you don't need us to stay here with you?" Qwypp double checked. Qwykk shot her a look of desperate annoyance.

"No, no, I'll be fine, honestly. As long as you two are patrolling the perimeter of the institution in minute detail, I feel absolutely safe."

"Right, then!" Qwypp smiled, relieved. "We'll be off! Ta for now. Have a lovely evening! Very nice sitting and chatting with you!"

"Indeed," Simon answered with a forced smile.

And with that, his two would-be protectors were out of his hair, and back out doing whatever it was they preferred to do.

Simon smiled with contentment. It was rather like putting a hamster on a wheel, he decided. "Now, let's see what's on BBC 2 tonight..."

*　*　*

Star Tao's van chugged up the motorway, carrying four unusual passengers, two of whom were injured and weary, and two who were acting contrite and guilty. Few words were spoken on the journey, though Jilly knew she was going to get a good talking to when they got home. Nothing had gone as they would have liked, except that no one was killed, a minor victory which almost paled in comparison to what was now at stake.

After a long, uncomfortable, and quiet trip, they drew near Knettles. The clouds had cleared as they arrived back in town, and an impressive moon hung in the sky.

"Right," said Qwyrk, breaking the silence. She looked at Star Tao. "I don't want you dropping us off. The last thing we need is to arouse any more suspicion from Jilly's parents, if they're home, and even if they're not, I still don't want you around, got it? So leave us a few streets up, and we'll walk from there, and you can bugger back off to wherever you came from."

"Fine," he answered in a sullen voice, but clearly in no mood to argue.

Jilly wanted to say something in his defense, but knew that this was not the time.

A few more minutes of uncomfortable silent driving brought them to within a short distance from Jilly's house, two streets over.

"This will do," Qwyrk said.

Star Tao pulled over the van, so that his passengers could get out. He tried to smile at Qwyrk, who ignored his poor attempt at a friendly gesture.

"Good night!" she said as she slammed the van door and began walking. "Blip, Jilly, come on! Best not stay out here too long." She didn't look back.

As they walked off, Jilly turned around to wave and smile at Star Tao, happy to defy Qwyrk's anger. He waved, backed up his van, and drove off.

"That was rather unkind of you," she said to Qwyrk with the same defiance. She knew she was going to get yelled at, so she didn't care at this point; Qwyrk could bring it on. To her surprise, she said nothing but just kept on walking, peering around, ever mindful of potential dangers.

A couple minutes' more walk brought them back to Jilly's home. Her parents' car was not there, she and Qwyrk both noted with relief. Without saying anything, she pulled out her key and unlocked the door, and in they went. Jilly thought ahead this time, and removed the note she had penned earlier for her parents. No sense in confusing them. She folded it up and went into the living room.

"Right then," she started, looking at Blip and Qwyrk, with a mixture of irritation and bravado. "Get on with it, I'm ready. You're going to give me a bollocking about all this, so just do it and get it over with."

To her surprise, Qwyrk's voice was soft and not angry, but more hurt.

"You lied to me Jilly. You promised me you wouldn't come anywhere near us tonight, and then the first thing you did when we were gone was to concoct some crazy scheme with Star Tao to get in his van and come charging in like the flipping cavalry. I mean, first of all, you got in a van with an adult you barely even know, then you rode with him all the way to Leeds, and ended up right in the middle of something ridiculously dangerous that you shouldn't have been anywhere near. Thank Goddess it didn't go any further tonight. We could have all been killed, and we might well have been, if not for Sir John. Now de Soulis has the dragon eggs, and it's only going to get worse."

"All right, fine," Jilly answered. "But it was as much Star Tao's idea as mine; it's not like I forced him to go, he wanted to. And we did help! We kept that family inside and distracted them; they never saw anything... well, not much anyway, and Jimmy's already seen you, sort of. But what if Mr. Eckelson had decided to go outside to look at what was happening? He would have had his head ripped off, or something horrible, and there'd be a boy without a father right now. It's because we were there that it didn't happen. That's got to count for something."

"Yes, yes it does, and I'm grateful that you two were clever enough to keep them occupied. You're right, you probably saved their lives. But that doesn't change the fact that you ignored me and did the exact opposite of what I asked, both of you. We got lucky tonight, but that's not going to happen again. De Soulis knows about us now. He's pissed off with us, and he won't be caught off guard next time. If he hatches those eggs, we've got a whole new pile of problems. I honestly don't know what I'm going to do right now; I'm going back home to see if I can get someone, anyone, to listen. But if they've all been charmed the way Blip and I were, we're in a right mess. Every hour that we don't stop de Soulis is an hour closer he gets to unleashing his hell on earth. I have to go now; I can't even stay here tonight. Blip is going to have to look after you."

"Fine," Jilly answered, resigned to her logic, though still in the mood to be snippy. "But you did just tell Star Tao to sod off by himself. So much for 'protecting' us mere mortals."

Qwyrk sighed. "I know, I was angry. Look, I'll find him, and have him either come back round here or at least let me know where he is, so that he's not alone. But I can't stay... uhnn!" She grimaced and rubbed her head as if pain surged through it. The side of her face still had a blue-green streak where the thorns had caught her.

"You're hurt," Jilly said with genuine concern. "Do you need anything? You should rest here awhile."

"No, I'm fine. I think it's a side effect of some sort of magic. But I don't have time to think about it right now. I'll clean up here a bit and then get someone to patch me up back home, if I can. It's not bad. I'll live."

Jilly wasn't convinced, and her worried expression gave her away, and she knew Qwyrk could see that.

Blip had remained silent throughout all of this, which was atypical of his normal verbosity. He sat on the couch with his hands folded, appearing pensive and staring into the distance, as if not even aware of their conversation. Indeed, he looked positively withdrawn, defeated, not at all like his usual pompous self.

"Um, Mr. Blip...ingstone?" Jilly hesitated. He didn't even look at her. "Excuse me... sir?" How she hated using that word! "Are you all right?"

"I've failed," he answered after a moment, not looking at either Jilly or Qwyrk. "I've let everyone down. Not only was I completely ineffective in battle, but the best I could manage to do was to get thrown head first into a window by an enchanted plant. I have been utterly unsuccessful and unworthy. Were it possible to tender my resignation from this venture, I would do so immediately."

There followed a brief, but uncomfortable silence.

"Well, lucky for us, you can't do that," Jilly said, with a half-smile, trying to cheer him up. It didn't work. Her smile disappeared as quickly as she had tried to force it. The fact was that all three of them were upset, and the only thing that had gone right that evening was that they were all still alive. She realized that her brief attempt to make peace was going nowhere. For his part, Blip let out a heavy sigh and said nothing else.

"Look," said Qwyrk. "I don't want to dwell on this. We got lucky, so let's just leave it at that. Jilly, you're staying here, no arguments. Blip, you're looking after her, no arguments. I've got to get the hell out of here and warn whoever will listen. I'll check in on Star Tao when I can, but right now, this is more important. Nothing's going to happen to him right away. De Soulis has work to do and doesn't care about anyone else. That's the one thing that may give us... me, some tactical advantage. I'm going now, so both of you stay put until you've heard from me. I'm not going to leave you in the dark, I promise. I'll let you know what's going on, but don't wait up for me, all right?"

"Fine!" Jilly said with a half-scowl, knowing Qwyrk was right, but not at all happy about it.

"Fine," Blip sighed, still staring off at nothing in particular.

"And you won't do anything foolish while I'm gone?"

"Well it's not like I can follow you or anything, right?" Jilly said in a tone that was perhaps more sarcastic than she intended. Never mind, it drove home the point, whatever that was.

"And that's a good thing... you'll see." Qwyrk managed a half smile of her own, but Jilly wasn't buying it. As much as she wanted to hug Qwyrk, to make peace and tell her that all would be well, there was just too much of an icky feeling for any real displays of emotion right now. As Qwyrk went to the washroom to clean herself up a bit, Jilly hoped, yet again, that this wasn't the last time they would see each other.

* * *

"Oh my Goddess, I'm so bored!" Qwykk whined as she and Qwypp wandered in and out of trees around the grounds, still trying to act like they were doing something important, but both beginning to suspect otherwise. "We've been here half the night. This is the fourth time we've walked around this place, and nothing's happened! My feet are starting to hurt! These heels aren't made for patrolling."

"Look, we're doing good work here, all right?" Qwypp countered, not yet ready to admit that maybe it was, indeed a waste of time. "We have no idea what's out there, and Simon and Qwyrk told us this was really important."

"But how do we know that? I swear I think Qwyrk's just laughin' at us behind our backs most of the time. Goddess forbid that we should be around, taking away her spotlight! How do we know she didn't just send us here to get us out of the way, so she can go off and be all heroic, and save the day, and... I don't know!" Qwykk's stroll became a stamp on the ground in frustration.

"Look, she was right about Simon, wasn't she?" Qwypp countered. "That bloke's like way old and super important, I think. If she thought we were just going to bugger things up, I don't think she'd have sent us over to him."

"He was one of those Temple guys, right? Night-time Temple something-or-others?"

Qwypp rolled her eyes. "Knight of the Temple, stupid. K-n-i-g-h-t, as in 'I dub thee Sir Very Important, Hoity-Toity, Look-at-My-Big-Sword.' Templars, they were called. Mean-arse bastards, they were. Nobody messed with them back in the Middle Ages."

"Why are they called 'middle'?" Qwykk mused, twirling her hair with a finger again.

"What?"

"Middle. Middle Ages. The middle of what? There must be like, First and Last Ages too, right? There can't just be a 'Middle.' That wouldn't make any sense. So... when were the First Ages? Crap! Are we living in the Last Ages now? Is that what this is all about?"

Qwypp sighed. "It's got something to do with being between Rome and nowadays, I think."

"But... Rome is hundreds of miles away from here, right?"

"Ancient Rome, you stupid cow! Ancient Rome and the modern world, and the Middle Ages were somewhere in between. In *time*. Get it?"

"All right, all right! You don't have to be so mean. I'm only askin' a damn question, I..." Qwykk let out a shriek and almost stumbled over. Her skill with walking in overly high heels saved her the embarrassment of landing face-first on the lawn.

"Qwykk, what the hell? Oh!"

Standing in front of them was a little mossy-green creature, looking rather like a miniature devil. He was about a foot high, had short horns protruding from his bald head, a bulbous nose, and wore a brown sack that looked like a badly-fitting toga. His yellowish eyes leered up at them, and he flashed a slight grin.

"Evenin' ladies, and greetin's! Lovely to meet ya out havin' a late-night stroll. I must say that were I to find meself in a state of poor health, I cannot think of two others that I would rather 'ave takin' care of me, and nursin' me back to health than you two. You are a credit to your profession, and I salute your 'ard work and dedication." He bowed.

"Who the bloody hell are you?" Qwypp demanded, now over her initial shock and well on the way to irritation.

"My name's Horatio, and I represent the local Union of Night-Time Nasties, Yorkshire Chapter."

"Lovely. What do you want?" Qwypp said.

"It has come to our attention that some very grave happenings have been, well, happening in this 'ere area for a bit, and we are gravely concerned about said grave happenings, and the grave ramifications of such grave disturbances."

"So, why tell us?" Qwykk interjected.

"Because you are the only two of your kind that seem to be in the immediate area, and so I was dispatched to deliver our warnings and concerns."

"What do you mean, 'our kind'?" Qwypp was getting alarmed and defensive, while Qwykk looked sweetly clueless, as always.

"Oh, give me a break, girls! While I must admit that you look absolutely fetching in those outfits, and under different circumstances, I'd be more than willin' to suggest some sort of naughty nurse thing for our mutual enjoyment..."

Qwypp was prepared to stomp on him.

"...you are as much nurses as I am the flippin' Duke of Cornwall. You're Shadow folk, and you have way more power than you're lettin' on!"

"All right, so we are, and you also know that we spend a lot of time beating the crap out of pillocks like you!" Qwypp was in no mood to be nice any more.

"Don't I know it! I've 'ad me arse 'anded to me on more than one occasion, thanks to you lot. But I ain't 'ere spoilin' for a fight. I ain't that stupid, honey."

"Call me 'honey' again, and I'll drop-kick you into the next county."

"Fine, whatever. Just listen up, all right? We Nasties, see, we have a system, and lately we've been takin' it a bit easy overall, we voted on it. We like to haunt old homes, scare children, break a few things, act all like poltergeists and such, but it's all in good fun, ain't it? A bit of mischief 'ere and there, a bit of havoc and chaos, just to keep the mortals on their toes. It's you Shadow folk who come in ruinin' all the fun and kickin' us around.

"Anyway, that's beside the point. I didn't come 'ere to debate the merits of our vocation. Somethin' bad is happenin', real bad, and it scares the crap out of us, got it? We like to have our fun, but this... this ain't fun. This is evil and madness and the end of the world as we know it."

"I knew we were living in the Last Age!" Qwykk blurted out, sounding panicked.

"Shut up!" Qwypp retorted, while Horatio looked lost.

"Right," Qwypp continued, "what's really going on? Tell me, or I'm going to thump you! And what do you mean we're the only ones up here? Why haven't you contacted Qwyrk? This is more like her king of thing, with all her brave heroics and shite."

"Normally, I would. But as I said, apparently, you two are the only ones in the area. She must have gone back to your world, or snuffed it, or something."

"What?! What's she been up to?"

"I 'ave no idea, honestly, but if she's gotten herself mixed up in this, she could be in real trouble, and it gives me no pleasure to say that."

"Mixed up in what? Tell us, damn it!"

"The return of William de Soulis," Horatio intoned in a solemn voice.

Qwypp and Qwykk looked at him with blank stares, his attempt to impress and terrify them all at once having failed miserably.

"De Soulis!" he said again. "Evil sorcerer? Wants to rule the world, and kill everyone who gets in his way? Strong enough to kick all our arses and plannin' on doin' somethin' else even worse? Honestly, what goes on in those heads of yours? Are you all just shadowy on the inside as well?"

Qwypp frowned, then grimaced, then screwed up her face, before the lightbulb went on over her head. "Oh, right! Qwyrk mentioned that bloke to us! Thanks for the help, Horatio. This has been a brilliant little chat. Go back to your mates and tell them not to worry. We'll get on it, all right? And don't be messing with us in the meantime, or we'll smack you good, got it? Come on, Qwykk." She turned and started off back toward the main building, Qwykk following along, still looking completely lost.

Horatio shrugged. "Well, I told them what I was supposed to. If that's the best the Shadows've got, we're all buggered." He turned and melted into the darkness of a nearby bush.

"What the hell was that all about?" Qwykk exclaimed, struggling to keep up with Qwypp in her high heels.

"Qwyrk wasn't lying, there *is* something really bad going on, and Simon is going to tell us exactly what."

"What did he mean about Qwyrk? She's not hurt, is she?"

"I don't know, but if she is, we're going to be kicking some serious arse, so you might want to change into something a little bit more combat-ready."

"Damn it, I hate doing that! It's so hard to find anything that looks good! Honestly, can't these army people be a little more in touch with fashion?"

Instead of agreeing with her, Qwypp just increased her pace.

* * *

Dawn broke here, in this cold, windswept place. Even in summer, it exuded a chill, its barren rolling hills concealing well the great fortress that had seen so much horror and pain over the centuries. Its high stone walls effused menace; a giant, rectangular tower in a fine state of preservation for its age. Even without a roof or a moat, it looked unassailable.

They stood nearby, the two who were still one, and looked at the impressive remains of Hermitage, imposing and grim even in ruin. Here is where it began, all those centuries ago, and here is where he would bring it all back.

"This is not the castle I remember," de Soulis mused, "but it is impressive, more so than before, and it will suffice. In fact, it may even be better. These walls are strong, and the floor conceals the tunnels underneath that no one would ever find."

"How do you know?" hissed Redcap. "What if others from a later time found them? Used them? Destroyed them? What if nothing is left?"

"You give these mortals far too much credit, my friend," De Soulis answered. "Even their protectors are pitiful. Look how we vanquished the Templar and the Shadow girl tonight. Two strong, healthy representatives of their forces, and yet they failed, miserably."

"The Templar did a fine job of running us through, or had you not noticed while plotting your take-over of this world?"

"He did not succeed, did he? And indeed, he caught me off-guard, I will admit. Nevertheless, the night was ours. Furthermore, I hid away some of my own magic in the large egg, knowing that I would need it to replenish myself after being imprisoned so long. You see? I have thought of such things and have taken a long view, preparing for all eventualities. That magic courses through me now, nourishing me and making me stronger with each passing moment. How do you think we were able to arrive here so quickly? My power is returning to its fullest, little fool, and once that happens, no Templar sword or Shadow magic shall ever touch me!"

Redcap growled, but as usual, said nothing more.

"Come," de Soulis said, cutting off the growl and walking down the hill toward the castle. "We have much work to do. We shall restore this place to its former glory. It will become a sanctuary, a place of arcane sorcery, from which I will rule this world."

"And I?"

"You... you shall be able to do whatever you wish. You may spread death and terror across the land as far as you are able, for all I care. Therefore, I say again: help me now, and soon we will be free of each other."

De Soulis sensed that Redcap decided to obey for a little while longer.

CHAPTER FOURTEEN

Qwyrk stood outside of Qwyzz's home yet again. It looked different now in the near-dawn light (Symphinity tended to follow the day and night pattern of earth, at least for the time being). She couldn't quite tell what had changed. Maybe he'd added a turret, or subtracted part of a crenellation, substituted a stained glass window for a later Tudor style, or some such thing. He was in the habit of changing the place's appearance all the time, so she didn't give it any further thought. She rang the bell, dreading what was about to follow. Sure enough, in a moment, a little stone figure peered over the edge of the roof, and spoke to her in a gravelly voice.

"Alloooooo! Who goes there?" Gargula bellowed down.

She sighed, and shouted up to him, "It's me, Qwyrk. I was just here yesterday, remember? I need to speak with your master right now. It's urgent, and I am *not* Attila the sodding Hun!"

"Ohhhh, urgent is it? Zat is what they all say! I for one, am weary of all of zese 'urgent' calls to my master and his abode. What could possibly be so urgent for ze likes of you, eh? Broken a nail and need ze master magician to fix it? Forgot where you put your shampoo and need ze master to conjure some more? Or maybe you misplaced your little brain and... ack!"

Qwyrk jumped up to the roof in one bound and grabbed the gargoyle by the throat. Her voice was calm, but deadly. "Right then, you miserable little stone piece of shite. This is how it's going to happen, all right? You're going to tell your master I'm here. You're going to tell him it's urgent, a matter of life and death, and you're going to do it right now, before I use your wretched little head to break down the door myself! Are we absolutely clear on this?"

Gargula's rocky eyes bulged wide. He swallowed hard, coughed up a few pebbles, and nodded his head.

Qwyrk smiled. "Excellent! Off you go then!"

"Zere's just one problem," he said with a defensive sneer. "My master is not here. No one has seen him tonight, not even ze lady of the house."

"What? Where is he?"

"I do not know. If I knew I would tell you, you horrid thing, but zat's just it! No one knows! We are terribly upset and worried; he should have been back ages ago. He never should have gone, in fact."

"Damn! Is the lady in? I'll see her."

He nodded.

"Well, then, let me in, you idiot! This could be even worse than I thought."

Gargula flapped his stony wings and fluttered down to the ground. Qwyrk followed after, making the jump from the roof and landing with a painful thud in front of the main door; she was still hurting from her scrap with de Soulis. "Where's Babewyn, by the way?" she asked. "At least she can be reasonable."

"She is busy at the moment, in ze cellar working on an

important repair. I can tell you no more, for it is privileged information for ze household only."

Qwyrk rolled her eyes.

The gargoyle thumped his wing on the door in several loud knocks. "Lady! Lady Qwota! Zere is someone here to see you. She is rude and obnoxious, but she insists zat it is urgent. Will you let her in please, so zat she will stop threatening me?"

Qwyrk scowled. Gargula sneered.

The door swung open and Qwota stood there, looking disheveled and tired. Her red velvet robe was a mess, her hair was frizzy, and she looked as if she had been crying.

"It's all right, Gargula, Qwyrk is welcome in our home anytime."

The gargoyle grimaced, Qwyrk smirked with satisfaction.

"Very well," he spat, "I now return to my roof position. I will warn you if enemies approach."

Qwota sighed. "You do that. Come in, dear."

Qwyrk entered, grateful to be away from that nonsense. The strange and cluttered house had changed even since yesterday, but she was too distracted by the news of her missing mentor to take any note of it.

"Qwota," she said, concern rising in her voice. "What is going on? Where's Qwyzz?"

Tears filled Qwota's eyes as she sat down on the sofa, and she burst out crying. Qwyrk sat down beside her, and put a comforting arm around her.

"Oh, Qwyrk, I don't know, but I know that something terrible has happened. Just last night, he told me he was beginning to become fearful that there were those on the council and in the land who were traitors, afraid that he was being watched, and that he might be taken. I told him that it was all in his mind and that he was working too hard, but he was adamant that he was being targeted. He said that he'd received an anonymous message warning him not to investigate whatever he was looking into. He wouldn't tell me anything else. This scared me, but he assured me he'd be all right. Then when I came home this evening, he was gone, and... and there were signs of a struggle. The back door was forced open, a flower pot was broken on the floor, and a chair had been turned over. Oh Qwyrk, I think someone came for him. Someone took him, they must have!"

She put her face in her hands and sobbed again, and Qwyrk hugged her close.

"Oh, my dear Qwota, I'm so sorry!"

"What's going on Qwyrk? What happened to him?"

"I'm not sure," she answered. "Things are just horrible right now, and I think someone, or maybe more than just one, knows about it."

"What things, Qwyrk? What's happening? If you know anything about what happened to him, you must tell me!"

Qwyrk sighed, and relayed the key events of the past few days, including last night's battle and defeat at the hands of de Soulis.

Qwota sat in silence for a while, looking pale.

"Do you think de Soulis came for him? Wanted him for some purpose?" Her voice was frail and shaking.

"He would never be able to enter our world," Qwyrk assured her, but how could she be certain of anything now? "Too many would have known, if he'd even tried. I think it's more likely that someone here took him, for whatever reasons."

"Someone working with de Soulis?"

Qwyrk hesitated, then nodded, hating the implications of what she was saying. "That would be my guess, as much as it disturbs me to say."

"But why, Qwyrk? Who? Who would want to help such a monster? And for what?"

"I don't know; it's been eating away at me. I have to find out, but I don't even know where to start. Who can I possibly trust here, now? Anyone could be a traitor. There may be just one, or a whole group of them, for all I know." Qwyrk put her face in her hands in frustration, and let out a heavy sigh.

"There must be something we can do," Qwota said.

"You didn't see or hear anything at all?" Qwyrk asked in desperation.

Qwota shook her head. "He goes out for walks sometimes, but he always lets one of the gargoyles know if he's going to be more than a short while. They always tell me where he's gone. They're rather vociferous, as you might have noticed." She managed a weak smile. Qwyrk returned a faint grin.

"I have a feeling that asking around in our world could be a bit dangerous right now," Qwyrk said. "I have to return to Earth, or I could end up missing, too. I'm going to do everything I can to find out what happened to him, and get him back."

"You think he's still alive, then?"

Qwyrk nodded. "I'm sure of it. Your bloke has a lot of specialized knowledge, and it wouldn't do for someone to eliminate him. He's valuable. If someone took him, it's because they want information."

"But, they could hurt him to get what they want..."

Qwyrk hadn't thought of this. "All the more reason I should go and try to find him." She held Qwota's hand for a moment, promised again to help, and kissed her on the cheek. "You be careful, all right? You know how to contact me if you need to. Ward your home, or something, and don't let anyone else in. I'll be back when I can."

Qwota nodded. Then Qwyrk rose and walked to the front door. She left without looking back.

* * *

Qwypp stormed back into the building, Qwykk stumbling along beside her, having given up and removed her shoes, which she held in one hand while hobbling on the grass.

"We're gonna get some proper answers, Qwykk. This is complete bollocks, and it stops now!"

"Maybe that Nasty was havin' us on?" Qwykk offered. "He was kind of sleazy. Maybe... maybe he was a distraction! To get us to come back here while the real threat was out there. Qwypp, what if we made a dreadful mistake and we shouldn't even be here!"

"I can't even believe I'm even saying this, but you're over-thinking it. Things are never that complicated, except in novels where they try to be clever. So just shut it. We'll go back to Simon. And let me do the talking, all right?"

Qwykk pouted, but nodded.

Without even trying to be subtle, they entered the building, stomped past the reception desk (fortunately staffed by a long-haired young man wearing headphones and rocking out, who didn't notice them), walked up to Simon's room, opened the door without knocking, and strode in.

"Right, mister Sir Templar Knight! I want to know what the bloody hell is really going on, and why I have to hear about it from some damned sleaze-ball Nighttime Nasty, when you could have just told us straight up what the score was, and... eh?"

They looked around Simon's room, but he was gone.

"Bollocks!" Qwypp swore. "Where is he? He couldn't have

gotten out of here, not without being seen. Oh, bollocks. Bollocks!"

"Well, if he's one of those Temple people, and he's old and powerful, he could do just about anything he wanted. Which is why Qwyrk wanted us to keep an eye on him, yeah?" Qwykk smiled, as if this made up for being insulted a minute ago.

"The window's not open," Qwypp observed, "so he must have gone out the front door, right past that moron at the desk. The bastard, he probably sent us off on a walk to get rid of us, so he could sneak out!"

"Or, maybe he was taken by force?'

"What?"

"Well, if that Horatio Nasty was right, and there's somethin' really evil going on." Qwykk's eyes grew wide. "Maybe he was abducted against his will!"

"Most people aren't abducted willingly, Qwykk."

"Well, yeah, but it can happen. I got abducted once by a fit elf chap. I mean it was a prank, and I kind of knew he was going to do it, but still, he carried me off, and everything, and nobody knew where we'd gone off to. Everyone got their knickers in a twist about it, but we were just spending the weekend in his woodland tree house, shagging and..."

"Look, I honestly, truly don't care about that, for once! If we lost Simon, we've really cocked things up. We may have to go back to Symphinity and get help. And what about Qwyrk? I'm so worried. She could be hurt. We've got to do something."

"But what? We don't even know what's going on. Simon may have just wanted a little fresh air and stepped out for a bit."

"Yeah, or, he may have been leading us on, or he may have been kidnapped. Come on, we've got to go!"

"Where?"

Qwypp took Qwykk's hand and dragged her out of the room.

"Just come on!"

*   *   *

Another sunny morning had come to Knettles, and Star Tao paced back and forth in front of the *Aloe Plant*, waiting for it to open. He'd slept in his van all night, or rather, had hardly slept at all. Even though Qwyrk had told him off, he still couldn't just walk away. He was worried about Jilly, and wanted to help. He'd tried to channel one of his guides for advice, but that hadn't worked at all. He kept getting a cosmic busy signal.

So here he was, pacing and fretting and turning over and over what to do.

"There's gotta be more info in one of them books in there, I just know it!" he said to himself as he strolled up and down the street. "And when I get it, I'm gonna go back and tell them all, and then she'll see. Then Qwyrk'll see I'm not a useless tosser. And Lord Blip will see that I'm a worthy follower!"

He contemplated getting a coffee while he waited, but decided that coffee did bad things to him, like make him jittery and unable to get a proper signal lock for channeling. Not that it was working well this morning, anyway, but best not to take a chance and make things worse. Someone might try to contact him, for a change. And besides, no place around here seemed to serve the organic oak twig tea that he preferred.

After an agonizingly long wait, the store clerk unlocked the front door, and Star Tao dashed in, giving a friendly good morning, but not even stopping to inquire about the status of his workshop. He went straight up the stairs, but stopped at the top of the first flight.

"Right! I'm gonna let me intuition direct me. Oh mighty guides, tell me which way to go. Lead me on the proper path to illumination and enlightenment. Oh Zixytar and Zzazznapo'ti'ak, help me find the answers that I seek!"

He was drawn to wander to his left, past a few bookshelves about random topics, including the ever-popular *Astral Telemarketers of the Seventeenth Plane: How to Communicate with and Banish Them*, and a small table displaying crystal balls. He stopped and gazed into one for a time, hoping to have a vision, but all he could see was the other side of the room refracted upside-down into a fish-eye shape. That, and the words *Made in China*.

He sighed in frustration and moved on.

He'd circled the entire first floor after a couple of minutes, but still didn't feel compelled to seek out any particular book.

"The energetic systems are a complete mess today; must be aggravated by last night's sorcery. Some twig tea would make it better." He sighed again.

In a flash, the answer came to him.

"Bollocks, I'm too chaotic! I've got to work more toward my inner peace. That's the only way I can fight this."

He closed his eyes and began a low hum, which segued into nonsense syllables. At least, that's what they seemed like, but he suspected they were far more than that. They were likely the secret language of the Galactic Star Brotherhood. He let himself move about the floor as he wished, without any regard for his surroundings, inspired by being in the moment, a pure, free soul, unfettered by the constraints of protocol and self-preservation. It was a beautiful moment of is-ness, a frozen capsule of Zen-like purity, when a light being is dissolved into the otherness of the absolute One, a single entity made universal, and conscious of all things in all other things.

And then he crashed into a bookshelf.

He stumbled and fell as a large paperback dropped from an upper shelf and knocked him on the head.

"Ow!" he yelled. "Bloody hell, that just ruined me moment! I was in it; I was one with the All, and it just got messed up. Thanks a lot, you stupid book, you..."

He picked it up and looked at the cover. It was old, covered in dust, sitting unnoticed on the top shelf for years: *The Life and Magical Works of Thomas the Rhymer.*

* * *

Dudley was a little unassuming man who enjoyed what he did: taking admission to Hermitage Castle, and helping out in the gift shop. He wasn't out there every day, but today, he was scheduled for a shift, and it was a clear, beautiful summer morning. He'd been up just after sunrise (an impressive accomplishment given the earliness of a Scottish summer day!) and was looking forward to it. Summer always brought more tourists, of course, and though it was better on days when few people were around, there was something relaxing about being so far out, away from the cities, the pollution, and the noise, especially out here. Things could be almost unnervingly quiet. Some people said that the whole area gave them the creeps, particularly if they were out here alone, but not Dudley.

Oh to be sure, the place had a dark and grim legacy, but that was a long time ago. Now, it was just a pile of old stones, as peaceful as you like. He didn't believe in ghosts, or curses, or any such rubbish, and he welcomed the solitude. Hours could pass without a single tourist coming by, and that's just the way he liked it. He could read, think, and be alone without any distractions.

And so this morning, like all the others, he arrived, parked his small car, and got his keys out to unlock the little visitor center. He was about to turn the key when he heard something, something coming from the keep itself. It sounded like a commotion, like stones being disturbed.

"No one else should be out here yet," he said to himself, wondering if some stray sheep had wandered into the walls, as sometimes happened. He put the keys back in his pocket and headed out to the castle.

The noises became louder as he approached, and sounded like large rocks, even blocks were being moved. He furrowed his brow in disbelief, and decided to get a closer look. He had no sense of danger, just an annoyance that something was disturbing his morning routine.

If it's sheep, I'll chase 'em off! He thought to himself. *If it's some kids, I'll phone the police!*

His irritation grew with each moment, and he now strode with purpose toward the keep. He noticed that clouds had started to gather in the last minute or so, even in the time it had taken him to walk from the gift shop down the grassy lane and up to the ruin. Dark clouds, looming and ominous.

Just a summer storm, he thought, and gave it no other attention. He rounded the corner and made for the entrance. It was an impressive archway, long missing its wooden doors, but it was the only entrance into the keep.

Screwing up his best authoritative voice, he walked through it, ready to tell off whoever was there, or at least frighten off the sheep.

"Right then!" he announced. "This here place is not open to the public for another half hour, you obviously haven't paid, and you're trespassing. So get the hell out before I call the... oh!"

He beheld a stunning sight. Inside, the castle was being rebuilt in front of his eyes. Stones reassembled themselves, new wooden beams appeared out of nowhere and rose up into the air, and in the middle of it all, standing there before him, was the oddest thing of all: a large shadow with glowing red eyes that seemed to be orchestrating the whole thing by moving its arms and directing the flying rocks.

Dudley's jaw dropped open, but he couldn't say anything. Stones and wooden beams flew right by his head on their way to various new resting places. As the figure first noticed and then floated toward him, all of his bravado drained away and he was terrified. It had to be at least seven feet tall, and it scared him. Oh, beyond scared, it terrified him. This wasn't even possible, and yet, it was happening in front of him. He watched wide-eyed as it stopped in front of him and observed him with its horrid red eyes, as if it were peering into his soul. It was violating and assaulting, but he couldn't move. He began to tremble, then shudder. He struggled to say something, anything, but the words wouldn't come.

The shadow observed him for another moment, and then reached out. Dudley gasped in disbelief as the thing's hand seemed to enter into his chest, to meld with him. He couldn't even feel pain as the hand emerged, holding his still-beating heart in its grasp. Finding his voice at last, he let out a muffled cry. As the light faded from his eyes, he saw that the thing seemed to smile at him, an evil smile that said it delighted in what it had just done. Dudley fell to the ground, dead.

* * *

Qwyrk walked out of Qwyzz's peculiar mansion feeling more

disturbed than ever.

"What the hell is going on?" she whispered to herself. "If Qwyzz is taken and missing, I can't risk going to anyone else here. Our enemy could be anyone. They probably already know I'm here. Damn it! So much for my brilliant idea."

She paced around in front of the house, feeling lost and desperate.

"Hey! You!" a gravelly voice called down to her in a stony whisper.

She looked up at the roof. "Gargula! I'm *so* not in the mood for you right now, so just leave off and go away!"

"No, zis is important!" He fluttered down to her and landed on the ground, with much dust flying about. "Zere is something *very* odd going on here. Monsieur Qwyzz is missing, but Babewyn and I saw nothing last night, nothing at all! It is our duty to stand guard at all hours. He never left zis place, as far as I can tell."

"Well, that just means that his abductors teleported into the house," Qwyrk offered. "It's something we can all do here."

"I know, I know! But my lady says zere were signs of a struggle inside. Why bother, when zey could have just zapped in and out, taking him and never being seen?"

"What are you saying? You think Qwyzz wanted it to look like he was abducted? That he planned to disappear?" She didn't like the implications of this at all.

"I do not know, but zere is something, how you say, 'fishy' about all of this. If ze master was worried about anything, he would have set up some kind of magical protection, to prevent zis very thing from happening."

Qwyrk's mind reeled. She couldn't accept what he was suggesting. Was Qwyzz the traitor? Had he arranged to disappear once he'd talked to her and learned what she knew? Was his talk with her all just an act? No, that was impossible. She'd known him for many human centuries. Still, she also knew that Gargula was loyal to Qwyzz and Qwota, despite his annoying demeanor. He wouldn't be suggesting anything untoward unless he truly thought something was wrong.

"So, any ideas?" she asked.

"None, whatsoever."

She glared at him.

"I am no strategist! I leave zat to the likes of you! But I would suggest leaving zis place and going back to ze Earth plane. It might be dangerous for you to remain."

"For once, I agree with you. Look can I trust you, Gargula? I need someone on the 'inside' here that I can count on. Qwota is too distraught, and she may be easy to compromise. In fact, she may be in danger, too. Goddess help me, I guess it has to be you. Can you help me?"

Gargula lifted one little wing in a kind of salute. "I swear by my homeland, majestic Normandy, land of apples and conquerors, zat you can call upon me in your hour of need to provide all knowledge zat I can, to help with ze vanquishing of those who need vanquishing, and to overcome ze, er, un-overcomed!"

He sounds like a French Blip, she thought, but she smiled and thanked him.

"I need to get out of here, just to be safe," she said, "but I'll contact you if I need you, thanks again!"

He bowed once more, and flew back to the rooftop, where he assumed his position. She turned and ran down the path back into the forest, fearful that watchful eyes may have already noted her presence here.

FOURTEEN

*   *   *

Jilly yawned for the umpteenth time. She'd barely slept all night, and with the arrival of the early morning sun, it became hopeless to try any more. Blip had sat in a corner of her room for hours, but had said nothing then, and little at all since Qwyrk left. Jilly was worried about him; all the life and pomposity had just vanished.

After her parents left for the day, she went downstairs, deciding to leave Blip to his funk. He hadn't answered when she spoke to him anyway. Now she stared out the main window restlessly, as if that would somehow resolve things. Odin came along, jumped up on the couch he was not allowed to be on, and sat beside her. He was a pain, but she appreciated his company.

She looked at the clock; it was well after nine, and still there was no word from Qwyrk, Star Tao, or anyone else about anything. Helplessness gnawed at her. What if they were in danger, or worse? She found herself missing Blip's endless verbose pontifications, and was only a little bit queasy about that. That fact was beginning to worry her more than the rest of the situation.

She heard light footfalls on the stairs, and turned to see Blip emerging at last. He walked in his usual haughty manner, but the fire seemed to have gone out of him, the arrogant confidence wasn't there. Could his defeat at the hands of de Soulis have been *that* demoralizing?

"Mister... Blippingstone? I'm, um, glad to see you. How are you? How are you feeling?"

Blip nodded at her but didn't say anything. He hopped up onto the same couch, far closer to Odin than she would have thought he would ever want to be. He sat there with his hands clasped and resting in his lap. He slouched and seemed to stare forward at the wall.

"Sir," she hated using that term! "I don't mean to be rude, but I'd appreciate it if you'd say something. I mean I know that things went badly last night, but it's not over yet, is it? We're still here, and we've heard no bad news yet. So, could you say something to me... please?"

He turned and looked at her, and managed a slight smile. "Of course, child. It's been terribly rude of me to ignore you and my duties, a terrible lapse in manners, inexcusable, even. We may as well continue your lesson today while we wait. I believe we were beginning a comprehensive, yet brief introduction to the fundamentals of Western Philosophy."

Jilly shuddered, but at least he was starting to sound like his old self again.

"No sir, what I meant is, we should talk about what we can do, especially if things go bad. We can't just run away."

"You saw me last night, my dear." His voice took on a more solemn tone. "I was wretched, abysmal, pathetic, and risible. I had my moment, I confronted the enemy bravely, and he, if you will pardon the vulgar expression, handed me my arse in mere seconds. I was made a fool before I could even strike a blow. What on Earth or any other world could I do to help now? I'm as pointless as a broken pencil, as weak as thinly-brewed tea. I'm as soft as a down duvet, and as phony as a barrister's wig."

"Uh... right, but, none of us did very well last night. We were lucky to get out alive, even that Templar, and he was quite strong."

"Precisely! So what makes you think we'd be of any further assistance now? We'd be better trying to engage de Soulis in a heated game of Tiddlywinks than trying to take him on in combat. We simply don't have the strength!"

"Well, not to go up against him in a fight, maybe, but there are other ways."

Blip eyed her. "Such as?"

"Well, some kind of magic, maybe? I don't know. I just can't believe that we're giving up so soon!"

"Qwyrk and the others are perfectly capable of dealing with this threat, I suspect. And if not, there isn't anything more that we can do, anyway."

"But this isn't like you! You're not someone who gives up! I've heard you talk over the last few days. Where's that confidence? Where's the Blip who told me about all of his accomplishments and deeds? *He* wouldn't give up!"

"I'm afraid it's all a bit of a lie, my dear, a fudge to hide the fact that I'm actually not particularly good at anything. Oh, I am blessed with greater-than-normal intelligence and eloquence, to be sure, but beyond that? Very little, it pains me to admit. Qwyrk is far more heroic than me, much as it pains at me to concede. Besides, she gave us strict instructions to wait here. I am to watch you and make sure that you do not try anything ridiculous again. And it's 'Mr. Blippingstone.'"

"And you're just going to take orders from her?"

"I must keep you safe, so there's sound wisdom in her plan. Not that I could do much of anything if I had to." There was a sadness in his voice.

"Well suit yourself, but I'm not just going to sit around and wait for my friends to be killed and the world to end!" Jilly got huffy again, having had about enough of his self-pity.

"And what do you suggest?" Blip retorted with a hint of sarcasm.

"I don't know! Maybe... maybe we should go back to the shop and find more books. We should at least find Star Tao and make sure he's all right."

Blip nodded. "A fine young man, indeed. It would be a shame to lose him."

"That's right, and it's *not* going to happen, yeah?"

A knock at the front door startled them both out of their heated words. Jilly looked at Blip with wide eyes.

"Who'd be here now?" she whispered.

Blip stood up at once and whispered back, "Stay down, child! We don't yet know what we're dealing with. This could be dangerous."

The knock came again, and this time was louder. Against Blip's orders, Jilly crept toward the side window and peered between the thin curtains. Relief and delight flooded into her as she saw Star Tao standing at the door, looking even more anxious and fidgety than usual.

"He's back! He's all right!" she exclaimed with glee, running to the door before Blip could say anything. "Star Tao!" She laughed as she flung open the door and hugged her friend.

He laughed and hugged her back. "All right, Jilly! Nice to see you, too!"

He hurried in, and she shut and bolted the door behind him.

Star Tao followed her into the living room, and made his obligatory obeisance to his lord. Blip was clearly still pleased by the young man's adoration, despite the depressing turn of recent events.

"What's that?" Jilly asked, pointing to the old book in his hand.

"Well, that's why I'm here," he answered. "I was right depressed after last night, so I went away and thought about it. I reckoned there must be more information in the store somewhere. So I went back first thing, and allowed me guides to show me the way. It was funny actually, I was wandering all about the first floor with me eyes closed. I banged into a few things, but then, this here book hit me right on the head. Literally, I mean, it fell down off of a top shelf and hit me. Must have been up there for ages; I doubt anyone even knew it was still there. So, I bought it, dead cheap, and had a look through it."

"What is it?" Jilly asked.

"It's all about the life and magic of that Thomas the Rhymer bloke, the one who banished de Soulis way back when. He was a powerful bardic master, who used songs and stuff to get the best of his enemy. Now according to this, he disappeared, married a Faerie queen, or something, and hasn't been seen since.

"Glorienne, yes, it's well known. She's quite reclusive and doesn't talk about it," Blip interjected. "I think they eloped to avoid her disapproving parents, and rightly so. It was a bit of a royal embarrassment, her marrying such a commoner. But he was quite good at what he did, and so he was allowed to stay with her, but he wasn't allowed to return to earth. Her father's anger even subsided a little after a few hundred years."

"But what good is that to us?" Jilly asked. "I mean, he may have been brilliant and all in banishing de Soulis, but that's not going to help us now."

"No Jilly, it can," Star Tao replied. "It got me thinking again. I have a special talent for communicating with other planes. You've seen it. What I'm sayin' is, if I really put me mind to it, I can contact Thomas, and channel him, and he'll come through. There are some spells and whatnot in here that may help us out, too. If he speaks through me, maybe he can work his song magic mojo and banish that dodgy old magic bloke again!"

Jilly thought about it for a minute, and then turned to Blip with a smile. "See? I told you we'd come up with something!"

* * *

De Soulis smiled, even though his murky face showed no trace of it. He might have even permitted himself a laugh, were he not so focused on his task. The heart of the foolish little man who had dared to confront him was now set on a central stone in the courtyard.

"He was brave, I will grant him that. For such an imp to challenge me, he shall have the honor of giving some of the first sacrificial blood needed to complete the task."

"Are we nearly finished?" spat Redcap. "These arcane workings are a bore to me."

"A little while longer, you vicious creature," De Soulis snapped, "and we shall be rid of one another for all time."

"You keep saying that!"

"And I keep meaning it! So shut your foul mouth and let me finish!"

De Soulis began his workings and conjurings yet again: intricate hand gestures and ancient words in long-dead tongues. A red glow emanated from the dead man's heart, and as more masonry shifted, it all began to take on a new shape, restored to its likeness from over six hundred years before, but changed, twisted into something new and terrible, far more terrible than the grim events witnessed here over the long years.

Dark clouds descended overhead, and thunder rolled across the sky. De Soulis threw his arms up in a wild gesture and the work was complete. Now, they stood inside a restored keep, its roof re-made, its wooden floors rebuilt, twisted and evil faces magically carved into the stones, iron braziers aglow with unnatural fire adorning the walls. It was everything it had ever been, and so much more.

He waved his hands again, then clapped them together, making a dreadful popping sound. A strand of reddish light shot from his grasp, aimed at the ground. It reflected and spun up like a tornado, growing in size and intensity, until it was at least half his height.

"What is this?" Redcap barked.

"There is another task yet to do, which I have no time for. The little one who saw us kill that Templar fool? I probed her mind while she watched us. She is an illuminator; she makes pictures. That is a useful skill, dear Redcap. If I am to be free of you, and you of me, I have need of her talents. She will create the sigils I shall need painted on the floor to awaken the dragons in the egg. When she is done, you may do with her as you wish."

He could feel Redcap grinning.

The whirlwind of light spun faster now, and a dark figure took shape inside of it. The lights sparked and hissed and gave way, fading to reveal a grotesque creature. It was half the size of a grown man, with long arms stretching almost to the ground ending in sharp talons, and short but muscular legs, with something like an eagle's beak for a mouth. And yet, its appearance was similar to a frog, like some horrid, twisted version of Blip. Its eyes glowed red, and when it opened its mouth, it hacked out an awful sound and revealed jagged teeth and a grey, forked tongue. It spoke no words, but eyed de Soulis with curiosity, as if unsure of the Shadow's identity.

"Ah, Croakbeak, my old pet. How delightful to see you again after so long. Yes, it really is me! I shall be happy to explain all in due course, but now, there is an important task that I wish you to perform."

Croakbeak grunted and nodded.

De Soulis projected a series of images into the creature's head. It swayed back and forth for a few moments, then grunted and nodded its head again that it understood. The lights whipped up and circled around it again in a fantastic display; then it was gone with a cloud of smoke and the stench of ozone.

De Soulis turned his attention once again to his reborn fortress. He basked in his work and imagined all that he would accomplish from here. He waved his hand a final time, and now, a stairway opened in the floor, until then hidden by his powerful wards until they could be unlocked again. De Soulis picked up the master egg, cradled it in his arms and walked down, down into the darkness and back into his ancient lair, where tonight, he would release the dragons and unmake the world.

CHAPTER FIFTEEN

Qwyrk was back on Earth, sitting on a rocky outcropping at Sutton Bank in the Yorkshire Moors, watching the morning mist fade in the summer light and feeling devastated and alone. As she'd moved farther and farther from Qwyzz's mansion into the thick clusters of trees, she began to feel uneasy. She wanted to get to her favorite place in the forest, where somehow, teleporting always seemed easier; it was a magical hotspot, or something. She'd been in such a hurry to leave Symphinity that this was the first location she thought to transport to, a favorite place of peace and tranquility when she needed to get away from it all. It was hardly that now, since the whole horrible situation raced through her mind over and over.

"Qwyzz is missing, betrayed by someone, or maybe he's actually the traitor. If he's not dead, he might be working against us. De Soulis has the big egg, and he's going to let loose the dragons any time. Crap."

Her hopes of getting some answers now seemed gone, and she couldn't bear facing Jilly and Blip just yet. There was one more option.

"It's up to the Templars and me now," she sighed, "I don't even know where to find them. Whatever's been clouding our minds must have got to them, too. If only Simon had told me where..."

She stood up and focused. A flash home and a moment later, and she stood in a copse near St. Cornelly's. Things were quiet and peaceful, but damn it, her head hurt!

"And *that* is why you don't do those kinds of teleportations too often, you cow!"

She looked around. "Seems all right," she said with relief. "So I guess de Soulis hasn't bothered to come back here yet and massacre everyone. Hooray. Now to go get Simon."

With no time to worry about barging past people this time, she walked across the lawn and right up to the front doors. No one was around at the moment, and she knew she'd be harder to see in broad daylight, anyway. She strode into the institution, walking past a young man at the reception desk who took no notice of her, as he seemed busy rocking out and head-banging to whatever music was playing in his headphones. Grateful for that bit of heavy metal distraction, she made her way upstairs and went straight to Simon's room. In spite of the urgency, she knocked, figuring he at least deserved some privacy and respect.

There was no answer, so she tried again. Still nothing. Her hand went for the door knob.

"I hope I don't have to break it in, because I really don't want to have to morph through it!"

To her relief, it was unlocked, but this set off alarms in her head. Sure enough, the room was empty. No Qwypp, no Qwykk, and no Simon.

"Crap!" she swore, frantic and looking around for signs of a struggle. There were none, but there was a folded piece of pink paper on the unslept-in bed. She snatched it up and opened it:

Dearest Qwyrk,

I know this is a long shot, but in case you come back here, Qwykk and I left I've enchanted this paper so that no one can see these words but you, in case you find it We were watching Simon last night like you asked, but then he wanted us to patrol the perimeter. We did, but a Nighttime Nasty named Horatio (says he know you?) showed up and told us there was way more going on than we knew (he was actually pretty helpful, go figure), so we rushed back here, only to find that Simon had gone. I think he lied to us to get rid of us, and then went off to fight whatever it is you're also dealing with. We're going to go back home and try to find out more, and maybe figure out where he is. Sorry about this, we really were just trying to do the right thing. Hope you're all right, please take care and get in touch as soon as you can.

Love,

Qwypp and Qwykk xxxx

Qwyrk half crumpled up the paper and let out a long sigh.

"Great, so now Simon's probably on a guilt trip and thinks he's going to go kick de Soulis' arse single-handed. Dumb and Dumber have gone back to the same place I just ran from, and they're going to get captured themselves or killed. And I still don't know how to find the Templars!"

She slumped on the bed and another wave of despair washed

over her, when she noticed a small amulet on the far corner of the nightstand. She picked it up and looked it over. It was engraved with a Templar cross on the front, and some Latin letters on the back that didn't seem to spell any recognizable words. It had a hinge, rather like a locket, so she opened it into its two halves. A green glow emanated from inside, but she couldn't see anything else. The light was hypnotic, and she tried to pull her gaze away from it, but couldn't. It held her, and now she sensed a presence in her mind, but not something evil or probing. It was more almost... bureaucratic? She was a bit like a phone caller who had been put into a queue, asked to press numbers, and subjected to 1980s smooth jazz. Except in this case, it was Gregorian chant.

What the hell? she thought.

It all became clear a moment later, when shifting images of knights in white tunics flooded her mind. Someone was communicating with her.

"You're one of the Templars! Brilliant! Look, I need your help, and..."

She couldn't finish her sentence. A voice sounded in her head:

Simon has gone and left this for you to find. He is taking his fight to de Soulis at Hermitage Castle, where the sorcerer now works to be reborn. We will be there as soon as we can. You must go, as well. There are no other Shadows we can trust. We have been betrayed. Someone from your world knows more than you and has helped de Soulis with his plans. Be on guard, and have caution for those you care for. All are vulnerable. Go. Go now to Hermitage, but wait for us when you arrive. The amulet will take you there.

She tried to ask in her head for more information, but the voice faded and the glow in the amulet receded. She had the strange feeling of having just listened to a mystical voice mail message. She closed it and put it back on the nightstand. She sat there for a few moments, taking it all in.

"Someone's betrayed us... who? Why? What on this Earth could they hope to gain by helping that sack of scum?" She shook her head. "Right. Now, do I go there, or do I check in with Blip and Jilly first?" She wanted to see her young friend again, especially after all that had just happened, but the danger at Hermitage was pulling on her.

"I could lose valuable time. I can't wait for the Templars to show up there. I have to try something. I'm sorry Jilly! I'll explain it all when it's over, if we're all still around!"

She stood up and concentrated on sending herself to that awful place.

"It's a long jump, longer than I'd usually make, but hopefully, they've set this up to work. It's probably going to hurt, though; not what I want to do before the fight of my life."

But she closed her eyes, focused on sending herself into the æther, and willed it to be so. In a moment she was gone, and the amulet fell back onto the nightstand.

* * *

"Now, just a damned minute young man!" Blip started with great annoyance. "I appreciate that you are a loyal follower of mine, and you've indeed shown yourself to be rather useful, despite your wretched appearance, but I think it's fair to say that all of this nonsense about you being in contact with higher spirits and galactic committees is just that: pure rubbish, balderdash, and bunk! I can't imagine why such entities, if they even existed, and I'm not implying that they do, would want to say whatever it is they have to say through you. It simply makes no sense!"

"I can't explain it, either, oh lord, I just know that I've always been able to do it, and from what I read in the book, I think I have a good shot at gettin' in touch with this Rhymer chap. See, he's an artist, like meself, and I have an affinity with other artists, on this plane and others. Except Jim Morrison; you never did tell me what happened with him..."

Blip just stared at him with a clueless expression. "I've no idea what you're on about."

"What exactly do you want to do?" Jilly asked, looking desperate but willing to give him the benefit of the doubt.

"I have to open meself up to him. There's some of his magic poetry in here, and I think if I put that out to the greater beyond, maybe chant it out loud, it'll attract his attention. He probably doesn't hear it much these days."

Jilly looked skeptical and sighed as she settled back in on the couch next to the dog.

"Look, I've done it before," he said, seeing her disbelief. "And if I can get ahold of him, I can have him talk through me, and tell us what to do. He knows that de Soulis bastard better than anyone, and it's our best shot."

Jilly took the book, looked at it, and tried reading an excerpt from the Tristan story:

> "This semly somers day,
> In winter it is nought sen;
> This greves wexen al gray,
> That in her time were grene.
> So dos this world, Y say,
> Ywis and nought at wene,
> The gode ben al oway
> That our elders have bene."

"Huh?" she said squinting and trying to read it again. "I'm quite sure I wasn't saying that even remotely correctly."

"It's the opening of his poem about Tristan and Isolde, the doomed lovers of Arthurian legend," Blip offered, having peered over her shoulder, one eye on the text and one eye on Odin, lest the beast get too close. "A rather fitting passage, I should say, about a lovely summer's day remembered, and how now winter is here, and how the good has gone out of the world... So, do you really think you can contact him? Do you even know how to pronounce the language?"

"Well, I'll just have to wing it, won't I? I find that when the energies take over, it ain't so much me doin' the talkin', anyway. That's what channellin' is, right? You're letting the entity do the talking, but it uses your voice. I'll just have to let the spirits guide me."

Jilly looked at Blip with some resigned desperation. "It's worth a shot." She shrugged. "What else are we going to do?"

Blip looked away for a moment, quite certain that a grand metaphor about a train running off a cliff's edge, or a swimmer being swallowed by a shark, or a train running off a cliff's edge and then being swallowed by a shark, was appropriate at this moment, but was unable to form it properly, so he let it pass.

"Very well," he said, with a dismissive wave of his hand. "Begin doing... whatever it is you do..."

"There's not much to it, really," Star Tao said, sitting down, cross-legged on the living room floor. "I just have to get comfortable and let me mind go blank."

An easy task, Blip mused.

"Jilly, let me have the book again, and I'll try just reading that little bit of it, the part you just read."

She passed it over to him, and he started reading aloud, over and over.

Blip was not familiar with the English/Scottish dialect of the text, but he was fairly sure that Star Tao's pronunciation was closer to Martian than to saying it correctly. Still, he went along with it, if for no other reason than they had no other other ideas.

After five or six repeats with no result, Jilly began to shift around a little on the couch. She looked at Blip.

He looked at the spectacle in front of them, and sighed. "Perhaps this is not the best use of our time," he started.

"Shhh! Uh, I mean no offense, my lord, but I'm just getting started. Have some patience."

Now that Star Tao had memorized his version of it (sort of), he closed his eyes and began swaying back and forth, putting his arms forward and paddling as if he were swimming. Blip had thought this couldn't get any more ridiculous, but knew now he was a tad mistaken..

After another three repeats of the verse, Blip had had about enough. He prepared to get up and leave the young man to do this all day if he wanted, when something happened. A red light began to form in the air above the carpet behind Star Tao. It grew until it was several lights, swirling and rising up, like a small tornado.

"Jilly!" he whispered. "Look there!"

She was already eyeing it. "Maybe it's actually working!" she whispered back. "He seems stuck into whatever he's doing."

"I don't know; I've never seen anything like this before. If the Rhymer wanted to speak through him, why would he need a light show?"

"Maybe it's what he does? I don't know, but we should be quiet and let him finish. Something's happening!"

The swirl had grown to the size of half a grown man now.

"Jilly, I don't like this. Something about it feels wrong. I say, young man! Stop whatever you're doing now! You've conjured up something, the likes of which I've never seen. Stop it! Stop it now!"

Star Tao opened his eyes, looking dazed. "What? What's going on?"

In the next moment, Croakbeak stood in the room, glaring at them with its hateful stare. It glanced about, and seeing Jilly, made for her with astonishing speed. In a second, it was before her and reached out. She shrieked as it grabbed her in its rough claws and threw her over its shoulder, turning to leave.

"Jilly!" Blip yelled, and threw himself at the monster.

Odin growled and launched himself at the thing, burying his teeth in Croakbeak's right leg. The monster howled and tried to shake the dog off, while Jilly pounded on its back. Blip leapt in front of it, throwing punches that had little effect. Star Tao was still so dazed from his self-induced trance that he hadn't even turned around yet.

"Let me go, damn you!" Jilly yelled, but its grip just seemed to tighten.

"Jilly, hold on! We'll get you!" Blip cried, but he could do nothing. The creature brushed him aside with no effort.

Star Tao turned about and jerked his head around, trying to clear his mind. "What the effin' hell? That's not supposed to happen!"

Croakbeak shook itself again and managed to dislodge Odin, who flew through the air and landed face-first on the couch. He turned and growled and prepared to pounce again, but the monster just waddled away, ignoring them all. As it returned to where it had materialized, the lights swirled around and encircled it.

"No!" shouted Blip, and he jumped at the creature, prepared to do anything to save Jilly. He was too late and crashed to the floor. In a flash of stinking ozone, Croakbeak was gone, taking her with it.

* * *

Qwypp groaned and opened her eyes. Her head hurt, her hands were tied behind her back, and her feet were tied at the ankles. She shook her head and looked around. She was leaning up against a stone wall. It was cool and dark, and smelled old and damp. She saw the barrels in the gloom and realized she was in a wine cellar. Qwykk lay nearby on her side on the floor, still unconscious. Her hands and feet were bound, too, but at least her olive green jumper and camouflage trousers were a bit more practical; the high-heeled combat boots... not so much.

Qwypp tried to clear her head and remember what had happened. After they left Simon's and made a quick wardrobe change, they'd gone back to Symphinity.

We came back to the spot in the Elder Wood, she thought, *but it was really dark. Okay, right, so then what? We walked for a bit. It seemed like we were being followed... oh, crap! Yeah, something hit us from behind; didn't even see it coming.*

"And now we're here," she said, "wherever that is. I'm sorry Qwyrk. We really effed it up."

Qwykk moaned and stirred.

"Qwykk!" she whispered, "come on girl, wake up! We're in trouble!"

She edged herself over to her friend and tried to nudge her awake.

"Qwypp?" she breathed. "What's happening? Where are we? My head hurts."

"Mine does too, love. Look, we got ambushed. Something hit us from behind when we got back to the wood. Now we're stuck in this place, some kind of wine cellar, but it could be anywhere. We may even be back on Earth. It's too dark to tell. Here, come on, try to sit up."

Qwykk struggled and managed to get herself upright. She leaned on a barrel and tried to shake her voluminous hair out of her face.

"It's amazing how you can do that, "Qwypp quipped.

"What?"

"That. That whole stylish thing. Even when we're somebody's prisoners and stuck in a cellar, you still manage to look gorgeous." She grinned.

Qwykk returned a weak smile. "Aw, thanks! It's a gift."

"We've got to find a way out of here."

"We can't even stand, how are we going to do that?"

"I don't know... look, do you get a sense of any magic around? You're good at that. We could at least find out if we're home or on Earth."

"I can't tell, really. I think I'm still too messed up from being smacked on the head. Oh Qwypp, what're we gonna to do?"

"Right, let's not panic. Whoever did this didn't kill us, so we must be worth something to them alive. It's like they just wanted us out of the way."

"You don't think it was Horatio and the Nasties, do you?"

"No, why would he warn us if they were just going to kidnap us later? He was telling us to go back to Simon, not away from him."

"I suppose. I wish Qwyrk had told us more."

"Me too, but you know her. Little miss know-it-all has to do everything on her own. She thinks we're too bloody stupid to handle things by ourselves."

"Well, we did make a right mess of this, didn't we? And we don't even know... if she's still alive."

A pang of guilt hit Qwypp as she heard these words. "Yeah, you're right, that wasn't fair of me. I'm worried about her, too. Look, Qwyrk and Simon were onto something, something they had to go and fight. It's got to be why Simon did the vanishing act. I'm guessing this is all tied to why we were even asked up north in the first place. Something really bad is going on; I mean, we came back home, looking for answers and help, and we get the lights smacked out of us within minutes of showing up. Somebody doesn't want us finding out, or trying to help."

"So what do we do?"

"For starters, we get the hell out of here, and then we start smacking some heads together to get answers. I'm tired of being nice and doing this Qwyrk's way. We'll show them we're not as stupid as they think, and that they messed with the wrong couple of Shadows!"

* * *

"You utter, complete, useless *idiot!*" Blip shouted as he punched and kicked Star Tao over and over, who was curled up in a fetal position on the floor while his lord administered a divine pounding. Blip jumped up and down in between hits and seemed on the verge of bursting something, if gods could, in fact, do that. "What the blue blazes did you conjure up, and where has it gone?"

"I don't know, lord, I swear! I didn't do it! It's not possible for channeling to work that way! It's like a telephone, not a fax! It doesn't bring things over to where you are. That's *never* happened before, I swear. And could you PLEASE stop hitting me, it hurts!"

"It's supposed to hurt, you pillock! And how do you know that you didn't manifest whatever that horrid abomination was? Your chanting could have opened some sort of extra-dimensional door to let that thing in, some diabolical wyrm-tunnel or whatever in perdition those scientists call those things. That creature could have gone back to whatever plane of existence it came from, and we'll never see Jilly again!"

"Wait! Whatever it was, it went for Jilly, right, not me, and I was closer to it. That means, it was looking for her, not us. That means it came here to get her specifically. Maybe it wasn't an accident, maybe he sent for her!"

"Possibly," Blip said, giving Star Tao one final punch before hopping up onto the couch to think. "But why? What would be so important about her? She's just a child."

"She has something that he wants, that he needs." The voice came from an elderly woman who stood in the doorway. She wore a simple brown wool dress with a grey jumper and a scarf tying back her long grey hair. "I'm sorry, you left the door open, so I thought I would let myself in, what with all that commotion that you just kicked up. I'm quite sure half the neighborhood has heard you by now."

"And who are you, madame?" Blip asked in an icy tone, still too furious to think clearly. "I'm in no mood to chit-chat." He didn't even stop to wonder why she could see him.

"Yeah," Star Tao rolled over and stood up, rubbing his aching parts. "And how do you know anything about this? What's your name?"

"Oh, I have many names, young man," she replied, letting herself in and closing the front door behind her. "I've been around a lot longer than you can imagine, and I've seen some terrible things in my life. But this town, this place, has always been my home, so I adapted and just went with the times. It's a bit of a nexus for weird and wonderful activity, so I suppose I shouldn't be surprised."

"Madame," Blip said, "it would help us greatly if you would tell us who you are. You seem to know something, so out with it. I mean no disrespect, but we have had a fairly dreadful twenty-four hours and things are only going to get worse..."

"Unless you and your friends can stop what he's about to unleash," she finished the sentence. "I know. I've dealt with him before. It was ugly then, and it's going to be worse now. These days I live across the street from this house and go by the name of Agnes Burdockweed. But back in the older times, folks around here knew me as Grandmother Boatford."

Blip stared, incredulous. "My dear lady, I am, for the sake of the heinous events that have transpired here these past few days, prepared to believe many improbable things, such as this vagabond being able to communicate with beings from outer space, or some such rubbish, but I hardly think that you can expect me to take in and accept the fact that you are, in fact, a 400-plus-year-old woman..."

"More like 650, actually," she interjected with a grin.

"...standing before me looking exceedingly healthy, despite your age, and I mean no offense, of course."

"None taken. But, Simon's older than me, and he stood guard over de Soulis and Redcap for centuries."

"Yes, but that's different... he's a Templar knight and his order is ancient and it wields powerful magics, and..."

"And I didn't? My prophecies were legendary, Mr. Blippingstone. They still are to this day. Of course, I threw in a few phonies once in a while. It kept people on their toes and taught them a valuable lesson. But the point is, my magic was strong, and given the severity of the whole business of keeping de Soulis in a box, I didn't like the idea of Simon being alone here, even in this out-of-the-way place. So, I chose to stick around, offer him some help, and counsel others as best I could. As the centuries passed, I simply gave up on the idea of passing over." Her expression turned more grim. "But I tell you, if de Soulis has his way, we'll all be passing over far sooner than we would like."

Blip relaxed his defiant stance, now a bit more convinced. "Well, what are we going to do? Something just took Jilly, thanks to this wastrel, and now we have two problems to confront."

"Oh, the boy had nothing to do with that," she said.

Star Tao's face brightened, and he flashed a smug grin. "Thank you, ma'am, that's what I've been sayin'."

Blip rolled his eyes.

"That thing was sent here by de Soulis to take the girl. He needs her for something. I suspect it's because she's an artist, and he needs someone with a physical body to draw his magical sigils and symbols and such, whatever he's going to use to finish the process of hatching the master egg, giving himself a new body, all of that. He must have seen her before?"

"She saw him," Star Tao answered. "Saw him kill somebody, and then she ran away, and bumped into Qwyrk."

"The young Templar," she answered with a hint of sadness. "Yes, that's just the beginning of what he'll do. He must have sensed her talents and spared her so that she could perform his tasks later. He's probably had his mind set on her since his escape."

"Ha! She'll never do it," Blip said with defiance. "I know her. She's good, noble, and strong. He's mad to think that she will enact his foul plans."

"She will if she thinks that he'll harm you, or Qwyrk, or her parents, or anyone else, and that is precisely how he'll threaten her."

Blip's heart sank. "So what do we do?"

"You finish what you started."

"Eh?"

"You go after him, and this boy contacts the Rhymer for help."

"What?" Star Tao and Blip said in unison.

"Dear lady, you don't really believe that this nonsense will work, surely?" Blip asked.

"I think that you undervalue him, and yourself, Mr. Blippingstone. Now, both of you, come here and take my hands. I'll send you after him, but the rest is up to you."

*   *   *

Jilly struggled, but the beast held on to her with its vice-like grip. They had passed through a bright red flash, and she could see through her dizziness that they were in a stone chamber. Dim light from candles flickered all around them. Still slung over Croakbeak's shoulder, she had a poor vantage point, and tried to move around to get a better sense of the room.

"Damn it, you're strong!" she swore.

"It has to be," a deep and ominous voice said, resonating against the rocky walls. "It is carrying a most valuable prize, one that I could not risk losing."

The voice sent chills through her. It was him. Unable to see him, she spoke again. "I saw you, a few days ago. You murdered someone by the river and threw the body in the water. You tried to get into my head then, but you..."

"I let you go? Yes, I did. I saw into your thoughts, that your illuminating talents would serve me, but I had more important matters to attend to. I knew I could find you again, so I let you be. Little did I know you were going to make things so easy by associating with that idiotic frog-thing and the foolish Shadow girl. They practically sweat magic; it was like you had a bright candle glowing over you the whole time. And I sensed that you were nearby last night, but that damned Templar wounded me just enough that I thought it wiser to leave.

"No matter. Croakbeak has been a most helpful servant in bringing you to me. I freed it before I freed myself, you know, so it could go and search for my prize. It found the wyrmroost and your foolish friends, but I kept it from feeding on them; it wasn't time. You're welcome."

He turned to face the creature. "Leave her here, my pet, and go, I will summon you again later."

It growled and set her down, softer than she would have expected. It lumbered off and seemed to disappear into the shadows beyond the candlelight's reach.

Jilly stood up and turned around to see her captor. She wished she hadn't. He stood towering above her, seven feet tall, at least. Even in the dim glimmering light, she could see his Shadow form, human shaped, almost muscular, with two glowing red eyes, eyes that burned with hatred and evil, with revenge and cruelty. He peered into her mind again, probing her thoughts, invading her secrets. It was horrible, could all Shadows do this? She tried to fight him, but he overpowered her with no effort. She felt tears coming to her eyes, even though she was in no pain.

"Stop!" she yelled out. "Please!"

And then it was gone. Her mind was her own again, but it was like he had taken something, stolen thoughts that were not his.

"Yes," he said. She sensed he was smiling, even though she could see no face. "This will do nicely. You are a fine illuminator and your work will suffice."

Jilly shook with fear, but she mustered up as much defiance as she could offer, determined not to let him see her terror, even if he could read her mind. "What do you mean, 'illuminator'? I have no idea what you're talking about! You've got the wrong person, and when my friends get here, you're going to get your arse kicked!"

De Soulis let burst a condescending chuckle. "Oh yes, the frog-creature, the bravado-laden Shadow, and the noble young Templar. They caught me unawares, when I was drained of energy in bringing forth the egg; it will not happen again."

His voice changed into a raspy growl. "Let me open her throat when you are finished! That will teach her to speak so to her betters!"

"Be silent!" the original voice countered. "I will do as I have planned and you will not interfere!"

The second voice growled.

Jilly, who should have been numb with terror, was more curious than anything. *What the hell? There really* **are** *two of them in there! That's right creepy!*

If de Soulis understood her thoughts, he said nothing.

"You make pictures, am I correct?" de Soulis said, interrupting her confusion.

"Yes, yes I do. You already know that, so I'm not going to deny it. What does it matter to you, anyway?"

He chuckled at her attitude. "Normally such insolence from a small rat would infuriate me, but I like you, child. Your defiance amuses me. I'm glad to see it, in fact. It shows you have a head of your own and won't collapse in a sobbing heap."

"Oh, you'll never see me do that, you bastard!" Jilly was working up a head of steam now.

The growl emitted again. Jilly lost some of her confidence.

"It is because of that," he continued, "that you are obviously intelligent enough to understand me. You will use your skills in illumination to make the signs and sigils that I need to complete my work. You shall have the paints and inks that you need, and will draw them as instructed on the floor of this chamber. While I could do so myself, it is time-consuming. I have many other tasks to attend to, and I suspect that you will be far better at it. This Shadow body is good for killing, not for art. Accuracy is quite important for these things, you see. Errors can lead to... complications."

"What complications? What will this do? Where the hell are we?"

"I shall not tell you; you know all that you must. And we are in my home, of course, Hermitage Castle. Well, not exactly as it is in your own time, but I have set about re-creating it to look as it once did. I must say the fortifications that were erected after my supposed death are most impressive, so I have kept those. I am remaking the interior, however, to remind me of those days when I was master of these lands."

"I don't care what you've done! I'm not drawing or painting anything that will help you!"

"Oh, you will, little one, you will. As I have said, I see that you are possessed of a good mind, a rare quality in a female, to be sure..."

Jilly scowled, wanting to hit him. But she knew it would be useless—and probably painful—so she held back.

"Therefore you understand the idea of consequences. If you will not help me, I will let Redcap rip out your friends' throats, one by one, in front of you. Oh, they will come for you, if that is a comfort to you at all. But they will fail. They will perish. Then it will be your turn."

Redcap's delighted laugh escaped from him.

"Or, you can do the work that I require, and perhaps, just perhaps, I will let all of you live. I will need servants in the new world that we will create, and it would be foolish to simply kill those who could be useful in some capacity."

Jilly had the passing thought that she was being lectured by an evil version of Blip.

"Even the Shadow may have her... uses," Redcap's voice cackled.

Jilly didn't want to know what that meant, so she just answered, "Well, I suppose in that case, I can't really say no, can I?"

"Not if you wish to avoid dying painfully, no."

"Right, then, so what do I do?"

She could sense him smiling again.

"You will paint a magical circle according to the dimensions that I give to you, here." He pointed at the floor where he stood. "You will need to draw seven sigils at precise points, again as I indicate. Each is important and represents a stage in the magical work. I will provide you with a parchment that shows the signs, and you will copy them exactly. A candle will be placed at each of the points to illuminate your work. It will not take long, but I need precision, and that is why I chose you. Fortune has favored me indeed that you were the first that I saw! You see? It is my destiny!"

Jilly looked at the floor. "How will I know where to start?"

"Ah yes, there I can help you." He raised his left hand and made a clockwise circling motion. A perfect circle of yellow light appeared on the floor, burned into the stone, with seven points marked equidistantly around it.

"You may now draw according to the pattern. Simply trace the line I have given you. You see? It is not difficult, and you will be finished in due time. I ask little of those whom I would have serve me. Do well, and I may be merciful, perhaps even generous. I shall leave you now. The paints and brushes you need are there, behind me, the sigil patterns on a sheet of vellum next to them. And, lest you think of running in my absence, Croakbeak stands guard in the dark, beyond your ability to see. Cease your work, or attempt to flee, and it will stop you. I honestly do not wish for it to harm you, but I cannot guarantee your safety. It is... rather wild, you see, despite my holding it in check."

"And what if it hurts me so badly that I can't finish your signs?" Jilly asked with smugness, thinking she had him.

"Then you will die."

De Soulis strode past her and disappeared into the same shadows as his foul courier. Redcap let out one final snort, maybe as a warning?

Foiled, Jilly sat back down for a moment looking at the glowing circle. She waited until she was sure he was gone, trying to keep her mind as blank as possible, in case he was somehow listening in. After a few minutes, she relaxed a bit. There was no real fear, just belligerence.

If he thinks I'm going to help him at all, he's a right idiot! She decided.

CHAPTER SIXTEEN

Blip and Star Tao emerged right after they left Jilly's home (or maybe a bit before) from a four-dimensional bubble surrounded by sparkling blue lights, materializing at the base of some low rolling hills that were rather barren and windswept. The sky overhead was grey, threatening rain.

"It seems far darker than it should be for mid-morning at this time of year," Blip noted. "It's also too quiet."

"Cor, that was groovy!" Star Tao blurted out, shaking his head and looking around at his new surroundings. "One minute we were at Jilly's, and now we're in this place. It was like we de-materialized and our atomic essences were shot through a tesseract, and reassembled in a nanosecond back on the prime material plane, but hundreds of miles away! That has got to be one of the most excellent experiences of me life!"

"Shhh! Keep your voice down, you miscreant!" Blip whispered harshly, looking a bit nauseated. "I have no idea what in the blazes you're taking about, and I don't care! We're here! And he could have spies everywhere!"

"Right! Sorry, my lord," Star Tao whispered back, regretting his enthusiasm. "What do we do now? I await your command."

"You're going to have to summon him: the Rhymer, Thomas. Somehow, you're going to have to contact him and ask him what on this Earth we're to do, because I must admit, for once, I have absolutely no idea. Yes, it's true. Even gods can be at a loss at times, however rare it might be."

"Don't worry, lord," Star Tao answered with a smile, wanting to pat him on the back, but not daring to be so presumptuous. "Everyone doubts at times. I mean, you didn't see that I had nothing to do with Jilly's getting taken, either. Uh, maybe I shouldn't have brought that up. Sorry."

Blip harrumphed, but said nothing else.

"Right," Star Tao continued, eager to make amends to his deity, "um, I'm gonna have a go, yeah? We'll see what happens. I think I still got that poem in me head, and maybe out here, I'll have a better connection."

"So, it's like one of those blasted mobile phones, is it?"

"Uh, not really, well... yeah, all right, a bit. But I just figured that since he was here all those centuries ago, right, maybe he's still got a connection to this place, a psychic link of some kind. Maybe he checks in on it once in a while."

"I suppose it's worth a try. Granny Boatford seems to think you can do it, Goddess knows why. Do... whatever you're going to do. Right now, it's all we've got. I'm going to make a quick reconnaissance of the area, and perhaps see what strategies may best avail us. Cheerio!"

SIXTEEN

* * *

Blip left him behind and climbed to the summit of the nearest hill. Looking out east, he could see the ruin of Hermitage in the distance. No, not a ruin. It looked as it might have done 600 years ago, rebuilt with a roof. It was a solid castle, almost like a dark stone cube set amongst the rolling hills, bleak and windy, a terrible place where terrible things had happened. A strange orange-red light emanated from the keep, lighting up the surroundings.

"Well, he's already gotten started on whatever the hell he's up to," Blip mused. "We must assume that Qwyrk was not successful." A slight tear formed in his eye, which he wiped away in haste. "Damned shame, that! I had my differences with her, but she could be quite the force in a fight. She won't be forgotten. *Requiescat in pace.* I suppose it's down to the Bohemian and me."

"Well, I wouldn't very well trust your chances in that case," said an impish voice behind him.

Blip almost cried out in shock as he turned to see a grinning Qwyrk standing a few feet down the hill behind him.

"Qwyrk! Damn you! You gave me a dreadful fright!" He ran toward her and jumped into her arms, almost knocking her backward, hugging her tightly. "Oh, thank all the powers! I was sure we were finished! Where have you been? What's been happening?"

Qwyrk winced at his new-found affection and at his iron-clad grip, tried to put him back down on the ground. "Now I know how Jilly felt," she mused under her breath.

"What?"

"Nothing."

Prying his arms off of her, she said, "We don't have the time for me to tell you everything, but it's bad, Blip. And why are you here, by the way? Don't tell me you left Jilly alone!"

Blip knew there was no sense in trying to hide what had happened.

"It's worse than you think, actually. De Soulis has her."

"What?" Qwyrk's face changed to an expression of horror.

Before she could even give him the verbal flaying that they both knew was coming, he interjected, "And before you blame me, understand this: de Soulis had marked her out as a target from the moment he saw her by the river. He needs her for something, and no, I'm not quite sure what, drawing magical symbols or some such. He sent a foul beast to kidnap her out of her home, right in front of us. It just showed up in her living room, snatched her, and vanished. There was absolutely nothing we could do; the young scoundrel down there will verify it. And if you don't believe me, you can go ask Grandmother Boatford, who apparently is still alive, thank you very much, and just happens to be living a comfortable modern suburban life in obscurity right across the street from Jilly and her family. It was she who sent us here, in some sort of magical, four-dimensional tetrahedral... triangular... triceratops... something or other. And so here we are. Yes, it's a ridiculous plot twist that wouldn't be welcome in a hack's first novel, but there you have it!"

Qwyrk looked as if her mind was reeling. "I feel sick, light-headed. Everything's just gone from really bad to utterly terrible in one go."

"Look, he's not going to kill her," Blip continued, seeing her distress. "Get yourself together! We haven't time for anger or senti-mentalities! He needs her, but he'll no doubt be counting on us to come and rescue her. The bigger point is, how do we do it? How do we play into that without getting ourselves killed? And how do we stop him? The end of the world is nigh, and our brave Jilly needs our help!"

Qwyrk took a few deep breaths, and Blip sensed a small amount of calm returning to her.

"You're right, Blip, as much as I hate to admit it. But this just makes things even worse. It's bad over there. Someone has betrayed us and is working with de Soulis. Qwyzz is missing. His wife is distraught. Everything's going to hell. The old Templar, Simon, has decided to make things right by coming here, apparently on his own. I have no idea what he thinks he can do. You haven't seen him, have you?"

Blip shook his head. "It's just me and the lad down there."

Qwyrk glanced down at him. Star Tao was seated cross-legged on the ground and seemed to be murmuring words. He was swaying back and forth with his eyes closed.

"I know I'm going to regret asking this, but what's he doing?"

"Hmm? Oh, channeling the Rhymer, of course. Thomas, that is. We think that if he can make contact, Thomas might be able to tell us how to defeat de Soulis, since he did it once before. Yes, that's how desperate we've become."

"Any chance of it working?" she asked, looking down at him blankly.

"Not one in a million, I'd say. But Granny Boatford seems to think that he has it in him. So, who am I to argue with northern England's greatest seeress?"

"All right, the whole idea that Granny Boatford is still alive is just starting to sink in," she said, "and it's bloody bonkers! Wait... you said she lives across the street from Jilly? And she sent you both here?"

"All true, I say, as mad as it sounds. Now, that must count for something. Either it's the most outrageous coincidence to be found as this grand tale unfolds, or perhaps fate is guiding us somehow after all. Maybe destiny has deigned to smile down upon us small and fragile beings who fail utterly to comprehend her mysterious ways. Mayhaps, even Lady Fortune has granted us one last boon to aid us in..."

"Blip, not now. At least it's something. I must admit, I don't have much else to offer. I got a message saying that some Templar knights would be on their way, but I have no idea when or if they will. We can't wait for them." She turned and looked toward the keep. "That's it, eh?"

"Indeed. A devilish-looking place if ever there was one."

"I'm kind of surprised he hasn't posted misshapen minions all over the place to guard it, with big blades on the end of long sticks. Isn't that what these evil overlord types are supposed to do? Orcs and things? I feel like there should be a ring we're meant to destroy, or something."

"I rather suspect he is leaving an open invitation to us. Who else knows he's here? Or can do anything about it? He's goading us, asking us right into his home for a most unpleasant tea party. He has all the advantages right now, so why should he fear us? I suspect that if he had wanted us captured, he would have done so by now."

Qwyrk nodded and started down the hill toward Hermitage. "Come on then, I think we should leave astral boy down there to do his own thing. Who knows? Maybe he'll come up with something useful? He's safer there than going with us, anyway."

"But where are we going?" Blip asked, hastening to keep up with her.

"To the keep, of course."

"To do what, precisely?"

"I don't know," she grinned, "we'll think of something along the way."

* * *

"How are we going to get out of here?" Qwykk asked. "This is so frustrating. I don't like not being able to escape from being tied up. Unless, of course, I want it that way…"

"I don't know," Qwypp answered, changing the subject, "but these unbreakable ties mean that we're probably still at home. On Earth, we could've slipped out of them, no problem."

"Hey, yeah, you're right! So, does that mean someone's holding us by magic?"

"I'd imagine so. I just wish I knew where we are. We can hardly see in here at all. That's pretty odd by itself. Somebody's messing with us. Who do we know that has a wine cellar?"

"Lots of people, really."

"No one in particular? Like an old boyfriend or something?"

"What are you saying? That I have an ex who's a crazed kidnapper that wants to… blow up the world or something?"

"No, I'm just saying we have to think of all the possibilities. Maybe somebody has a grudge against us, or Qwyrk, I don't know. "

"Yeah, all right, fair enough. But I can't think of anyone who's that messed up. I mean, I've had my share of losers over the centuries, but none that… well, there was that one, what was his name? Weird and creepy bloke, it didn't last long. Sorry, I think I've blocked it out."

"Never mind," Qwypp said. "I had one of those, too. Creepy and angry. I was just tossing out ideas."

"So, what do we do?"

"Pssst!"

"Pssst, what?" Qwykk asked.

"I didn't say it!" Qwypp shot back. "Who's there?"

"Over here!" a tiny voice whispered. "I can help you."

"Who are you?"

"That is not important; it's best that you not know, so that I am not discovered. Just whisper again so that I can find you. My eyes are not as good now as when I was young!"

"We're over here," Qwykk offered.

"Qwykk, be quiet! We don't know who this is!"

"Oh, stop your whining! I am here to help. If I can find your hands and feet, I can release you from your bonds."

"Wait, how do you know we're tied up if you can't see us?" Qwypp queried.

"Because you would have already run away if you could have."

"All right, fair enough, we're over here."

They heard what sounded like a small animal—but heavier— make its way across the floor. Qwypp could feel something fiddling with the ropes binding her hands. It was like a stone tool cutting the fibers. In a moment, her wrists were free, and her rescuer worked on her ankle ties. These were unloosed, and then the creature moved on to Qwykk.

They were free in just a few moments, and stood up, stiff and aching, shaking their limbs out and regaining their balance.

"Right, so what do we do now?" Qwypp said.

"Follow the sound of my voice. I will lead you to a small side door, and from there you can escape. When you do, run! Don't dally outside."

The voice led them on. Though it sounded small, it was as if it were wearing heavy boots as it trotted along the stone floor of the cellar. Whatever it was, neither Qwypp nor Qwykk cared at this point.

"I can't see anything," Qwykk complained again.

"Shhh! And watch out!" it warned. "There are big barrels every-where. Just keep moving towards the sound of my voice. We're almost there."

They seemed to twist and turn and change directions several times. Soon, they heard their liberator again. "Now, in front of you, slow down and put your hands out. You will feel a door, with a large latch. It is unlocked. Use it to make your escape."

Qwypp did as the voice directed, and was delighted when she grasped the latch.

"Thank you, thank you so much! Can't you tell us who you are?"

"No, it is better that you do not know at this time. Perhaps later, if all is resolved. But understand that things are very dangerous right now, so be careful. Find your friend, the one called Qwyrk. I don't know where she is, maybe on Earth. Go there! You are not safe here. Now, farewell!"

And with that, whatever it was scampered off.

Qwypp turned the latch and pushed the door. The first rays of light peeked in, and she marveled at how well it had blocked the outside brightness.

"Bollocks, this'll be nasty," she said.

"It's going to be like the worst hangover ever, isn't it?" Qwykk asked. "My head already hurts."

"Worse, love. Squint and let's go. We're getting out of here!"

* * *

Jilly completed painting the circle, following the guide of the magical light de Soulis had left for her. Her knees and bum hurt and her back was sore from leaning over. Worse, she had black stains on her fingers, and they smelled horrible. Whatever it was, it wasn't normal paint; she didn't want to think about what might be in it. Now, even with a dark circle marked on the floor, the light still shone on either side of her lines. It was eerie. She gazed at the vellum with its strange symbols. It showed at which points they were to be painted and in what order. But they made no sense.

"This is ridiculous," she said to herself. "It's just a bunch of silly squiggles. What's he going to do with all of this?"

She examined the first design and studied its shape. It was geometric, a five-sided figure, but had smaller, more ornate markings inside. *They look like letters, but I can't read them,* she thought, deciding it would be better not to talk, just in case Croakbeak was still there somewhere in the darkness, listening, and it could understand her. She'd also decided against testing de Soulis' warning not to try to escape.

She looked again at the pattern, and then at where she was supposed to paint it on the floor. Each location was marked with a point of enchanted light, a small beacon that cast its own shadows across the rough stone floor. There was no ambiguity about where they were to be placed and how. *I can't put them in the wrong place, he'd see it right away,* she pondered in frustration. *But I don't want to do this the way he wants me too, because obviously, something terrible will happen.*

She sighed, and was about to resign herself to just getting on with it. Then she had an idea. It was bold, it was stupid, and would most likely fail.

*But he **did** say they have to be painted exactly as they are here...* She suppressed a smile, in case the beast was watching. *I can do that... sort of. It's worth a try.* Picking up a brush and the stinky paint, she knelt down and began work on the first sigil.

SIXTEEN

*   *   *

"So," Blip mused, "we're just going to walk into his dungeon, announce ourselves to his servants, and say 'Greetings, monsieur de Soulis, hope you're quite well, love what you've done with the place, we've arrived to hash things out at last, have a good scuffle, finish the job, and may the best team win!'" He and Qwyrk had reached the bottom of the hill. The path leading to Hermitage lay before them, open and without obstacles. The sky grew darker by the minute, and a few drops of rain were already falling.

"That's not such a bad idea," said a voice back down the path, coming from the direction of the visitor's center and parking lot. They turned to see an old man walking toward them. He was clad in chain mail, over which he wore a white tunic with a red cross on the front. He carried a sword at his side, and he strode with a confidence that seemed out of place.

"Simon," Qwyrk said, shaking her head and walking toward him. "No, no Simon, don't do this. It's suicide. I know you were the guardian for all those centuries, but this is different. His strength is unnatural now, and he'll kill you without even thinking about it."

"I think you rather underestimate me, my dear. I wasn't appointed to watch this monster for all that time because I was reckless and foolish. I've a good deal more fight in me than you might think. And I didn't come alone." He motioned with his head to look behind him. Qwyrk saw several knights, all dressed like Simon, carrying large swords, their heads covered by full helmets. They were an impressive sight, something not seen by many over the last 700 years.

"I could only muster twelve in such a short time, but that will be enough to make things difficult for our adversary." The knights arrived behind him and bowed their heads in salute to her, but kept the helmets on and said nothing.

Qwyrk smiled big, for the first time in a while. "So, should we just go knock on his door, then?"

"I think that's an excellent idea," Simon said. "He's not going to stop us. Given his arrogance, he either doesn't even know we're here, or he thinks it doesn't matter. Both could lead to his undoing."

"Goddess, I hope so," said Qwyrk. "I'm so sick and tired of this! I came up north to get away from all the chaos in London. I just wanted a bit of a break, and it's been a complete disaster."

"Well, when we're finished, you can have a long holiday."

"I intend to."

"This is spectacularly splendid!" Blip clapped his hands together. "It will be like the Armada in 1588 all over again, except on land, and with magic and dragons. But otherwise, just the same, just the same! We shall fight on the seas and oceans, we shall fight with growing confidence and growing strength in the air, we shall defend our island, whatever the cost may be. We shall fight on the beaches, we shall fight on the landing grounds, we shall fight in the fields and in the streets, we shall fight in the hills; we shall never surrender!"

"That was Churchill, Blip, not Queen Elizabeth."

"Yes, yes, I know, but it was a rousing speech regardless, and I see no reason why we can't mingle historical events for inspirational purposes. Damn it, woman! This is the best I've felt in days, don't ruin it! Sir Simon, you would not per chance, happen to have a suitable weapon? A sword? A dagger? A mace? I want to be in the thick of the fighting, dealing out appropriate punishment to these evil-doers."

"Blip, I'm not sure that's a good idea..."

"Here," Simon smiled, reaching into his boot and pulling out a stiletto-type blade. "Have this, and go forth to wreak havoc!"

"I really wish you hadn't said that," Qwyrk sighed.

Blip beamed and accepted the weapon. "And so I shall, good sir knight, so I shall! Ah, it will be a day of glory. And if we should fall, songs will ever be sung in our remembrance. Forward brave knights! Let us take this castle and save the day!"

And with that, he strode off toward the keep, dagger held high. Qwyrk almost put her face to her palm, but decided that for group morale, it was best to do nothing. She fell in with the knights, and off they went.

* * *

"How is your work proceeding, little one?" De Soulis' voice echoed off the stone walls. It sounded as cold as they were. Jilly couldn't see him beyond the glow of the candles (which never burned down, she noted). She shivered and tried to keep her thoughts under control again. If he suspected what she was planning...

"Well enough. These sigils are tricky, so I'm taking my time with them," she lied. They were actually easy. It was what she was doing to them that was the tricky part.

"Do not stall hoping that you will be saved, child. Your friends are already here." He glided into the light without a sound, his red eyes boring into her.

She gave him a look of surprise.

"Oh yes, the frog fool and the one with ropes for hair are out in the hills, quite nearby. I have no doubt that the others will arrive soon, if they yet live. I have help in other places, you see, so I cannot guarantee that they will be able to join us. But I do hope they can; it would be lovely to bring them all together for such a momentous occasion."

"Why are you doing this?" Jilly asked with a slight annoyance that was genuine not just bravado. "What are you trying to do?"

"Those questions are not your concern. Suffice to say that some are meant to rule, and most are meant to be ruled. I am among the former, you are among the latter. But, there is no shame in this. You are what you are, and you have uses, as I can see. Now, how is the work progressing?"

"I've done four of them, and the fifth is almost done," she said suppressing her anger at his arrogance, and wanting to ram her paintbrush down his throat, if she could find it.

"Good, very good. Let me see." He moved to the first sign and looked at it.

Please don't notice, please don't notice...

She almost sighed with relief when he nodded and moved to another.

"These will do, well done. Hurry now, child. Finish your work. Perhaps I will reward you by seeing what your labors are for. It will be quite beautiful, I can assure you."

"What? What are you going to show me? I have a right to know if I'm doing all the work to paint these!"

"Ha! You are a precocious one, indeed. I like that, but have a care not to test my patience too far. Very well, your insolence amuses me. I will show you soon. For now... work, and know that you are helping to create a new age in this world. Perhaps you will be rewarded for it, perhaps not. I'll see what my mood is when the deed is accomplished."

His shadow glided out of view again and into the darkness. She heard nothing, no door opening or shutting, no footsteps on stairs (if he even walked down stairs or walked at all), so she had no way of knowing where she was. And there was still no sound from the creature that had abducted her.

If only I could get Odin to be that still and quiet, she thought. She burst out laughing at her own joke and the absurdity of this whole situation. In response, she heard a low, nasty grunting coming from the shadows.

"Fine, all right, all right! I'm working!" she yelled out. Her heart raced. So that thing was still out there after all.

At least he didn't notice. She almost smiled.

＊　＊　＊

Qwypp and Qwykk emerged into the blinding light of day, squinting, swearing, hands over eyes, yet trying to be mindful of tripping.

"Shut the door," Qwypp whispered, "and be quiet! We don't want anyone to know we got out."

Qwykk closed the cellar door, and trying to stay quiet, they ran as fast as they could to the nearby forest, not looking back at where they'd been.

"Where are we?" Qwykk asked, barely able to see anything. "My head feels like it's burning up, and I'm dizzy."

"Mine too. I don't know where we are, and I don't even care. Come on, let's keep moving. We have to get as far away from here as we can. Someone may have already seen us. I'm not being put back in that old cellar."

They stumbled forward for a few minutes more, entering the more muted lighting of thick tree cover, and waiting to get their daylight sight back. All was quiet and peaceful.

"If we're being followed, they're doing a damned good job of hiding it," Qwypp observed. "Everything seems a little bit too normal. I don't like this. We're lost and basically helpless. Bollocks, what are we going to do?"

"Wait... this looks familiar," Qwykk remarked, looking around.

"Yeah, now that you mention it, you're right. I'd swear this is Elder Forest. I don't reckon I've been right in this spot before, but the trees are the same, the landscape's the same. We must have been held near where we arrived and got jumped."

"Who has a house or a cellar around here?"

"I don't know, but we'd better get out of here and head back to Earth."

"Fine, but what then?"

"Let's go back to Simon's room at that retirement home. Maybe there are some clues there, like where he went."

"That's not much to go on."

"Yeah, but it's all we've got right now. Come on, we'll go there first, and if we don't find anything, we'll think of something else."

"Like what?"

"Like... I don't know, we'll just come up with something. It's what we do, right? I mean, we can be brilliant, yeah? We've helped lots of people over the centuries. We can do this!"

Qwykk nodded. "Fine, but let's get going. Being here is makin' me nervous."

"Me too, come on take my hands and concentrate..."

A few moments later, they stood in a copse of trees looking at front entrance of St. Cornelly's. It was calm, though a few people milled about near the front doors.

"We don't have time to be sneaky," Qwypp said. "I vote we just barge right in. It's not like they're going to notice us much in this light, anyway. We know where we're going, so let's just get this over with."

Qwykk nodded, and with that, they stormed off across the lawn, and right up to the entrance. One elderly woman was standing between them and the doors, admiring the stone architecture on the arch above. She held a notepad, writing down comments.

"Like I said," Qwypp noted, marching up to address the lady. "Um, excuse me, we have to get through, it's kind of an emergency, can you move for us please?"

"What on earth! Who said that? Where are you?"

"I'm right here, ma'am. Now, I don't have time to explain, but we have to go in there. Lives are at stake, the world could be in danger, and every minute counts. Think of it being like one of those crime or hospital shows. It's urgent."

The woman gasped at Qwypp in horror, mouth agape and muttering. She dropped her notepad and staggered back a few steps.

"Now, be a love won't you, and let me and my friend past, thanks very much. It's all for the best, I promise. What's the matter? You look like you've seen a ghost!"

And with that, they slipped through the door, leaving the poor woman to mull it over.

Once inside, they made their way past a young man who was getting off of his shift. He was wearing headphones and rocking out to whatever was playing through them. Ignoring him, they made their way back to Simon's room, which was unlocked. They slipped inside and closed it.

"I'm going to lock it, just in case," Qwykk offered.

"Good idea. Now, what should we be looking for? Did Simon leave us any clues? He wanted to get rid of us so he could go do something, so I don't think he'd want to help us, but, maybe Qwyrk came back and... wait, look! There's my note to her! It's been crumpled up. That means she must have read it!"

"But what if it wasn't Qwyrk? What if one of our kidnappers found it, or someone else, and she never even saw it? It could have been one of the people here, for all we know."

"Yeah, it could be, but maybe we got lucky and she did find it. Maybe she left it here to let us know she did." She un-crumpled it and looked it over to see if Qwyrk, or anyone else had left a new note.

"Hmmm. I don't see anything. Hey, what's that?" Qwypp reached for a small amulet on the nightstand.

She picked it up and turned it over.

"What is it?"

"It looks like some kind of locket. It's got a latch. What happens if I open it..."

Green light poured out of the opening, and Qwypp heard a voice in her head.

Simon has gone, and left this for you to find. He is taking his fight to de Soulis at Hermitage Castle, where the sorcerer now works to be reborn...

* * *

The keep was large, imposing, threatening. Qwyrk, Blip, Simon, and the Templar knights stood outside of its large wooden double doors, which were closed and barred. The sky overhead was dark grey now, and a light rain fell. The wind whipped up, emitting a haunting howl as it swept over the rolling hills. It was not a pleasant or a natural sound.

"Interesting. He's remade the castle with his magic to look as it would have in his time," Simon observed. "He's gaining strength. This keep was built after he was killed. I suppose he had to use what was here, and not try to reconstruct his old fortress. That tells me that he hasn't gained his full power, or hatched the young dragons yet. He must be waiting for something, some preparation must need to be finished before he can do it."

Qwyrk thought of Jilly trapped in there, and a chill ran down her back that had nothing to do with the weather.

"Look, it's good that we've made it this far, but we're right outside; why hasn't he tried to stop us yet?" she asked.

"Maybe he's not yet powerful enough to extend his sorcery beyond the keep itself. It must have taken quite a bit of effort to recreate a place of this size, and he might be weakened now, which would be to our advantage. Or perhaps in his hubris, he thinks he doesn't need to try. Maybe all he wants to do is keep us outside long enough for him to hatch the egg. And if that happens..."

"It's not going to be pleasant for any of us," Qwyrk answered. "So, what should we do?"

"Since he's not tried to stop us, I think the direct approach is the best option."

"It shall be just like D-Day," Blip offered up. "Yes indeed, a direct assault to secure a foothold, and from there, we will spread out and conquer!"

"Yeah, just like that," Qwyrk said, "minus the channel, the ships, the guns, the element of surprise, the troop numbers... have I left anything out?"

"Hmmph!"

"No need for subterfuge," Simon said. "We'll just do this the easy way..."

"There's an 'easy way'?" Blip asked.

Without answering, Simon raised his voice to a shout. "William! It is Simon! You know we are here. We have come to settle this, and put an end to these vile doings. Cease your cowardly hiding in your pathetic keep, and open these doors to us. If you are truly the magnificent and terrible lord that you imagine yourself to be, prove it once and for all, lest I proclaim you to be the half-wit and coward that I've always known you are, hiding behind baby dragons when you've no real power of your own. What a wretched turn of events for one so formidable. Receive us now, you imbecile, for we will wait no longer!"

"Well," muttered Blip, "*that* should speed things up a bit."

The Templar knights, who had until now been silent, roared their approval, drawing their swords as one, swearing and shouting insults in Latin.

"I suppose if one is to be obliterated, exiting this reality with Latin curses on one's lips is a rather elegant way to go," Blip said with approval. Qwyrk shot him a look.

To everyone's surprise (or maybe to no one's at all), the doors creaked, and swung open and outward, dragging along the ground, and making a horrific grating sound, almost like a scream. Qwyrk and Blip had to cover their ears with their hands, but Simon and the Templars endured it.

The rain now fell in sheets, but through it, they could see a murky stone hall (or perhaps it was a courtyard) beyond, with pillars forming a row away from them. A reddish-orange glow permeated the air, but illuminated little, save a solitary Shadow standing at the far end, its hateful red eyes piercing the dark. It appeared to be alone, but Simon knew better. He smiled and drew his sword.

A dark and cold voice spoke. It seemed to come from the Shadow, but also from inside their heads at the same time. It was fierce, direct, and brief.

"It is good that we meet again, dear brother."

CHAPTER SEVENTEEN

Jilly concentrated, working to finish the last sigil. She ached, and the cold room gave her a chill. The stench of the paint was becoming unbearable, but she pushed through it all. Forcing back a shiver, she drew the last letter inside the final sign, and sat back, admiring her handiwork. *If I get away with this, it'll be brilliant! I can't wait to tell Qwyrk!*

Her face darkened. "I've been working so hard on this rubbish, I'd almost forgotten about her," she whispered. "Oh, Qwyrk, I'm sorry we argued; I'm so sorry about it all." She fell silent for a bit.

I don't even know if she's still alive. What's going to happen to me now? I don't trust this bastard at all; there's no way he's going to let me go... or live. I wish I could figure out how to get out of here.

A wave of panic rushed over her as the reality of everything hit her all at once. She was alone, afraid, and she fell down in the circle and started to shake while tears filled her eyes. She dropped the brush, and put her face in her black-stained hands, trying to muffle her cries.

It's all hopeless! I'm going to die down here, alone. Mum and dad will never know what happened to me, and even if Qwyrk's alive, I'll never...

She sobbed again. "I could yell for help, but what's the point?"

The creature was still there in the darkness, she knew, watching her.

De Soulis probably told that thing to eat me. I'm cold. I want to go home. But I can't just sit here. Right, then...

She took a deep breath and dried her eyes a little with her shirt sleeve.

There's nothing else for it. Maybe I can convince him that the sigils are ready.

She stood up and called out in a loud voice: "Hello! Anyone out there? Mr. de Soulis! It's me, Jilly! I'm done. I've finished painting everything. You can come have a look if you'd like. I think it came out quite well. It should do the trick. Hello! Are you there?"

Her voice echoed in the chamber and then fell silent. For a moment all was quiet. Then she heard a shuffling noise. Something was moving, moving toward her, in fact. She shuddered.

"Hello?"

The heavy dragging of feet slowly sounded closer and closer.

"Look, I'm done... all right? I did what you wanted. You said I'd be rewarded. What I'd like is to go home now. I think that's fair. That's the only reward I really want, anyway. You got what you wanted, and it looks brilliant... at least *I* think so! Why don't you come back and have a look? Hello?"

Then she saw it. Her abductor shambled into view. Croakbeak opened its maw and let out a low squawk, an awful, rumbling sound. She saw its teeth in its beak and heard its heavy breathing. She swallowed hard, and her heart raced as she watched it observing her, tilting its head from side to side. Jilly was sure she was being sized up to be a tasty meal.

After a moment, it crouched, not taking its eyes off of her.

"Oh no," she whispered through tears, terror filling her. "Oh, no, please no! Not this! Not this!"

She screamed as Croakbeak flexed its claws, let out a howl, and sprung into a leap, charging straight toward her.

* * *

"Brother? Simon, what the hell?" Qwyrk stared at him in shock as the rain poured over them.

"Yes, it is true. William de Soulis and I are brothers, born of the same womb, though history has forgotten me, which is as the order intended. Even as a boy, he was... cold, unstable, incapable of empathy. I do not know why; none of us did. Our mother least of all. He... broke her heart. I opposed him, did what I could to prevent his excesses, but he became too powerful. Why do you think I was chosen to be his jailer for all these centuries? No one else would have been suitable, and that's why I am here: to mend the mistakes I have made."

"Oh, there shall be mending this day, dear brother, many mendings, in fact," de Soulis answered. "I shall avenge the wrongs done to me, and reclaim what is rightfully mine: my power, then my body, and then my lordship of this realm!"

A low growl followed de Soulis' boast, and the voice changed. "Enough of this banter! Let us kill them and be done with it! I have no more patience with you, and I will be free! Their scent is strong, and I yearn for fresh meat!"

"Ah, good Redcap," de Soulis retorted, "ever the temper of an angry child! The hour is upon us, all things are now in motion, and our liberation is at hand! Can you not wait even a short time longer? Another hour to avenge centuries of wrongs? Would you undo all that I have accomplished? I promised you blood, and you shall have it, starting with these good knights, though I wish to spare my brother and the Shadow woman. The frog beast you may also have."

Blip grimaced and clutched his blade. "Just try it, you scoundrel!" he belted out, probably with all the bravado he could muster. Which was not much at all, Qwyrk decided.

De Soulis chuckled and motioned to them all. "Come in, come in to my new... my old home, my friends! Please, take yourselves out of the rain and accept my hospitality. Just because you are going to die this day does not mean that you should spend your last hour being battered by the elements."

"William, we should settle this, you and me alone," Simon answered. "There is no need to involve the others, let them go." Qwyrk shot him a look that was both astonished and annoyed. The knights held their swords, but said nothing at all.

"Simon, dear brother, where would be the amusement in that? You must know that you have no hope of besting me alone, but why surrender so easily? At least try; at least show me that you have some of that same spirit with which you locked me away for so many centuries. It did, after all, take so many of you to accomplish the task then. Do not be a fool and think that you can vanquish me on your own. Of course, asking you not to be a fool is in vain, I suppose. Nevertheless, I want to see the hope drain from your faces as I destroy all of you, one by one."

"Look," Qwyrk shot back. "I'm getting bloody sick and tired of you and your incessant bragging, Mr. Big, Bad, Warlord-Pillock who wants to rule the world! I've heard all this crap before, you know, by folks way more impressive than you. If you think you have what it takes to finish us off, than get on with it, or just shut the hell up!"

De Soulis laughed. "I like you. It will be a pleasure to show you just how wrong you are... and just how painful torture can be."

Qwyrk sneered, unimpressed. "You're all talk, sorcerer. Weak, limp words, and weak, limp other things, too, I bet. Wouldn't surprise me if that's what's behind all of this. What happened, oh mighty dark one? Some peasant girl wouldn't let you get off with her back in the day? Maybe she laughed at your undersized manhood, so you had to take it out on everyone? Or maybe your mummy didn't give you enough love, so you're going to get your own back by destroying everything that crosses you?"

"Qwyrk!" Blip hissed. "I do not think that provoking him is prudent at the moment! Clearly, he's angry enough as it is."

"I'm spoiling for a fight, Blip," she whispered back. "And pissed off enough that I'm fine with getting him all riled up; maybe he'll actually shut the hell up and do something. Besides, you've seen what an arrogant knob he is. The angrier he gets, the more likely he is to get careless and make mistakes, like back in Leeds."

He gave her a skeptical look.

"All right, we cocked it up, but we didn't know what we were dealing with. Now we do! So, instead of complaining, maybe *you* should try taunting him a bit, yourself... you're good at annoying people!"

"Hmm? Oh well, right. I'll have a go, then." He raised his voice to a most authoritative tone. "Ahem... You sir, are the very essence of perfidy! A balatronic blowhard of farcical proportions, who suffers from delusions and phantasms of the mind so immense as to dwarf even the lowest and most wretched inmate of Bedlam! I firmly believe that you are no wizard at all, but merely a cuniculous fraudster of the lowest order! You are barely even a music hall conjurer who should be performing for pennies at a carnival, if I dare say. And so, I name you a buffoon, a scoundrel, and a mendacious cockalorum, and I declare that when *I* am properly seated in the House of Lords, you shall have a thing or two to answer for. Thank you, and good day, sir. Hmph!"

"Right then, we may as well be off," Qwyrk sighed. "Blip's just won this thing single-handed."

"You're being sarcastic and petulant again, aren't you?" he snapped.

∗ ∗ ∗

A green light flashed as they materialized, staggered, and fell to the ground. Then, there was nothing but black... then a blur, then some sensation, and the feel of fresh, damp air.

"Oh, bollocks, I think I'm going to be sick!" Qwypp groaned. Qwykk said nothing, but rolled over, moaned, and proceeded to do just what Qwypp feared.

"Crap!" Qwykk managed to say after a few unpleasant moments. "What the hell just happened? My head is poundin' and spinnin'... and I need some mouthwash! Ugh. At least I missed my hair. Remember that time in Barcelona when I didn't and..."

"Love, please just shut up!" Qwypp stammered, not ready to sit up yet, for fear of the consequences. Holding her stomach, she looked up and tried to take stock of their surroundings. They were lying in a shallow dell. The sky was grey and dark, windy, and a light rain fell. A glowing light shone in the distance, beyond the next hill.

"I think we're here. I think we made it!"

"Where's 'here'?"

"The place; the place where Simon went. I think Qwyrk's here, too. That amulet must've transported us. Damn bit more unpleasant than our usual teleporting, which isn't so fun itself! It must be magically attuned to Simon, or something; I've seen that kind of thing before. Good for security and the like; makes you wish you'd never tried it. Probably feels even worse for humans, like it's the morning after seven pints and some vodka shots. Right, I'm going to risk sitting up."

"Careful with that! My head's still spinning."

"We don't have a choice, Qwykk! This isn't a hangover, and we can't just lie around waiting for it to go away. We've got to help, there's nothing for it."

She sat up and immediately regretted it, emptying her own stomach on the grass.

Qwykk grimaced. "Yeah, I'll wait here until you're done with that."

A few more agonizing and gross minutes passed, and then they were both teetering on their feet.

"So, now what?" Qwykk asked, still shaking her head.

"We go toward the light, and I don't mean that in some sort of New Agey, peaceful, near-death way. There's something bad over there, something that's dangerous and horrible. That's why we were asked to come up here with Qwyrk and told to look after Simon, and I'll bet anything it's why we were kidnapped and put in that cellar."

"So... why are we going over there, again?"

"Because Qwyrk and Simon need us, you stupid cow! Are we just going to let our friends face whatever's out there and do nothing? We've come all this way, so let's at least have a look and see if there's anything we can do to help."

"All right, all right, I'm sorry, but look, we ain't in any shape to do anything. This is *worse* than a hangover; I feel like crap!"

"Me too, but it's not going to stop me this time; I mean it. Look, we're always saying that we feel like we're second fiddle to Qwyrk, right? How she always gets the praise and we're just the sidekicks? How they wouldn't even ask us to help if it weren't for her being there? Why do you think that is? It's because we're pillocks and cock-ups who act like university freshers away from home for the first time, when we should be doing our job. It's an honor, what we do, but we treat it like some stupid joke! Why they didn't just sack us a long time ago, I don't know, but Qwyrk saved our bums there, too. Maybe we can make a difference this time. Maybe we can show them and ourselves that we're not all that bad at this whole 'watching and protecting' thing. And maybe we can actually help out Qwyrk for once, and not be the arse-pains that just get in the way!"

Qwykk gave her a weak smile. "That's quite a speech, love. I can't think of a worse state to go into a fight than we're in right now, but what the hell, eh? All right, I'm in, let's do it!"

* * *

"Childish taunts do nothing, I'm afraid," de Soulis said as he sneered, "for I hold the center of the board; the strongest pieces are mine. You play at my game, and I make the rules. And I'm afraid that checkmate is now imminent. Shall you resign? Or will you struggle on to the bitter end?"

He moved toward the edge of the castle door. A cape of purple mist swirled about his form, sometimes blurring his shape, at other time enhancing it as he floated over the ground.

"Come, come." His voice was icy and he motioned them to approach. "I *mean* it, do enter my home, and save yourselves from this rain. There is no reason to perish in such misery. I am nothing if not generous to my most esteemed foes."

Qwyrk kept her eyes on him at all times, not moving. Simon did the same. The knights held their ground while Blip fidgeted, looking uncomfortable.

"I could compel you all to enter, but I'd rather that you do so freely," he said after a moment, in an annoyed voice.

Still the group refused to move.

"Very well. Qwyrk, is it? Perhaps this will motivate you... Croakbeak! Come to me!" His voice amplified and took on other layers of sound, weaving in a magical summoning that made two, three, maybe more voices, echoing in a cacophonous choir. It grew ever louder and hurt their ears. The air seemed to vibrate.

Then, the terrible shriek of the beast sounded in the hall, just out of view. The noise of its horrid feet slapping on cold stone followed, step after step, as it drew nearer. In a moment it joined its master, and it wasn't alone.

"Jilly!" Qwyrk screamed in horror, putting one hand over her mouth.

Jilly squirmed in the creature's arms. She yelled and pounded at it, trying to twist free of its grip, all to no avail. Croakbeak held her firm, and ignored her.

"Let me go, you damned bollocky piece of crap! When I get free, I'm going to make you wish you'd never been... born, spawned, whatever!"

De Soulis laughed and patted the creature on the head, stroking it like some perverse hunting dog. It was impassive, but seemed to emit a slight croak of approval.

"Young Jilly, you see, has been most helpful to me," he said, turning his attention back to his foes. "She has kindly agreed to draw the symbols for my magical circle. I need only await the proper hour, and the work will be accomplished. The little beasts will hatch and the world will be undone. I understand that she's made a fine job of it all, and is to be commended. She said so herself. She boasted about it. I shall inspect her art again shortly to determine if she speaks the truth. If so, it is almost enough for me to spare her life, almost. I just wanted to let you know, dear Qwyrk, that your little friend shall be the undoing of all of you."

"Jilly, no!" Qwyrk blurted out, feeling light-headed and nause-ated. She struggled to remain standing, and fought back tears. "What were you thinking? How could you do this? Do you know what you've done?"

"He said he'd kill you all, and mum and dad if I didn't," she yelled back, still squirming and trying to free herself. "I didn't have a choice, Qwyrk, I'm sorry! I'm so sorry!"

"There's nothing more for it, then," Blip announced, "we may as well rush in and finish this campaign, and hope that the Goddess is with us."

"No," Simon countered, "not yet. Hold your ground for a moment, and we will see this through together. We'll go to him as one, not like some wild pack of berserkers."

Paying no attention to them, de Soulis once again motioned to the company.

"Now, I shall ask one final time, will you join me inside, or shall I have Croakbeak rip this child in half in front of you?" Jilly winced in fear. Simon nodded to her.

Swallowing her fear and rage, Qwyrk took a hesitant step forward, then another. Blip did the same. They were halfway to de Soulis before Simon motioned the knights to follow suit.

"Qwyrk, no!" Jilly pleaded through her tears. "It's hopeless! You know it is. He's just going to kill you. Run while you can! You can regroup later or something. Don't worry about me. Please! Just get out of here!"

Qwyrk ignored her young friend, ignored the pounding rain, and increased her pace, each step becoming more and more precise. Her walk became a march. Blip fell in step with her, and then so did Simon and the Templars, their swords held before them; one purpose, one goal.

This ends now, you bastard!

She sensed that de Soulis smiled, a broad smile hidden in the dark of his form, but it was one she couldn't see.

* * *

He sat on the wet ground, oblivious to the elements, chanting a few lines of old poetry over and over.

"This semly somers day,
In winter it is nought sen;
This greves wexen al gray,
That in her time were grene...

"Oh great Rhymer, oh great Master Thomas Erceldoune, please hear me, and please speak to me. I need your help more than anything else. Come to me now, hear your devoted and faithful servant, come to me in this hour of great need!"

The rain fell steadily now, and Star Tao had to concentrate not to wipe it off his face.

Bollocks! Me plats are gonna get ruined in this! This is a right waste of time. No, I can't get distracted. Focus! Remember what the old Granny lady said. You've got this, mate!

He squinted his eyes shut even tighter and began chanting again, louder and more forcefully with each pass. As if in response, the rain seemed to fall even harder. He started to shake; he felt sick. Cold shivers poured through him, then flashes of feverish heat, like some nightmarish rapid flu. Something was wrong.

"Bloody hell, this has never happened before!" he said out loud, doing everything in his power to keep his eyes shut. "Crap, I'm gonna puke... focus, focus!" In the next instant he knew he would pass out and that he had failed.

* * *

"Welcome, dear friends."

De Soulis gave a mock bow as the company entered into his remade keep. The doors slammed behind them.

The castle interior glowed in myriad changing colors, first blue, then red, then purple. A hearth burned with a yellow fire, but somehow, the glow was unnatural, like everything else here. Garish tapestries hung on the rebuilt walls in a mock medieval style, depicting scenes of extreme violence. Timber beams loomed overhead, giving weight to the high ceiling. Two gothic door arches on the far wall opened into the dark and stone steps beyond. Several large wooden tables and chairs were set in the hall, adorned with table cloths, pewter goblets, and pitchers of wine.

"I see you've been busy, brother," Simon remarked, "indulging in extravagance and reminiscing about old times?"

"Creating the lifestyle to which I am accustomed, dear brother. I fear that the quarters you chose for me all those years were a bit, shall we say, cramped? I rather thought I would make things a bit more pleasant for myself. Do you like what I have done?"

"It looks as evil and off-putting as it did then," Simon replied with no emotion. "So I suppose you are to be congratulated on consistency of taste, if nothing else. Are the torture chambers ready? Or will you have to wait until the builders can get them installed? What's the going hourly rate for building a rack these days?"

De Soulis smirked. "Everything here is because I wish it. My magic returns to its full potency, you see, and as the hour of the hatching approaches, so does my strength grow."

He motioned for them to look up. High above, among the beams and rafters, the master dragon egg floated, spinning slowly clockwise. Surrounded by green swirling mists, the light made a sharp and unpleasant contrast to the reds and purples of the hall. There seemed to be cracks along one side of the shell.

"Is it not beautiful, my guests? A thing of perfection that will unleash perfect destruction, under my command. Those marvelous little creatures will grow quickly and do my bidding. It shall not be long now; we need only wait for the appropriate hour, and then I will descend into the depths and recite the proper incantations. Your little friend here was quite helpful in that regard, I must reiterate."

Jilly grimaced, and Qwyrk tried to take no notice.

"So, where are all of your evil minions?" she interjected instead with sarcasm, her eye never wandering far from Jilly (who by now had stopped struggling against her captor and just scowled at him). "I would have thought an army of undead, or goblins, or some such would be swarming in here, pointing their rusty old weapons at us. Isn't that what you dark lord types like to do? Provide a bunch of stupid monster fodder so we can fight against them and get worn down while you sit on your big arse throne and laugh?"

"Oh, I do have my loyal servants," de Soulis assured her, "and should things go the wrong way, I could summon them in an instant. But for all of your hubris, I cannot help but note that you have not yet tried to attack me again, Qwyrk. You succeeded before, for a short while... what stops you now?"

"Perhaps something about you threatening to tear my friend in half? Yeah, that might just be it."

He laughed. "You care for her, even now, knowing that she has helped me? Knowing that her fine artistic skills shall destroy everything you hold dear in this world? Like so many of your kind, you are weak, soft. You prove to me again why you and your council are not fit to rule, and why there are others far more suited."

"Long have I said this!" Redcap spoke up. "They are frail and pathetic! I am disgusted to be one of them!"

"Who's helping you, you bastard?" she spat, not caring if she asked de Soulis or Redcap. "You couldn't have done this on your own. Who's helping you in Symphinity? If you're going to kill us, at least let me know."

"I will tell you nothing," de Soulis responded, having once again suppressed his violent counterpart. "It is far better that you go to your end forever wondering, never knowing. But come, sit and have a last glass of wine before we bring things to a close. I assure you it is a fine vintage, the best you will ever have. And please," he waved his hand dismissively, "do not think I would be so base as to try to poison you with drink. There are far more interesting and amusing ways for you to die."

"And none so appallingly stupid as being bored to death by your speeches," Qwyrk sighed. "Look, I'll make a deal with you. You shut the hell up, let Jilly go, and you can face me right now, one-on-one, in front of everyone, and we'll see who's got more going for them. Sound good? Maybe you'll kick my arse, but at least I won't have to listen to any more of your crap!"

"Qwyrk, no!" Jilly shouted, and she began to struggle again.

De Soulis guffawed. "You are an amusing lot, I will say that much. All right, very well, I accept, noble warrior. Croakbeak! Let the child go."

The beast squawked and dropped Jilly to the stone floor. She grunted and picked herself up. She started to run toward Qwyrk, but Qwyrk held up her hand.

"No Jilly. No. Please stay back. I have to do this. Just get out of here. Find Star Tao and get the hell out, both of you!"

"Don't be stupid!" Blip shouted at her, clenching his fists and gripping his stiletto. "You know damned well what happened to you the last time! You don't stand a chance!"

Jilly held her ground and stared back and forth between Qwyrk and de Soulis, while Qwyrk pleaded with her facial expressions for Jilly to run.

Simon had said nothing the whole time, but he held forth his sword as if to strike, and the knights did the same.

"Now, now, brother." De Soulis waved a mocking finger. "She did promise me a single-handed combat for her friend's life. Do not spoil my generosity by thinking to come to her aid. I kept my end of the bargain; you must allow her to keep hers, if you have any sense of the chivalry and decency that you lot like to boast about. I'll finish you off soon enough."

He turned back to Qwyrk, bringing up his fists as glowing light began to swirl around them. He uttered some unintelligible words in an ancient language. She swallowed hard but prepared herself to dodge his first attack.

He swung a fist at her, like a punch, and a bolt of golden light shot from it. Qwyrk leapt to the left, just dodging it. The energy hit the floor behind her and dissipated. Before she could collect herself, he let loose the other which caught her on the left shoulder, ripping her shirt, knocking her backwards to the ground, sending waves of burning pain through her body.

"Qwyrk!" Jilly screamed, tears filling her eyes, but she didn't move.

One of the knights drew a dagger and prepared to throw it at de Soulis. Without looking in the young man's direction, he ordered, "Toss that toy at me, Templar, and I'll instruct Croakbeak to devour little Jilly. And what a sight that would be. That goes for all of you. Any further interference and you will regret it."

The knight pulled back, and Simon nodded to him, motioning to put away his weapon.

Meanwhile, Qwyrk had roused herself from the floor and stood up, a grim smile on her face. "Is that all you've got? Kind of pathetic, really, hiding behind your bombastic, pretty lights. Having a go at me from so far away, too? What's the matter? Scared to get any closer? Afraid of getting your balls kicked by a girl?"

Jilly grimaced at Qwyrk's taunts. "No, Qwyrk, no! Stop it!"

"I am just beginning, I assure you." He waved his hand before him, and Qwyrk was jarred by a jolt to her midsection, like she'd been punched in the stomach. Gasping, she doubled over with the wind almost knocked out of her, but stayed on her feet and forced herself back upright.

"Not bad," she hissed, "but I have a few tricks, myself." She made a fist and thrust it in the air in front of her. She yelled out in pain as a pale blue light, like a bolt of lightning, shot from her hand and hit de Soulis square in the chest. It pulsed around him like an electric surge, before dissolving into sparks and vanishing, leaving a cloud of foul-smelling smoke rising from the Shadow's form. He gasped, staggered for a moment, and looked at her, as if in surprise.

"You're not the only one that can manipulate energy, you bastard!" she said in a breathy voice, not willing to admit how much it hurt to do it. "There are plenty of Shadows who can, more than you think. Imagine what'll happen when we all get a hold of you."

"I am truly impressed," de Soulis replied. "Perhaps you have greater merit than I had thought. But clearly, you cannot sustain such an attack for long. It is obvious that you are already weakened. Another few of those, and I won't have to do anything. You shall kill yourself for me, robbing me of some fun, but making my task far easier."

"Let me finish her!" Redcap interrupted.

"Stay silent, wretch!" de Soulis warned. "I forbid you to speak now."

Redcap howled as he struggled to gain control of their body. For a moment, the Shadow twitched and shuddered, but the sorcerer's power had grown too strong. Redcap retreated, and de Soulis was triumphant once again.

* * *

The company of knights watched, bewildered looks on their faces, but Qwyrk saw that Simon understood just how strong his brother had become in such a short time. There was fear in his voice as he spoke.

"William, if you kill Qwyrk, or the young girl, I shall ensure that your punishment will be beyond your comprehension. You will beg for a hell to relieve you from it." He took a step forward, brandishing his sword. The knights fell in behind him, ready to strike at his command.

"Bold words, brother, but can you back them up? I think you cannot. I have changed my mind. Let us see how well you can fight at your age; this should keep you engaged for a time."

He spoke a few words in the same arcane language and the air around the edges of the hall began to ripple and pulsate, like a desert mirage. In a flash, creatures emerged from nothing. They stood about five feet tall, were arrayed in a variety of old, battered and rusty pieces of armor, carried spears and poleaxes, swords and axes, and had bristly faces with tusks, like warthogs. They grumbled and grunted and pressed inward in an odd waddling march, their beady yellow eyes looking at the knights with hungry glee.

"Oh great, he's finally brought out his rubbishy minions," Qwyrk sighed, exasperated.

"Wirry-cows?" Simon spat. "Really, brother, is *that* all you could find to follow you on such short notice? Your standards have fallen since your younger days."

Nevertheless, he and the rest of the Templars were put on the defensive and assumed a position at each other's backs, as they watched the creatures advance. A few dozen would have been little trouble, but soon, there were fifty or more.

"Stand your ground! Wirry-cows are stupid, but in large numbers, dangerous enough." Simon ordered. "Show no fear! Do what you have trained to do!"

In an instant, the beasts were on them. The clanging of metal and weaponry, the cries and yells of both sides as they bore down on one another filled the hall. The chaos spread as smaller groups broke away and knights made their way into new fighting positions, behind chairs, on top of tables, against walls.

* * *

Qwyrk struggled in her pain to take in everything and to see if Jilly was safe, but she couldn't locate her. She brought her attention back to de Soulis, who was clearly watching the ensuing combat with amusement.

As if in answer to her worry, Blip yelled out, "Jilly! Where are you girl? Aaahhh!" He ducked as a random axe swung at his head, bearing down on him.

* * *

"Great Minerva's girdle!" Blip swore, as the axe just missed him. "This will not do at all!" He turned all about to locate the perpetrator of this obvious outrage. But the clamor raged all around, and his attacker had disappeared back into the melee. In a moment, more fighting overwhelmed him, and he found himself yet again ducking, jumping, and trying to run to get out of harm's way. He swung his dagger in front of him, trying to hit something, anything, and clear a path so he could locate his young charge. Somehow, he made it to an overturned table, and hid behind it, trying to size up the scene. It wasn't good. Jilly was trapped behind another table on the other side of the hall, though for the moment, the wirry-cows had not seen her. But Croakbeak could be anywhere...

* * *

De Soulis raised his fists, prepared to launch another attack on Qwyrk. She knew that if he hit her again, she wouldn't be getting up.

There was a loud bang, and the doors of the keep flew open and off their hinges, startling everyone, even de Soulis. A forceful wind rushed in, carrying with it a torrent of unnatural rain, blowing almost sideways, and causing most to turn away and shield their faces. It upturned the tables and chairs nearest to the door, sending them sprawling in different directions. Many of the wirry-cows fell over or crashed into one another, and began swearing at each other in their guttural language. Fist fights broke out among a few of them, and some even seemed to forget the Templars they'd been fighting. Others looked to the entrance and gasped in fear or excitement.

A lone figure stood in the doorway, oblivious to the natural forces. In her pain, Qwyrk strained to see who it was. Soon enough, the wind died down, and her eyes widened.

"Star Tao? What the bloody hell?"

Star Tao took one step into the keep, then another. Despite the raging storm, he was completely dry. His face was devoid of any expression, and his eyes glowed a brilliant white, lighting up his face. He strode forward with determination, never taking those magical eyes off the sorcerer.

He spoke. The voice that came from his mouth was rich with authority and tradition, but it wasn't his. It was sweet, like audible honey, and seemed enhanced by an echo and otherworldly musical tones.

"William de Soulis," he said, "you are not permitted to be here. Your punishment was for eternity, and so it shall be again. You will do no more harm. You will surrender. This ends now." As he moved, he seemed taller and more assured than ever. If not for his clothes and hair, Qwyrk would not have recognized him.

"Good Goddess, I do not believe it!" Blip exclaimed in the stunned silence that followed, pumping his fist in the air in triumph. "He's done it! The miscreant has succeeded! He's channeled Thomas the Rhymer!"

CHAPTER EIGHTEEN

"Erceldoune," de Soulis said with a light laugh, but there was less confidence in his voice than a moment before. "You are an unexpected guest, truly. I... had not anticipated this, I admit. The boy you have possessed to make yourself manifest on this plane is strong, but why take his body? Could you not tear yourself away from your lovely harlot Glorienne for even a few hours to return and save this world that you profess to care so deeply about?"

"Had I the time to prepare," Thomas spoke, "I would have done so, but your presence left me no choice. The hour is short, but this vessel is adequate for what I must accomplish."

"And what is that, Thomas? You must know that it is too late? The circle is set, the sigils are ready, summer solstice is upon us, and soon the beasts will hatch. At that moment my power shall reach its peak and I shall be whole again. Perhaps I will steal away the body of the young man you now hold. It might be a strong form that could serve me well for a few years."

Jilly clenched her teeth. "Just try it, you bastard!"

"As ever, your arrogance borders on the comical," Thomas replied, increasing his stride. De Soulis took a step backward. "You were never that special in earlier times, William, just clever and strong enough to terrorize the ignorant and the superstitious. It took us some time to learn how to contain you. You possess great power, just not the wisdom or talent to use it properly. And that, my old enemy, makes you even more dangerous than if you were a master at what you do."

He brushed past Simon and the rest of the Templars. The scattered wirry-cows nattered among themselves, seeming curious and fearful.

"But I have gained much in power and wisdom these many centuries, more than you can know," Thomas continued. "I take responsibility for this calamity now and will end it the way it should have been ended then."

His right hand glowed with a brilliant white hot radiance.

"What is this? What is *this*?" Redcap hissed. "How dare you let this half-wit poet anywhere near us? Stop him, you senseless wizard, stop him now!"

"Be silent, fool!" de Soulis ordered, but Redcap would not. Their form began to twitch, writhe, and clutch at itself, as if trying to shed some garment.

"No! I will no longer do your bidding, William de Soulis! Free me now, you mortal scum, free me from bondage to your idiocy!"

Star Tao had reached the conflicted Shadow and drew himself up, meeting de Soulis face to face. Qwyrk, Jilly, Blip, Simon, the knights, and even the wirry-cows watched motionless, not daring to move, even to breathe.

"This, William, is to be your proper fate. This will undo the wrongs of those times, and set things right. This will stop you from causing harm again. Let it be so!"

He plunged his sun-like hand into the sorcerer's chest. De Soulis and Redcap screamed together, an appalling cacophony of sounds that echoed through the hall, forcing everyone to cover their ears, and some fell to their knees. The wirry-cows bellowed in terror, and many fled from the hall. A few retreated to the shadows or hid behind overturned tables, whimpering and cowering.

After a short time, Star Tao drew his hand out of the sorcerer's form, and he pulled with him... an old man? Qwyrk shook her head, removed her hands from her ears and stared in disbelief. The others joined her in amazement. The Shadow body of Redcap fell backward and into a heap on the stone floor, where he lay still.

Star Tao held the man by the collar of his charcoal-colored woolen robe. His hair was white, thin, and shoulder length, and though he was clean-shaven, he bore a strong resemblance to Simon. He gasped for air, and looked at Star Tao and the others in shock.

"H-how? How did you do this?" His voice seemed weak and insignificant now. "My mortal body was destroyed!"

"Your essence resided in that Shadow, and so I drew it out and gave it back the form it would have had."

De Soulis groaned and gazed up at the ceiling, but said nothing, still caught in the Rhymer's iron grip. Thomas let go of him and he slumped to his knees.

"But no one could do that!" Simon stepped forward, looking as shocked as the others. "We tried, Thomas, goodness knows, we tried! Their forms were bound together, and nothing could separate them."

"I have learned much in the centuries since those dark days, and my power has grown beyond what you can know. I have partaken of elder faerie magic long since forgotten even by many of that race. It is a harsh, vital, and dangerous lore that few can learn, much less wield. I make no claims to being its master, but I know enough now to harness some of its secrets."

"Then why the bloody hell didn't you just fix this problem when it first happened?" Qwyrk was angry now, and ignoring the pain in her battered and bruised form, she strode up to yell at his face; the fact that Thomas inhabited Star Tao made it that much easier to vent. She was just fine with smacking him, if need be. "He's been on the loose for two days, and you could have just stopped him anytime you wanted to? And after all the crap we've gone through?"

"The realm of my dwelling is not so close to this world as yours, Shadow woman, and I do not know what occurs here, when it occurs," Thomas replied. "The young lad who contacted me did not succeed on his first try, or his twentieth, from what I gather. It took great strength and determination for him to part the veils between our realms. He has a true gift and is to be commended for his skill."

Qwyrk bristled at the thought and stared down at the floor.

"My time here must end now," he continued. "I did not undertake this task lightly, and it does not come easily. There are forces even beyond my control, or yours. You will soon face a greater danger than de Soulis. A reckoning is coming, a price must be paid. Remember that."

"What price? What are you talking about?" Qwyrk looked back up at him.

"I cannot stay longer," he replied. "Already I can feel the pull of the Noble Realm. Farewell friends, I have done what I can, you must complete the task. Quickly, guard William de Soulis; do not let him..." Star Tao's body began to sway, prompting Qwyrk (against her better judgement) to grab hold of him and try to keep him standing.

"Damn it, Rhymer, you don't get to go yet. I have questions for you!" Qwyrk shouted, but there was a burst of sound, like all of the notes on a harp played in a quick glissando, and Star Tao fell forward on his knees. He shook his head a few times and rubbed his eyes.

"Cor... that was brilliant!" said a familiar voice. Qwyrk scowled.

"Um, I'm sorry to interrupt, but I just noticed that Redcap's gone and so's Croakbeak," Jilly said. "And I think that's more important right now... just saying."

"Damn it!" Qwyrk swore, "Why weren't you knights paying attention, or something? Do I have to do everything?"

"We were as shocked as you," one of them offered in a humiliated tone. "Especially since we didn't think it could be done. The other Shadow must have slipped away, it was an easy mistake to make, with him being... shadowy and all. And there are those beasts," he pointed to the cowering wirry-cows, dazed and strewn across the hall. "They were more than a bit distracting!"

"Well now that the little murdering psychopath is free, we may all be in even bigger trouble," Qwyrk answered. "At least de Soulis reined him in."

Jilly screamed, startling everyone.

"Oh, he tried, he tried, that much is true." Redcap stood holding Jilly in his arms, a sharp dagger at her throat. But his voice sounded more human, and he had a form. He was a young man, handsome, with scruffy brown, curly, shoulder length hair. His clothing was antiquated and bland, in mottled browns: a leather jerkin, rough pants and boots. He giggled and waved the blade about. There was wildness in his grey eyes, a cold look that betrayed his nature. No empathy, no kindness. No sanity.

"I am free... at last! At long last after all those centuries trapped with *him*," he mused, punctuating his unsteady words with chuckles and heavy breaths. "I can do what I want, go where I want. It will be like old times, yes I think it will. Ha! I can, I can take things, and hurt people, kill them even... and no one will, no one will stop me, for I am the feared Redcap. I don't know why I even have that name, I barely ever wore the thing, it was, more of a symbol, a magical symbol, you see, and..."

"He's completely lost his mind," Qwyrk said. "I mean even more than already if that's possible." She never took her eyes off of Jilly.

"The trauma of the separation, I would say," Blip observed, "snapped what little was left. Be careful, he's like a rabid animal that's been cornered."

"I heard you! I am not, and I have not!" Redcap screamed, holding the knife point dangerously close to Jilly's throat. "You take that back, you horrid woman and you repulsive jirry-jirry creature! You're a disgrace to our kind!" Tears flowed down his face now and his hands grew shaky.

Qwyrk watched him like a hawk, waiting for her moment. *One mistake, you little bastard! I will take you down, and I will kill you!*

"Qwarrel? Qwarrel?! Oh come on, I don't believe it!"

Qwyrk and the others turned their gaze to the main doorway where Qwypp and Qwykk stood, looking like hung-over, drowned rats.

"Oh Goddess, no!" Qwyrk said. "Are you bloody kidding me?"

Qwypp stomped in, taking no heed of anyone or anything else, and headed straight for Redcap. "You right bastard! You've got some nerve showing your pretty boy face here; I thought you'd disappeared for good ages ago!" Qwykk ran along behind her, almost falling over twice, but trying to look indignant and authoritative. It wasn't working so well, since she doubled over and seemed ready to be sick.

"Get away from me!" Redcap shouted. "I don't know who you are! But I mean it; I'll kill her! I'll kill this precious child! I'll do it!" Jilly gasped as the knife stuck into her skin, almost drawing blood.

"Don't know who I am?" Qwypp shot back. "I'm the one you jilted, you twat! You told me you loved me and promised me that we'd be bonded forever! Then you ran out on me for someone else. Broke my heart you did! I never saw you again. Remember? Like over a thousand years ago?"

"Wait..." Qwykk said, snapping out of her poor state. "A thousand years ago? Hold on! That was when this bloke told me that his lady had left him, and he was despondent, so I took pity on him, and... you know. Next thing he's telling me he loves me, and then runs off when I start getting too close. Hold on, he said his name was... Red. You bastard! That was *you*! You dumped my best friend and then used me!"

"Oh, Qwarrel, you sick puppy," Qwypp said, her icy cold stare going to sub-zero.

They headed for Redcap, who was shaking now. He stumbled away from Jilly and dropped the dagger.

"Qwyrk!" Jilly yelled and ran to her at last. The two embraced, and turned to watch the ridiculous scene unfolding.

"I have never seen either of you before, you pathetic cows," he sneered, "for I would have remembered such vileness if I had been in the presence of either of you. You make me ill, away with you!"

"Qwarrel, love... that was the wrong thing to say," Qwypp quipped with a smile.

She unleashed a right cross against his jaw that sent him sprawling to the floor. She followed with a boot in his behind and several kicks to the stomach that doubled him up in agony.

"Qwykk, dear," she said in a sing-songy voice, "would you like to have a go?"

Qwykk smiled, looking much better now. "Thank you, I'd be delighted!"

* * *

In the chaos of Thomas' arrival and departure, the remaining wirry-cows became restless. They looked afraid, but when the Rhymer vanished, they began to grumble and fidget, getting their courage back. They began to howl in unison. Then they clanked their weapons. They looked hungry.

"That does not sound like a good thing," Blip observed over the din of their cacophony.

In a moment, they'd sprung up and attacked the knights, and a new melee began. Qwyrk shouted for her friends to take cover. Jilly ducked behind a table as arrows and the occasional axe or other airborne missile flew by in random directions. Qwykk and Qwypp did likewise (after several more well-placed kicks and punches to their mutual jilter), while Blip stood about, looking confused, wanting to join in, but remaining still, like a deer in headlights.

"Blip!" Qwyrk cried out, and that seemed to snap him out of his trance. He looked around, held up his weapon, and with a courage that surprised her, fell on one of the nearby beasts, swearing and yowling as he vigorously stabbed the air, but not so much his opponent.

He was so busy trying to hit something, anything, that he didn't see Croakbeak circling, stalking in the far darkness of the great hall.

* * *

Qwyrk didn't have time to worry about anyone else now, as she turned to see de Soulis looking weak and frail, slumped down on his knees. He raised his head toward her, looking pitiful and weak. For a moment, she almost felt sorry for him. Almost. But his weakness started to fade and a fire returned to his eyes.

"Do you really think I have lost all my power? My magic is bound to me!"

He launched into the air, leaving an astonished Qwyrk behind.

He flew up into the rafters, reaching the egg, where he circled around it, gazing with an admiration that Qwyrk thought bordered on manic.

"It's so beautiful!" he declared in a loud whisper.

"You're just about done, you sick git," Qwyrk shouted up at him. "Why don't we end this now? You were so eager for a one-on-one before, what say we finish it, eh?"

She levitated off the floor, but it wasn't easy and took too much effort. She flew into the air and up toward him.

"Qwyrk! Please! Be careful!" Jilly shouted after her. Another arrow whizzed by her head and she ducked.

"What do we have to do to make you shut the hell up and get back into your toilet prison?" Qwyrk cursed.

"Nothing at all, little wretch, for it shall never happen!"

"We'll see about that!"

She flew up fast beside him and threw the hardest punch she could, a real punch intended to connect with his jaw. He swerved, avoiding the worst, but took part of it on his chin. Growling, he reached out with fury, grabbing for her throat. She ducked, but caught his arms with her hands, and they struggled to break free of each other's grip and attack again. They turned in mid-air, almost upside down. Then righting themselves and whirling from side to side, they dropped into a free fall, away from the egg, and straight toward the ground.

"Qwyrk!" Jilly screamed.

They came to an abrupt halt a mere five feet above the floor, as if they had hit a surface, but their struggle continued, oblivious to their surroundings.

"Yield to me, little Shadow. You are strong, and I may yet let you live if you flee now!"

Qwyrk grunted, trying to get leverage. "What is it with you evil overlords and your mock generosity? Get the hell over it! I'm taking you down, Billy boy, literally!"

She freed herself and grabbed his robe. Pain surged through her body, but she held on as he fought in desperation to break her grip. Calling up more strength than she thought she had left, she cried out and hurtled him toward the floor. He shrieked as he fell toward the ground. His body hit the flagstones with a sickening thud and was still.

Silence fell over the hall as everyone, even Qwyrk herself, looked on in disbelief.

She descended to the floor, made a rough landing and stumbled. Jilly ran to her and put a supportive arm around her friend.

"Well then," Blip offered, seeing her across the hall, "that is the last we shall see of this malefactor." Qwyrk, being held up by Jilly looked over to him, staring at de Soulis' body. He offered her a slight smile. "Damn good job, young lady, damn good job. In fact, I would say excellent!"

*   *   *

He should have been dead. But of course, he wasn't; that would have been far too easy. He stirred as life surged back through him.

"I am not defeated yet, you insignificant fools!" de Soulis howled, rising to his feet in front of the shocked gathering. "There is still time!"

With a wave of his arm, an inky blackness enveloped him and emanated outward, a thick smoke that soon surrounded them, burning their throats and making them choke and gasp for air. And then he was gone.

"Damn it!" Qwyrk choked, flailing about in the darkness. "I've got to get after him! We can't lose him!"

In another moment, the smoke began to lift. As the others hacked, spat, and took deep breaths, Qwyrk scanned the hall in haste, seeing that de Soulis had disappeared. She cursed, but saw a small trail of smoke floating out of the left doorway, into the darkness.

"He's still going to do it, or at least try," she said.

Still wracked with pain, and taking no heed of Jilly or the others, she made for the doorway, and plunged into the dark.

* * *

"Qwyrk!" Blip shouted, still clearing his throat. "Where are you going, girl? You're in no shape to do anything. Let these otiose, useless knights take care of it!" After seeing a knight standing next to him, Blip looked up and felt a bit embarrassed. "Er... sorry, chap, no offense meant. Simply a figure of speech, you know."

The knight nodded, but Blip didn't know if that was an "apology accepted" or some disdainful version of "sod off."

"She cannot face him alone. He is still too dangerous," Simon said, drawing his sword and making his way through the haze for the same doorway. Not looking back, he held up his left hand to warn off any would-be followers. "Stay here! Finish off those vile creatures!"

Blip wanted to stop him, or at least follow after and do something to look heroic, or even useful, but he just couldn't summon the will for it. He cursed himself. And then Croakbeak pounced.

* * *

Qwyrk was well out of earshot, feeling her way down a winding stone stairway, trusting her heightened senses to keep her safe. Step by slow step, she edged farther into the depths of the castle. The air grew colder and damper. To her surprise, a gnawing fear began to nibble at her. She tried to talk to herself to keep it at bay.

"This is not a nice place, and that's just what he wants. He's playing with my mind. Probably more of his magic tricks. But if I can just keep from falling to the bottom and breaking my neck, that would be lovely. Or at least not look like an idiot doing it. Or not get set upon by whatever else he's conjured up. Wirry-cows? Really? That would be a stupid way to go. Come on, Qwyrk, focus! This is not that hard; it's just another save-the-world-and-have-a-pint-after scenario, eh? You'll be laughing about this with the girls tomorrow. And right: what the bloody hell are they doing here?"

She reached the bottom of the steps, where a dark corridor led away from her. A faint light shone from somewhere in the distance.

"Of course, into his inner chamber. Just what he wants." She sighed. "Let's get this over with."

The pain in her body was getting worse; she was bleeding from several small scrapes and out her nose, but she ignored it all and set off down the hall.

EIGHTEEN

* * *

Blip hit the stone floor hard and the wind burst out of him as his weapon fell from his grip. He had the sense to roll over before Croakbeak could swipe at him from behind. He rose to his feet, flailed about and swatted with his bare hands in front of himself, frantic to keep the creature at bay.

"Back, you foul beast! Away with you! I am a master of many martial arts, and I shall use them if I must! You do not want to face the wrath of the ancients!"

Croakbeak let out a squawk that sounded rather like a laugh, which Blip found insulting. It pressed in, forcing him to the ground and trapping him under its body, its maw open and closing in for the kill. Drops of its drool spattered on the stone floor. With his left hand, Blip pushed back against the monster's face, a battle that despite his strength, he knew he was losing. His right hand grasped for the handle of the stiletto. He looked around for assistance, but there were no Templar knights nearby, because the damned wirry-cows were once again attacking them.

"Unhand me, you repulsive creature! I'm warning you, this is your last chance, I... oh, damnation!"

Croakbeak leaned in to finish him, its sharp teeth inches away from Blip's face. He stretched his arm so far that he thought it would break, but at last, his fingers touched the smooth handle of the weapon. Blip smiled.

The creature lunged to make the killing bite. Blip grabbed the weapon and thrust his right hand forward, straight into its maw. Croakbeak's eyes bulged in shock, and it tried to look up. A razor-sharp stiletto protruded from the top of its head, covered in black blood.

"Enjoying the taste of my blade, eh? I rather suspect not!"

It choked and gurgled, twitched and shook. The life drained from its face. It loosened its grip on Blip and fell forward. Quite forward, in fact, pinning Blip underneath its lifeless body.

"Ooofff! Damn it, will somebody get this abhorrent thing off of me?"

* * *

She stood at the door of the keep, wearing a poncho. Her cowboy hat was soaked, but at least her aqua T-shirt underneath (the one with the map of Texas on it) was dry. The rest of the tour group had decided not to walk up this far from the bus, given the sudden inclement weather, but of course, she just had to see, just had to get a closer look at all the shifting lights. Now, she said nothing. She had just watched a bunch of warthog-faced goblins fighting a group of men dressed like knights, and a young man with funny hair had pulled an old man out of a thing that looked like a shadow, who then proceeded to fly into the air and fight with the elf she'd talked to yesterday.

Dottie Lee Jefferson screamed, turned, and ran as fast as she could back to the bus. This was absolutely, positively the last time she would ever leave her home town again.

* * *

Qwyrk heard de Soulis' voice echoing down the hall as she approached. She stopped short of the chamber and remained in the shadows, just out of the flickering of the torchlight. Peering in, she saw what she most feared.

De Soulis knelt in the middle of the circle, chanting guttural words which no one understood or would ever wish to. His hands made motions, as if he were tracing words in some unknown alphabet into the air. Qwyrk realized that he was oblivious to her, and she was determined to take advantage of that. But as she moved toward the circle, she smacked into some kind of barrier, as hard as glass and charged like an electric fence, which sent her sprawling back onto the stone floor. De Soulis never opened his eyes, never even noticed.

Cursing, she roused herself painfully from the floor and looked around, trying to see anything that might be of use in breaking the barrier, but the room was empty. She stumbled back to the chamber entrance, gasping and feeling light-headed.

De Soulis' chanting grew louder; the circle and its glyphs and symbols began to glow, turning from a pale glow to a bright gold.

"Crap!" she swore, feeling more helpless with each passing moment.

She heard someone approaching behind her and turned, not even caring at this point. "Now what?"

"Qwyrk! Stay back!" Simon hissed, grabbing her shoulder and pulling her back into the hall's shadows away from the light.

"We have to do something!" she retorted. "After all this, he's still going to do it, the bastard!"

"No!" whispered another voice. "No, he won't!"

Qwyrk watched in horror as Jilly came running up to both of them; all of her hope vanished.

"Jilly," she sighed. "Please, just get out of here. No matter what happens, you have to get yourself to safety. Take Star Tao if you can, and Blip, *please*..."

"No, Qwyrk, wait. It's not over yet. Just watch!"

Qwyrk shook her head in despair and looked back to de Soulis.

He seemed serene as he uttered his arcane spell, unaware of their presence and absorbed in his dark work. Now they could understand his words.

"This is the time. Let it be so. Release the creatures and let my power return to me. The hour is here, and the work is done. Let it be so!"

The circle's light blazed up and heat emanated from it in all directions. De Soulis smiled and let out a contented sigh as he gazed upward, his ancient face filled with a peace she didn't think possible.

Qwyrk grabbed hold of Jilly, certain that the end had come.

"Goddess, I'm sorry," she whispered, tears filling her eyes. "I tried. Forgive me."

The ground shook, startling them all. De Soulis opened his eyes and looked around, alarmed. Clearly, something was wrong.

"What is this?" he growled. He turned and saw his three enemies at last. "What is this? What have you done?"

Jilly freed herself of Qwyrk's embrace and stepped forward, a mischievous smile on her face. "I just did what you told me to do. Oh... bollocks, I'm sorry! I just remembered, I forgot to add in something."

"What?" De Soulis shrieked. "What have you done, you foul little imp? Tell me now!"

"Well, I would, but since I don't know for sure, I think you'll find out on your own in a minute."

The ground shook again and de Soulis howled as the glowing glyphs along the circle perimeter increased in intensity and began to sputter, sparks flying from them in all directions. He fell to the middle of the circle, twisting, contorting, and screaming in awful ways. A beam of light shot forth from his mouth, and then two more followed, one from each of his eyes. The air around him rippled in the heat, and he trembled.

Qwyrk grabbed Jilly and Simon came up to take hold of them both.

"Jilly!" she yelled, "What did you do?"

A pulse of energy burst from the circle, knocking them over as it dissipated in every direction, and extinguished most of the torches. The glyphs sparked their last and died out. The magical circle disappeared, its dried ink turning to an ashy powder and scattering. De Soulis lay in a heap on the floor, unmoving.

Qwyrk roused herself, yet again. "I'm getting well sick and tired of getting knocked over, you know."

Jilly smiled. Simon kept his gaze on his brother.

She looked Jilly straight in the eye. "Seriously, what did you do?"

"Well, he told me the glyphs had to be drawn exactly as they were on his scroll, no changes at all, or the whole thing could backfire. I knew I'd have to do them how he wanted, but I cheated a little. I drew them, but I used the shadows and contours on the old floor to hide the fact that I didn't finish all of them just right. I'd leave out part of a line, and let the pattern on the floor fill it in. I do it all the time on rough paper to create, well, shadows. It makes interesting effects. I figured that would mess things up real nice when he got around to using it."

"But, how did you know it would work?"

She paused for a minute. "I didn't, but it was all I had, so I took the risk. He said it had to be perfect, and I was gambling on my artistic license to cock it up." She grinned.

Qwyrk burst out laughing and hugged her close. "You are one hell of a young lady, my dear, and don't you ever forget it!" Jilly laughed and hugged her back.

Qwyrk noticed that Simon had left them and walked into the

remains of the circle.

"Simon!" she called out. "Wait!"

He knelt down and rolled his brother over. De Soulis' face looked much older now. It was grey, withered, corpse-like, and his thin hair had all but fallen out. He tried to lift an arm, but could not. His empty eyes looked up at Simon, and he opened his mouth.

"Brother," he faintly whispered. "It did not have to be like this. We... we could have ruled together, you and I. Why would you not see, why would you not..."

"From the day you were born, you were a curse on us all," Simon answered. "Your mad schemes are over at last. There will be no return to a prison for you. Your journey ends here."

He reached out and took his brother's neck in his hands. De Soulis tried to cry out, but no sound escaped. Simon tightened his grip and twisted de Soulis' neck sharply to one side. There was a faint snap, and then William de Soulis fell still. A hollow and agonizing moan filled the room for an instant, and then it was gone. Simon let the lifeless body fall to the floor. It began to crumble and turn to dust, the centuries catching up with it in mere moments. Soon only the robe remained, in tatters.

Simon stood up and returned to Qwyrk and Jilly, no expression on his face.

Qwyrk regarded him with surprise and even a little fear, and wished that Jilly hadn't had to witness another killing. She understood why the Templars were so feared in their time.

"I know it needed to be done, Simon," she offered, as he walked by her.

But he said nothing, so she said nothing more. She smiled at Jilly, who tried to smile back, but they stood there for a long awkward moment before following him back up to the hall.

EIGHTEEN

* * *

They emerged from the dark steps into a dimly-lit hall. A few torches still shone. The surviving wirry-cows had fled. Unfortunately, a few of the knights were wounded, and two lay still on the ground.

"The magic that is sustaining this place will not last much longer," Simon said. "We should leave soon; it will revert to its modern ruin, but in case anything left over comes crashing down, it's best not to be here."

Qwyrk nodded. "I have to get the egg first."

She looked up and saw that it still floated among the rafters, but it was no longer spinning, and no glow came from it. She breathed a heavy sigh of relief. Willing her pain-wracked body to levitate one more time, she flew up. Taking hold of it, she descended, landing a bit harder than she had wanted to. She needed this day to be over soon. And a hot bath. And a massage. And a pint or two. Or three. Sod the fact that alcohol had no real effect on her at all.

"Here," she handed the egg to Simon, "I expect you lot will know what to do with it. I'd be thrilled never to see it again, so make sure I don't, all right?"

He smiled and took it from her, handing it off to one of the knights, who wrapped it in his cloak. "We'll keep it safe," he promised.

Qwyrk saw the dead and wounded Templars. "I'm sorry, Simon, so sorry."

"We all know the risks," he said with sadness. "They will be given proper burials, and the living will be cared for superbly."

"We did it. We really did it," Jilly said after a moment of uncomfortable silence, looking around in disbelief. "I mean, all of us, we all did something important here, didn't we?"

Qwyrk smiled and put her arm around her, hugging her. "We did indeed, my dear. We did!"

"Hm, well worth risking everything for," Blip muttered, still stumbling a bit from his close encounter, as he wandered up to them, having at last extricated himself from Croakbeak's bulk. "I was glad to send that thing back to perdition!"

"Blip, you were brilliant!" Jilly said with a big smile, seeing Croakbeak's corpse lying nearby.

"I *was* rather marvelous, wasn't I?" he said in triumph.

"Here we go," Qwyrk rolled her eyes.

Blip grunted a bit and rubbed his ribs.

"You're hurt!" Jilly exclaimed, reaching out to him and touching his shoulder.

"I'll be all right, girl, but thank you for your concern. I can assure you that Bernard Beresford Bartlesby Blippingstone the Third shall not be vanquished by one demonic monstrosity. Why, it's just like that time back in 1527, when we…"

"Blip, not now," Qwyrk sighed, though she smiled as she said it. Everything was actually getting back to normal, whatever that was.

* * *

"Damn, he's a bit of all right, isn't he?" Qwypp said, looking over at Star Tao, lying up against a wall.

"What, him?" Qwykk shot back. "Eh, whatever floats your boat, love, but he's not my type at all!"

"Well, good thing for me then, isn't it?" Qwypp answered with satisfaction. "He looks like he could use a helping hand, and it turns out I've got two right here. I think I'll take a chance to give this brave young warrior his ample reward. To the victor goes the spoils and all that..."

"All right, but just not in front of everyone, all right? I still feel a bit sick, and I don't need any help."

"Yeah, you're funny. Why don't you go try to pull one of those Templars, or something? That should be a real challenge, even for you!"

Qwypp left a bewildered Qwykk behind (who was clearly wondering what was so special about these knights that she couldn't pull one with ease), and strolled on over to Star Tao.

"Well, hello there!" Qwypp said with an eager smile, kneeling down and reaching out to lay a gentle hand on his chest. "You've had a bit of a bad fall, love, but I'm going to take care of that, no worries at all. And can I just say that whole... whatever it was you did, was cracking! Don't know where a human learned how to do that; you'll have to tell me all about it. I mean, when you're feeling better, of course. But for now, why don't you just let Qwypp take good care of you."

Star Tao groaned and squinted, trying to focus on her, but it didn't work too well. But she knew he could see a cute, pink-haired young lady caressing his chest, and that was good enough for now.

He looked up at her and smiled in that silly way he was so good at doing. "Cheers! I think I can get up now, if you'll help me, that is."

"Oh, I can help with a whole lot of things..." she grinned as she helped him sit up.

*　*　*

"I don't know, and I really don't want to know," Qwyrk, who stood nearby to Qwypp and Star Tao, said, too exhausted and in pain to be grossed-out.

"So what do we do now?" Qwykk asked, pacing about, and looking like a lost puppy.

"Now, we leave this awful castle and find a better place to tell each other about what the hell happened and what we each know," Qwyrk said. "There are still a whole lot of questions I want answered. Just because we beat the bad guys doesn't mean this whole bloody nonsense is over."

Simon nodded, looking around at the magic coming undone. "And the sooner the better, I would say."

"What about those things?" Jilly asked. "Those cow things. Are they still a problem?"

"The wirry-cows? The rest of them will likely scurry back to wherever they came from," Qwyrk answered. "Without a strong leader to hold them together, they're cowardly and pathetic."

Jilly looked relieved.

With that said, they began to filter out of the keep.

"What are you going to do with Qwarrel?" Qwypp asked one of the knights as she held her arm around Star Tao's waist to steady him.

The Templars had Qwarrel in tight restraints, and he wobbled on his feet, still weak from his sound beating at the hands of two jilted lovers.

"He's a bit too battered and bruised to be much of a danger to anyone now, I should think," the knight answered. "But we'll turn him over to the council and let them decide."

Qwypp suppressed a laugh, but she obviously took some delight in seeing her old boyfriend's arms wrapped up in leather bonds as he was forced to get to his feet and march out with them. She watched for a moment, but then brought her attention back to the young man in her arms. Qwyrk watched the whole thing, rolled her eyes, and tried not to think about it.

Outside, the clouds began to part, letting through a bit of midday sun.

"I wasn't sure we were going to see that sight again," Qwyrk smiled.

"Well, it *is* Scotland, so you never know," Jilly joked.

Qwyrk burst out laughing, which made her sides hurt, but she didn't care.

CHAPTER NINETEEN

Qwyrk stood again outside of Qwyzz's impressive forest home, admiring the ramshackle oddness of it all. She stepped up and rang the bell, but no insulting gargoyles appeared this time. There was a long silence, and she tried again; still nothing.

"Looks like no one's home," she mused out loud, to make sure she was heard.

Then the door opened a crack, and Qwota peered out. Seeing Qwyrk, she let out a gasp.

"Qwyrk! Oh, thank Goddess you're alive! There has been so much distressing news lately. I feared the worst! Won't you please come in?"

"I'm all right here, just for the moment," Qwyrk smiled.

"Are you in a hurry?"

"Yeah, something like that. I just wanted to let you know that, we were able to defeat the one behind all of this, William de Soulis. He's dead, in fact; dead as a doornail. Simon the Templar finished him off personally, I watched him do it. And we got back the dragon egg. We saved the world yesterday. Hooray for us."

"Well, that's... that's remarkable, but, but you still haven't found my beloved Qwyzz?"

"Actually, see, I think we have. You've been playing me for a fool, Qwota, and I don't like being fooled. I had a chat with my mates Qwypp and Qwykk over there, and the place they were held sounds an awful lot like your wine cellar. Also, Babewin told me that Qwyzz never actually left the premises. So, I reckon he's still down there, and not by choice. Now, we're going to march down to that impressive cellar of yours and you're going to show me where he is, and we're going to set him free, or else you're going to regret it."

Qwota grimaced, threw open the door, and raised her hands to strike some magical spell at Qwyrk.

"I wouldn't recommend that," Qwyrk warned in chilly voice, stepping to one side. Behind her, at the edge of the forest clearing, stood Simon, crossbow in hand, pointed directly at Qwota's head. He was backed up by a regiment of Templars, and next to them, Qwypp and Qwykk stood nearby in their camouflage outfits, looking agitated. Blip stood behind them with his dagger drawn and wearing a shiny new monocle.

"Go on, you disgraceful cow," Qwypp threatened with a slight smile. "Just give us an excuse!"

Qwota's lower lip began to tremble, and she burst into tears.

"You fools! You've all ruined everything! We could have made the world new again!" Her sobbing became hysterical as she collapsed to the ground.

"Sorry, having a really hard time feeling any sympathy." Qwyrk answered. "Get off your arse and take me to him, or I'll pick you up and carry you down there over my shoulder!"

A short time later, they were in the cellar, walking down the main aisle between the barrels. Simon kept his crossbow trained on her and made sure she was well aware of it.

"This is it, Qwyrk!" Qwypp said, looking around and smelling the air. "This is where we were held prisoner, I'm sure of it!"

"I don't doubt it," Qwyrk answered.

"But, who freed us?"

"That would be me!" a small stony voice answered.

"Babewin!" Qwyrk smiled.

"You horrid little wretch!" Qwota spat. "You did this, you freed those tarts, and then you led them all back here! You have betrayed me!"

"And I would do so again," Babewin answered. "I serve Qwyzz, and all that is good, not your evil plots and plans. I saw what you were doing, and I suspected your villainy, but I needed to be sure. When Qwyzz disappeared, I first feared that he was lost somewhere else, but when you arranged to have those two lovely ladies abducted..."

Qwypp and Qwykk beamed.

"...I knew that you were the culprit behind his disappearance. But he does not seem to be here, or I would have freed him myself!"

"Oh, he's here," Qwyrk answered, "he's just hidden, isn't that right? Release him now, Qwota, and maybe the council will be a bit more merciful with you."

Qwota scowled and waved her hands while speaking arcane words. A door came into view on a wall in front of them.

"Open it," Qwyrk ordered.

Qwota pulled a key from her belt and placed it in the lock, which glimmered, and then the door swung open by itself. Inside, Qwyzz sat at a rough wooden table. He looked tired and forlorn, but otherwise well.

"Qwyzz!" Qwyrk ran to him and embraced him.

Qwyzz returned her hug, but barely acknowledged her.

"Qwota?" he stuttered with a heartbreaking sadness. "I don't know what led you to betray me. I cannot understand. Can you just tell me why?"

"Why, Qwyzz? *Why?* Have you not seen what they have done?" she pointed in the general direction of the knights that had accompanied them. She raised her voice further.

"Humans have despoiled their precious Earth, and we sit by while they do it! They have no respect for the old ways, no respect for the very world that gives them life! They do not deserve to live in such a world; they do not deserve to live at all! William de Soulis would have changed that. Yes, he was evil, but he would have cleansed the world with those dragons and made it new again. Then we could have dealt with him and put him back in his prison, or even killed him, or whatever was needed.

"I arranged it, you see. I saw to it that Simon was evicted from his wretched hovel so that someone, anyone, could come along and accidentally open the seal; clearly, some dolt did it!"

"Well, thank you very much," Qwyrk snapped, "you caused a hell of a lot of damage and accomplished absolutely nothing. I hope you're proud of yourself."

Qwota shot her a hateful look. She turned to Qwyzz.

"I put you down here because I couldn't have you interfering. You know all about William de Soulis and would have advised the council. I created a spell to cloud all of your minds, just enough to slow you down. And I convinced them to send that wretched jirry-jirry to the girl to hinder Qwyrk from discovering what was happening."

"Eh, what?" Blip grunted.

"That is powerful magic," Simon observed.

"I've been studying," Qwota half smiled, "while he," she pointed at her husband, "wastes his time on old wines and rebuilding this house every damned week!"

Qwyzz sat in silence for a bit, sadness and pain on his face. "And would you have killed me... to achieve your wish?" he asked.

"If need be," she answered with no emotion. "That was not my intention, but you and everyone else were expendable for the greater goal."

"I think we've heard all we need to from you," Qwyrk said, anger swelling in her heart. "Maybe humans have cocked things up, and yeah, maybe things are getting dire in their world, but you had no right to do this; no right at all! I look forward to watching you answer for all of it. Maybe you'll end up sharing a cell with Qwarrel."

"This is all too horrible," Babewin sighed, "I do not know what to think. I need fresh air. I must return to the roof and wake up my useless Gargula. Call on me if you need me, master!" And off she hopped, her stone steps echoing through the cellar.

Qwyrk helped her old mentor to his feet, and they made their way out of the damp and musty cellar. Once back in the safety of the house, she wrapped Qwyzz in a warm blanket, and set him down on his beloved velvet sofa.

"A spot of port would be lovely," Qwyzz said with a little smile.

"Have the whole damned bottle if you want," Qwyrk smiled back, fetching it for him.

She looked up to see the knights escorting Qwota away, with Qwypp and Qwykk volunteering to go with them.

As they were leaving, Qwyrk addressed Qwota one last time. "You couldn't possibly have done all of this without help."

"No," Qwota answered with an arrogant smile. "No, I couldn't." And then she turned away and said nothing more as the knights took her outside.

* * *

Jilly paced in her living room on a cloudy afternoon. Two days had passed since the events at Hermitage and no one, not even Blip, had popped in to let her know what was going on. Star Tao had gone off who-knows-where ("I bet he's seeing that tarty pink-haired Shadow girl!" she thought more than once) and she was lost in ignorance. Her parents, as usual, were at work, and had never even seemed to notice that she'd been away. She was starting to realize just how much that hurt.

Odin came bounding into the room, wagging his tail. Jilly smiled.

"At least you're here, old friend!"

"He's not the only one," a familiar voice said in response.

"Qwyrk!" Jilly yelled and almost jumped into her friend's arms as she entered. "You're here, you came back! And I can still see you!"

"Ahem..."

Jilly looked over to see that Blip stood a few feet away. She ran to embrace him. "And you, of course, Mr. Blippingstone!" She grinned.

"There, there, child. Lovely to see you as well, but remember, we must observe some teacher/student protocols, you know."

Jilly kissed him on the head, and he winced. "I'm glad to see you, too!" She turned to Qwyrk. "How did you get in? Oh, never mind. You can pretty much do what you want, right?"

"Well, I don't always like to just materialize into people's houses. It's a little bit dangerous and invasive, but I figured that since it's still day out, it might be best to be a bit more sneaky about it."

"So, what's going on? Did you find out who was behind it all?"

Qwyrk's face darkened, but she filled in Jilly on everything that she'd learned. Blip tried to interrupt several times to put his own spin on it. Jilly was glad he was feeling better.

"So, there are others who helped make all this happen?" she asked as Qwyrk finished.

"I'm afraid so, "Qwyrk nodded, "but they're probably going to lie a bit low right now, scared of getting caught and all that. I don't think we have much to worry about, at least for now. I'm asking around, and there's a whole investigation starting up. I'll have some work to do for a bit, but we'll catch them."

There was a knock at the door. For the first time in days, Jilly wasn't afraid to answer it. She swung the door open, and sure enough, Star Tao stood there with a big grin on his face.

* * *

"Hello, Jilly!" Star Tao reached down to hug her.

"I thought it might be you. Come in!"

He stepped into the living room behind her. "All right, Qwyrk?"

Qwyrk was actually happy to see him, and greeted him with a quick embrace. This time, he didn't try to make more out of it.

He did, however, bow to Blip, who happily received his obeisance.

He'd barely sat down, when Qwyrk blurted out, "All right, so just how did you do it? The Rhymer channeling thing? That was well impressive, I have to admit."

"Don't know, really. I didn't have a plan, I just kept on trying. Something kept pushing me to keep going. I felt sick and wanted to stop, but I couldn't; there was just too much at stake. Somehow, I reached him. Surprised the hell out of me, actually. It was definitely the best channeling I've ever done."

"Did you have any control over yourself?" Jilly asked.

"Well, it was like I was still inside me, but he was in charge. I could feel meself speaking, but the words were his. I remember when I put my hand into the spook, I was thinking 'this is brilliant!' But it wasn't me choice to do it, I guess."

"And then he was just gone?"

"Yeah, he was there, and then I was me again, but I kind of blacked out. I woke up in the arms of your fit friend," he smiled at Qwyrk, who had a sudden need to go to her happy place.

"Speaking of which," he smiled.

Qwyrk shuddered at what he might say and wished Jilly would leave.

"She's helped me out quite a lot with me workshop."

Qwyrk breathed a sigh of relief.

"Yeah, with her contacts, we got twenty-five people signed up for tomorrow, it's brilliant! She's going to help me out with teaching."

"Won't that scare some people?" Jilly asked. "They won't see her properly."

"Well, maybe, but I figure those who are advanced enough spiritually to take one of *my* workshops should be ready for it!"

"Well," Qwyrk fake-smiled, "good luck with that!"

"I should go, actually," he said.

"Oh, what a shame," Qwyrk said before she even realized it. Jilly glared at her.

"We still have loads of things to do before tomorrow. After that, we're going to pop down to Devon for a week or so, and visit me cousin. But I'll be back, Jilly, don't worry!"

"I can't wait," Jilly said with a big smile. "Go and have a brilliant workshop and holiday, and tell me all about it when you come back!"

"Oh, I almost forgot!" he said. "I found this scroll on your doorstep."

He handed it to her. Jilly untied the ribbon around it, and unrolled it.

"It's a hand-written note," she said, "from Granny Boatford! It says: 'Well done, all of you. It's nice to know I'm not the only one who can keep an eye on peculiar things. If you need anything, or just want to chat and have some tea and biscuits, you know where to find me. Love to you – Granny B.'"

"So, I guess you have a friendly new neighbor," Qwyrk grinned.

"Yeah, it's a bit odd thinking there's a 600-year-old woman living across the street, but after all that's happened, that's kind of tame, I suppose," Jilly answered.

"It *is* quite the *deus ex machina*," Blip observed. "I wonder how she came to be living in immediate proximity to this home?"

"I don't know; a mystery for another time, I guess," Qwyrk smiled.

"Righty, then, I should be off." Star Tao stood up and hugged Qwyrk and Jilly again and bowed one last time to his lord.

"Best of luck, young man," Blip said with smug satisfaction. "I've no doubt that we'll meet again. Now be off with you, and do... whatever it is you're going to do."

"I shall, oh lord, and I will make you proud!"

Star Tao smiled, and then stepped out the door and on to other adventures.

"Fine young lad, that," Blip mused, "the very best sort."

"Um, Mr. Blip? Sorry, Blippingstone..." Jilly looked apprehensive.

"I suppose 'Blip' is acceptable," he replied. "It's become a sort of term of endearment, one could say."

"Yeah, it has!" Jilly's face brightened. "Um, would you mind if I had a bit of a chat with Qwyrk alone? It's just, there are some things I want to talk about with her."

"Of course not, child. In fact, I think I shall go for a walk. There appears to be some rain coming, a good time to go out and think. Did you know my new cane also transforms into an umbrella? And yes, of course, it sings!" He smiled and winked. "But when I return, we will begin work anew on the great works of the philosophical Western tradition! We shall make a start with Hegel."

"I'm counting on it!" Jilly grinned as he excused himself, a smile that faded into resigned exasperation as soon as he was out the door.

"He's really not that bad, you know," she offered to Qwyrk, obviously trying to convince herself as much as her friend.

"No, but neither is a headache, if you take something for it." Qwyrk smirked.

"So, what happens now?" Jilly said after a moment of giggling. "I'm going to lose the ability to see you soon, aren't I?"

Sadness came to Qwyrk and she nodded. "I'm afraid so. I don't know how much longer it will last, but with de Soulis dead and Redcap locked away, it can't be long."

"Do you have to go soon?"

Qwyrk nodded. "I wish I didn't, but there's more questioning that the council needs to do, and then they could well send me out to look for more answers. Or, I might have to stay here. I don't know yet. We have to find out who helped Qwota and why she was so easily swayed."

Jilly smiled but had tears in her eyes. Qwyrk could feel her own eyes stinging a little.

During an awkward moment of silence, both smiled sadly and said nothing, but eventually, Jilly couldn't hold back any longer. "Oh Qwyrk!" she sobbed, burying her head in her friend's chest. Qwyrk tried to be strong, tried to comfort her, but it wasn't going to happen. She let loose and cried along with Jilly, holding her tight.

"You're the best friend I've ever had, Qwyrk. I know we fought, and got angry with each other, but you understand me, and you're like a big sister to me, and..." She sobbed again. "I can't bear the thought of not seeing you again! I mean, *literally* not seeing you."

"Oh, my dear one," Qwyrk cried, stroking her hair. "I'm not going away forever. You may not be able to see me properly, and I might be busy, but I'll still check in on you, and Blip will be here... all right, that probably just ruined the moment."

Jilly laughed in spite of her sadness, and in a moment, Qwyrk joined in. They laughed and cried and laughed again and finally just held each other.

"Whatever you have to do, you *will* be careful, right?" Jilly asked, wiping her eyes.

"No, I thought maybe next time, I'd do something different and be reckless." Qwyrk winked.

"You'd better come back and visit often!"

"Believe me, not even the prospect of listening to Blip blather on about Kant could keep me away. I'll be back when I can, I promise."

"Can I ask you a favor, before you go?" Jilly laughed, drying her eyes.

"You can ask anything you like," Qwyrk answered stroking her hair. "Except, I can't get rid of Blip, I think you're stuck with him. I don't know about Star Tao, though..."

Jilly grinned. "No, silly. Will you let me finish drawing your picture, so I have that to remember you by? I never got to before."

"You still want to do a portrait of me?"

"Of course! If you don't mind. I mean, I could take your photo, but I'm not even sure that would work. It would probably just be all grey and shadowy."

"Jilly Pleeth, of course I don't mind; I'd be honored! I've never had my portrait done before. But Goddess, I'm a mess! Give me two ticks to clean myself up!" She wiped her eyes.

"No worries." Jilly smiled, reaching for her sketchbook. "This is going to be the best drawing I've ever done!"

* * *

Grey clouds swirled in the sky; rain was on the way. Simon looked up at them for a moment.

"At least they're all natural," he smiled.

He shoveled the last few piles of dirt into place and tamped them down, pleased that he hadn't scratched himself on that perfidious rosebush. The pink flamingos would have to go, though. And that damned garden gnome.

"Is this really a good idea?"

He looked up to see Qwyrk hiding out of view in the nearby trees.

"It makes perfect sense," Simon answered. "Even if any of our enemies found out about de Soulis and everything that happened, no one would dream that we would return the egg to the same place. That would just be crazy!" He grinned.

"And you're keeping an eye on it?"

"Of course; left alone, it won't hatch for another 500 years, plenty of time for us to make plans about what to do with it. And I don't have a home in Knettles anymore, so the order has arranged for me to live nearby and keep an eye on things here. It was pretty easy to convince the Ecklesons that they needed a gardener. This place is a bit of a disaster, after all."

"Watch out for their son. He's a bit too sharp for his own good, and he may well suspect that something's up."

"All well and good. I like an active young mind. Maybe we can recruit him when he's old enough!"

"Simon," Qwyrk moved out from the trees and walked up to him. "Are you *really* going to be okay? I mean, you've been through a lot, what with you having to... you know."

The old knight smiled and gave a little nod. "It wasn't the best solution to begin with, leaving me as a guard. It was just all we could think of. Over time, as the years turned to centuries, no one seemed to come up with anything better, and I sort of gave up on even suggesting a new answer. I was losing my mind in that place, talking to things that weren't even there... at least I think they weren't. But I'm glad he's gone. And this gives me a new purpose! Maybe I can start a whole new gardening business... call it 'Temple Landscaping' or something. It would be a nice change."

Qwyrk smiled and gave him a hug.

"Take care of yourself, Simon. I've no doubt we'll meet again."

"I do hope so; the last week has been the most excitement I've had in centuries! I could do with a little more," he said with a wink, "but maybe not for a month or two!"

*   *   *

Neither of them noticed a young boy watching from his first floor bedroom window, who shut his curtains in fear, because the new gardener was talking to a pair of glowing red eyes.

*   *   *

Jilly sat in the park under her favorite tree enjoying the warm sunlight of a summer afternoon. It had been a week since Qwyrk left to do whatever it was her superiors wanted. She might be gone a long time, and who knew what other dangers were out there?

"She'll be back, though," Jilly said to herself. "I know she will."

In the meantime, Blip promised to show up every day with plans to further her education. She wasn't sure if that was a good thing or not, but it gave her a regular connection to their unusual world.

She took out her sketchbook looked again at the drawing she had made of Qwyrk.

"Best picture I've drawn... so far!" she said to herself. "I wish mum and dad could see how important this is, but at least I've got my new friends, and they're brilliant. And I helped save the world, thank you very much! I can do anything, even be a great artist. And mum and dad will come around; maybe I can even tell them about all this someday.

"Just remember," she said with a smile, thinking about Qwyrk's parting words to her: "Keep dreaming big and don't give in to fear and doubt. Be yourself, make beautiful things on your own terms, and don't give up, because that's where the real magic is."

ACKNOWLEDGEMENTS

When writing a book of any kind (even one as silly as the present volume), there are always those people behind the scenes who make the whole process easier (or at least less painful), and sometimes even fun. Thanks so much to my agent Maryann Karinch, for believing in this series and wanting to get it out into the world as much as I do, and big thanks to Armin Lear for providing a home for it and for future volumes!

Huge thanks to my wonderful partner, Abigail Keyes, for enduring these stories as I dramatically read them out to her (audio book style), and for being an eagle-eyed editor who has found far too many mistakes and made this book much better than it was.

Thanks to my readers, Heidi Waterman and Samara Metzler, for their feedback and suggestions for improvement. Thanks also to my lovely blurbists: Peter, Diana, Laura, and Elizabeth, for providing not only quotes, but also valuable feedback and suggestions of their own. And special thanks to Freya, for inspiration and insight.

Any remaining mistakes are my own, though I might try to blame the Nighttime Nasties for them.

Coming in November 2021

LLUCK

All Qwyrk wanted was a few winter days of rest and relaxation in the small town of Knettles in Yorkshire, but of course, it all goes wrong immediately. She'd like to spend time with her young human friend, Jilly, but Jilly and her not-so-imaginary friend Blip have met a remarkable boy named Lluck, who can bend events to his favor.

Lluck is on the run from two big goblins with unnatural powers. On top of that, Qwyrk meets a mysterious and enchanting woman who's also looking for the boy. And hiding in the darkness, something else wants Lluck for itself for the impending Winter Solstice, but why?

Lluck is the second in a series of four novels about the comic misadventures of a group of misfits at the edge of normal reality in modern northern England, a world of shadows, Nighttime Nasties, witchy magic, remarkable Indian Fae, would-be superheroes, a lazy Komodo dragon, and more elves... though they continue to be a bit silly.

Sign up for Tim's mailing list and get a sneak preview of the book as a free gift!

https://timrayborn.com/lluck